ALSO BY THIS AUTHOR

The Fenwold Riddle

As David Evardson:
Gelding For Beginners

www.DaveEvardson.com

The
Fenwold
Inheritance

DAVE EVARDSON

CONTENTS

AUTHOR'S NOTE

The Fenwold Inheritance is intended to stand on its own, but may also be read as a sequel to The Fenwold Riddle, published by Fireship Press in 2012 under its Cortero Publishing imprint.

I wrote The Fenwold Inheritance during a year tinged with darkness. That I came through that period with a finished novel and (I hope) my sanity still intact I owe mostly to my wife and dearest companion, Julie.

I am grateful to Yarburgh Writers Group, as well as to Mick Hayward and Brian Green for their encouragement. I dedicate this book to Brian's memory – a dear friend, the world is a poorer place for his passing.

CHAPTER ONE
APHELION

Boone felt for the wristband on his cot-side table. Its feint *buzz* and repeating light-pulse were enough to disturb his shallow sleep. Yawning, he applied gentle pressure to its pliable face, but although the buzzing ceased, the flashing persisted.

That meant a message.

"Oh, no. What time…?"

"What's the matter, Gideon?" The bulge beside him pulled testily at the night sheet. "I've only just got off. It can't be start of watch already."

He accessed the text. "It's the Commander," he said, throwing back the cover on his side. "Lights."

The small sleeping room illuminated dimly as he swung his legs over the edge of the cot. He should be used to the austere conditions by now, but still he winced when the soles of his feet touched the ice-cold floor.

"She wants to see all five watch captains right away. Must be something important if a simple log entry won't do."

Zelda leaned up on one elbow and grinned hopefully. "Maybe the shuttles are back with glad tidings?"

He thought her optimism misplaced. That wasn't Commander Karlin's way. For her, good news could always wait. Still, he returned Zelda's smile as he hastily pulled on his shoes, slacks and tunic and headed for the door.

"Wait, Gideon. Haven't you forgotten something?"

Dutifully he returned to the cot and kissed her lightly on the cheek.

She smiled. "Off you go then."

On his short walk to the control deck he silently cursed his bad luck. The youngest watch captain on record, he was keenly ambitious and usually first to know what was on the Commander's mind. But her last duty roster switch had aligned her with Green Watch, and it rankled that his rival Phil O'Grady would already be clued in with what was going on.

Boone strode along the dimly lit corridor, up two stairways to the flight deck, and into the meeting room. A quick glance through the gloom told him he was the last to arrive. Heads turned and, at a nod from Karlin, he took a seat.

The senior officers – three men and two women – wore identical silver-grey slacks and tunics, only distinguished by the small coloured insignia depicting each of the five watches. From close up Blue and Orange captains looked fresh enough, summoned only from recreation and vacation spells. But the Yellow Watch Captain's bleary eyes and huddled attitude made it clear that she, too, had recently left her warm cot to attend this unscheduled session at the bidding of the woman who now stood before them.

"Sorry this couldn't wait until our next scheduled senior officers' meeting. The sooner we resolve this issue, the better. I assume you're all familiar with my recent log entries concerning the shuttle mission?"

A couple of heads nodded, in spite of Karlin's rhetorical question.

"In that case, you know all the facts, barring one – which is that the shuttles have just returned with identical reports."

Though in different states of alertness, each of the five faces perked up expectantly. All sagged with disappointment though when she delivered the awaited verdict.

"I'm afraid this planet is unsuitable for settlement."

Boone shuffled in his seat. "Did you say that it's *not* suitable, Commander? But earlier probes reckoned it to be our closest match ever. Size, temperature, vegetation – it was supposed to meet all the criteria. There was even spectrometric evidence of a ni-ox atmosphere. Surely our instruments didn't lie?"

"No, Captain Boone, the science lab got it right. The atmosphere is breathable. But it's already supporting a race of intelligent bipeds."

O'Grady leaned forward. "Commander, I have to ask why that should be an issue. Remember, I was next to you on the bridge when the first shuttle reported the nature of these creatures. They're not humanoid – and by all accounts there aren't too many of them either."

"Both our shuttle crews obtained some fairly good images." She leaned forward and touched the console in front of her. A hologram flickered into life from a small projection box in front of her, eliciting sharp intakes of breath from her audience.

"As you see they appear reptilian – though that's only a visual assessment. You'll also note that their hands are well developed – enough for them to manipulate simple tools. They number several thousands. They herd other animals and seem to be nomadic. Our shuttles detected no permanent settlements but there's every indication that, barring outside interference, they'll become civilised in terms that we could recognise."

"I still see no problem, Commander." O'Grady slapped a palm on the plastic arm of his chair. "We have the weaponry. We could easily eradicate these primitive reptiles before they have a chance to develop any further – and take the planet for our own!"

Boone fought his fatigue and turned to face his adversary, trying hard to disguise his natural dislike of the man. "I strongly disagree with the Green Watch proposal. Our mission guidelines clearly advise against hostility towards intelligent life forms."

O'Grady was quick to respond. "And I say that our mission guidelines are just that – guidelines. Our main objective is to find a habitable planet and settle on it. Well, after centuries of searching, here we've found one at last. This is a golden opportunity. We may never get another one. Successive generations have considered and discarded more than fifty planets because of their inability to support human life. We can't turn this one down – it's a gift from God. Does Red Watch really want to throw it back in His face!"

Although Boone spoke in even tones, his anger was hard to conceal. "Commander, I don't think a just God would condone the destruction of a burgeoning civilisation merely to suit our own needs."

Before O'Grady could respond, Karlin held up a hand for silence.

"I hadn't intended to put this to the vote, because I took the view that the conquest of an incumbent intelligent race wasn't an option. However I take Captain O'Grady's point as to the absolute authority of the guidelines. So before we go any further I think we should resolve this issue for good and all. I'd like a show of hands in favour of the use of force to establish our domination of this planet."

"Before we do this, Commander," Boone said, "shouldn't a question of this importance be put to the full Joint Watch Committee?"

She brushed his question aside. "I'll ratify our decision with the JWC later. Now, those in favour, please."

O'Grady's hand was in the air almost before she'd finished speaking, while Boone's arms remained firmly folded across his chest. The Blue Watch leader clearly struggled with the question, her eyes darting from one to another of her colleagues' faces. At last, though, she too raised a hand in favour of an armed invasion. But Yellow and Orange obviously came to the opposite conclusion, for after a while they, like Boone, folded their arms resolutely.

"All done?" The Commander studied each face in turn. "In that case, the motion is defeated. I hope you accept that, Captain O'Grady?"

Clearly disappointed, the Green Watch captain pursed his lips. "Of course I accept the majority decision, Commander. But I have to ask: where do we go from here? It seems we'll never find a suitable planet that isn't already occupied."

Even Boone saw the logic in O'Grady's remark. But he had great respect for the Commander's intellect. He voiced his thoughts.

"Ma'am, if our treatment of this planet's inhabitants wasn't your original reason for calling this meeting, then I suspect you already have a proposal regarding Captain O'Grady's observation."

She rewarded his comment with the ghost of a smile. "Recently I've been thinking a lot about our situation. Worst-case scenario is that we search indefinitely for a suitable unoccupied world. We could in theory resign ourselves to that prospect. The Salvation is, after all, self-sustaining – albeit with the occasional need for economies, depending on our proximity to a solar energy source. Leaving aside how that might affect morale, at around eleven thousand, our on-board population is nudging its comfortable physical maximum. We would soon be forced to impose strict reproductive management."

"But that would go against the religious codes of some of our people," the Yellow Watch leader observed.

"It would be a difficult issue, I agree, Captain. That's why I'm proposing a fundamentally different course of action. Though our solar batteries can be cantankerous, our engineers assure me they can produce enough energy to make the journey that I'm proposing. I think you all know what I'm talking about.

"And before any of you asks the question, if we start out now, without mishaps, the journey should take about sixty years."

Boone looked at his colleagues' expressions. He too had wondered about the Commander's proposed course of action, though he'd never discussed it openly. He hadn't wanted to be the first to suggest what many would interpret as accepting defeat. Apart from that, there was always the chance that their distant goal might not yet be safe to inhabit. It would require a giant leap of faith. But there was another reason, and Karlin must have read it in their faces.

"I know, people," she said. "Sixty years is a long time to wait for the achievement of our next objective. Most of us won't live to see its fruition – certainly not I – perhaps none of us sitting here. I think for that reason we must be careful how we present the idea to our fellow passengers. But I believe with sensitive preparation they'll accept it as the only alternative. And before you ask, Captain Boone, I'll be calling an emergency meeting of the JWC for their ratification of our decision."

After a short pause she added, "Well then, shall we take a vote? Please raise your hand if you accept my proposal."

She looked around the group and smiled at her officers' unanimity.

"Thank you all. Captain O'Grady, since it's your watch, I'd be obliged if you'd plot a course for home."

CHAPTER TWO

IN A NEW LAND

A demonic howl emerged from the midnight forest, riding the moaning wind down towards the riverbank, and snatching Marshal Dominic Bradley away from his dreams. Through bleary eyes a pale wintry moon revealed that his four companions had heard it too.

They were all scruffy, trail-weary individuals in dishevelled hunters' gear. Their weapons – bows, short swords and knives – lay ready for use beside their exhausted bodies. Too tired to clear away the remains of their rabbit supper, they had chatted only briefly around the flickering campfire before surrendering to restful sleep after their recent exertions.

Now, though, all five were wide-awake.

"By the Gods, what was that?" The fisherman Sean was least accustomed to the sounds of the forest, and urgently pulled his young son Toby closer to his side.

But the lad slipped his father's grip and sat upright. "I know – it was a wolf!" he gasped. "Isn't that right, Miss Sylvia?"

The young huntress raised her head from Dominic's breast and rubbed her eyes. "Yes, Toby. You and I had an argument with some wolves on our journey to the north, didn't we?"

The boy blinked. "Yes, but the dragon roared and breathed fire and scared them away!"

Rajeev Shah, Dominic's youthful deputy, said, "I doubt if we'll find friendly dragons on this side of the Wall, Toby."

Bradley shook his head. "I wouldn't be too certain of that, Rajeev. But just in case there are none of those metallic beasts around to defend us, I think we'd better take shifts to tend the fire."

He shivered, silently cursing himself for having neglected their only source of heat and protection from wild animals. He stretched out the fingers of his right hand and held them up against the night sky, where scudding clouds gave way to intermittent glimpses of the feint starry tableau beyond.

"I'll stay awake until the Moon's moved a span, then I'll rouse you to do the same, Rajeev. Sean, take the third shift if you will."

The fisherman nodded. "All right, Marshal. But Toby and I must be getting back before daylight. His mother will be worried."

By now Dominic's senses were fully primed. "I understand, but what about the raft?"

"You'll need it here, I know," Sean said thoughtfully. "When we're ready to leave, I'll wake you. Then, if you'll come through the culvert with us to the Fenwold side of the Wall, you can bring it back here after we've gone."

"I'm not sure I could bring it back on my own, Sean. You'd best give Rajeev a shake as well when you're ready to go."

Sited on a rise just above the riverbank, their simple bivouac offered shelter enough, with protective hides above and behind, where the sombre forest loomed only a couple of furlongs inland.

Nodding towards the woodland Sylvia said, "Sean, don't you want to stay and see what treasures the Ancient Ones left for us here? After all, that's why we made this journey."

The fisherman smiled. "A part of me does, I must admit. But Toby's been through so much these last few days, what with the trek as captive to that outlaw, and then the extra leagues to help you open the culvert through the Wall. He's endured enough. I want to get him back home as soon as possible."

He looked down at his son and whispered, "See, he's already asleep. He's worn out. When you've done here, secure the raft well above the bank on the Fenwold side. Don't think of trying to pole it downriver – you know how treacherous these waters can be, and you're not yet good enough sailors to make that trip. In any case you'll need the raft here later for re-entry. Return on foot beyond the old bridge and light a beacon. My kinsman or I will sail over from Nearbank and bring you across. You can tell us of the Ancient Ones' wonders then. You'll not be staying here much longer, will you?"

Dominic shrugged. "A day or two, long enough to find out what's here. I suppose we could have gone into the forest today, but after a good night's rest we'll be better prepared for whatever's in there. We'll take stock, then retrace our steps, collect our horses from your village and return to the Capital. Now that the Wall's breached at last, I'll need to report back to the Council. They'll want to organise the settlement of these lands as soon as possible."

Sean said, "You'll mention my request to the Council, won't you – that my village provide the ferry service for the new settlers?"

"Of course. We'll need boats large enough to take horses and other livestock. Only your people have the skill to build and operate such craft. And I'll suggest the Council help you establish a new port on the south bank, nearer to the Wall."

Sean nodded approvingly. "That'll shorten the crossing by more than a league. Perhaps we'll even establish a new village. And don't worry – we'll build the craft to do the job. It's our speciality." His gaze rested on Sylvia's drooping eyelids, and smiling mischievously he whispered, "But I suspect you've some other important business to take care of on your return to Fenwold. A wedding, perhaps?"

Seeing the fisherman's grin reflected on Rajeev's boyish face, Dominic only drew Sylvia closer to him and said quietly, "If you'll just throw some wood on the fire, I think you two should try to get some sleep."

* * *

Early next morning after they'd said their farewells to Toby and his father, Dominic and Rajeev brought the raft back through the culvert. Using the metal handles placed on the tunnel wall at intervals by their long-dead forefathers, they only needed to resort to the oars to paddle the makeshift vessel the few strides back to the riverbank, where Sylvia waited to help them ashore. The two men pulled the raft partly out of the water and Rajeev staked it where it lay, while the Marshal walked towards Sylvia's open arms, and the couple embraced.

Sylvia stood away. "Did they get off all right?" she asked.

"Yes. They should make the crossing point in a day and a half. They'll be picked up from there and be home on the south bank by tomorrow evening."

"It's good to think Toby will be back with his mother at last," Sylvia said. "He's been such a brave lad. That was thoughtful of you the other day to make him an honorary deputy marshal – I'm sure it made him feel the trek had been worthwhile. It's painful to recall what he went through at the hands of that outlaw."

"What you both went through," Shah said.

She turned her face towards the forest then, and Dominic knew she must have been reliving those horrific days as hostage to the red-haired outlaw. He drew her closer, one hand instinctively grasping the hasp of the knife at his belt.

"You've nothing to fear from Red now, my love. I only wish we could have taken him alive to stand trial as an example. But as he was trying his best to kill me, we had little choice in the matter. In any case, he's dead now, and we should be satisfied with that."

Shah grimaced and said, "Perhaps it was a blessing that he perished here. I wouldn't have relished his company on the trek back to Nearbank as prisoner to stand trial. It'll be easier now he's out of the way."

Dominic glanced at the spot by the Wall, closer to the forest, where he and Rajeev had burned the outlaw's remains the day before, according to custom. Then he shifted his gaze towards the woodland.

"What's done is done," he said. "But now we have only good things to look forward to. Come on, both of you. Let's see if we can find some of those treasures we were promised."

* * *

Approaching the woodland's edge Dominic thought it looked no different from the forest inside the walled enclave of Fenwold – centuries old tall, mature trees, separated by clustered thicket and saplings, dark and brooding, and all festooned with invasive runners of rampant ivy.

But there was one important difference on this side. Though there were animal tracks, worn clear by the repetitive use of wolf, fox and deer, none had been broadened out by the regular passage of human hunters. Proof came from the behaviour of small creatures – mainly rabbits and birds – which made no attempt to fly or scamper away at the approach of the three intruders. Instead they clung onto branches or sat wide-eyed among the grasses, bemused rather than fearful.

Sylvia broke into his thoughts. "It seems a shame, in a way, that before too long these animals will have to learn to be afraid for the sake of their own survival."

Rajeev added, "They'll have to watch out for themselves when our settlers move in and make this place their own." Then after a pause he turned to Dominic and asked, "What kind of treasure did Cara say we'd find here?"

"She only used the word 'treasure' when Red asked her about it, but I believe she only repeated it to curb his impatience. Her first reference was to science, knowledge and things we'd find useful."

"Hmm," said Shah. "I think you're right. It's a bit vague though, isn't it? 'Useful things' could mean just axes and saws. We could send for our village blacksmith Don Benson to make as many of those as we need. As for knowledge, we already have plenty of that, don't we? And what is 'science' anyway? I didn't want to admit it in front of that outlaw, but I've never heard of it. Is it some kind of food?"

"Rajeev, this is no time to be negative. Think of the journey we three have undertaken because of the riddle the Ancient Ones left to guide us – the hardships, the ordeals. Think of the trouble they went to in bringing us to Cara's house in that northern town, not to mention building an impenetrable concrete wall strong enough to keep our people inside Fenwold for eight hundred years! They surely wouldn't have done all that just to deliver simple tools, knowledge we already have and a simple plate of food! No. I'm expecting something much more here – something beyond our dreams!"

The deputy still looked dubious, so Dominic placed a friendly hand on his shoulder and his other arm around Sylvia's waist saying, "Come on, you two. It can't be much further. Our treasures have to be here in the forest."

But now the absence of wide tracks proved problematic – they had to resort to using their machetes to clear a way forward. This slowed their progress, so that even Dominic thought the Ancient Ones weren't making the final stage of their quest particularly easy.

Rajeev wiped beads of sweat from his brow. "You were right to delay this until today, Dominic. We'd never have managed it without food and rest."

"Don't go thinking I foresaw all this hacking, Rajeev. I just thought it best to start this final task with a clear day ahead of us."

The cutting continued unrelentingly until, about a furlong inside the forest, they arrived abruptly at an inner margin. Here all three stopped, astounded – and, for a moment, dumbfounded – at what lay before them.

Rajeev broke the silence. "By the Gods of the Sacred Wall! Whatever is all this?"

Dominic gasped. "This has to be the place we're looking for."

They had emerged on the edge of a clearing, so huge that it appeared to have no visible limits. The space was occupied by countless plain, flat-roofed, windowless buildings of various heights, but mostly with standard floor dimensions of about ten strides by twenty-five. Each had large double doors, flush to the walls, but lacking conventional handles.

"How are we supposed to get at the treasure?" Sylvia asked, pushing vainly against the nearest door.

Rajeev pointed out a pad of buttons with markings on them. Touching some of these he said, "This is how. But I suppose you have to know which ones to push – a bit like the tiles that gave us entry to Cara's house in that northern town, and then later to open up the culverts in the Wall. It's a sort of code."

Dominic frowned and tapped his tunic pocket. "Except that then we had this key to show us which tiles to press. I see no such instructions here. We need someone to tell us which symbols will open these doors."

Sylvia said, "And the only person who can do that is Cara, but we left her back in that northern town. Perhaps we needed more information from her. Remember, she was cut off in mid-speech because Red damaged those batteries on the roof."

Dominic said, "She told us enough to get us this far. And when you say we left her there, we only left her likeness. What did she call it?"

"A hologram?" Rajeev offered.

"That's right. She said she wasn't real – only an image that the Ancient Ones created to speak to us."

"In other words her image could be here too – is that what you mean?" Sylvia suggested.

His voice lacked its earlier confidence. "It's all I can think of."

"But if Cara's here, how are we going to find her among all this lot?"

He could only offer a typically logical response to her question. "Apart from tracking, how do you find someone in the forest?"

Rajeev suggested, "Call out their name, I suppose."

"Come on then. All together – three times."

So they joined voice and shouted the hologram's name. "Cara! Cara! Cara!"

Nothing. They tried again. "Cara! Cara! Cara!"

Rajeev said. "This is stupid. We're wasting our time. Perhaps we should try to break down one of these walls."

"Wait!" Sylvia urged. "Shut up for a moment!"

They stood in silence. "Can't you hear it?" she said.

"Hear what?" Rajeev asked sulkily. Dominic shrugged.

"Follow me," she said, and walked gingerly between two of the buildings, her companions in tow. As they edged forward Bradley became aware of a distant high-pitched buzzing, whose volume increased as they progressed further. After turning a few corners they found themselves before a small, square building with more clear space around it than the others.

"It's loudest here," Dominic said. "This must be the source of the sound."

"And look at this building. Recognise it?"

"It's Cara's house!" Sylvia said.

Rajeev added, "It's the same size and shape anyway. And look at the roof. There's a rail all the way around, just like the other one had. I bet there's even a mechanical dragon up there, breathing fire to keep the ground clear of vegetation. It must be round the back."

There was no doubt in Dominic's mind. This was an exact replica of the building to which they'd been guided by the ancient riddle, in the northern town on the other side of the Wall. There the hologram Cara had given them instructions to wake the machine that opened up the culverts in the Wall where it crossed the river. Then thanks to Sean's skill as a raft maker they'd passed through the nearest culvert into this new land, inaccessible to their people for the past forty generations. Here was their inheritance, their destiny.

"But there had to be five of us to enter the other house," said Rajeev. "We're only three. Toby's gone home and Red's dead. So how do we get in?"

"There aren't any tiles here to press," Sylvia observed. "Perhaps it's not so complicated. We've already been led here by calling Cara's name. She's probably expecting us. Why don't we just knock on her door?"

Without waiting for the others to agree, she confidently walked up to the flush double doors and knocked twice.

The buzzing stopped and the three unkempt travellers stood expectantly. After the briefest pause the doors opened with a *swish*.

Amazed, Dominic led them across the threshold.

CHAPTER THREE
GIFTS FROM THE GODS

Though it was only a matter of days since their first audience with Cara, it seemed to Dominic that a far longer time had elapsed – probably due to the excitement of recent events. But despite that interval he thought he remembered the drill.

The moment he, Sylvia and Rajeev stepped onto the black circles in the middle of Cara's chamber, the ambient lighting dimmed and the three familiar pillars rose from behind the white rail in front of them, each emitting a beam of pure white light. This triad of radiance fused to form the flickering, three-dimensional half-sized figure of Cara, mouthpiece of the Ancient Ones – and, it would appear, custodian of their bounties. Their historic benefactors had made her appear pure and untouchable – which, being transparent, he imagined she must be – her wispy blond hair cascading over a flowing pure white gown. Her image soon stabilised to radiate the sublime reality of a benign presence, generating an aura of truth and trust.

"Good morning, Dominic, Sylvia and Rajeev," she said.

Bradley caught his breath at the shock of the hologram's greeting. He was amazed that this non-being should not only instantly recognise them, but also remember their names. He found it strange too that her voice should sound soothingly like his own mother's, as he recalled it had done at their previous meeting. But he suspected the same was true for Sylvia and Rajeev, for each of them looked upon the image with expressions of almost childlike expectation. He coughed nervously.

"Good morning, Cara. By what kind of magic do you recognise us?" Then he added uncertainly, "You are Cara? The one who spoke to us in the northern town?"

The hologram answered him.

"Beverton. That's the name of the town where we first met. I explained to you then that I am not a real person, but an image generated by machinery – different machinery, but the same image. I've kept a record of your visual and genetic identities, along with your names, of course. It's just a question of cross matching. There's no magic involved. It's basic science."

Rajeev and Dominic exchanged inspired looks. 'Science' clearly represented much more than sustenance for the body, after all.

Dominic hoped Cara wouldn't find his next question too cheeky.

"But how can you possibly see people? You seem to be made of nothing but beams of light."

"That's correct, Dominic. But there are cameras both in this room and the entrance chamber. They are simple devices for collecting and recording images. I can tell from the recorded visual data that you have straight black hair, and that Sylvia has brown eyes, with bone structure suggesting an attractive face. There is evidence of a scar on one cheek."

Sylvia seemed unshaken by Cara's remark. "That's from an injury in the blacksmith's forge when I was a child," she explained.

"I see," said Cara, pausing only briefly as if to commit even this snippet of trivial information to her memory. Then she added, "But such things as this help me construct a visual image by which I may recognise you at our next meeting."

Though a thousand questions jostled for supremacy in his mind, Dominic realised there was no time to waste in satisfying his idle curiosity. "Cara, I'm afraid we can't stay here for long," he said.

"Of course you can't," Cara said. "You have to go back inside Fenwold to organise your people to migrate here, if they're to make use of the technology bequeathed to them. The three of you couldn't possibly establish a settlement on your own. Besides, it's too late in the year to begin the migration – it would make sense for you to return in the spring. Are there other survivors inside Fenwold?"

He smiled, surprised by her question. "So, there are some things you don't know."

"Of course. I have no presence south of the river. What I can't observe, I have to be told. Please answer my question."

Though her words might have constituted a rebuke, her intonation didn't suggest annoyance.

"Yes. There are many people in Fenwold – just lately too many for the land to support them, in fact. That's one of the reasons why the Council sent me to find a passage through the Wall."

"Did you use the riddle?" she asked.

He was speechless for a moment. Then he stammered, "You know about the riddle, then?"

Here Sylvia chimed in. "I told you before we set out on this quest, Dominic. It was all planned. The Ancient Ones arranged for the riddle to be recited after forty generations – eight hundred years. Cara confirmed this back in Beverton – don't you remember? She said that was how long they thought it would take for the plague to completely die out. And that old woman's reciting of the riddle set in motion the chain of events that brought us here today. Isn't that right, Cara?"

"Yes, Sylvia."

The three stood in silence for a moment, dirty, ragged and trail-weary. Though they had made half-hearted attempts to clean themselves in the shallows earlier, the water had been so cold that their efforts had made little improvement. But regardless of their appearance Dominic was certain they all shared a profound sense of solemnity, and also privilege, to have been chosen to stand here and speak with their ancestors. At the same time he thought it strange that the future of Fenwold should now rest in their six grubby hands.

After a while the hologram flickered, and added warmly, "Young lady, you have wisdom."

Though he didn't turn his head Dominic sensed Sylvia's superior sideways glance. He hoped Cara didn't detect his discomfort. He was very fond of Sylvia and had come to admire her frequent flashes of inspiration, but still he sometimes felt the need to re-establish his authority. Besides, it was time to ask more important questions.

"Cara, when we return to Fenwold, our people will ask about the treasures we've found. What can we tell them?"

The hologram responded without a pause. "Tell them that our stores here include everything your people will need to establish a city, supported by agriculture. You will find machines to help you clear the forest, to till the soil and harvest crops; prefabricated dwellings that can be erected quickly; systems for delivering water and power to your homes; motorised vehicles to help you travel further out and make this world your own; and many other useful things."

For once Dominic was lost for words, and it fell to Rajeev to fill the chasm of silence.

"Motorised vehicles? What are they?"

"Put simply, wagons propelled by their own internal power."

"You mean, without horses?"

"Yes."

"But we have plenty of horses, Cara. Why should we need these motorised wagons?"

"You'll find motor vehicles much more efficient and reliable."

The deputy seemed sceptical. "I don't see how. Horses have served us well enough for generations. Does this mean our blacksmiths will no longer be needed?"

"No," said Cara. "Skills learned in the forge will be of great value in assembling and maintaining the machinery."

Then she said something that Dominic found extraordinary – not because of its literal meaning, but because it seemed to demonstrate a quality that he wouldn't have expected in a hologram. That quality was consideration.

"But Rajeev, don't think that you must abandon your old ways. We only want to give you the choice. If you wished to bring horses through the culvert – which should be possible using properly designed craft – you could breed them and train them to perform any function, be it for work, transport or leisure."

This seemed to satisfy the deputy's concerns. Dominic knew that Rajeev loved horses at least as much as humans, and was bound to defend their usefulness.

Cara continued, "But these are mere details. There is one treasure I haven't mentioned, which we hope you will put to good use. For without it, you are unlikely to develop your dominion of this new territory as anything more than ignorant masters of machines that you don't understand."

Dominic raised an eyebrow. "What treasure is that, Cara?"

"Knowledge. In the warehouses you'll find teaching devices, from which you and your children may access everything we knew. Don't ask me to list the types of wisdom available to you there – they are too many and varied. I have a programme for your introduction to these things – as with all the other treasures."

Sylvia said, "You mean we can only get into the different stores in a certain order. You won't let us in until you think we're ready. That's why there are those buttons with symbols on the outside, right?"

"Correct, Sylvia. We call them keypads. The symbols are the visual depiction of numbers – one, two, three, etcetera. I will tell you which numbers to press when it's time to access each store. You must use numbers, surely? They were always a part of your spoken language."

"Yes, of course we use numbers," Dominic said. Then he frowned. "But why do you say 'spoken language'? Is there some other kind that we should know about?"

"Yes, Dominic. I shall introduce you to the written word – the ability to record your thoughts and deeds, and read what others have thought, said and done, even though you may never have met them. Your ancestors agreed to relinquish these skills when we enclosed them inside Fenwold."

"Why would they do that?" Rajeev asked.

"Because of the incredible power of reading and writing. With these abilities your society would have developed too quickly, and you would soon have discovered how to breach the Wall before it was safe for you to do so. But they are yours now that the plague is gone – and I promise you that they will completely alter the way you live."

Dominic frowned. "Cara, I don't fully understand everything you say. I realise there must be much for us to learn. For the time being we'll have to take your word for the importance of these new tools. But in order to work, horses must be fed. What will feed these machines?"

"You're right, Dominic. They do need food. And that food is called electricity. I'll teach you about it in time. For now, understand that it's a natural form of energy that we've been able to generate on a huge scale and transmit to wherever it's needed. But you'll learn about these things later. Are there any other matters you would like to ask me about before you leave?"

Wide-eyed, Rajeev and Sylvia shook their heads. Dominic could only stammer, "N- no, Cara. My mind is so full with all this information – I certainly couldn't absorb any more. Thank you for answering our questions."

"You're most welcome, Dominic. When you leave this building, walk towards the one opposite. Its doors will open when you approach. Just inside you'll find a small object. Take it and leave the building quickly, because the doors will close and lock after a very short time."

"What sort of an object?" Dominic asked. "Is it a weapon?"

"No, but it will provide evidence that you have been here. It's powered by a tiny battery that has a limited supply of electricity, so don't use it until you really need to."

"How do we make it work?" Sylvia asked.

Stooping, Cara mimed the actions that she now described. "Place it on level ground, or on any flat surface. Then either with a finger or gently with a foot, press the raised button in the middle. When it clicks, stand clear."

"Is it dangerous, then?" Rajeev asked.

Cara smiled. "No, Rajeev. But if you stand too close when it operates, its effect may be spoiled."

Dominic frowned. "How will we know when to use it?"

"You will know," she said. "Now, go back into Fenwold and tell your people what awaits them here."

CHAPTER FOUR
HOMEWARD BOUND

Mid-morning of the following day saw them pass back into Fenwold through the culvert, leaving the makeshift raft securely moored close to the Wall. From here they set off eastwards along the north bank of the river.

"Do you think this rain will let up soon?" Sylvia asked glumly before they'd travelled fifty strides.

"I doubt it," said Dominic. "Look at the sky. The rain cloud spreads without a break from the Wall behind us as far as the eastern horizon."

Rajeev said sulkily, "I wish I had my deerskin cape and leggings with me. At this rate I'll be drenched before mid-day."

After all they'd been through, Dominic sometimes found it hard to recall that his companions were still teenagers – his juniors by four years or so. Recalling their courage and loyalty, he couldn't find it in him to rebuke them for the occasional complaint.

"There's a limit to how much gear we can carry on foot," he said sympathetically. "But we've a change of clothing in our packs, so we can dry off when we reach the bridge. That'll be mid-afternoon at the latest. Under its shelter we'll soon get warm and dry again before setting out for the crossing point in the morning. That's only another half day's walk."

Sylvia grabbed his hand. "The bridge! Don't you remember? That's where we first…"

He frowned and squeezed her hand tightly, swivelling his eyes in Rajeev's direction and hoping she understood his silent plea for discretion.

She frowned back at him. Clearly she didn't share his unease, so he'd have to finish her announcement before she embarrassed him.

"That's where we first saw all those bats," he said. "Yes, of course I remember. It was quite a sight."

She gave a little laugh. "Dominic, don't worry. Rajeev knows about you and me. He and I have been friends since we were kids. He's like my third brother. We don't have secrets."

He glanced across at his deputy, who thankfully now walked a little distance away from them, his expression hidden because he was looking inland towards the forest. For once Dominic silently thanked him for having some tact. He had to remind himself that village folk were far more open than his friends back home in the Capital – not that he held that against them. Sylvia's parents had treated him like their own son this past year, even offering their home as his headquarters during the war against the raiders.

Sylvia broke into his thoughts.

"Dominic, what happens after we've crossed the river and retrieved our horses?"

"First I'll have to report to the Council in the Capital."

"What about Rajeev and me?"

"I thought you'd want to go home and see your parents again. I don't think you'd like it much in the Capital."

"How do you know what I'd like? I bet it'll be more exciting than dreary old Crowtree."

"But your mother and father will be worried about you. I'm sure they can't wait to have you home safe and sound again. And I'll have lots of boring business to take care of. There won't be much time to spend with you and show you around."

"That's all right. I don't need a nursemaid. I can look around on my own if you're too busy. Besides, Mum and Dad already know I'm with you – we sent word with those traders after your accident, remember? They won't mind waiting a few days more. Come on, Dominic, let me go with you!"

Her mention of his shoulder dislocation reminded him how useful she'd been, even if she hadn't been invited on this momentous journey. She'd manipulated the joint skilfully and there was now hardly any pain. Also he recalled her wilfulness, and that forbidding her was useless, for she would only sulk and make his life a misery until she got her own way. So he did what any man would do under the circumstances. He prevaricated.

"All right, Sylvia. We'll see. I'll think about it."

"Well, don't think about it for too long. I don't want to set out from Nearbank not knowing where I'm going."

He merely nodded and turned his face into the rain.

* * *

Later that evening under the bridge they made love to the screeching of bats and herring gulls' raucous cries. The bridge being an enormous structure of considerable width, Rajeev had had the discretion to make his bed far enough away to give them some privacy.

As they lay listening to the eerie echoes of the river's motion on its endless journey to the Great Sea, they spoke more of their future together.

"Dominic, what will our wedding be like?"

"Our wedding?" he teased. "Who said anything about a wedding? Ouch!"

He should have learned by now that she never pulled her punches. He knew there'd be a bruise in the morning from the one she'd just delivered to his ribs. Now she grabbed a handful of his chest hair and pulled it gleefully.

"You were saying, Marshal Bradley?"

"All right! All right! There'll be a wedding."

When she let go he added, "But I want it understood I was forced into it by a vicious, cruel, heartless little squirrel!" And they kissed, long and lovingly.

"So," she repeated, "what will it be like?"

His eyes had a faraway look. "It'll be like nothing you've ever seen before. By tradition it should be held at your home in Crowtree. My parents and friends must come from the Capital. I hope the village can accommodate them all."

"Don't worry," she said. "We'll manage. And afterwards?"

"Well," he drawled, gently fondling her breast, "More of…"

She removed his hand. "No. I meant, after all that."

"Oh. Well, it depends on the Council – where they want me to work and whatever commissions they have for me. We'll have to wait and see."

She looked up at the concrete canopy above them. "I was right about this bridge, wasn't I? When I first saw it I said that human hands must have put it here – even if we couldn't imagine how the Ancient Ones had done it. It's a shame they destroyed the road surface above though. We could easily have walked across to Nearbank."

"They disabled it to discourage mass migration until the time was right. They seem to have thought of everything."

After a pause Sylvia said, "I hope the Council makes you a marshal in the New Territory. I'd like to be a part of its development. Couldn't you ask them?"

"Yes, I suppose I could. But in the end, they're my employers. I have to go where they think I'm needed."

"Who are these Council members? Are they very fierce old men?"

He laughed softly. "No, not really. Not most of them anyway. My Dad's a Councillor, and he's a nice guy – much like your own father in many ways."

"I think I remember you telling me that he was a farmer."

"He owns farmland, but he pays others to work it. Years ago he became a trader – not the travelling kind, but one that travelling traders work for."

"He must be very rich."

"Comparatively, I can't deny it. But our fortune rises or falls with that of Fenwold as a whole. If its produce diminishes, then so does the trade."

"It sounds complicated. But don't apologise for your family's wealth. If your father's successful, I bet he's worked for it. Didn't you want to help in the business?"

"I enjoyed growing up on the farm and helping with the menial work. I'm not so keen on sitting around, telling other people what to do. I prefer to get my hands dirty – to get involved. I suppose that's why I opted to train as a lawman."

"There must have been something else."

"What do you mean?"

"Well, I'm sure you could have found a 'hands-on' job somewhere in your father's trading organisation. Why choose such an extreme occupation as you did? Oh, I bet I know!"

"Oh, you do, do you? You think you know everything about me, don't you? So, what does the great Sylvia Storey think drove me to become a marshal?"

"Some girl turned you down – though I can't think why. Am I right?"

He looked at her for along time, trying to measure the extent of her wisdom. Then he yawned and said, "The past is gone, Sylvia. I'm tired, and you must be too. Let's go to sleep and dream about our future."

* * *

A mighty flash of forked lightning illuminated the expanse of the brown, churning river, briefly revealing the fishing village of Nearbank on its opposite shore. The vision was short-lived though, and the depressing gloom soon resumed its dominion over the bleak estuary. Though it shouldn't have come as a shock, the deafening thunderclap that followed stopped the three weary travellers in their tracks, its amplified roar jarring their nerves and shaking the ground beneath their feet. The rain still poured and they were thoroughly soaked again.

Dominic peered upwards. Great banks of dark, rolling cloud obscured the sun, and he searched for that part of the sky where some dim light filtered through. From his observation he reckoned the time at a little after midday. The looks of relief on his companions' faces reflected his own thanks that at least they should need to walk no further.

"By the Gods," Rajeev complained as he slung down his packs, "Will there never be an end to this foul weather?"

With an ironic grin Sylvia replied, "Cheer up, Rajeev. It's not even mid-winter yet. Be thankful it hasn't snowed again."

Dominic said, "Never mind that. Did either of you two think of packing any dry kindling? We're going to have to light our fire in the rain."

Even as he spoke, the dependable deputy pointed at one of his bags, made of stout, well-stitched leather. "You'll find some in there. But we'd best get a shelter up before we open it."

They foraged the woods for anything that would burn, lunched on half-cooked rabbit and mouldy bread, and then rested protected from the worst of the weather by a rough arrangement of hides supported by poles and branches. This also shielded their campfire, of necessity a meagre affair in case it set their shelter alight.

"Do you suppose they'll see the flame, Dominic?" Sylvia asked.

"It depends how hard they're looking. It's not much of a beacon, but they might see it through the gloom. Though even if they did, I couldn't blame them for waiting for the weather to improve. We'll have to be patient."

But after a while Rajeev sat bolt upright and pointed. "Look! Isn't that a sail?"

The rain having now subsided to an idle drizzle, Dominic peered out across the murky water a full league or more towards the southern shore, where the now familiar white sheet billowed and bobbed about upon the river's turbulent surface.

"Yes, I think you're right! Our fishing friends certainly keep their promises. I wouldn't have chosen to make the crossing in these conditions."

Rajeev's face turned ashen as he gulped and said, "Nor would I, Marshal. But I've just remembered – that's just what we're going to have to do when yon boat arrives on this shore!"

Dominic recalled the discomfort of their earlier crossings. "Hmm. I can't say I'm looking forward to it. But we have to be grateful to Sean and his cousin for coming to fetch us."

"Thankful?" Sylvia said. "It's they who should be thanking you for rescuing Toby from that vicious outlaw!"

Rajeev mused, "I bet they'll have some sort of reception prepared for us when we land. And Marshal, forgive me for saying this, but…"

"But what?"

"Well, knowing how hard you find it to accept praise, and how eager you must be to start for home, I hope you won't shun their tributes and hurt their feelings."

Dominic laughed. "You two think you know me inside-out, don't you?"

Sylvia said, "We know that once your eye's focussed on a target, you don't let anything distract you from it. This time, just try and have some patience and take some time to accept their thanks, won't you?"

"Yes, yes. All right," he muttered uncomfortably. "I promise not to disrespect their wishes."

Rajeev clearly wasn't going to leave it there. "And you'll have to do the same when you get back to the Capital, you know. I'll bet you'll receive a real hero's welcome there."

Still truculent, he brushed aside his deputy's comments. "Hero's welcome? Whatever for? You and I have merely performed our duties to the best of our abilities. I expect only the back-pay that's due to me – nothing more."

"Rajeev's right, you know, Dominic," Sylvia insisted. "What you call 'only your duty' has changed Fenwold's future forever. Now that you've broken through the Wall, there's all that new land to save our people from famine – not to mention the wonderful things that Cara spoke about. How can you make so little of it?"

"I was in the right place at the right time. That old woman might have recited her riddle to any other marshal she happened upon. And besides, I didn't do all this on my own. Think of all the help I had along the way from brave young village folk – like you two."

"Well," Sylvia said, "I for one wouldn't mind a bit of fame and flattery. What about you, Rajeev?"

"Me? I haven't done that much. I just came along for the ride."

She sounded exasperated. "Oh, no. Don't tell me you're going to be a shrinking violet, just like him!"

"No, not at all. But before our quest to breach the Wall, don't forget it was he who organised us to face and defeat the raiders. Without him, they'd have enslaved or destroyed us. That alone deserves some special honour."

Dominic sighed. "As I've said many times before, I was merely the motivator. It was you and others like you who found the courage to face those outlaws. You're the ones who deserve the accolades."

The deputy looked puzzled. "Well, I may not know what an accolade is, but I do know that none of this would have happened if you hadn't come along. You might as well accept it, Marshal. You're going to be everybody's favourite. So why not enjoy the experience?"

Realising he wasn't going to win the argument, Dominic shrugged and peered out across the river. Through a much lighter drizzle the boat bobbed about at a point roughly a quarter of the way across.

"If you two don't mind, I'm going to shut my eyes for a while. Give me a kick when they land, will you Rajeev?"

What his deputy and Sylvia had said was true. He'd never been able to handle praise. It always embarrassed him. He recalled now how he'd hated the passing out ceremony on completing his training, almost a year ago. Looking down from the dais as the Senior Councillor handed him his marshal's emblem, he found it hard to stand straight and smile, or to return the looks of pride on his parents' faces. He felt the world sensed and silently ridiculed his discomfort, and he was never so relieved as when he stepped off that platform to merge into the crowd again.

But now as he drifted in and out of sleep thoughts of the ceremonies to come floated in like dark clouds across the otherwise bright blue sky of his impending career. Hard work, outlaws and impenetrable concrete walls – these were the stuff of his life, issues he knew how to deal with. But ceremony, officialdom and all its trappings – he'd sooner leave all that to someone else. He wasn't much looking forward to reporting back to the Capital either. He only wanted to get back to work.

But there was one ceremony that didn't loom ominously. Rather it rose like the bright morning star above a clear horizon, lightening his mood and lifting his spirits. That would be the day when he travelled back to Sylvia's home village of Crowtree and formally asked her father for her hand in marriage. As he dwelt on that heart-warming prospect he fell into a deeper sleep.

It was brief.

His first thought as he felt the sharp *thud* in his side was, "I know I asked you to give me a kick, Rajeev, but not quite so hard!"

His eyes opened to reveal that it wasn't his deputy who'd delivered the kick. How could he? For a heavy set brute dressed in the tunic and breeches of a Council lawman had him securely restrained. A second officer, with difficulty, held Sylvia in his grasp, while she spat and struggled. And the third was the owner of the primed crossbow now aimed at Dominic's torso, as well as the military boot that had struck him so forcefully. His blood froze when he recognised the stern voice that now addressed him.

"Marshal Dominic Bradley, I am charged by the Fenwold High Council to place you under close arrest and to deliver you to the Capital for trial."

He struggled to respond, because his throat was completely dry. Puzzlement, anger – he recognised these emotions. But there was also a tinge of fear – similar to the trepidation he'd experienced while climbing the Wall at Crowtree several months earlier. He fought its effects and worked his tongue to produce saliva. Colonel William Carson had been a thorn in his side during his training at the Academy, but he was determined now not to let him know that he was afraid. He sat upright.

"Trial, Sir?" he demanded as forcefully as he could. "May I ask on what charge?"

Carson corrected him. "Not 'charge' – charges – seven counts of dereliction of duty and one of involuntary manslaughter."

Bradley looked him in the eye. "Let me stand, please Sir."

Carson jerked the weapon to indicate his grudging assent. "Slowly though – and don't think about diving for your weapons. They've been removed."

Bradley hadn't expected otherwise. He knew these men were drilled to perfection. He got to his feet.

"Who accuses me?"

"The High Council." This was a tribunal elected to govern Fenwold between infrequent meetings of the full Council.

"And what does the High Council hope to achieve by bringing these ridiculous charges?"

"No more ridiculous than a Council marshal who talks in his sleep! Looking forward to some ceremony or other, are you? I can't comment on the Council's motives. I only know that when you're found guilty you'll face ten years' hard labour after being publicly stripped of your commission!"

He delivered these words with a sneer, which broadened to a callous smile as he turned to his men and announced, "Now, that should be a ceremony I wouldn't want to miss!"

CHAPTER FIVE
A MUTED REUNION

"I don't know what to say to you, Marshal."

Sean ran his hand through his hair in frustration, while his wife and son Toby stared anxiously from the kitchen of the simple cottage.

"When Colonel Carson asked us to take him across to the north bank, he said it was to surprise you. I had no idea he intended taking you prisoner."

Dominic placed a reassuring hand on the fisherman's shoulder.

"Don't go blaming yourself, Sean. Carson always was a sneaky devil. He was right about surprising me though. For a moment when I saw him standing over me, I almost believed he'd come to escort me back home for a hero's welcome."

"But why didn't he just wait here for my cousin to bring you back to Nearbank? Why suffer the discomfort of that stormy crossing?"

Dominic's half-hearted laugh was ironic. "Because he knew I'd suspect something as soon as Luke mentioned his name. Even if he'd convinced you all that his intentions were genuine, he knows I wouldn't trust him if he said the Sun was going to rise in the morning."

Sean nodded. "I see. So he wouldn't want to risk your escaping into the forest with your friends."

He gestured to Dominic to take a place at the table, while his wife and son served the supper.

"Not that we'd have done that. Living as outlaws in that dense woodland wouldn't be a pleasant prospect. I couldn't spend the rest of my life as a fugitive. And though I despise the man, I can't deny he's good at his job. He'd track us down eventually. No, I'd sooner get this stupid business over with. I may have made some mistakes in my dealings with the raiders, but I don't believe any of my actions were criminal. I have to return to the Capital and clear my name. He knows that too, which is why he's allowed me to stay with you here until we start back."

The fisherman nodded towards the door to the rear of his cabin. "Well, if you did decide to make a break, now would be your best chance. It's dark and families are busying themselves with supper. You could be away clear into the forest before the guards outside knew you'd gone."

Dominic shook his head. "There's no need. I'm confident I can squash Carson's trumped-up charges. Besides, do you really think I'd make you an accessory? Of course I wouldn't – and he knows that too."

Sean shoved the food about on his plate and said slowly, "I know, Marshal. You're an honourable man. But what will happen to Sylvia and Rajeev?"

Though lacking his usual hearty appetite, Dominic forced himself to eat, not just because he knew the household could ill afford to waste food, but because he had no idea when or what his next meal would be. Not all deputies were as adept at cooking as Rajeev. The thought brought a faint stinging to his eye.

"They have nothing to fear. Neither of them can be blamed for my decisions. Getting mixed up with me was just their misfortune."

His host laughed nervously. "I'm sure they don't see the situation quite like that, Marshal. When I spoke to Sylvia earlier she seemed distraught to think what might happen to you."

Dominic gritted his teeth and gripped his knife tightly.

"What I couldn't do to that swine for causing her this anguish! Carson always hated us younger marshals for being chosen instead of him to lead the fight against the raiders. He's acting out of pure jealousy. I need to talk to Sylvia and make her see how flimsy these charges are."

Sean frowned and said meekly, "I'm afraid you won't see Sylvia again until all this is over."

"What makes you think that?"

"She told me that Carson had ordered Deputy Shah to escort her back to her home village of Crowtree, where Rajeev is to serve under her brother – apparently he's the resident marshal there."

Dominic nodded. "Yes, I appointed Jack to that position. What you say confirms that Carson doesn't intend to charge Rajeev for merely following my orders. I'm relieved to know that. But he hasn't done this out of the goodness of his heart."

"What do you mean, Marshal?"

"It's clear the swine wants Sylvia and Rajeev far away from the Capital during my trial."

Sean studied the piece of fish on the end of his knife. "I see. You told me Crowtree is in the southwest, and the Capital is on the east coast. How far away is that? About three days' journey?"

"Without a change of horses and in good conditions, yes. And winter's already made its entrance."

"So, it's going to take several days to have them called as supporting witnesses."

"Yes. Not that I'd choose to put them through that ordeal though. I'm confident I can speak for myself. It's true that I did make some mistakes."

The fisherman banged his fist on the table, rattling the dishes and cutlery and making everyone sit up and take notice.

"But, by the Gods, Marshal, surely these are far outweighed by your achievements?"

"Thank you for saying so, Sean. But don't forget – I know Carson only too well. He'll twist the facts to show me in the poorest light. He'll claim I merely helped a few villagers face up to that rabble of raiders in the southwest – just as many of my brother marshals did in their appointed regions. That was our prime objective after all – the culmination of our gruelling course of training at the Academy. Failure wasn't an option for any of us. We were just doing our jobs. That's how he'll paint it. Then he'll parade my mistakes before the Tribunal and try to exaggerate them out of all proportion."

"But what of the rescue of my son and your Sylvia from the clutches of that vicious brute of an outlaw? And then there was your quest to conquer the Wall and discover the treasures of the Ancient Ones."

Having finished his meal, Dominic sat back in his chair. "Much as it was important to you, Sean, the rescue mission may be seen by the Tribunal as a mere sideshow at best, and possibly as a reckless act. They might even question the necessity of risking our lives on such an escapade."

The fisherman looked exasperated. "But what about the Wall and the treasure?"

Dominic sighed heavily. "I have no proof that we found treasure. There was a gadget that the Ancient Ones' representative Cara gave to us, but Carson's men confiscated all our gear. He's probably had it destroyed by now. No, my friend, I'm going to have to go back to the Capital, state the truth as I know it and make the Tribunal believe me."

"And if they don't?"

"I'm not even going to consider the possibility."

The fisherman smiled. "It's good to hear you say so, Marshal."

Dominic also found some humour in the situation. "And if I do end up in prison, when it's all over, perhaps Sylvia will wait for me and I'll join her people in Crowtree as a simple farmer!"

The fisherman laughed and placed a fraternal hand on Dominic's shoulder. "I'm sure that girl would wait for you till the end of time, Marshal. And if you don't find a refuge in the south, I hope you know you'll both be welcome here. Perhaps we'll even teach you to be a real sailor at last!"

As, still smiling, they clasped hands in friendship, the door burst open and Carson's imposing frame appeared in the doorway.

"That's it, Bradley," he sneered. "Have a laugh while you can! You'll not be finding much cause for merriment where you're going. And here's another reason to wipe that grin off your face. I've been talking to that young girl you brought up here with you and, on top of all the other charges against you, I'm pretty certain I can make a case of abduction of a minor. That'll be enough to double your custodial sentence. I've already advised her to give up any hope of waiting for you. You'll both be middle-aged by the time you're released."

Carson's satisfied smirk caused Dominic to spring forward angrily, his right fist clenched ready to land a blow on his prominent and suddenly inviting chin.

"Go on, you young upstart!" Carson growled. "Strike a senior officer! Add a few more years to your sentence!"

Sean grabbed Dominic's hand and beckoned to him to sit down. He did, but he was still seething. "Sylvia is eighteen," he hissed. "She followed me of her own free will. I even tried to send her home with the traders, but she refused. Rajeev can vouch for that."

"Oh, I've no doubt he can. Anyway I'm not disputing what you say. But the way I see it she was still seventeen when you failed to persuade her to return home. It's an unfortunate technicality, I know, but enough, I think, to convict you of abduction. You know how slapdash these simple village folk are about the precise timing of events. They don't celebrate birthdays, for that very reason. You'll find it impossible to prove she was eighteen when she latched on to you. The only safe verdict – for the benefit of vulnerable young girls who fall under the spell of predators such as you – is to punish you as an example to others. We can't allow lecherous marshals to use their office to lure innocent young girls away from the safety of their homes and families."

Dominic seethed as he digested Carson's words. And though he knew it was futile, he asked, "Can I see her?"

The senior lawman raised his eyebrows. "Given the nature of the charge – no, you may not see her. She and the deputy leave for Crowtree first thing in the morning."

He turned as if to leave, but then paused and sneered cruelly. "But think about this, Bradley. You claim this girl followed you of her own free will, yet it seems she can't get back to her home village fast enough. I heard her ask your deputy if they could start out tonight. Fortunately he has the sense to see the foolishness in that. But it's plain she's eager to see the back of you."

"You're lying!" Dominic said accusingly, rising to take a step towards Carson. But he was restrained again by Sean's hand on his arm.

"Why should I lie? She seems an intelligent girl. Even if there's doubt about her precise birthday, she'll have worked out by the seasons that she's an adult by now, and free to go wherever she wants to. And she wants to go home. She's had enough of you. It seems to me she's weighed up her chances and decided to cut her losses. After all, there must be plenty of eligible young warriors back home in Crowtree. I can't say I blame her."

Deflated and confused, Dominic was for once at a loss for words.

Carson concluded, "We four will start out for the Capital at mid-day. I advise you to get yourself cleaned up and mentally prepared. We've a long journey ahead of us. And you've some hard questioning to face before you begin your sentence."

CHAPTER SIX
A FATHER'S WELCOME

"My son, in spite of what's happened, it's good to see you home safe."

Councillor Bradley's declaration was nervous and stilted, as if carefully rehearsed during the short walk from the family mansion to the Council House. It was here in one of its gloomy basement cells that Dominic was confined until his trial. Only a pale wintry light filtered through the small grill near the ceiling, and the guards had lit the wall candles even though it was mid-morning. For the moment forgetting his dismal surroundings young Bradley rose from his cot and grinned when he heard his father's voice. The old man had never been fluid in his conversation – his thoughts were usually occupied with business deals and trading ventures. But Dominic was by now used to his father's apparent lack of emotion, often wrongly interpreted by many as coldness.

"It's good to see you too, Dad."

Resisting an urge to step closer and hug the old fellow – which he knew would embarrass both of them – he merely extended a hand, fighting the stinging behind his eyes when it was accepted heartily. He read genuine affection in his father's half smile, mixed with concern for the predicament now facing his only son. But even this must require much effort, for as they lowered their hands he sensed the awkwardness returning.

"Have a seat." He pulled forward a wooden chair from the corner of the cell, while he made do with the edge of his cot.

"I'm glad they did as I asked and left your hands unbound," his father said.

"Thanks for that. I wondered why they were suddenly so trusting. Did you have to put up a surety?"

The Councillor brushed the matter aside with a sweep of his hand.

"How's Mum? Couldn't she face seeing me here?"

The Councillor averted his eyes and shrugged. "Your mother isn't feeling too well today, I'm afraid."

Dominic tried hard not to react to what sounded a lame excuse. It was more likely that she wouldn't want to be seen anywhere near this place. Straight-faced, he merely said, "I'm sorry to hear that. Tell her I hope she'll be better soon."

His father coughed nervously. "She sends her love, naturally. I'm trying to persuade the Tribunal to grant you bail until the trial. It'll be more fitting for her to welcome you back to your proper home."

Dominic forced a smile, even though he felt a pang of guilt that he found it hard to love his parents in equal measure. He did love them both, of course, as any dutiful son would. After all, hadn't they each encouraged him to follow his chosen career, even to aim for its pinnacle by becoming one of the Academy's brightest graduates? But he felt his father's pride was felt genuinely for him on a personal level, whereas his mother paraded his successes as trophies to elevate her in the eyes of her society friends. He'd always told himself that this was just her way. He didn't doubt her affection, even if it wasn't always obvious. In any case he didn't expect to get the chance to mend their relationship in the near future, because the likely outcome of his father's request for bail was surely a foregone conclusion.

"I've disappointed you, Dad. I'm sorry about that. I don't know how this happened. I was expecting to come home to cheers and laurels, until Carson brought this catalogue of charges. I didn't think I'd done so badly. And if I made mistakes, I can promise you that I always acted with the best of intentions."

His father surprised him by touching his shoulder reassuringly.

"I'm sure you did, son, and you shouldn't apologise for your actions. I know the standards you set yourself have always been far higher than most. But there's something you must understand. Carson is only a tool for others – albeit a willing one. It's my belief that these exaggerated charges have been brought for political reasons."

Dominic perked up. "Really? How do you mean?"

"There've been quite a few changes since you left the Capital for Crowtree last summer. Beyond your basic training, you were chosen for special tuition from a group of wise people who were convinced it was time – and in Fenwold's best interests – to find a way to the far side of the Wall. But that policy was supported only by a narrow majority of Councillors, including two of the three Tribunal members in office at the time."

Dominic shrugged. "I recall there was a noisy minority who didn't go along with the plan, though I can't say I took much notice of them. I was too busy concentrating on my training, and the only discouragement I had was from Carson. That was understandable though, because he wasn't chosen to lead our force in spite of his seniority. I'd have been miffed too if I'd been in his position. But are you telling me that the Council no longer supports mass migration beyond the Wall? And what about my tutors? Don't they have a say in the matter?"

The Councillor's grave expression deepened further, and there was a rare tinge of bitterness in his tone. "They've been effectively silenced, and threatened with imprisonment if they persist in their teachings. Those who now dominate the Council are dead set against any faction that might challenge their authority."

Dominic frowned. "But don't they understand the importance of the new lands beyond the Wall? Even without the great store of treasures waiting for us there, access to these virgin lands solves our over-population problems at a stroke. Surely they can see that?"

"I've no doubt that some of them can – even if they say they doubt your word. I've tried to work out why they should want to discredit your discoveries, and the only conclusion I can draw is that they're afraid of the consequences, and the impact on their comfortable positions here."

"But that's ridiculous! Opening up the far side will *increase* trade, not diminish it!"

His father shook his head. "I know, I know. But it will do more than that. It will empower the poor farmers who move there and help develop this new world. It will cause upheaval for the structure of society in Fenwold itself. Your teachers must have told you that people naturally fear change – and that's especially true of those in power."

Dominic recognised the wisdom in his father's words.

"But what happened to bring about this sudden alteration in the Council's power base, Dad?"

"Our majority was always narrow. It took ages even to win agreement to fund the training of marshals to fight the raiders. As for conquering the Wall – the opposition always fought to prevent it, claiming it was a fanciful scheme based on superstition and wild guesswork. That's why in the end only one man could be spared to undertake that quest. Many doubted that you'd succeed – even on our side."

His son sighed. "I didn't realise my position was so precarious. I should have taken more interest in politics, I suppose. My mind was too focussed on my main goal."

"There's nothing wrong in that, Dominic. And there's one thing I want to say to you now, whatever happens."

The Councillor looked his son in the eye and said, "I can promise you that I never doubted you. And even if this madness prevails and your efforts come to nothing, they can never take away my pride in what I know you've achieved."

There was a brief silence between them then, conveying that deep paternal love that the staid old Councillor had never been able to put into words.

"But, to answer your question, our faction included a number of older Councillors, and two deaths were sufficient to tip the scales against us. I don't suspect foul play. A sudden sickness claimed the lives of several elderly citizens here in the Capital. Councillors may be powerful people, but they're not immune to the diseases that strike from time to time. With two of your strongest supporters gone, a proposal was carried to appoint a new ruling High Council comprising two of their people and one of ours. They now had the majority they needed to overturn existing policy and make new executive decisions, and they wasted no time. Their first act was to withdraw support for their predecessors' quest to breach the Wall. By this time word had come that you were heading north on your journey to contact the Ancient Ones. It was easy for them to ridicule an expedition said to be based principally on some doggerel resembling a children's rhyme."

Though he knew his father's words shouldn't affect him in this way, Dominic suddenly felt very foolish, and he nodded glumly.

"The Fenwold Riddle."

"Yes. And though several of us were convinced you'd found the link that pointed from across the centuries to Fenwold's destiny, our opponents made light of the riddle and rubbished the idea that it could lead to any significant discovery. But they were obviously scared enough of being wrong that they felt a need to discredit you personally in the eyes of the populace. In this they recruited Carson and his investigators to root out anything that might show you in a bad light."

Dominic smirked ironically. "I bet he was only too glad to help them."

"We both know he was jealous to death that a younger marshal had been chosen to lead the quest. When word came through from traders of your success in defeating the raiders in the south-west, he sent out scouts to follow your tracks and sniff out your every error or stroke of bad luck."

Another sardonic smile crossed his son's lips. "They must have been spoilt for choice."

Looking sad, his father placed a hand on Dominic's forearm – a physical gesture that he found both surprising and comforting. "You always had a tendency to be hard on yourself, son. Who doesn't make the odd mistake in their work, especially when they're young? It's how we learn and improve."

Then with down-turned eyes Dominic said bitterly, "I made my biggest mistake on day one."

"You mean, losing your deputy?"

Dominic nodded and said sadly, "I'll never forgive myself for putting Vin Colby in harm's way, Dad. I should never have gone along with his idea to make camp in such an exposed position. But we were both tired and damned hungry. And when I saw he was hit, all I could think of was getting out of there."

"If you hadn't, you'd have been dead too, no doubt."

"Well, yes, but …"

"But nothing. You had to make a hard decision, and it was the right one. When the Tribunal questions you, just tell them the plain truth. That's your best course of action. Meanwhile I'll find witnesses who'll testify to your good character. And there must be plenty that you helped on your mission who'd speak up for you, surely?"

Dominic had already thought long and hard about this.

"I had two companions on my journey north – Sylvia Storey and Rajeev Shah. They displayed great courage, and I trained them to become capable warriors. But in many ways they were naïve. I think a clever prosecutor would portray them as being too close to me – too much under my control. And their youth would detract from their credibility. My accusers would only trash their testimonies and write them off as fawning sycophants."

He didn't add that he was still bitterly disappointed that Sylvia hadn't found a way to stay with him, rather than give in so readily to Carson's demand that she return directly to Crowtree with Rajeev. Outranked by Carson, Rajeev could be forgiven for simply obeying a direct order. But as a free adult woman, Sylvia needn't have abandoned him quite so meekly.

Then he recalled other friends he'd made during the quest.

"There's the fisherman Sean – Rajeev and I rescued his son and Sylvia from the clutches of an evil outlaw known as Red. You'd have liked Sylvia's father, Tom Storey, Crowtree's headman. He treated me like his own son. I trained and appointed his natural sons, Jack and Liam, as lawmen in my absence. There was Don Benson, the Crowtree blacksmith – a very clever and even visionary man, whose skill in making the weapons and physical defences for the village proved invaluable. Then there were all the young people of Crowtree and Ashwell who trained hard to become warriors fit to fight and defend their villages. Any of these would support me loyally, I know.

"But they are all simple folk, unpractised in the ways of wheedling lawyers and unscrupulous politicians. My accusers would run rings around their testimonies and make them look foolish."

What a pity, he thought, that he couldn't employ Cara's idea of the written word, avoiding the need for his friends to attend the Court to testify in his favour. But that seemed to him now to be nothing but a foolish dream.

"So, yes, Dad, I met many whom I now count among my friends. But I wouldn't want to subject any of them to such an intimidating ordeal."

His father set his jaw. "Don't be too hasty, son. I've found that good people will do what's necessary for loyalty's sake, especially where the cause is a just one." His left eyebrow twitched and with a flicker of a smile he added, "And you might find you have friends in surprising places."

Dominic was intrigued. "What do you mean?"

"You didn't think I'd let you face your impending ordeal without arranging some professional representation, do you?"

"But, Father, I don't need…"

"You need as much help as you can get. I know you've always resented my buying you any advantage, but on this occasion I have to insist."

"Insist? On what?"

The Councillor cleared his throat and said nervously, "I've arranged for someone with exceptional legal expertise to represent you."

Dominic's expression turned from one of amused surprise to incredulous indignation.

"Dad, don't tell me it's…"

"Now, son, you have to accept that Pieter was Gretchen's choice – and you know the reason for that. That doesn't alter the fact that he's the best man for the job."

He wondered if his father saw the irony in that remark. But he only took a deep breath and said, "I apologise, Dad. You're right. I should – I do thank you for doing your best for me. I wouldn't be a man if I couldn't put aside my bitterness and make use of his talents. Besides…"

He paused, and his father frowned the unspoken question.

He was going to tell him about Sylvia. But what point was there in referring to a relationship that no longer existed?

"Never mind, Dad. I'm grateful for anything you can do. When will he see me?"

"Later today, after lunch."

CHAPTER SEVEN
FRIENDS AND FOES

"How are you, Marshal?"

The huge figure hung in the doorway, gangly and awkward. Over two strides in height, Pieter Jennings had to duck to clear the doorjamb, as he wiped a big hand on his breeches and thrust it clumsily in Dominic's direction.

His familiar gawkish smile kindled memories for Dominic of their long friendship through school and the Academy, even after they'd chosen different career paths. It was a shame they'd parted on such bad terms, and although the cause of their quarrel seemed devastating at the time, now somehow it was just a remote and trivial episode.

He took Jennings' clammy hand and offered him the hard wooden chair saying, "As well as you'd expect me to be under the circumstances, Pieter. How about you?"

"Oh, I'm fine. Gretchen and I have been following the tales of your exploits with interest – some of them quite incredible. But you know how the traders like to add spice to their news. They've had you up the Wall, over the Wall, talking to the Gods – even getting advice from the Ancient Ones! But what can't be denied is your success in clearing the raiders out of the southwest. It makes us proud to know you."

"It's a shame the Council don't see things the same way, Pieter. In any case, I can't take all the credit – I had a lot of help from the farmers and their families."

Jennings smiled. "Still the modest one, eh?"

Dominic shrugged and asked, "How's Gretchen?"

"Very well. She sends her – regards."

"Tell her I said 'Hello'."

"Of course. Now, we'd better get down to business. But before we start I want you to know that I'm in complete agreement with your father about the motives behind these charges against you."

"You mean, that they're political?"

"Yes – although I'm not sure our knowing that fact helps us very much."

"How could it? If those in power want to see me discredited, what chance do I have? It goes without saying they'll have appointed judges who see things their way."

Jennings nodded gravely. "They're taking no chances. The High Council itself will hear your case. It comprises two of the ruling party's people and one of your father's friends – he's quite a frail old fellow though, and only there because the Tribunal has to reflect the political make-up of the whole Council."

Dominic raised an eyebrow. "And who owns this friendly face?"

"Ahmed Ali."

"I know Ahmed. He's partnered my father in many business ventures over the years. He's a decent chap, but he's not especially forceful."

"I know, but at least you'll have one ally on the bench," Jennings offered.

"And another one representing me."

His advocate blushed. "I'm glad you harbour no hard feelings. I was sorry we had to fall out as we did, especially right on the eve of your departure. There was no time for us to discuss things rationally."

"Don't worry, Pieter. I'm over it now. Anyway it's a common enough story. When two friends fall for the same girl, there has to be a loser. Besides, Gretchen made it clear she could never be a lawman's wife. Nor do I blame her for that. She made the right decision. I hope I'm grown up enough to admit that the better man won."

Clearly keen to change the subject Jennings said, "But what of your adventures? You didn't really get to meet the Gods, did you?"

Dominic laughed and shook his head. "No. I did climb the Wall though – and was later helped to the other side by a... "

Here he paused, realising that even his intelligent friend would have trouble with the concept of a hologram without having seen one. So he chose his words carefully.

"I was helped by a messenger sent by the Ancient Ones."

"A messenger? But how could a man travel from the past?"

Dominic sighed and smiled. "I didn't put that very clearly. It wasn't a living person – only a representation. And it was a *she*, not a *he*."

The look of scepticism on Jennings' face told him he'd already said too much.

"I want to know more about these things, Dominic, but I'm afraid there's no time just now. Promise me this though. When you're giving evidence, try to avoid referring to any event that the court might not understand. They'll see it as a threat and it won't help your case. Just stick to the relevant facts."

"All right, I'll try to do that. But it's all relevant to Fenwold's future."

"Even so, take my advice and save it for later. First we have to get you cleared of these charges. Have they been put to you formally yet?"

"Not really. Unless you count Carson's gleeful outpouring when he arrested me. I know there are several relating to honest mistakes I made."

"I agree – and I hope we'll convince the Tribunal that that's just what they were. But how do you think Carson's men gathered all this information about you?"

"It wouldn't have been so hard. I did nothing secretly. In all my planning I confided in Tom Storey – the Crowtree village headman. I wouldn't have had the villagers' cooperation if I hadn't. It would have been easy for Carson's smooth-talking investigators to wheedle the details out of Tom. He's a pleasant old chap who loves nothing better than a chinwag over a couple of beers. If that's how it happened I forgive him now unreservedly. In any case, what does it matter? I'd have admitted the facts freely if they'd bothered to ask me. For the sake of the Gods, we're only talking about simple professional errors of judgment!"

Jennings nodded. "There are seven such charges – plus one connected count of involuntary manslaughter. As you say, they seem the kind of misfortunes that could befall anyone on active duty under dangerous conditions. We'll go through them one by one and make sure you can recall all the pertinent circumstances."

"Do you really think that'll make a difference?"

"I might be able to argue that they be treated as military issues that should be dealt with via normal disciplinary channels. That should at least buy us some more time. But it's the ninth charge that's going to prove our biggest challenge."

"The abduction? It's ridiculous, really. Sylvia – she's Tom Storey's daughter – followed us secretly and we had no choice but to take her along, if only for her own protection."

"But they claim she was a minor. Did you know that?"

"Yes. No. I can't be sure. There was so much more important stuff going on. It didn't occur to me to check."

Jennings looked straight at him. "Dominic, if they ask you about… If they want to know whether… "

Dominic lowered his gaze and said dejectedly, "I can't deny it, Pieter. I fell in love with Sylvia. We spoke of marriage. We made love. As far as I was concerned she was an adult woman."

"I see. But where is she now?"

"That's what's hard to understand. She went back home to Crowtree with my deputy, Rajeev Shah. All right, Shah had no choice in following Carson's direct order. But Sylvia could have chosen to come with me if she'd really wanted to. Instead she went back with him. I feel she's abandoned me."

"Why should she do that?"

"I've done nothing but wonder about that since they threw me into this cell. Maybe she didn't feel strong enough to help me face this ordeal – though many times I've seen her display the courage of a young wolf."

"But if she's just a simple village girl, she may feel unable to face the complexities of court proceedings in the Capital. That would require a different kind of strength."

Dominic sighed. "Or could it be that her feelings just aren't strong enough? I couldn't blame her for having second thoughts about getting involved with a Council marshal. It wouldn't be the first time, would it? How many successful lawmen do you know who can boast a wife and family? Not many, I'll bet. Maybe the solitude of bachelorhood comes with the badge of office."

Jennings shifted uncomfortably on the hard chair. "You really do have it bad for this girl, don't you, Dominic?"

"By the Gods, Pieter, I surely do – though it was never my own choice. It's as if she's a potion that I need for my very existence! My dreams are filled with thoughts of her – the tone of her voice, the warmth of her physical presence, the smell, taste and touch of our intimacy. They come out of nowhere to taunt me during the solitary hours. I'm telling you, the prospect of a prison sentence is nothing compared to the torture of having to do without her!"

Jennings breathed a thoughtful sigh. "How long a ride is it to Crowtree?"

"Normally I'd say three days. But with a change of horses, a good rider could do it in a day and a half."

"Right then. I'm going to organise a courier."

"What if she won't come?"

"She has to – she's your key witness. I'll make sure she understands how serious this could be for you. If her feelings are true, I'm sure she'll come. I only hope we can get her here in time."

"What do you mean?"

"Oh, don't say they haven't told you! The trial's due to start tomorrow morning. We'll have to try and string out your defence on the lesser charges."

"But do you really think Sylvia's testimony will impress the Tribunal?"

"I don't know. But one thing's for certain. Without her in that witness box, I'm afraid your chances are pretty slim."

CHAPTER EIGHT
THE ORDEAL BEGINS

Early the following morning Dominic was shaken awake by one of the two guards assigned to his 'protection'. Aside from his father and Pieter Jennings, he'd had no other visitors. It was understandable. His old Academy friends being scattered across the enclave on various law keeping duties, it was likely the news of his arrest hadn't yet reached most of them. It would take all of Jennings' skill to avoid his conviction being a mere formality – part of the necessary process to discredit the old Council's plans for Fenwold's development.

The guards said nothing to him as they escorted him into the courtroom – in reality the Council chamber within the ancient building that had always been used for government purposes, even by the Ancient Ones – according to commonly held belief anyway.

In spite of its age it was still magnificent, its exterior faced with a hard stone that had withstood the rigours of the centuries. The internal decorative features were too intricate to have been fashioned by his contemporaries – the perfectly concave architraves, and exquisite ceiling mouldings from which hung the remains of once beautiful glass chandeliers. How they were meant to function nobody knew, because they'd never supported wax candles, though a few of the funny little glass and metal appendages still remained. Oddly under the circumstances his gaze fixed momentarily on one of these and he realised that, although no-one had a clue how they had ever illuminated this hall, he was convinced that the answer lay in Cara's description of the power source she'd referred to as electricity.

From below the dock Jennings smiled a greeting, which Dominic tried his best to return. A man in a tunic of official green, whom Dominic took to be the court clerk, sat straight in front of the main bench. Carson sat not far from him, arms folded and face fixed with an acid grin that bragged of a foregone conclusion. Then Dominic glanced to the rear of the chamber where rows of chairs were arranged for public use. Clearly the populace hadn't yet caught wind of the hastily arranged trial, because only three people sat there – his anxious looking father and a couple of his old Academy co-students, both now fellow marshals. Could the High Council's haste in bringing him to trial reflect their fear of too much of a public show? He nodded towards his few supporters and smiled gratefully at his father for finding at least two friends who would, if nothing else, provide a degree of moral support.

"All rise!"

Everyone stood as the three members of the High Council entered from a side door and took their seats behind the main bench.

"The Court recognises Fenwold High Councillors Rankin, Miller and Ali as competent to hear this trial. Prisoner, confirm your name and rank."

Dominic looked across at the Tribunal, only one of whom he recognised as Councillor Ahmed Ali. The kindly old man looked weary, his expression also betraying a degree of embarrassment, no doubt uncomfortable to have to sit in judgment over the son of his old friend and colleague. The other two looked anything but embarrassed. They fixed Dominic with stony stares, leaving no illusion that he might expect anything approaching a fair hearing under their prejudicial direction.

"I am Dominic Bradley, appointed Marshal and Surveyor of the Wall by the Fenwold High Council."

One of the newer Tribunal members spoke in stilted tones. "I am Councillor Rankin. I have to inform you that the previous High Council acted illegally in this matter, so that your title of Surveyor of the Wall is no longer recognised. We do, however, accept your appointment as a Council marshal. We are here only to examine your conduct since receiving your commission."

"Sir, members of the Tribunal," Dominic said as respectfully as he could manage, "Part of my mission was to find a way through to the far side of the Wall. Not only have I accomplished this, but I have made contact with the Ancient Ones through their…"

He paused, again partly because he was reluctant to use the word *hologram*, but mostly in response to the wild expression on Jennings' face, silently shrieking at him not to go down this avenue. In any event Councillor Miller's harsh voice filled the hiatus.

"We'll have none of this fanciful nonsense, Marshal Bradley! You have no witnesses here to corroborate such rubbish. Therefore you will not insult the Tribunal by alluding to what comprises nothing more than fairy tales and superstition. You are forbidden to make any further reference to matters relating to the Wall. We are concerned only with your conduct as a Council marshal – which, by all accounts, leaves a great deal to be desired."

Jennings addressed the Tribunal for the first time. "Councillors, as advocate for the defendant I must object to Councillor Miller's prejudicial comments."

Miller leaned forwards, his face red with indignation, and he seemed about to vent his anger, when the clerk approached him and whispered something that clearly took the wind out of his sails.

"All right. I withdraw my last remark. But you would do well to remind your client to stick to matters pertinent to the charges in hand." He turned to address Dominic. "I will say this only once, Marshal Bradley. You will either confine your remarks to the subject of your behaviour, or you will be returned to your cell and we shall hear the evidence against you in your absence. Do you understand?"

Inwardly seething, Dominic realised it would do him no good at all to give up the opportunity to answer his accusers, however futile his efforts might turn out to be. So he curbed his temper, gritted his teeth and said, "Yes, Sir."

Here Jennings spoke again, with a confidence and force that quite surprised Dominic. "Councillors, before these charges are announced I wish to move that this Court is not competent to sit in judgement over what, essentially, are military matters. They should instead be dealt with as disciplinary issues by a properly convened Court Martial."

Miller was visibly taken aback by this proposal and spat some whispered words in the clerk's direction. After a few moments he sat back in his chair and declared smugly, "Mr Jennings, are you denying that this Tribunal is the highest authority in the whole of Fenwold?"

The advocate's former spirit seemed to elude him. "Well, no Sir, but…"

Miller cut him short. "In that case, you must accept that it is competent to sit in judgement over whichever case it chooses to."

Jennings stammered, "Well, yes, I do accept that. However I would suggest that a Court Martial would bring a degree of military experience to the proceedings."

"Hmm," Miller huffed. "No doubt it would also bring some of your client's close associates to the proceedings. It's our opinion that a civil hearing is likely to be more impartial."

Jennings opened his mouth, but Miller cut him short. "The matter is closed, Mr Jennings."

Client and advocate exchanged dour glances, and Dominic shrugged as if to say, "Never mind. It was a good try." He could only hope that Pieter might find other ways to delay or extend the hearing so that Sylvia could be brought from Crowtree to speak for him before the trial ended.

The three Councillors now conferred in whispers, following which Ali addressed Dominic in a friendly tone. "Marshal Bradley, I am authorised to explain to you how these proceedings are to be conducted. The clerk will announce each of the nine charges against you in turn. He has committed them to memory from sworn declarations by Colonel Carson's investigators. If necessary they will be called on for corroboration."

Dominic thought how ridiculous it was that the court's deliberations must rely entirely upon the clarity of one man's powers of recall.

Ali concluded, "You will have the opportunity to answer each charge in turn." Then he nodded to the clerk, who turned to face Dominic and address him in clear, neutral tones.

"Charges numbers one and two will be taken together, as both relate to the death of your deputy, Vincent Colby, at the beginning of your mission. You chose to make camp in the heart of raider territory, in a forest clearing barely a league from the safety of the village of Crowtree. Your negligence left you open to attack, and as a result your deputy received what proved to be a mortal wound. You barely escaped with your own life. You are therefore charged first with dereliction of duty and second with involuntary manslaughter, since your ill-advised decision led directly to Deputy Colby's death. How do you answer these charges?"

Although Dominic had re-lived a hundred times the events of that terrible evening, the turmoil of the past few days and his uncharacteristic lowering of spirit had served to dull temporarily the pain of his loss and the associated feelings of guilt. Now, however, the horror of that raider attack leapt vividly to the forefront of his thoughts, forcing him to fight a sensation of intense nausea that welled up from the pit of his stomach. He couldn't deny that he'd expected, at the very least, harsh criticism for Colby's loss, and he'd made no secret (to those closest to him) of the guilt he felt – mostly for being forced to leave his friend to the raiders' mercy in that desolate clearing. He'd admitted more than once to Sylvia and her father that he accepted responsibility for what happened, and he saw no reason to deny it now.

"Sir, Councillors, I admit that it was a bad decision to make camp in that clearing. But we were trail-weary and hungry." He omitted to say that it had been Colby's suggestion that they break their journey in that place. He hadn't mentioned the fact even to Jennings. To try and attach any blame to his subordinate would be nothing less than cowardly.

"As I later discovered, we had missed the opening to the main trail leading to Crowtree, which was overgrown through neglect. Because of raider activity the villagers had taken to using forest trails for safety, but we had no way of knowing that at the time. Even if we hadn't stopped where we did, a league or two further would have brought us to Ashwell, the raider gang's stronghold, where we would have ridden straight into their camp. While I accept responsibility for the decision I made, I don't accept that the outcome was inevitable. It was just our bad luck that a raiders' hunting party was in the vicinity at the time. My escape and subsequent capture by some Crowtree hunters was the only stroke of good fortune that came my way that night."

Rankin sneered. "So I take it you plead *not guilty* to the charges on the grounds of bad luck?" He turned and exchanged mocking grins with Miller.

Again Pieter Jennings interrupted, this time more forcefully. "I must ask the Bench to give my client the courtesy of a fair hearing!"

The Councillors, clearly unaccustomed to criticism, looked exasperated, but on further consultation with the clerk they were seen to defer.

"All right!" Rankin said testily. "We're all new to these procedures. Let's get on with it!"

The clerk looked across to Dominic. "Is the prisoner ready to plead?"

Dominic could only look down and mumble, "To manslaughter – not guilty. To dereliction of duty, I plead guilty."

"Very well," Rankin said. "The clerk will commit the prisoner's pleas to memory. Let's hear charge number three. I suggest after this that we break for lunch."

Dominic suspected that Rankin and Miller were interested more in filling their bellies than dispensing their peculiar version of justice. But he realised their selfishness could work in his favour, and glancing down at Jennings he noticed his advocate was half grinning, equally glad of anything that might induce a delay.

The clerk coughed and said, "The third charge is also one of dereliction of duty. On your first night in Crowtree you were alerted to a fire at an outlying barn. You called for all able-bodied villagers to attend the fire where you directed its extinguishing with some degree of success."

"With a considerable degree of success," Dominic corrected him. "We were able to save several barrels of precious barley grain."

"Silence!" Rankin roared. "You will refrain from speaking until the charge is fully announced!" Then he looked down at the clerk saying, "I don't think we need to hear so much detail. It's irrelevant whether any of the peasants' – er, villagers' – stores were saved or not. Get on with the charge please."

The red-faced clerk paused to gather his thoughts. "You realised too late that this fire was a diversion on the part of the raiders, who meanwhile broke into the unprotected main village barn and absconded with a large quantity of produce. As a result the village headman was forced to impose rationing. How do you plead to this second charge of dereliction of duty?"

Dominic looked down at Carson, whose supercilious expression hadn't changed. In some respects he had to admire just how thoroughly the Colonel's investigator had conducted his enquiries. Again he imagined how his dear friend Tom would have willingly opened up to the officer's seemingly harmless questioning, vividly describing the quenching of the fire as an example of quick thinking on Dominic's part. But the Crowtree headman wouldn't have realised that the purpose of the gentle interrogation was to find a flaw in Dominic's judgment. He could only be relieved that no reference had been made to the deaths of two elderly women who had tried bravely to impede the raiders' progress. No doubt Tom had chosen to omit the details of their sad loss.

"Sir, Councillors, I admit that I should have realised the raiders' true intentions. And although I went on to train and prepare the villagers to defeat the outlaws, that doesn't excuse me from my initial error. I plead guilty as charged."

He now glanced across to the public area where his father sagged with head in hands. He was shocked to realise that, for the first time, he really was seeing his father as an old man. This redoubled the guilt he felt for the shame he'd brought on his family. He found it touching that his two friends had their arms about his father's shoulders, supporting him in this hour of need. One of them glanced at Dominic, flashing a weak smile that helped raise his spirits by the tiniest degree, and he held onto that image as he was escorted back to his cell for lunch.

* * *

Later when the trial resumed, Dominic was disappointed to see that his father sat alone. His two friends had, for some reason, deserted him.

The afternoon was taken up with the clerk's announcement and Dominic's subsequent pleading in respect of five further charges of negligence. All of these concerned minor errors of judgment on his part during his leadership of the Crowtree villagers in their struggle to defeat the raiders. Any attempt by Dominic to mitigate the charges by referring to his successes were quickly slapped down and declared inadmissible or irrelevant by Rankin or Miller. He wasn't really surprised either that Jennings found few opportunities to interject on his behalf, other than to complain about prejudicial comments from the Bench or minor aberrations from standard procedure. Invariably, given the way in which each charge was put in isolation, it was impossible for Dominic to deny that he was technically guilty of negligence, however minor the degree.

Only just before it would have been necessary for the wall candles to be lit, Rankin ordered that the proceedings be adjourned until the following morning. At the end of the trial's first day, Dominic had admitted guilt to seven charges of dereliction of duty, denying only the charge of the involuntary manslaughter of his friend and colleague, Vin Colby.

Pieter Jennings came to see him in his cell just after his evening meal.

"Has your father been to visit you?"

"No, Pieter. I'm glad really. I don't want to be reminded how badly things have gone today – nor to see how miserable it's making him. What happens tomorrow?"

"We'll hear the prosecution's abduction charge. I suspect they'll put Carson's investigator on the stand as it's too complicated for the clerk to remember everything clearly."

"When did your courier leave for Crowtree?"

"Soon after I left your cell the evening before yesterday. I found two good men who agreed to ride through the night. They reckoned they could change horses at a farmstead they know about half way to Crowtree. They planned to ride all day today on a couple of hours' sleep."

"Good men indeed," Dominic said. "But even if they make Crowtree tonight, they'll not get Sylvia back here in time to speak for me tomorrow. Is there any other way you can delay the proceedings?"

"I don't know. I can prevaricate to a certain degree. I'll do what I can. I don't suppose you could feign illness?"

"And risk having them hear the most serious charge without my being present? I don't think so, Pieter."

Jennings shrugged. "Perhaps you're right. Leave it with me. I'll try and think up a lengthy speech to slow things down a bit. It'll give me something to do tonight – I know I won't be able to get much sleep."

Dominic sat on the edge of his cot with head in hands.

"Don't you find it tedious, having to remember so much?"

His friend laughed nervously. "I wouldn't have become an advocate if I hadn't been blessed with a good memory, Dominic. Why do you ask?"

"One of the things the Ancient Ones' messenger told us about was something she called the written word."

"I've never heard of that. What does it mean?"

"I'm not sure I fully understand, but it's a system for recording events and even ideas in a permanent form using a sort of code of special markings on a suitable surface. Someone could make the record in one place, and then someone else could interpret and read it out in another. There are whole storage houses full of these writings about the Ancient Ones and even our own origins, just waiting for us on the far side of the Wall. And so many other such treasures." He waved a hand at the cell walls. "They make all this seem so trivial."

Wide-eyed, his old friend stood and stared at him.

"Dominic, I had no idea. I'm so sorry I didn't let you talk about this earlier."

"No, you were right. Today's proceedings were more urgent. But if you can spare the time now, I'd be happy to tell you of my meeting with the Ancient Ones' representative, and about the great stores of science and knowledge waiting for us on the far side of the Wall. Could you stand that?"

Jennings pulled the chair closer to the cot, resumed his seat and said eagerly, "Just you try and stop me!"

CHAPTER NINE
DELAYING THE INEVITABLE

"That's quite a find, my friend. Where did it come from?"

Dominic peered into a small fragment of mirror glass, scarred and pitted with age, which he'd perched precariously on the sink in the corner of his cell. Grinning, he turned to greet Pieter Jennings who had intruded on his morning ablutions.

"What, this ugly mug? I've had it since I was born, as far as I recollect!"

If Pieter had expected to find Dominic in the depths of despair, his expression now belied it, for his client's irrepressible humour soon brought a smile to his own face.

"That's the spirit, Dominic! If you can keep that frame of mind in court today, we'll give those old fools a battle they won't forget!"

Though his smile remained fixed, Dominic was sure Pieter must know his humour was purely ironic, a mask to hide the desperation he was truly feeling just below the surface. But he fought hard to keep the mask in place.

"Battles I can do, Pieter – against men though. Not rats like Miller and Rankin."

"Yes, they are a bit rodent-faced, aren't they?" Jennings mused. "I wonder if we can distract them for a while with some suitable bait?"

"Oh, you've been working on your delaying strategy, have you?"

"Been giving it some thought anyway. I only hope it'll buy us a couple of hours. If we can just extend the trial for another day, or even two…"

"It seems unlikely, Pieter. They managed to race through most of the charges yesterday. There's only one to go. But I know you'll do your best."

"Of course I will. And this last charge isn't as straightforward as the others. It's also far more serious. I'll make sure it's given due attention. But you still haven't told me where the mirror glass came from."

"Oh, that? I found it at the back of the cabinet by the sink. Only the Gods know how long it's been in there."

"Can I have a look?" Jennings took the ancient shard and examined it. "So that's what I look like – what a good looking fellow! It's been a long time. There aren't many surviving fragments of this stuff. It breaks so easily. From its shape and jagged edges I'd say this was a remnant from a much bigger piece. I wonder how old it is?" He handed it back to Dominic.

"Eight hundred years at least. That's how long ago Cara said the Ancient Ones last walked the Earth, and only they could have made it."

"Cara – she's the woman who you said appeared as a – what was it? A hologram?"

"That's right. Anyway I thought I'd try and smarten myself up for today's performance. But I shouldn't have bothered – even this dirty glass shows how terrible I look – more awful than I'd imagined. And there isn't much I can do about it – I don't even have a comb, let alone anything sharp enough to shave with. I'd probably arrest anyone who looked like I do. A criminal if ever I saw one!"

Jennings laughed. "Now who's being prejudicial? Anyhow don't worry. I'll send out for a barber to come and smarten up your appearance."

"Thanks, but do you think there's time?"

"I'm sure of it. When I came in I passed Rankin and Miller on their way to the refectory. If I know those two they'll be stuffing their faces for as long as it takes to make you as handsome as me!"

* * *

"Distinguished Councillors, we all appreciate the serious nature of this charge. For an adult male to take advantage of an underage female is, I am sure we all agree, a highly immoral act as well as an illegal one. In fact, I would go so far as to suggest that the moral repugnance the act invokes far outweighs any legal considerations. Nevertheless our forefathers deemed it necessary to put laws in place in order to protect potential victims and provide suitable guidelines, outside of which public sanction becomes a necessary deterrent and punishment.

"Now, with regard to the guidelines…"

"Wait a moment please, Mr Jennings!" This exclamation came from the exasperated Councillor Miller, whose ruddy complexion seemed to Dominic to be as much the result of indigestion as of frustration. He hoped so anyway.

"How much more of this diatribe have we to put up with? Do we really need to hear a lecture on the complete laws of Fenwold? We all know how very clever you are, but that isn't the reason we're here."

At this point – and for the umpteenth time – the clerk whispered some words of advice to the Councillor at which, with pursed lips, he rasped, "The clerk reminds me that you have every right to speak on matters pertinent to the case. However I would…" (and here he paused, adjusting his expression as if to reflect the distaste he must be feeling in mouthing his next word) "… *respectfully* request that you have regard to the limitations on our time and good humours."

Jennings scowled and said, "I am very sorry, Councillor, but I was unaware that the Court's deliberations on a charge of such a serious nature should be subject to niggardly time constraints. I feel it most important that my client be given every opportunity to defend himself, if for no other reason than to obviate the later need for a re-trial!"

Dominic was amazed how Miller's facial expression seemed capable of so many degrees of infuriation. In fact he wondered if the old fellow were about to suffer some kind of seizure. It was at this point that he thought Pieter Jennings showed impeccable timing by pulling a masterstroke in the art of prevarication.

"Oh dear, Councillor," said the advocate with credible concern, "Are you not feeling well, Sir? If so I would certainly have no objection to a temporary recess."

Rankin offered Miller a sip of water and they conferred in whispers, pointedly excluding Councillor Ali from their consultation. Then, partly recovered, Miller gasped, "Yes, yes. Thank you. We'll break early for lunch and resume the case this afternoon."

* * *

When the Tribunal reconvened Councillor Miller appeared to have recovered from his earlier seizure, but he was now more subdued, leaving Rankin to conduct the hearing. But while Dominic was glad to hear less from the volatile Miller, he knew from earlier exchanges that Rankin's fevered partiality could be more than a match for that of his colleague.

Also there must be a limit to what extent Pieter Jennings might apply his oratory skills to stretching out the proceedings. His old friend must have used every device in his repertoire to try and extend the hearing, but by not long after lunch it was clear that his talents and energies were all but spent.

It was at this point that Carson's investigator took his place on the witness stand. Smartly dressed in his marshal's tunic he looked the epitome of military reliability. As the first independent witness the clerk formally swore him in.

"Do you swear by the Gods of the Wall that the evidence you are about to give is completely true?"

"I do so swear."

Then, prompted only by a nod from his smug-faced superior, the fellow commenced his testimony.

"I am Marshal Norman Claridge, appointed by Colonel Carson to investigate the alleged misconduct of the accused, Marshal Dominic Bradley. My initial investigations concerned the charges already heard, but it was during my enquiries into those issues that I learned of this most serious crime committed by Marshal Bradley."

Jennings interrupted. "Councillors, I must ask the witness not to make judgements. Whether or not my client has indeed committed a crime on this count has not yet been determined."

Rankin gave an exasperated sigh. "All right, all right. I can assure you that the Tribunal's verdict will disregard everything but issues pertinent to the administration of justice in this case." He then addressed the witness. "Marshal Claridge, we could avoid using up valuable time with defence objections if you'd do as Mr Jennings suggests, and stick to the facts."

Claridge looked only across at Carson, whose slightly raised left eyebrow appeared to ratify the Councillor's instruction.

"Sorry, Sir," Claridge muttered, and coughed before continuing, "During my enquiries at Crowtree and the near-by village of Roundhill, I learned that Marshal Bradley had set out on an expedition to the north, accompanied by a deputy and a young female. Questioning those who knew this girl revealed that she was strongly influenced by Bradley, to the point of infatuation. This wouldn't have been a serious issue had it not

75

been the case that she was only seventeen years old at the time. Knowing that taking a minor without parental consent amounts to abduction, I reported these facts to my superior."

Rankin looked scornfully at Dominic, and seemed to take a leering delight in carefully phrasing his next question, which he delivered painstakingly.

"And may we ask the accused if he took advantage of this innocent young girl's attentions?"

Although he'd rehearsed his response to this inevitable question on countless occasions over the past couple of days, Dominic now felt a stab of shock strike at his inner core. Sweat beaded on his forehead and he fought to stop his hands from shaking. Conflicting emotions of rage, embarrassment and guilt waged battle inside his head and the churning of his stomach made him nauseous. He thought again of his parents' shame and at first avoided looking towards the rear of the chamber where his father sat. But it was impossible. He had to face his fears. He glanced at the old man – and was amazed to see that he was smiling! It was a serene smile that radiated parental love, and as a devoted son Dominic tried to return it. At the same time he thought, "May the Gods bless you for supporting me!" and was certain his father heard his unspoken words. It buoyed him too to see that a group of people – perhaps as many as a dozen – were now taking seats upon the public benches close to his father. He found courage in his father's eyes, took some deep breaths, held tightly to the front of the dock before him and tried hard to concentrate. Standing as straight and proud as he could, he turned and faced the Tribunal.

"Councillors, you have heard me honestly admit to charges concerning mistakes I made on this, my first mission as a Council marshal. You have not allowed me to mitigate by recounting the many successes I achieved in organising the farmers to face and defeat the raiders."

Rankin interrupted. "Because these are not relevant…"

But Dominic didn't let him finish. "My reputation and years of my life are at stake here, Sir! I demand that you let me have my say!"

Shocked, the Councillor looked down at the grim-faced clerk who nodded almost imperceptibly.

Lips pursed, Rankin sat back, shrugged and merely waved a hand as a sign of conditional deference.

Dominic continued, "Don't worry. I'm not about to go into detail about the positive aspects of my mission. I only want the chance to explain fully my relationship with Sylvia Storey, the young lady in question. Let me declare openly now, without shame, that I love Sylvia, and that it was – and still is – my intention that we be married. However, I swear by the Gods of the Wall that I did not abduct her. In fact, when she joined us uninvited on our journey northwards, I did my utmost to have her sent back accompanied to her home village. But she refused to go, leaving me no other choice but to keep her with us for her own protection. At this point there was nothing between us. In fact, it wasn't until much later, after the snows started, that we declared our feelings for one another."

The courtroom was silent for a moment. Then Rankin leaned forward with a twisted grimace and said, "But Marshal Bradley, you haven't answered our question."

Dominic took another deep breath and looked him in the eyes. "Sir, if it gives the Court any pleasure to hear it, yes – we were lovers and we made love – as consenting adults."

Rankin sat back again, grinning broadly. "Ah! Well, that's the unpleasant bit out of the way. The only item in question now would appear to be this. You say you were both adults – consenting or otherwise – but how did you know she was eighteen when you – when these events occurred? Did she tell you as much?"

"No, Sir, she didn't. The question never arose between us. But I had two reasons for being sure of the fact. First, having lived among the good folk of Crowtree throughout the summer, I knew them to be a close community, moral and law-abiding. I worked with and trained several of their youngsters and found them to be respectful and obedient to their parents. Sylvia was like her friends and siblings – honest and true. She would never have done anything to shame her parents, nor to place me in such a position as you are suggesting. Second, she told me when we first met that she would be eighteen later in the year. I told you earlier that the snows had arrived before anything passed between us. She was a woman by then."

Rankin sniffed. "Is that it? Well, Marshal, it appears to me that both of your arguments are based on little more than convenient supposition on your part."

Here Pieter Jennings interjected. "With respect, Councillor, the charge itself is based on supposition. Under our ancient laws the prosecution carries the burden of proof. No man can be tried and convicted on the basis of conjecture."

Rankin consulted with the clerk, and this time their whispered discourse was lengthy. At last Rankin gestured to the clerk to address the Court.

"As I explained to Councillor Rankin, there have been instances in the past where there has been doubt, but where a guilty verdict has been handed down based on the balance of evidence and the need to protect vulnerable young people."

Jennings spoke again. "I have heard of such examples. And although I have not committed their details to memory, my recollection is that in those cases there were hints of intimidation, for example where the accused took advantage of a simple-minded victim."

Rankin leered, "Well, for all we know, this Sylvia Storey may indeed be simple-minded!"

At this, there came an unexpected response from the back of the hall.

"I can assure you she is not, Sir!"

Taken aback, Rankin peered into the late afternoon gloom. "Light the candles! Stand forward, that woman, and state your name!"

The room was hushed. Supported by her man's arm the elderly woman walked slowly to the front, like him unkempt and obviously weary from a long journey. But she stood her ground and did as Rankin had commanded.

"My name is Amelia Storey, Sir. This is my husband, Tom, headman of the village of Crowtree. We are the parents of Sylvia Storey."

CHAPTER TEN
A CRUCIAL TESTIMONY

Dominic stared in disbelief. That Tom and Amelia Storey now stood in the courtroom seemed an absurd impossibility. Jennings' courier couldn't have made the journey to Crowtree and back in less than two days. They must have started out independently. But why would they? And where was Sylvia? He peered to the back of the chamber, but she was nowhere to be seen.

But all that must wait. Here was her mother, apparently wanting to testify – on his behalf, he hoped. He hissed an instruction to his advocate.

Evidently Pieter Jennings understood his client's prompting well enough, for he addressed the Tribunal urgently. "Councillors, Marshal Bradley asks that this woman be allowed to give evidence!"

The travellers appeared bedraggled and exhausted, their garments wet and mired from the muddy track, faces drawn and dirty, a trail of boot prints marking their path from the rear door to where they now stood in full view of the court. Rankin peered down at the spectacle before him.

"Are you asking us to hear testimony from a pair of common tramps?"

Dominic had spent the summer as the Storeys' houseguest, and in all that time he had never heard Tom Storey raise his voice in anger. But the old man did so now.

"Sir, you do me and my wife a great injustice! We've suffered a long and arduous journey to get here – the last four leagues on foot because our horses went lame on us! We came straight to the courthouse out of a sense of urgency, so we've had no opportunity to clean up. And if you lack the common decency to treat us courteously as fellow citizens of Fenwold, I demand at least that you show some respect to my office of headman of the village of Crowtree!"

Rankin only sniffed and turned to confer in whispers with Miller, while Ali strained to catch the drift of their conversation. Clearly still suffering from the aftermath of his earlier seizure, there was irritation in Miller's demeanour as he spoke.

"We've had no notice of this so-called witness, Mr Jennings! I see no point in wasting further time with these theatricals!"

Jennings didn't try to hide his exasperation. "Councillors, I am certain the clerk will confirm that the prior notification of witnesses is a mere courtesy – not a legal necessity."

The clerk was already nodding and for once both Rankin and Miller were rendered temporarily speechless. Councillor Ali however seemed to spring to life and leaned forward.

"In the circumstances I can see no reason why we shouldn't hear Mistress Storey's testimony. Clerk, please swear in the witness."

He did so, after which the Crowtree headman's wife smiled at Ali. "Thank you, Sir. Will it be all right if I speak from here? My back's playing me up and I'm not sure I have the energy to climb the steps into the witness box."

"Yes, of course, dear lady. In fact you can have a seat if you want to." He addressed one of the guards. "Fetch a chair for Mistress Storey, would you?"

This done, she thanked him and he continued, "You know that the Court is trying to determine your daughter's age at the time these events happened – and that your evidence on this point will directly affect the outcome of the trial?"

"Yes, I understand that, Sir. That's why I'm here. Sylvia was a harvest child. She was born eighteen years ago, just as reaping began. I recall it clearly, because Tom chided me that I'd planned it to avoid doing my share of the work in the fields." Here she turned and smiled at her embarrassed husband. Then she added, "But I knew he was only joking."

Judging by their sullen silence and dour expressions, Miller and Rankin clearly didn't see the joke. Councillor Ali continued, "And when did your daughter leave to follow Marshal Bradley?"

"Harvest was well under way when we first missed her. We were terribly worried for a while. But then one of our sons told us she'd confided in him about her intention to join Dominic – Marshal Bradley. We were relieved at that, because he'd become like a third son to us. We knew he wouldn't let her come to any harm."

Throughout her testimony Carson was seething and at times almost writhed in his seat. He glanced repeatedly at Miller and Rankin, obviously frustrated that neither of them challenged her testimony. Suddenly he got to his feet and blurted out, "This is all woolly thinking! Harvest never takes place at exactly the same time! It depends on the weather and growing conditions! The girl could still have been underage!"

Pieter Jennings now spoke. "The Colonel's observation is correct, of course. But in the absence of factual evidence to the contrary, the balance of probability has to be that Miss Storey had reached majority by the time my client agreed to allow her to join his expedition."

Carson stood open-mouthed for a moment, but appeared to be lost for a coherent argument. Angrily he sat down and glared at Dominic.

Councillor Ali, clearly enlivened by the recent turn of events, seemed now to be enjoying his role as spokesman for the Tribunal, while his colleagues on the bench remained tight-lipped and sullen.

Smiling, he rubbed his hands. "It's getting cold. I think we should adjourn until tomorrow morning. By then the Tribunal should be in a position to deliver its verdict."

* * *

Dominic rushed to greet Tom and Amelia Storey as they entered his cell, accompanied by Pieter Jennings. Dewy-eyed he embraced each in turn saying, "How can I ever thank you two for all you've done on my behalf! But how did you get here so quickly – and where is she?" He peered past them, hoping to see their daughter lingering in the corridor.

Tom said, "Forgive our appearance, Dominic. We're grateful to your friend here for taking us to the washing facilities just now, but I'm afraid we've used up all of our changes of clothing. You want news of Sylvia, of course. Well, when I told the Tribunal that our horses had gone lame, it wasn't the entire truth. Our whole journey was dogged with bad luck. First there was the weather – the rain hasn't let up since we left Crowtree four days ago, and there's flooding in several places. We're lucky in the southwest where the drainage is good, but nearer to the coast the ground's all clay and some poor people are being washed out of their homes. It's dreadful…"

His wife interrupted. "Oh, for the sake of the Sacred Wall, Tom! Are you never going to put this poor boy out of his misery?" Then she winced in pain and declared, "Oh! My back!" and dropped the bag she was holding onto Dominic's cot while he helped her to a chair.

Her husband continued, "Eh? Oh, sorry, Dominic. Sylvia's mare shied crossing a ford and threw her. She broke her leg – Sylvia, that is – the mare's fine."

Dominic's concern was now urgent. "Where is she, Tom? Did she make it to the Capital with you?"

Mistress Storey replied breathily, "The Gods sent us a stroke of good fortune. We met Advocate Jennings' courier and he brought us to the livery post. The kind folk there helped fit Sylvia with a makeshift splint, and provided us with fresh horses. I wanted to leave her and hurry on to the trial, but she insisted on making the journey, in case her testimony was needed. Of course it slowed us down to walking pace, but the courier said he thought there'd be time. He was only just right, by the look of things! Anyhow, she rode with us and we found a medic here to fit a proper splint. He says it's not a complete break – the skin isn't broken, only bruised – but she'll need to rest the leg for a good while."

"Poor Sylvia! Where is she now?"

Tom answered, "The medic runs an infirmary not far from here. Sylvia can stay there for a few days, and meanwhile I'll need to arrange for a cart to take her home. I must admit that's a journey I'm not looking forward to."

At this point Dominic's father entered the cell. "Forgive me, Mr Storey. I overheard your conversation. Your daughter must stay with us until she can walk again."

Tom glanced at Dominic, who quickly made the necessary introductions. Then, wondering how his mother would react, Dominic said, "Are you sure about this, Dad?"

"Of course. Your mother and I had a long talk last night and she regrets not coming to see you. But she really has been quite poorly and miserable with winter chills – she can't seem to shake them off, poor woman. I'm sure she'll want to do whatever she can to help."

"Please tell Mistress Bradley we're very grateful, Councillor," Tom said, while his own wife, appearing more comfortable, smiled and nodded.

"I'll tell her. I can't stay long here because there are some people I have to see. I came to tell Dominic we believe the recent elections were rigged. We suspect at least one of the tellers accepted a bribe from the opposing party. We'll soon have enough evidence to justify fresh elections. We're also fairly sure Colonel Carson is in their pockets."

Even though his father's news was positive, Dominic found it hard to raise a smile. Sylvia was now at the forefront of his thoughts. He ached to see her, frustrated that she couldn't come to him, while he wasn't yet free to go to her. And knowing she must be only a few streets away was of little comfort to him. But he wouldn't parade his anguish before his friends and family.

"How does all this affect the trial, Dad?"

"It would mean the Tribunal carried no authority. And as the bogus ruling party, with Carson's help, chose to twist some minor military errors into spurious criminal acts, the entire basis of the proceedings is undermined."

Dominic managed the ghost of a grateful smile.

Then he turned to Sylvia's father and asked out of politeness, "How did your harvest turn out?"

"Very well," Tom said brightly. "We even had a surplus to sell to the traders. Oh, I nearly forgot. Sylvia made you a cake. It's in the bag along with some other things she wanted you to have." Then he said apologetically, "I'm afraid it's a bit overdone on top – you probably know cooking's not one of her foremost talents."

This cheered him somewhat. "That's thoughtful of her. I'll enjoy going through her gifts later. I hope meanwhile you'll thank her and send her my love."

Jennings said, "If you'd all excuse us, I think Dominic and I should spend some time now preparing for tomorrow."

The Councillor said, "Yes, of course. I hope these good people will do me the honour of accepting my humble hospitality during their stay in the Capital. Meanwhile, I think you should know there's a lot of interest in this trial now the word's getting around. People are wondering why it was brought with such undue haste and there are many who resent the Tribunal's attitude to justice. I think you'll see a lot more supporters on the public benches tomorrow, Dominic."

Then he embraced his son and said, "Take heart, my boy. You've many friends here, you know."

Later that night in the quiet of his cell Dominic opened the bag of presents that Sylvia had sent. He ate some of the cake, which tasted delicious only because she had made it. She'd also sent him items of warm clothing, socks and pants, as well as hazelnuts and sweet dried berries. Though small things, these were all signs of her love – and it shamed him now to think that he'd ever doubted it. Chewing on some dried fruit he casually cast the limp sack to one side. It gave a dull *thud* as it hit the wall beside his cot, so he pulled it back towards him and felt inside.

He rummaged through the loose wrappings that he'd put back in the sack, and then plunged his hand into its corners. There at the very bottom he felt something small and hard. Drawing out the article, he removed its linen kerchief wrapping, and stared in amazement at what now lay in the palm of his hand.

It was something he'd seen only once before, and thought never to see again.

* * *

The courtroom buzzed with excitement as Dominic took his place in the dock. There was little room left on the public benches and he thought he even heard some muted applause from the rear of the chamber as he entered.

When the Tribunal members entered the mood took on a darker tone, with murmurings and even some barely stifled booing.

"Silence!"

The clerk's reedy voice failed to bring the unruly crowd to order, and it was left to Councillor Rankin to bang his clenched fist repeatedly on the bench in front of him. As he did so he yelled, "Quiet! This is a solemn court of law and those attending should show it due respect! I'll have the chamber cleared if this goes on!"

It was then that Dominic noticed at least four extra guards posted around the hall, all with loaded crossbows in full view. Glancing across to the bench, he also detected something different about Rankin and Miller – something in their expressions. Then he allowed himself the faintest smile, for he realised the nature of this new demeanour. It was fear. These so-called leaders were afraid of the people who were supposed to have elected them.

Rankin spoke almost in a monotone that suggested he'd committed his short speech to memory.

"We have reached the following verdicts. We find the accused not guilty of abduction."

An almighty cheer arose from the assembly, so loud as to rattle and shake the huge glass chandeliers until Dominic thought they might fall and shatter onto the joyful crowd below. When at last silenced by the repeated banging of Rankin's fist, the people listened attentively as he continued.

"We also find the accused not guilty of the involuntary manslaughter of Deputy Vincent Colby."

This announcement brought more cheering, only this time slightly more subdued. Rankin paused when it subsided, long enough for Dominic to realise that his final declaration was likely to prove less popular.

Rankin coughed nervously and opened his mouth to speak.

"Just a moment, Councillor," Dominic said calmly but clearly. "Before you sentence me for mistakes I freely admitted to, allow me to show you something."

Rankin's expression turned to thunder. "How dare you interrupt the Tribunal's verdict! I'll have you removed! Guards, seize the accused and take him to his cell!"

But Dominic had foreseen Rankin's reaction, noted the two cell guards' positions, and now deftly dodged past them and leapt across to the bench, where he crooked his left arm around Rankin's neck, while holding the shard of ancient mirror glass close up against his jugular.

The courtroom was hushed. Dominic declared, "Friends, I apologise for disrupting the proceedings, but I've known all along that justice was never to be dispensed here. I respect the rule of law, but I refuse to submit to a corrupt Council that abuses the law for its own ends! There's something important I want to share with you. I fear that if I don't do it now, I will never be given the chance again! Pieter, catch this!"

The surprised Jennings caught the small object that Dominic then threw down to him.

"Place it on the floor and gently press the central button with the sole of your foot. You should feel a *click*. Then stand away."

He had wondered whether to forewarn his advocate of his plan, but realised it would place him in an untenable position. Instead he'd decided to gamble on his old friend's compliance at this crucial moment. At least Jennings could claim to have gone along with Dominic's demands for Rankin's sake. Still, Dominic prayed to the Gods of the Wall that Pieter would do as he said.

Jennings stood immobile for a moment, clearly shocked by Dominic's action and perplexed by what he was being asked to do. He held the object in the palm of his hand, staring at it as if trying to comprehend the function of the protruding central button and what looked like small coloured gemstones arranged around its perimeter.

"Put it on the floor, Pieter," Dominic repeated.

Bending his knees, the advocate placed the object in the centre of the clear space between his seat and the front bench.

"Now press the button."

Gingerly he stood upright and put out his right leg, gently applying pressure with the ball of his foot until a distinct *click* echoed around the hushed chamber. Then he stood back.

As if coaxed by some inner fire, the stones began to glow, their hue and brightness increasing with intensity until shafts of colour shot upwards and touched the courtroom ceiling.

This brought a collective *gasp* from the assembly, for none of those gathered here could have witnessed such a sight before. But what ensued was so astonishing as to smother any further vocal reaction. The lights danced – for a while formlessly – until fusing into the transparent but sharply focussed shape of a female figure, clad in a white flowing garment, and twice the height of an average woman.

Pieter, white faced, glanced up at Dominic, who had now released his grip on Rankin. With a questioning look he mouthed one word.

"Hologram?"

Dominic nodded.

While the audience quaked, the giant image spoke in a gentle, reassuring voice that nevertheless filled the auditorium.

"Citizens of Fenwold, have no fear! I am neither human nor demon. My name is Cara, a messenger sent by your ancestors, those whom you call 'the Ancient Ones'. Your wise Councillors sent Marshal Dominic Bradley to find me, by following clues in a riddle passed down through forty generations. We inhabited the entire world beyond the Wall and created many wondrous things. When a plague threatened to destroy Mankind, we shut some hardy volunteers inside the Wall, until it be safe to inhabit our world again. That time has come for you to resume possession of the lands beyond the Wall. For those who wish to join Marshal Bradley, many wonders await you there. I shall be there too, to advise and guide you in your new lives. Those of you who choose to remain in Fenwold will benefit also – but this will take time. Meanwhile I urge you to listen to Marshal Bradley and follow his advice."

Then as suddenly as it had appeared, Cara's image flickered and faded, leaving those present in a state of silent bewilderment.

Dominic knew he must seize the moment. Now was the time to take his biggest gamble. He addressed the gathering.

"Friends, you have heard the voice of the Ancient Ones. I know what you've just witnessed must seem like magic – but believe me, it's not. The Ancient Ones were people, just like us. What they did, we can do. Imagine a future with the advantage of such knowledge – the kind of knowledge that can produce something as wonderful as Cara's image!

"It's my belief that the recent election was rigged. On top of that, I put it to you that these latest events call for fresh elections. Do you agree?"

Assenting voices rang around the chamber. "Yes! Let's have fresh elections!"

Rankin now stood away from Dominic and screamed, "Don't listen to him! This is trickery!" Then he yelled at one of the guards. "You there! Silence him! Shoot him!"

The soldier approached the bench, his primed crossbow aimed in Dominic's direction. But from the floor below the bench the fellow thrust the weapon up to Rankin, saying, "I'll not do your dirty work for you. Do it yourself!"

Rankin took the bow and looked at it quizzically. "But I've never... I don't know how..."

In a flash Carson strode up and snatched the weapon, deftly aiming it at Dominic's heart. "But I know how to," he said. "I'll shut this young whelp up for good and all!"

As he spoke the other three armed men approached him. He snarled, "It's all right, lads. I can deal with him myself. You don't need..."

But when he glanced around, it was to see their bows pointing at him. The senior officer of the three addressed him.

"Put the weapon down, Colonel Carson. You're under arrest."

CHAPTER ELEVEN
A NEW BEGINNING

The military guards – the four he'd seen for the first time today, plus his two familiar cell guards, moved immediately to drag Rankin, Miller, Carson and Claridge into a cowering group on the floor below the bench. The senior man among the military addressed Dominic.

"What shall we do with them, Marshal?"

Dominic hadn't dared imagine or form detailed plans in the event that his ambitious gamble might pay off. His first thoughts were of Sylvia, but his immediate duty now must be to help create some semblance of order out of this present chaos. He glanced across at Councillor Ali's smiling face and realised that he, being the only remaining Tribunal member at the bench, was at that moment technically in charge of proceedings. Having him ratify Dominic's extreme actions would be invaluable just now. He would have to risk that Ali might choose to condemn his recent act of defiance. He took a deep breath and said, "Councillor?"

Ali didn't hesitate. "Better lock them up for the time being," he said, and looked out from the bench at the turbulent crowd. Then he addressed the four sorry-looking captives. "By the looks of things, gentlemen, it'll be for your own protection as much as anything. If it's found that any of you has broken the law, you'll receive a fair trial – fairer than the one you reserved for that young lawman, at least." He nodded in Dominic's direction, and then added, "Otherwise you'll be freed."

To the guards he said, "Take them to the barracks prison. They'll be safer there."

By now Pieter Jennings had joined the group below the bench. Dominic's father also pushed his way through the crowd, with Tom and Amelia Storey close behind him. Dominic moved to descend the steps to floor level, but Ali hissed across to him, "No! Address the people again, Marshal!"

The Councillor waved an arm to indicate the mass of excited citizens and urged breathlessly, "Speak to them. Seize the moment!"

Looking at the faces of the people before him, some agitated, some bewildered, he knew that Ali was right. He resumed his place on the raised platform and shouted, "Quiet, please everybody! Listen to me!"

The hubbub receded.

"I returned here only recently from my expedition to help the farmers defeat the raiders and to seek out Fenwold's inheritance on the far side of the Wall. I've seen only a part of the new lands but I can assure you there's a treasure store of wisdom out there, beyond our wildest dreams! Everything Cara told you just now is true." He indicated the cowering four below him. "For some reason these men didn't want to believe that these good things exist, and brought this trial to discredit me and the wise old Councillors who sent me out on my quest.

"I told you earlier that I respect the law – and I meant that. Because of the confused situation there will have to be new leaders." He glanced behind him to see that Ali nodded his approval. "For the time being though, the Capital will remain under martial law until fair elections can be arranged. Now please disperse peaceably."

Relieved as the crowd vacated the chamber, he singled out the senior officer among the guard. "Can I have a word with you, Major?" He crouched as the man approached. "I didn't realise there'd be this much support. What's the position with the military?"

"It's believed only a few of the top rank were in their pockets, Marshal. The people appear to be with you, and I'm certain you'll have the army's support as well. That goes for the local marshals and deputies too."

"Good. Apart from Colonel Carson, who's the senior ranking officer at the barracks?"

That would be Colonel Rodriguez, Marshal."

"Yes, I think I know him. Is he still his own man?"

"As far as I know his hands are clean, if that's what you mean, Sir."

Dominic recoiled at being addressed so, but couldn't throw the Major's genuine respect back in his face.

"Please go and tell Colonel Rodriguez what's happened and ask him to come to me here, after placing under arrest all suspected corrupt senior officers."

The major looked unsure and glancing up to Ali he asked, "Can I tell him on whose authority, Councillor?"

Ali stared out across the floor of the chamber at the dispersing crowd and with a sweep of his arm declared, "On their authority, Major. The citizens of Fenwold."

* * *

Dominic descended from the bench to greet his father and the Storeys with embraces before vigorously shaking hands with Pieter Jennings.

"Well, Dominic," his father said proudly, "It seems the people support you. What happens now?"

"As I said, fresh elections. I'll have to ask you and Councillor Ali to organise them – I wouldn't have a clue where to begin."

"Yes, of course – we'll see to it. But that's not what I meant. What are your own plans? I'm sure you must realise, the way the citizenry reacted today, that you'd stand a very good chance yourself if you stood for the Council."

Jennings' eyes widened and he said eagerly, "Your father's right, you know, Dominic. These people would follow you anywhere."

Dominic laughed nervously. "What? Me? A politician? No, I'm sorry. That's not a life I ever envisaged. It's hardly a full-time job anyway."

His father said, "Normally I'd agree with you, son. But under these circumstances I wouldn't be so sure – especially with the colonisation of the new territory beyond the Wall to organise. Somebody's going to have to mastermind the selection of migrants, consider the effect on those left behind, the pace and nature of the settlement itself – and how law and order are to be established there. It's no small thing, my boy."

Dominic shrugged. "Dad, that's why you're a politician and I'm a lawman. You have the ability and vision to consider all the things that need to be done. My job is to see that those things get done without anyone coming to harm. That's what I've been trained to do."

Pieter said, "He speaks from his heart, Councillor Bradley. But the new colony is going to need a figurehead – someone to run things on a day to day basis, and see that the Council's wishes are carried out."

Tom Storey added, "Yes, that's right. And if that someone already had a direct line of communication with the Ancient Ones through that amazing thingamajig – well, so much the better!"

Dominic smiled nervously. "Hang on a moment please! I'm not sure I like where this conversation is leading. I'm trained to be a Council marshal, not a…"

Pieter supplied the missing word. "Governor?"

Dominic stammered. "If that's what you call it – yes. I mean, no."

His father laughed. "You're saying you're not qualified for that role?"

"Well, yes, obviously. I mean, that's what I'm saying."

"Who else in Fenwold *is* qualified?"

"I don't know. How should I? There must be somebody."

Tom mused, "But how could there be? It's an entirely new situation."

His father folded his arms and said, "Quite. I couldn't have put it better myself, Tom. Well, I think that settles it."

With fixed expression Dominic said, "Settles what? What do you mean?"

In measured tones his father declared, "When we have our new Council, I intend to propose they appoint you Governor of the New Territory."

* * *

The little infirmary sat literally around the corner from the Council House. Unlike the still magnificent government building, it comprised a hotchpotch of makeshift wooden shacks, connected by adjoining doors and corridors. Dominic had come with Tom and Amelia Storey, who had brought Sylvia here a couple of days before.

The trial and ensuing business having kept him away from his beloved, he was now impatient to see her again. He hesitated though when they reached the main entrance, unsure of his way around.

"Don't you know this place, Dominic?" Mistress Storey asked.

"Not really. My family have their own medic. Sylvia will convalesce at my parents' house as soon as she can be moved."

His eyes swept the exterior. "I can't get over what a tumbledown place this is. Do you know it's reckoned to be a hundred years old?"

"Yes, I can believe that," said Tom, poking a finger into a piece of rotting window frame. Then looking up he observed, "Some of those loose roof shingles could do with attention. I hope the building's outward appearance doesn't reflect the quality of medical care Sylvia can expect here."

Dominic was hoping that too, but was relieved on this point when they stepped inside. The entrance hall buzzed with activity from medics and nursing staff, all clad in clean linen housecoats.

"I wouldn't blame you if you couldn't remember which room she was in, Tom. This place is laid out like a warren!"

Her back now much improved, Mistress Storey grabbed his hand saying, "I remember. Follow me!"

She led him through the maze of corridors and public wards. He tried to memorise the route they took, but soon lost all sense of direction. Eventually, Tom panting for breath several strides behind, Mistress Storey brought them to an abrupt halt before a cubicle door.

"This is it!" she announced. Now he faced an army of confused emotions. His desire to see Sylvia again made him feel like an infatuated adolescent. But then the thought of her injury filled him with great concern. They went in.

He stopped, turned and put a finger to his lips.

"Hush! She's asleep. What have they done to her, Tom?"

"It's standard treatment for breaks apparently. They build up a plaster casing that hardens so the two bits stay together until the bones knit."

"How long will she be like that?"

Mistress Storey answered him. "As she's young, they say the bones should mend fairly quickly. But they must be sure before they take it off. It could be spring before she can safely put her full weight on her leg."

Tom must have read the disappointment in Dominic's face. Taking him to one side he whispered, "I know how you feel, son. But you'll have to be patient – just think about your spring wedding!"

He turned back to look at his daughter. "She looks so serene. It seems a shame to wake her."

Amelia giggled. "We made a lovely daughter, didn't we, Tom?"

Then she said, "Oh, I've just remembered, my dear. Mistress Bradley wanted us to help her arrange our room. You know she's not been well – I can't leave her to do everything herself."

Tom frowned and protested, "But the Bradleys have servants, dear."

Exasperated, she said, "Oh, sometimes, Tom! Perhaps the Marshal would like to have a moment alone with Sylvia. We had a good chat with her last night. We know she's in good hands here. We can come and see her any time, whereas Dominic has many other duties to attend to. Now, come along and don't be so selfish!"

Tugging her husband's hand she pulled him away through the door saying, "We'll see you later, Dominic."

At last they were alone, though despite her mother's chivvying Sylvia still appeared to be asleep. Should he gently shake her or call her name? No, he would savour the moment and look at her for a while. He'd almost forgotten how beautiful she was, even with the scar from her childhood accident. Her eyelashes were long and she'd a healthy blush in her cheeks in spite of her fall. They must be feeding her well. He ached to touch her. A little kiss could do no harm.

He approached the cot and slowly lowered his face to hers until their lips met. He felt her stir ever so slightly and savoured the warm sweetness of her mouth. Her lips parted and there was brief contact between the tips of their tongues. The taste of their youth, their smouldering love almost overwhelmed him as he sensed her consciousness gathering. Her arms reached up to embrace him and her fingers teased the short hairs on the back of his neck, deliciously stimulating his desire for her. She opened her eyes, and regarded him sleepily. He drew away for a moment to savour her innocence, but she gently pulled him in close again for a long, sensuous kiss that swept aside his recent miseries.

When at last he drew away he realised that his fingers had found an unbuttoned opening in her shift, where they now gently caressed her naked breast. Casually she removed his hand.

"Oh, it's you, Dominic," she said.

He sat up. "And who usually comes in here and wakes you in such a way?"

"Oh, the medics are wonderful here. There's nothing they won't do for you." Then she giggled.

Would he ever get used to her peculiar brand of humour? But he smiled. "How about another kiss? I've missed you such a lot."

"Help me sit upright, will you. But be careful – I mustn't move the cast too much. Ouch! Careful, I said!"

"Sorry. Did you hear what I asked you?"

"Yes. You can have a kiss when you go, but we must be careful because a nurse could come in here at any moment. And if you've got any other ideas, just remember with this cast on I couldn't possibly…"

He grinned hopefully and said, "Oh, I don't know. Surely there's a way…?"

She pouted. "Well, whether there is or not I'd rather wait until after the wedding. I want it to be something special that we can both look forward to. You know – perfect."

He shrugged and then smiled. "It will be, my love. Meanwhile I'll just have to exercise some self-restraint. But it's not easy with you lying there looking so gorgeous. You're not in any pain now, are you?"

"Not if I keep still. The worst is when I get an itch on my leg – it's impossible to reach under the cast and scratch it."

Dominic slid a hand under her cover and grinned. "Do you want me to try? Where does it itch?"

"Get your hand out of there, Marshal Bradley. It's not itching just now in any case. I think we should talk about something that'll take your mind off whatever it's on at the moment. Tell me what happened after that horrid man Carson arrested you."

Just the mention of the crooked Colonel's name was enough to dampen Dominic's ardour. He recounted for her the events of the past few days, and the ordeal of his false trial.

He ended by saying, "Worst thing of all was not having you there to support me."

She took his hand. "Oh, my love, I'm so sorry. You must have thought I'd abandoned you. When Carson told me they were going to charge you with abduction of a minor I was at my wit's end. Of course I knew he couldn't force me to return to Crowtree. I could have followed your party to the Capital if I'd chosen to, and he couldn't have stopped me. I considered it of course. But what would be the point? I couldn't prove my age to the Tribunal, just by stating the fact. They'd claim I'd say anything just to save you – and they'd have been right. No, I knew I needed a reliable independent witness – someone who was there when I was born."

"Of course – your mother."

"Right. And the dear old thing took no persuading. Nor did Father. We set off almost straight away. Just as well, because we didn't know the trial had already started."

He said, "They wanted to rush it through to stop my friends drumming up any public support. Lucky for me they wasted time trying to create the semblance of a proper trial, when all along anybody could see it was nothing but a sham. They'd have done better to have locked me up and forgotten about me – or silenced me for good."

"Dominic! Don't say things like that! Anyway, there were others who knew about the Ancient Ones' treasures and the Fenwold Riddle. The truth would have come out in the end."

"Perhaps. Did I mention they might offer me the job of Governor of the New Territory?"

Her eyes widened. "Dominic, that's wonderful! That means you'll be able to see all of Cara's visions become real!" Then she added coyly, "I don't suppose you'll want the encumbrance of a wife while you're busy overseeing things."

He chided her. "Don't be silly. A Governor needs to be settled as well as focussed. It's an ideal job for a family man. But it won't be an easy life for either of us. We'll both have to work very hard – as will all of those who choose to join us."

She grabbed his arm. "It's exciting though, isn't it? Who would have thought that a simple country girl would end up a Governor's wife in a strange new land?"

"You'll always be more than just my wife, Sylvia. When I think back over the past year, I realise how many times you've been there for me, and that final masterstroke of sending me Cara's gadget in the sack of gifts your parents brought for me. Without that, the people would never have rallied to my cause as they did."

Then he frowned. "Mind you, I could swear Sean told me Carson's men had thoroughly searched all your baggage back in Nearbank. I'd assumed they'd found and destroyed it there and then."

With a throwaway shrug she said, "Oh, no. I managed to hide it from them."

"That's obvious. But how?"

Blushing she said, "If you must know, I had it hidden in my undergarments!" Then with an exasperated sigh she snapped, "Why do you have to know every last detail? Just shut up and kiss me!"

CHAPTER TWELVE
WHILE DESTINY SLEEPS

Monday 28th June 2984

My name is Krania Bradley. Today was my first day at school and also my fifth birthday. That's when all children here start school. First we learn reading and writing but I can already read and write a bit because my Mummy taught me how. This diary is Mummy's idea. I think it's fun anyway. Mummy is very good at reading and writing because she is a teacher at the academy where the older children go. Mummy teaches history there. She says I am cleverer than Daddy because he can't read or write very well at all yet. She says that it's because he's too busy being Governor. That means he is in charge of everything here in the New Territory. Besides Daddy never went to school. Except where he learned to be a marshal in Fenwold, on the other side of the big Wall.

Friday 11th February 2985

I like going to school because my friends are there. We each have our own teaching console. Mummy says it's so that we can learn at our own pace. I had geography today. I learned that the New Territory is very small compared to the whole world. Even the land of Fenwold inside the Wall is quite small. Fenwold and the New Territory lie on the east coast of a land that the Ancient Ones called Britain. Britain is a small country surrounded by sea. There are lots of other lands across the sea but the only people live in Fenwold and the New Territory. I have never been to Fenwold inside the Wall. I think I would like to go there some time. My Grandparents live there, also my Uncles Jack and Liam, who are both marshals.

Wednesday 12th July 2986

It's very warm today. It's been a lovely summer and Mummy said I could take time off school because I was doing so well. She and Daddy took me camping for a few days in the forest on the west side of the New Territory, near the landing strip. We went there on horseback. Daddy and Mummy ride very well and they are teaching me. They shot some rabbit for our supper with their crossbows. They are very good shots but when they asked if I wanted to try I said no. I asked Daddy what the landing strip was for and he said for aircraft, but Cara told him that we're not ready for flying yet. I've seen video of aircraft on my teaching console. I would like to fly in one someday.

Saturday 15th September 2987

I'm very excited because Mummy, Daddy and I are going to visit our relatives in the village of Crowtree in Fenwold. It's because Uncle Jack is getting married to a lady called Lucy and there will be a big wedding. We will have to take the ferry through the culvert in the Wall and across the river. Then we will travel by horse and cart with Andreas the trader to the southern edge of Fenwold. Daddy says it should take us about five days to get there. He says it will be interesting to see how Mummy gets on without her gadgets. Mummy says it will be interesting to see how he gets on without Cara. Mummy laughed when she said it and Daddy pulled a face. I think it was meant to be a joke, but I didn't really understand it.

Thursday 4th December 2988

I have a cousin! Andreas brought the good news that my Aunt Lucy has had a baby girl. Her name is Emily. I wish I could see her but Dad says we can't spare the time for another visit.

It's snowing outside. I like the snow when it's fresh and you can make snowmen but when it melts and goes slushy it's horrible. It's very cold outdoors too so we muffle up in furs or some special blankets that Cara gave us. She is very good to us. Every few weeks she tells my father the codes to open up another container or warehouse put here for us by the Ancient Ones. Then the settlers go inside and bring out all kinds of useful things.

Right from the start she has given us prefabricated houses. A house can be put together in a week or so. But Dad says it's hard to keep up with the numbers of settlers from Fenwold. So some people build their own log cabins from felled timber. He calls this the 'old way' and doesn't seem to mind very much. He says there's plenty of room for everyone who can help to work the land.

Thursday 22nd January 2989

Mum says she's never known it so cold. Even the river froze over and Dad says it's too dangerous for the ferry to bring more settlers across from the south bank and through the culvert. The weather has stopped the house building too. Mostly we stay indoors and read or watch video about the Ancient Ones. We have electricity to keep the house warm and power the video and other gadgets. It's beamed from sunlight collectors on the Moon to our powerhouse and stored in big batteries, then transmitted to our homes. I said we'd probably freeze without electricity but Dad said the people who still live in Fenwold get along very well without it, because there's plenty of wood for them to burn from the forest.

* * *

Krania stepped inside Cara's room and heard the familiar *swish* and *clunk* of the doors closing behind her. She felt uneasy, almost afraid that she might be rebuked for leaving it so long since her last visit. She knew this was irrational because Cara wasn't human, merely a hologram, and unlikely to get upset about such a trivial thing. It was true that Krania's visits weren't all that frequent now. When she'd first asked her parents if she might enter the chamber alone – seven years ago on her tenth birthday – she'd been so thrilled at their agreement that she'd almost gorged on that permission, for fear that it might be withdrawn without warning.

But why should it be? Cara was everyone's friend after all, and certainly posed no threat. The settlers of the New Territory owed their very existence to her – or, more accurately, to the technology that made her. So Krania had learned to ration their meetings, thereby heightening the novelty and anticipation of their conversations. Aside from that, there had been other distractions lately.

Almost two months had passed since her last visit, but she knew the drill. As soon as she stepped onto the middle one of the five black circles, the ambient lighting dimmed and the familiar three pillars rose from behind the plastic rail in front of her, each emitting a beam of pure white light. This triad of radiance fused to form the flickering, three-dimensional half-sized figure of Cara, mouthpiece of the Ancient Ones, and custodian of their bounties. They'd made her appear angelic, her wispy blond hair cascading over a flowing pure white gown. When her transparent image stabilised Krania felt the heightened sense – as she always did – of a benign presence that generated an aura of truth and trust.

"Good morning, Krania," she said.

Why did the shock of the hologram's first greeting always make her catch her breath? Could it be because she was amazed that Cara should instantly recognise her and remember her name? Or was it that her voice sounded unnervingly like that of

Sylvia, her mother? She should be used to these tricks by now, but they always unnerved her. Still, she was determined not to give the appearance of being overawed.

"Morning, Cara. I won't ask you if you're well, because I realise by now that such pleasantries are irrelevant to you. Incidentally, do you recognise everyone after their first visit here?"

"Oh, yes. I have a record of everyone's visual and genetic information. I can even identify blood relationships. For example, when I first met you I knew that Dominic Bradley was your father."

"That would be reassuring for him," Krania muttered casually, and then bit her lip for making such a cheap remark.

Though her quip brought no reaction to the hologram's expression, by way of atonement she said, "I mean, that's very clever. But how can you do that just on a single viewing?"

"As I said, it's not just visual. There are instruments in this room that take all kinds of readings, including sweat and iris analysis. It's just a question of cross matching to existing genetic records. It takes a fraction of a second. But I'm not infallible."

"Really? You mean, even you can get things wrong sometimes?"

"Yes. For example, if there is close visual and genetic resemblance between two people, I might mistake one for the other."

"Such as twins, you mean?"

"Possibly. Or blood relations who are very close genetically. But it's not often a problem."

"But it's not *you* that sees people, is it? You're just composed of beams of light after all."

"That's correct, Krania. There are cameras both in this room and the entrance chamber. But I can tell from the recorded data that you have your father's short, straight black hair, brown eyes like your mother, and that your bone structure suggests a very attractive face. I suspect you have no shortage of prospective boyfriends."

"Oh, I see. And how do you know I'm even interested in boys?"

"You have had your seventeenth birthday since your last visit, Krania. You are a young woman now."

Krania frowned, slightly embarrassed by this last observation. How much did Cara actually know about her? Quite a bit, she supposed, considering the number of meetings they'd had. There'd been lots of stuff she'd divulged – especially when younger – some of which she now wished she hadn't. Lately she'd tried to be less candid, more guarded. For she realised that when Cara spoke to her parents they were bound to discuss her. But today she wanted more than just a superficial chat.

"Can you keep a secret, Cara?"

Evidently this was one of those questions that tested Cara's logic circuitry, because her image gave the faintest wobble before she responded.

"It depends. If the information affected the progress or security of the New Territory or the well being of any of its inhabitants, I would have to inform your father. In the case of a more trivial issue, I would have no problem in treating it as confidential if you so requested. Why? Do you have a secret that you want to share with me?"

"Not a secret as such. But I need to talk to someone who won't repeat everything I say to all and sundry."

"What about your close friends?"

"My friends? Are you joking? I might as well broadcast my innermost thoughts on vid-link as entrust them to those blabbermouths!"

"I'm sorry, Krania. I cannot make or share a joke, as you know. Nor do I have a template of attributes defining what constitutes a normal friendship. I used the term 'friends' generically as a mere suggestion of an alternative to expressing your concerns to me. But tell me what is troubling you, if that is what you wish."

"And you promise you won't split?"

The hologram image wobbled again, but quickly settled.

"Yes, I promise. Unless what you're about to say threatens the progress or security of the New ..."

"All right! I got that the first time round. Now, listen – please."

"I am listening, Krania."

"It's about Mum and Dad."

"What about them?"

She hesitated, and then said slowly, "I don't really like them much any more. Is that a bad thing to say? No, sorry, I realise you can't make that sort of a judgement. I don't mean that I don't... love my parents. Of course I do, for all they've done for me. I certainly don't want to hurt them. But I find them so... so boring! Their lives are so humdrum, and they can't see it. And they want me to be the same as them. But I don't want to be. I need to be different. I want to do things, to go places!"

Without emotion Cara asked, "Do what? Go where?"

With a puzzled frown Krania murmured, "I don't know." Then defiantly she looked straight at the hologram. "But don't go thinking this is all just to do with adolescent hormones, Cara. All my friends seem to talk about is gadgets, boys, marriage and babies. And I'd like to have all that too one day – but not yet. I feel I have something more to give to the world – and more to take from it as well!" She lowered her voice again, as if afraid that she'd spoken out of turn. "I'm not making much sense, am I?"

"Yes, you are making sense, Krania. You are a gifted young woman at the peak of your mental and physical potential. Genetically you are the product of parents who had similar attributes in their youth – even if you now see them as spent and boring. But you mustn't write them off quite so casually. Nor should you strike out aimlessly to satisfy your natural ambition. You have proven yourself a superior student, but you still have much to learn. You also have much to contribute to your people's development. You must build on your strengths and suppress your weaknesses. And I know this is the hardest thing to ask of you, but have patience, and you will find your place in this new world – your destiny!"

In spite of Cara's earlier assurances about her physical health, Krania had to fight to stop her knees from buckling. She hadn't expected what amounted to a computerised version of an emotional outburst. Then she wondered: did the hologram's words constitute a wisely reasoned prophecy, based on the vast store of information accumulated about her over the years? Or was Cara's speech merely a pre-programmed stock response to a confused teenager's ramblings? And if she asked Cara to say which of these her words of counsel had been, how would she reply? Truthfully, she assumed.

But she decided that she wouldn't ask Cara, because she wanted to believe that her advice was genuine. And she promised herself this. She would take Cara's advice and be patient. She would give it three months, and if destiny didn't come along and shake up her world by then, she knew she'd be forced to do something really drastic!

CHAPTER THIRTEEN
DELIVERANCE

"Eight hundred years!"

Stooping in deference to his advanced years, the tall uniformed figure silently mouthed the words into the void, his tired grey eyes surveying the tableau spread out before them.

It was a momentous occasion, and just cause for celebration. But Commander Gideon Boone considered any display of emotion unbefitting of his rank. Steeped in the traditions of unerring duty and selfless leadership, he made it his rule to avoid the vulgar demonstration of grief or jubilation. Besides, there was a small issue that put a brake on outright exuberance. Even so, he allowed himself a short, silent prayer of thanks. Thanks to his ancestors for launching the Salvation, this ship that had brought his people safely back to their home system. And thanks to their God for protecting the vessel, along with its precious human cargo, now so close to its long promised destiny.

"Destiny!"

This time his voice broke the silence. But although the word rose as a shout in his dry throat, it left his lips as a whisper, temporarily misting the transparent panel in front of him. Without shifting his gaze from the cold, dark vacuum of space, he reached for the water flask at his hip and took a sip. Though weary, his still keen eyes peered out beyond the void, across so many million leagues of emptiness, to feed upon one bright source of light, not yet a discernible disc. Yes, it was just a single star. And yet, if pressed, even this staid and stuffy old leader of men would admit that its sight filled his eyes with wonder, and his heart with gladness.

He shivered. It was bitterly cold here, and he could have obtained this view from the comfort of his own quarters, or from the control centre on the bridge. In fact he knew that at this moment everyone awake on board would be watching this same image by way of the many screens littering the ship's warren of cabins, offices and common areas. But to relish the sheer spectacle of space, for Gideon Boone there really could be no substitute for the Salvation's observation deck – even with minimal background heating, the ship's energy being so precious. In fact the near-freezing chill enhanced the sense of isolation, making him starkly aware of his own vulnerability. It was strangely comforting. Against the backdrop of the universe, he felt closer to its Creator, and privileged to glimpse the enormity of His works.

His thoughts turned to his cargo – his fellow settlers and crew. They now numbered close on twelve thousand souls, every one of them looking to him for leadership. No doubt they shared his feelings, and would expect him to address them at such an important time.

His index finger found a small depression on the console at his collar and, applying the slightest pressure, engaged the comms link. He gathered his thoughts. Then with measured tones his avuncular baritone boomed forth to command their attention.

"This is Commander Boone. I am looking out upon a sight that gladdens my heart, and fills me with thanks and humility. I know you must all be watching it too, and share the sense of wonder and fulfilment that I feel at this moment.

"More than eight centuries ago this star liner set out from the plague-infested planet that we call Earth. Its contingent of barely one thousand volunteers – our courageous forefathers – went forth into the unknown of deep space in the hope of securing humanity's survival. There was no guarantee of success. But they took with them the tools they would need to accomplish their mission – technology, skills, courage and –

most important of all – faith. Faith that God would guide, protect and deliver their descendants to a safe haven. After more than seven centuries of searching, no habitable planet was found. Therefore sixty-two years ago it was decided to return to Earth in the hope that we would find it free from contagion and able to support our race once more. Well, it's taken a little longer than we envisaged, but here we are at last.

"The Salvation's proximity to our home solar system offers an ideal opportunity for me to confirm what is now, in any case, an open secret throughout the ship. The on-board computers concur on this most important point. Taking account of observations relayed by the surviving orbital monitors, alongside all reasonable probabilities, I can tell you that the risk of plague remaining on Earth may now be considered to be negligible. Our planet will once again maintain human life."

His lower limbs buzzed to a spontaneous vibration through the close lightweight mesh forming the floor beneath his feet. This transmission wave conveyed the tide of joyous whoops, cheers and foot stamping that swept through the ship in an unrestrained reaction to his announcement. Uncharacteristically, he allowed himself the faintest glimmer of a smile, before concluding his address.

"You must know that the bright star we now see directly ahead of us – though still no small distance away – is the one we call the Sun. Slightly to its right, we can see the largest planet of the Solar system, Jupiter. From where we sit telescopic inspection will reveal it as a crescent, orbited by several satellite moons. In a matter of weeks we shall have crossed its path and that of the asteroid belt and, soon afterwards, the orbit of the fourth planet, Mars. We shall proceed from there to lock onto a fixed position above the surface of the Earth's own Moon. We'll then send an exploratory shuttle to locate the designated landing site and, if all appears well, begin the re-colonisation of our planet.

"In short, my friends, you have my permission to rejoice. We are going home!"

* * *

"Home! Home! We're going home!"

"He did say it, didn't he? We're going home to Earth!"

"I wonder what it'll be like - I can't wait!"

"Just think of walking on solid ground!"

"Feeling the wind!"

"Climbing trees!"

"Swimming in the sea!"

"Living in houses!"

"We're actually going!"

"At last! At last!"

In the Red Watch Senior College recreation suite groups of excited teenagers reacted joyously to the Commander's words. The refectory throbbed to the din of some four hundred boisterous students, shamelessly displaying a euphoria that was the antithesis of Boone's unruffled dignity.

In the forward starboard corner of the suite members of the Skiffle clan leaped and danced, arms around one another's shoulders, whooping and cheering with unbridled jubilation. Some of its dozen or so members sported false hairpieces, aping their ancient musical heroes. These wigs flapped about comically as they jigged up and down to the lively music playing on their local audio channel.

Other Red Watch clans hugged and shook hands in the same natural outburst of revelry that consumed the whole refectory. Dozens of screens, around which they'd gathered following the rumour that 'Old Boone' was about to address the ship, still displayed the subject of their celebration. But by now most had downloaded the image onto the optic memory chips clipped into their temple implants. They only needed to flip a mental switch to view it as they cavorted in response to the Commander's announcement.

Soon parents and other family members piled into the hall to join the teenagers. This being a designated family night, when the students – who lived apart from their mothers and fathers in the college dorms during term time – invited their kin to share a light meal and some gentle recreation. As they drifted in the youthful exuberance subsided, giving way to greetings and excited conversations that settled to a more restrained level as gifts were received and domestic trivia exchanged. With this sudden influx, the refectory now struggled to accommodate a gathering that easily exceeded its designated capacity of twelve hundred.

A male student greeted his family at one of the corner tables.

"Mum, Dad, welcome to our little soiree! You've heard Commander Boone's announcement, of course."

Both parents nodded and smiled, while their son felt a vigorous tug on his jacket sleeve. He teasingly looked about him, pretending not to notice the small person who eagerly sought his attention. But then he relented and looked down in feigned surprise.

"Oh, hello there, young man – isn't it almost your bedtime?" The little lad pouted, then smiled and gave his big brother an uninhibited hug.

"Hiya, Martin!" the child sang out. Then he added glumly, "Mummy says I can only stay for an hour, then I've got to go home on the nursery shuttle."

"Never mind," his brother grinned, "we can have lots of fun before you leave. We've got all the latest games of course, but I've brought my chessboard in case you'd rather play that. And we've got a special fruit drink on tap tonight – it's called strawberry."

The little boy beamed. "Wow! I've never tasted that! Can I have some now?"

"In a minute – let our folks get comfortable first. Mum, would you like a drink? Dad?"

His mother smiled. "It's a long time since I tasted strawberry, Martin. I thought the last hydro-crop failed five years ago and couldn't be revived."

"I seem to recall that too, son," his father said. "The whole crop had to be recycled."

"You're right, of course." Then, pretending to lower his voice to a whisper, he said, "Don't tell Stinker here, but we managed to synthesise the flavour in the science lab."

The little boy pulled a face. "Don't call me that! You're the stinker, not me. Anyway, what's sinter-size mean?"

His father stroked the little lad's hairless head and explained, "It means it's not the real thing, but as good as. Now, why don't you take Mummy over to the bar and collect a jug and four beakers, while I have a chat with your big brother here. Oh, and you might fetch a few plates of nibbles while you're at it."

His wife took the hint and grabbed the child's hand before he could protest.

Martin tried to recall if he'd done – or neglected to do – anything recently that might displease his father. He obviously hadn't sent them away just so that he could pass the time of day. His recent exam results had been okay, or at least he'd thought so. He was well on track to follow his chosen career of political history – as his father had done with great credit, being now a member of the ship's Joint Watch Committee. Martin was truly proud of his father, and would never intentionally do anything to displease him. His furrowed brow must have betrayed his concern.

"It's all right, son – don't worry. I haven't got you on your own to give you a lecture – quite the opposite, in fact. I wanted to congratulate you on your progress, and I know how embarrassed you get if I praise you when other people are around."

Martin's concern gave way to relief. "Oh, well, thanks, Dad. But I didn't think I'd done particularly well. For one thing, my pure history's a bit shaky."

"Don't fret about that. I was chatting to your lecturer last week. Your main problem is just to do with memorising dates – but you can always get that sort of thing from the databanks. What's important is your ability to interpret events. It's excellent – and your arbitration and leadership skills show great potential too."

"Really? Did old – I mean, did Mr Harrison say that?"

His father laughed. "Did I ever tell you Herbert Harrison and I were in the same clan? He was a dry old stick, even then – he never showed any emotion. But he's got a good heart. And he rates you highly, Martin. He says you've got a future in politics."

The youngster looked puzzled, and suddenly pensive. "Future? How can we know anything about the future? In a few months from now we'll all be starting a new one, won't we?" He looked around the refectory. "That's if this rusty old crate can make the final haul to Earth."

"Oh, I wouldn't worry, son. I'm no technician, but they say we'll be able to tap into the Sun's energy soon and build up our reserves. Though I gather it's been touch and go covering these last few million leagues. But I understand what you're saying.

After wandering around the universe in the Salvation for centuries, it's going to seem strange for us to rest our feet on solid ground at last. But you know, Martin, it's precisely because of the uncertainties that lie ahead of us that we'll need our political historians more than ever before. Scholars and thinkers like Harrison, who can reach back into the past, and help us face the new problems that are sure to confront us."

His son frowned quizzically. "The way you put it, I'd say you had some specific issue in mind."

The short silence that followed was just long enough for Martin to realise he'd struck a chord. His father glanced right and left, and shifted his seat in closer to him. Then he spoke in little more than a whisper, forcing his son to ignore the chatter of the surrounding families.

"I wouldn't try to hide anything from you, Martin." He glanced over to the refectory counter, where his wife exchanged pleasantries with a neighbour, while their youngest tugged at her sleeve.

"I'm going to tell you something that's been kept from us for eight hundred years. It's something only the senior historians have known about – a kind of secret they've been entrusted with. Harrison asked – no, instructed me to tell you – because, well, he believes you're going to be needed."

Martin's face became a deathly white. The prospect of approaching responsibility was starting to look just a bit scary. Still, he managed to blurt out, "Why couldn't Harrison tell me himself? And what about the other four watches? Surely they have some good people?"

His father was already shaking his head. "You know Harrison. If it's not in his lecture notes, he stutters. He's known me long enough... And as for the other watches, some of their political historians have their own agenda." He stared vacantly at the tabletop as he said this.

"I don't get it, Dad."

His father sighed. "Look, your mother and brother are on their way back. Shut up, and listen to me, and listen well. We think we're going back to an uninhabited planet, right?"

Wide-eyed, Martin said, "Dad, everyone on the Salvation knows that's precisely *why* we've made this journey."

"Well, the truth is, we're not."

"What do you mean, Dad? Oh, I get it. There'll be wild animals, of course. That's only to be expected. But we have weapons so that isn't really a problem, is it?"

His father looked straight into his eyes. "It's more than that, Martin. It seems there are..."

But before he could finish, his wife and younger son had returned, and in a trice four brimming beakers of sticky red substitute fruit liquid were being poured. It looked as though his father's opportunity to deliver his weighty message had been lost. Then, as each held their drink, ready to take a slurp, Martin had an idea.

"Wait! Let's have a toast!"

"Yeah! Let's have some toast!" yelled his little brother.

"No, not that kind of toast – a toast *to* something. Dad, you decide – what shall we drink to?"

He looked into his father's eyes, desperately willing him to take the hint and somehow find a way to finish his announcement. He thought he detected a look of understanding as the four beakers met over the centre of the table. But although Wakefield's lips framed a muted smile, there was no mistaking the underlying gravity in his voice as he completed his tidings.

It was with a single word.

"Survivors!"

CHAPTER FOURTEEN
DISSENTING VOICES

"Cold enough for you, Jessica?"

Martin's classmate twisted her lips at his feeble attempt at humour. Then her expression turned quickly to a smug grin as she reached into her bag and unwrapped a foil insulation blanket, which she draped casually around her shoulders.

"Some of us came prepared," she said. "I'll be warmer in a few seconds."

He pouted and folded his arms tightly in a vain attempt to suppress an overwhelming need to shiver. Crossing the Martian orbit turned out to be something of an anticlimax - as everyone had known it would be. But that didn't prevent about thirty people making the trip to the observation deck for the occasion. Only a few had remembered to bring extra layers of clothing in deference to the minimal background heating here, and most kept their arms and feet moving to maintain blood circulation.

The red planet itself wasn't visible, being far along its orbit on the other side of the Sun. The small crowd comprised in the main political historians from all five watches – enthusiasts who wanted to be able to say, "We were there." Some had come up during their designated sleep periods, just to be present at the exact moment of transit.

Martin's friends and co-students Jessica and Leonard accompanied him, and all three stared out silently in awe at the inky blackness. The two boys shivered bravely until their thoughtful companion took two further film blankets from her bag and handed them one apiece.

As they sheepishly unfolded the insulators she said, "Doesn't the Sun look wonderful - a lot bigger than it did a few weeks ago?"

Leonard nodded. "I've never seen a star as anything more than a pinpoint of light before now, except on video or telescopically. By the time we make Earth's orbit it'll look really huge."

Martin said, "I remember my grandmother telling me that her own grandmother was just a little girl when the ship passed through the Alpha Centauri system. That's a double star, you know. Grandmother's description was only second-hand, but she did her best, and she made it sound wonderful. Now that would have been a sight to see from this deck! Archive video can never do it real justice. Of course, when we're closer to the Sun we'll need eye protection to prevent retina damage."

A couple of Green Watch students slouched close by. One of them, a brutish lad called Raymond, turned to spoil their innocent wonder.

"Never mind retina damage - it's damage by savages that we'll need to watch out for!"

Jessica frowned. "Savages? Whatever are you talking about?"

"Oh, come on! Don't tell me you Red Watch idiots are the only ones who don't know! Don't your Committee people report back important issues? It came out at this week's meeting. We're going to find Earth teeming with dangerous natives!"

Martin bit his lip for a moment. He knew – as should Raymond – that sensitive issues were not to be broadcast lightly, and his father had explained to him that this one was subject to a Confidentiality Order. Raymond's father was also a Committee member, and if he had divulged anything to his son, then he should have sworn him to secrecy too. But from what his own father had told him, he knew that the Green Watch historians held views far removed from those of their own. Red Watch thinkers counselled stealth and restraint, rather than risk panic and over-zealous reaction to what, after all, was still now only conjecture. He couldn't keep silent in the face of Raymond's extreme claims.

"Don't talk such rubbish, man! We can't possibly make such trite judgements from this distance! As with any planet our scientists examine, *if* we discovered intelligent bipeds, we might find them to be just like us!"

Raymond sneered. "They might be like you." Then he turned to his Green Watch companion, nudging him and smirking. "Probably lacking in the brain department, like most of you Red Watch wimps!"

Martin gritted his teeth, determined not to let such a stupid remark provoke him. Leonard, however, had listened in anger and was now seething, raising a clenched fist ready to knock the smirk off Raymond's face. Only the intervention of his two friends prevented an unpleasant incident that might have led to his suspension.

Raymond turned away, clearly ruffled but still truculent. "My Dad says our historians have got it right. As soon as we get to Earth, we should hunt down the savages and let them know who's boss!"

* * *

Less than a week later, the chilly observation deck was as full as it had ever been - at least, within the memory of anyone now living on the ship. Eight centuries earlier, no doubt the area would have been just as crammed with spectators. But on that occasion they would have been apprehensive evacuees, taking a last look at their stricken planet before zooming off into space in search of salvation. Martin wondered if they could have foreseen this day, so far into the future, when their own descendants would at last return to re-colonise the Earth.

"You're looking thoughtful." Standing beside him, Jessica turned her eyes away for a moment from the expansive surface of the Moon, which hung like a huge, pockmarked balloon, barely a hundred leagues beneath them.

He turned to her and smiled at her observation. "I was lost in the past for a moment there, I'm afraid."

"As usual," she laughed. Then she returned her gaze towards the spectacle below. "It's really breathtaking, isn't it? So cold, yet so beautiful."

He nodded. "You and I are privileged to live through these times, Jessica. We're very lucky."

As he spoke these words he wondered just how true they really were. Perhaps there was no such thing as absolute luck, or privilege. Maybe, like those coins of ancient currency, they each had a flip side, a balancing element. Yes, they were fortunate to find themselves here at this historic moment, as role players at this important landmark for their civilisation. But he knew also, from recent discussions with his father and his mentor, Professor Harrison, that the immediate future held many uncertainties – even dangers. And one important lesson in particular that they'd dinned into him was that privilege, however grand, however glorious, was invariably accompanied by the solemn weight of responsibility.

But for now at least, he felt he could set aside his natural doubts and misgivings, and relish what was, after all, a very special moment. He glanced again at Jessica and was cheered by her radiant smile, so childlike and innocent, as her bright eyes continued to feast on the novel spectacle of the Moon's craters and plains. Then she turned her head to smile at him again, and for the first time, instead of a teenager's features, he realised that he was looking at the face of a young woman. And for a brief moment he fancied he saw his own fear and apprehension reflected in her eyes. But it could just have been his imagination.

"Red Watch Group K, please vacate the observation deck! There are still several hundreds queuing to access the viewing area! Please move out quickly and in an orderly fashion!"

Their train of thought was arrested by the brusque announcement from the public address system. It made them smile because the speech simulator hadn't been updated in this part of the ship for at least a hundred years, and the mechanised female voice sounded so old-fashioned. It reminded Martin of his great-grandmother, whom he remembered only very vaguely in the flesh, although he'd 'met' her several times in hologram form. The incongruity of the computerised voice seemed to amuse most of the people there, but they didn't hesitate to obey the announcer's command. Obediently they made their way towards the near-by shuttle station, where monorail cars waited to take them back to their various quarters and duties.

Just as Martin stepped aside to let Jessica board one of the cars, he felt someone's hand touch his shoulder, causing him to jerk his head round to see who it was.

"Dad! I didn't know you were here. Jessica and I got permission to skip a class…"

"It's all right," his father reassured him. "I didn't come to give you a ticking-off. What was it like?"

Jessica stepped back onto the platform. "Oh, hello, Mr Wakefield. It was stunning. Haven't you seen the Moon yourself yet?"

"No. I've been a bit preoccupied. I came down to speak to you both. Harrison told me I'd find you here."

Martin looked puzzled. "Oh, right. Do you want to step aboard then?"

His father looked around at the milling crowd of people and, twisting his lips thoughtfully, said: "No, I'll tell you what. Why don't we walk back, via the pedway?"

Martin didn't much fancy a walk. They'd been standing on the observation deck for a full twenty minutes, and he didn't know about Jessica, but his feet were aching. However he didn't want to appear a wimp, so he used the time-honoured male ploy of using a pretended concern for the female's well being to cover up his own reluctance.

"Um, I don't know, Dad. I'm not sure Jessica's up to it. Poor girl's been standing …"

Jessica however, perceptive as ever, cut him off in mid-sentence.

"Oh, don't be silly, Martin. It's only six furlongs. It won't hurt us."

Martin ginned weakly, shrugged and said, "All right." They cut a path back through the crowd towards the nearest pedestrian exit, from where they began walking along the tunnel, in silence at first. Martin grimaced a bit because of his aching feet, and glanced longingly across at the escalator that ran alongside them. Silently he cursed the fact that it had been out of order for decades, deemed undeserving of precious power and maintenance effort.

Wakefield must have sensed his son's discomfort and, far from expressing any pity or concern, delivered a brief lecture on the need for everyone to take regular exercise. "You'll see a big difference when you're living down on Earth, young man. It's all very well spending time in the gravity simulator, but you'll find it's hard work coping under Earth's atmospheric pressure. You really must keep your body in shape. Your mother and I walk these tunnels whenever we can."

Martin sighed impatiently. "Dad, I don't mean to be disrespectful, but I do spend time in the gym. And I doubt that you came all the way to the observation deck just to give me a pep talk on personal fitness."

Wakefield shrugged. "Yes, you're quite right. I do have something important that I need to talk to you about, and this is a good place to do it. It's only a fifteen minutes walk to the Red Watch main hub, so I won't waste time on trivia. I've just come from a meeting of the Joint Watch Committee. It's been confirmed from our unmanned monitoring shuttles that there are indeed human beings on Earth – in numbers probably equal to or even exceeding our own."

Jessica gasped. "Humans on Earth? But, how…" Then a knowing look replaced the frown on her face. "So that's what that idiot Raymond was ranting about…"

Wakefield stopped and turned to his son, saying with a whimsical smile, "Crikey, Martin, you really can keep a secret, can't you?"

Martin gave Jessica a sheepish look. She scowled at first, then said, "Don't worry, Mr Wakefield. Your son was born to be a diplomat. He wouldn't snitch if his life depended on it. But for my benefit, I think you'd better start from the beginning if you don't mind."

They walked on and Wakefield spoke while the youngsters listened.

"All right – here's the story. I can tell you now because it's going to be common knowledge soon in any case. When the Salvation set out to save humanity from extinction, nobody could predict with certainty that its mission would be successful. So our clever ancestors hatched a second plan, which involved creating a huge safe quarantined area on Earth, surrounded by an impenetrable concrete wall."

"Concrete!" Jessica was impressed. "That was a widespread building material on Earth, wasn't it? I've seen pictures of it, of course. But why not use synthetic materials?"

Wakefield smiled. "They had those, of course – but not in the required quantities. The components of concrete were readily available in the area they selected. In any case, they didn't have much time. From its inception to virtual annihilation the plague took just eight years. And they needed a barrier that was as much as half a furlong high in places, and something like seventy leagues in length."

Jessica's eyes widened as she tried to imagine such a structure. "Wow! That must be a sight to see!" Then she looked embarrassed, and said, "Oh, I'm sorry for interrupting you, Mr Wakefield."

"That's all right. A thousand courageous volunteers settled inside this enclave, which was given the name of Fenwold. Apparently the name reflected its topography – flat land to the south and low rolling hills to the north. It was first stripped of all the trappings of civilisation, so they'd have to survive using basic methods of subsistence – hunting and growing their own food. And so determined were they not to fail, that those first settlers pledged to conceal from their offspring all knowledge of preceding history and technology. This was necessary so as to delay for as long as possible what they knew to be inevitable."

Here Jessica cut in. "That someone would find a way to break out."

"Exactly. And that mustn't be allowed to happen until sufficient time had passed to ensure all danger of infection was eradicated."

"Eight hundred years!" Martin interjected, feeling particularly perceptive.

But Jessica was clearly way ahead of him. "And I suppose you're going to tell us that they have in fact broken out?"

Wakefield nodded. "About twenty years ago."

Then it was Martin's mind that raced. "If that's the case, they've not done themselves any favours, have they, Dad?"

"Probably not. Had they remained within the confines of the Wall, we might easily have left them alone – for a reasonable time, at least."

"But, wait a minute," Jessica said. "The Earth's a big planet. Is there no way we could, well, make our settlements around on the other side, or at least far away from them?"

Wakefield shook his head. "If only things were that simple. There's a bit of a problem. You see, our forbears left a treasure trove of technology and knowledge that, by now, the survivors will already have begun to make use of. We ourselves badly need access to those resources if we're to establish our home on the planet. The on-board computers have just released an inventory – and, believe me, it really is astonishing. There's enough machinery and materials to build a dozen cities, for a start. Then there are enormous stores of the finest ancient artworks, and great libraries of real books with characters printed on paper pages. It just goes on and on. It's ironic really. The store was set up to help whichever one of the two groups eventually made it safely across the yawning chasm of time. But I don't think it was ever foreseen what might happen if both groups survived."

Jessica frowned. "Look, I know this probably sounds a bit simplistic, but if these resources are so extensive, couldn't we, well, share them?"

"That's exactly what Harrison and I have suggested. But Green Watch in particular argue that we'd only be delaying the inevitable."

Martin said, "You mean, that attempts at social integration invariably end either in total submission of the inferior group, or in bloody warfare."

"Yes. And by now, the Earth-dwellers probably see the treasure trove as their birthright. They're not going to be too keen to share it with a bunch of visitors from space. It's likely they'll want to defend what they believe to be their rightful property."

Martin was almost afraid to ask the question that was forming in his mind. "So, Father, what course of action does the Joint Watch Committee recommend?"

By now they weren't far from the public area, so Wakefield stopped near the end of the otherwise empty pedway tunnel and spoke to them quietly and solemnly, out of general earshot. His serious expression reflected the gravity of his announcement.

"This won't be general knowledge for a couple of days yet, so keep it under your hairpieces. By a vote of three to one, with one abstention, the Green Watch motion was carried. A party of ambassadors will be despatched at the earliest opportunity, offering assistance to re-settle the Earth-dwellers back behind the Wall. If the offer is rejected, then we shall take whatever action may be necessary to enforce their re-settlement."

CHAPTER FIFTEEN
OLD ACQUAINTANCE

"But, Governor - Sir! Plot twenty-four ninety-seven was promised to me and my family!"

From across his desk the man who answered to Fenwold's Council for upholding the law in the New Territory eyed the young petitioner with curiosity and suppressed an understanding smile. Determined to show neither reaction nor emotion, he sat stiffly with arms crossed, aloof and impartial. And yet he couldn't help feeling some sympathy for this excitable young fellow, who from his windswept appearance had only recently arrived on the ferry from Fenwold. He didn't seem especially articulate, and Governor Bradley hadn't caught his name when he'd first mumbled it. But his clothing – the campaign-weary uniform of a Fenwold deputy marshal – bore clear testament to the arduous journey that he and his family must have made in hopes of starting a fresh life here in the New Territory.

In his mind Bradley was transported back twenty years to his own arrival as founding settler here in this amazing place beyond the mysterious Wall. He was sure he couldn't have looked much different then from this unshaven, longhaired, almost exhausted, yet still fiery individual who now pleaded before him. And there was something almost familiar about the young man's face, something that touched a chord far, far in the depths of his memory. But his expression remained stern and blank. He knew he must, as always, set aside any natural partiality, and show no favour.

The case was an emergency dispute that required immediate adjudication. He had found the litigants waiting at his office earlier that morning, causing him to miss his customary mug of tea and chat with his clerk, Stephen Cooper. The clerk had quickly summarised the facts of the case, but hadn't had time to prepare any paperwork. He now sat quietly on a chair in the corner, listening and taking notes.

In contrast to the dishevelled-looking deputy, the opposing appellant, seated calmly beside the young lawman, was smartly dressed, well-groomed and about five years his senior. His name was Trevor Smart, and Bradley knew him well. He had never much liked the chap, finding him boastful and arrogant – but of course he wouldn't allow that to affect his judgment either.

"Governor Bradley, with all due respect to..."

Smart cast a condescending sideways glance towards his opponent, and continued before the latter had any chance to repeat his name, so denying him the opportunity to assert his right to be there.

"... to our young friend here, I must remind him that there is a strict, first come, first served system of allocation of accommodation in the settlement. I see no reason why anyone – even a deputy marshal – should be allowed preferential treatment. Actually, I could equally claim favour based on my own profession – as you know, both my wife and I are instructors at the Knowledge Centre. I came here ten years ago with my parents and have played no small part in helping build up this community. Now that we have a child, my wife and I are in desperate need of a place of our own."

The younger man responded with poorly concealed anxiety. "I'm not asking for special treatment, Sir. I was forced to stay inside Fenwold beyond my tour of duty, to put down an uprising of slaves over in the east. Else my family and I should have come sooner along with my brother and his wife to be close to them. I was told the next plot – number twenty-four ninety-seven – was to be reserved for us. Please Sir, we've had an awful journey, and now your people are telling us we've got to wait for another house to be constructed, further away from our kinfolk."

The two opposing supplicants, having put their respective cases, now looked across the table at the Governor, to await his wise verdict. They would have seen before them a middle-aged man who was nevertheless still fit and handsome, and whose rugged features told of an active and eventful youth. His manner exuded seniority, demanded respect, and promised equanimity. They could expect nothing less – however much they might be hoping for more. Bradley, well used to these occasions, automatically assumed the well-practised attitude that he felt befitted a responsible decision-maker. He sighed deeply, unfolded his arms, placed both elbows on the desk and interlocked his fingers to make a rest for his strong, solid chin. Then he fixed his gaze on the embroidered saddle-cloth that hung on the back wall, a simple yet treasured gift from grateful villagers following his earlier campaign to rid the south-west corner of Fenwold of the feared raider gangs. Thus his eyes were focussed exactly halfway between the two expectant faces. He'd learned this trick years ago, to avoid accidentally appearing to favour one or other of the parties seeking his justice.

At this point he always gave the appearance of taking his time. To announce his decision too soon could smack of carelessness – even if he had already made up his mind. But in enforcing this hiatus he was also compelled to silently go over the main points of the case again, just to be certain. Except that, lately, his mind had taken to wandering – and wondering, only very briefly, just what useful purpose he was serving here. Twenty years ago he'd been plain Dominic Bradley, Special Marshal, Surveyor of the Wall, charged with finding a way to break through the physical barrier that had kept his people imprisoned for eight centuries. This he had achieved, as well as having played a leading role in the defeat of bands of murderous raiders who threatened the peace and structure of civilised society. He had become something of a folk hero, lauded and respected throughout Fenwold and credited with many deeds whose inaccuracies were laughable – slaying dragons being among the most farcical.

Since then he'd devoted many years to nurturing and directing the development of the New Territory. They'd been good years of hard work and fulfilment, with the help of his devoted wife and companion Sylvia. And she had given him the most wonderful gift of a daughter, now a young woman, their beloved Krania. But now – what? He was still active, and as strong as the younger lawmen. Well, maybe not as fit or agile as he used to be. Perhaps the best of his years were behind him. Still, he felt he had more to offer than merely to sit behind this desk dispensing decisions about petty land disputes and trivial breaches of contract.

"Governor Bradley?" Stephen Cooper approached the desk and poured out a beaker of water, which he then pushed towards his boss, almost too noisily. The sudden movement caused the Governor to blink several times. Cooper then shoved forward a sheet of notepaper, which Bradley glanced at with a squint.

He silently chastised himself for having allowed his eyelids to droop – if only for a few seconds, or so he hoped. But it gave a bad impression – he must watch that in future, and for the present, regain control. He glanced with gratitude in the clerk's direction, and silently thanked the Gods he had the knack of selecting loyal staff.

He coughed, raised and took a sip from the beaker, then said, "Thank you, Stephen." He quickly gathered his thoughts. "Well, gentlemen, I have come to a decision. I must precede its announcement by saying that – even though one of you will consider it imperfect – my verdict is final and according to our regulations, cannot be subject either to appeal, or to further discussion. Is that understood?"

Both men nodded.

"I sympathise with the plight of the Deputy Marshal here, especially since we share the same profession. But we have to have our rules of settlement in the New Territory, and we can't be seen to show preference – even if that's not our intention."

He looked at the young deputy. "I'm afraid that whoever promised you plot number twenty-four ninety-seven, young man, didn't have the authority to do so." He looked down again at Cooper's note. "My clerk tells me an identical prefabricated dwelling is currently being erected at plot number twenty-five zero-one, and should be ready for habitation in three weeks' time. Your family is to have that. Meanwhile you'll be allocated a temporary living unit within the new arrivals' facility."

He then rested both hands on his desk, pushed himself up out of his chair, and held out his hand, first to the successful applicant, who shook it once, before turning to leave the office, sporting a self-congratulatory grin. Then Bradley faced and offered his hand to the disappointed young lawman.

"Never mind, lad," he offered in a genuine attempt at consolation. "Three weeks will pass more quickly than you think. I'm sure you and your family will make excellent additions to our community." He checked that Smart had left the office, then continued, "Actually, you've really got the best of the bargain. According to my clerk's note the dwelling for plot twenty-five zero-one isn't exactly identical, despite what I said earlier. In fact it comes from a new batch, and apparently it's got more features than the earlier ones – better sanitary fixtures, and suchlike – your wife will love it. And you know, it's probably best not to live cheek by jowl with your brother and his family. It's good to remain friends, but at a little distance is best. Believe me."

He extended his hand again, and the young man took it, nodded and said, "Thank you, Sir. It's been a great honour meeting you again."

Bradley frowned. "Again? I'm sorry – I don't recall – I'm afraid I must be getting old... Have we met before?"

The young man's eyes glazed over, and he gazed into the distance, as if he were savouring a very fond memory. "I was a hungry little boy in charge of a corn wagon, driving my father's best horse like a madman, to bring my old Great Aunt Forty from Roundhill to Ashwell to see you before she died. She had important news for you, but I'll never forget that you insisted we eat and drink first."

"Roundhill?" Dominic couldn't hide his astonishment. "How old are you, son?"

"I'm twenty-eight, Sir. I'd have been just eight then – too young to truly understand the importance of my Great Aunt's message. But she insisted it be delivered to you. When I – all of Fenwold – learned of the outcome of your interpretation of her riddle, I vowed to become a deputy marshal and one day follow in your footsteps, perhaps to meet and serve you again."

Here the young man stopped abruptly, his face flushed, as if afraid that he'd said too much.

But on hearing his revelation Bradley stepped up closer to the deputy and clasped both his shoulders with big, avuncular hands. He looked directly into his eyes, as if to seek out that little boy from Roundhill, the boy who had played such an important part in forming the destiny of each and every inhabitant of Fenwold.

"By the Gods of the Wall!" he said. "I knew there was something familiar..."

Now it was Bradley's turn to reflect, to relive those days of glory, of his great quest, of the riddle that had been passed down through forty generations, and entrusted to him to interpret and act upon.

It had been a good while since he'd recited it, but he brought it to mind now as readily as ever.

When a good man comes where Forty dwell

It will be time these words to tell

Look east at the river as far as you might

Till you come to a tower where once was light

Within that tower a key hangs down

That opens a door in a northern town

Above that door a dragon grins

Unlock and enter – the quest begins

Forty had been this deputy's great aunt, the fortieth in her lineage to learn and convey the riddle devised by the Ancient Ones, that would lead the occupants of Fenwold to the lands beyond the Wall. Some also called it the Wall of Death, because until then such had been the fate of any who had attempted to conquer it.

The young lawman smiled at him now, though clearly a little disconcerted, since the Governor still had hold of him by the shoulders. Seeing his embarrassment Bradley took a step backwards, but couldn't resist reaching out for his hand for a third time.

"It's as well you didn't tell me this before, young man. I'm afraid my impartiality would have been sorely tested. You and your wife must come and meet my family so that we can bore them all with talk of the old times – don't worry if you can't remember much – it's all still crystal clear to me! Give yourselves time to get settled – as well as you can, anyway. And I'll see if there's a suitable vacancy in the Marshal's office – I'm sure there'll be no problem. By the way, twenty years ago at Ashwell, amid all the excitement, I never got round to asking you – nor did I catch it earlier on – what's your name?"

"Forty-Two, Sir. My mother's name was Forty-One, but she died in giving birth to me. I was still struggling to learn the riddle at the time, which is why my Great Aunt had to tell it to you."

Bradley's jaw dropped, and the deputy explained. "The tradition was to be continued indefinitely – just in case, I suppose."

Then he left the office, leaving the Governor smiling, slowly nodding, and murmuring, "Of course. Of course."

And for the thousandth time, he marvelled at the wisdom and foresight of the Ancient Ones, whose ability always to provide a contingency plan never ceased to amaze him.

* * *

Krania slammed the front door shut and flung her schoolbag onto the hall floor.

"In here, K!" her mother shouted from the kitchen.

Though Krania heard her, she opened and slammed two other internal doors before approaching. After all, parents were there to be ignored. Not just misheard, but pointedly ignored. She slouched in.

"How was school?"

"Okay," she drawled, opening the fridge door. "Is there any milk?"

"There should be. But don't go spoiling your appetite for supper. And how you can drink it chilled I don't know. As far as I'm concerned, there's nothing sweeter than fresh milk still warm from the cow's udder."

"Yuk!" Krania's face twisted. "That sounds disgusting! And so unhygienic too! Honestly, I can't understand how you survived childhood on a farm."

"Well, I did. And by all accounts it's not doing your young cousin Emily any harm. By the way, one of your pigeons landed in the loft this morning. There'll probably be a note from her."

"Oh. Thanks."

"You don't sound very excited at the prospect. I think it's a wonderful way for you two to keep in touch."

"Huh! Well, it was all right when she was only five and I was her big cousin. I felt more comfortable with the things we wrote about. But now she's eight, she asks about more grown-up things. You know, boyfriends and all that. Things that shouldn't concern her yet."

Her mother smiled. "Children grow up faster in Fenwold, Krania – especially in the villages. They have some schooling these days, but they still have to muck in and help their parents about the house or on the land."

She turned to look wistfully out of the kitchen window. Krania knew the next bit, so she mouthed the words silently behind her back as her mother said, "I remember I went on my first hunting party when I was seven, and shot my first rabbit soon after." She turned around quickly to catch the last traces of mimicry slide from her daughter's face, and then said sternly, "I expect Emily's at least as grown up as her big cousin."

Krania blushed and said quietly, "I'm sorry. But I wish I could talk to her face to face rather than having to write things down."

"Well, why not go and see her? I'm sure my brother Jack and your Aunt Lucy would be thrilled to have you stay for a few weeks."

Krania perked up. "Wow, Mum, that would be great! I suppose I could travel down with Andreas next spring. But I should be starting college – if I graduate."

Her mother gave her a sideways glance. "You'll graduate. And a few weeks away from your studies won't hurt. You'll soon catch up. You ought to see something of the world outside the New Territory."

"How long do you think it would take to get there?"

"It's not that far really, but some of the terrain is rough and the ancient roadways broken up. There's the ferry crossing each way too, of course. And it'll depend on Andreas' itinerary. Do you remember when we made the trip for Jack and Lucy's wedding? Four or five days should see you in Crowtree. It would certainly be an adventure for you."

"Yes. But what about Dad?"

"Don't worry about him. I know he's over-protective towards you, but that's mostly because of some of the odd boyfriends you bring home."

Krania giggled. "Well, I can't help it if I'm attracted to weird people. I don't like normal, boring boys. I prefer a bit of eccentricity – a promise of excitement."

Her mother eyed her coyly. "I think that's what he's afraid of. Anyway, leave it with me. I can usually persuade him to see things my way."

"I've never asked you – was it love at first sight between you and Dad?"

Sylvia laughed. "Not at all. I remember finding him arrogant and chauvinistic when I first met him. But I felt he was special in some way. Do you believe in destiny?"

Krania recoiled mentally, recalling her earlier talk with Cara. Had the hologram reneged on her promise of confidentiality? She answered her mother's question guardedly.

"I don't know. Destiny's a remote concept when your life seems so ordinary. I'm not sure I'd recognise it if walked up and hit me."

"A part of you will know – and you'll act accordingly. But you might not realise it's your destiny at first. When you do, it'll surprise you."

"Ooh, Mum, stop it! You're making it all sound so spooky. Look – I'm getting goose bumps!" She held out her arm for her mother to see.

Sylvia laughed. "Sorry, K. I didn't mean to frighten you. All I meant was that – for some people – destiny can sort of creep up on you. When it does, don't fight it. You won't be disappointed."

"All right, Mum. Piece of profound parental advice number forty-six received loud and clear! But there's just one thing that puzzles me."

"What's that?"

"Well, if you usually get your way with Dad, how come you're the dutiful housewife? I've never known him cook or help with the daily chores."

"Ouch, Krania! That was below the belt! But you know that being Governor of the New Territory is more than a full-time career. I, on the other hand, have a straightforward day job. Neither he nor I like the idea of slave help, so that means we have to fall back on the traditional family division of duties. Anyway, I do what I want with my spare time. And there's one very important thing I learned about your Father in the first month of our marriage."

"At the risk of not wanting to hear this – what would that be?"

"He's probably Fenwold's worst cook!"

"Huh! And I'll bet he never tried to learn. By the way, he's late, isn't he?"

"Yes, he called to say he had to go and talk to *her*."

"Ah. He certainly seems to spend a lot of time at Cara's house."

"Yes. He always has done. It's the first thing he does every day when he leaves the house."

"Oh well, I suppose you can count yourself fortunate that she's only a hologram."

"I have to keep reminding myself of the fact. But I often wonder why the Ancient Ones had to make her look quite so attractive."

"Easy. I expect her graphic designer was a man."

"You could be right. But, to be fair, we have to remember that Cara is the fount of all knowledge as far as the New Territory's development is concerned. Still, I often wonder what they talk about in their one-to-one sessions. Philosophy? Our sex life?"

"Mum! You're embarrassing me!"

"Oh, I'm sorry darling. Let's change the subject then. School?"

"Not much to tell on that subject. Oh no, wait! There is something new. They're going to take us on a field trip to see the power house and the landing strip."

"Oh? When's this going to happen?"

"In about a month's time I think. My class will be the first group to go."

"Really? But you've seen the landing strip before, haven't you? When we took you out camping, remember?"

"That was years ago Mum. I recall that I didn't like it very much. It was disgusting – we lived like animals. We had to use a stream to wash in and go to the toilet in the woods. I was so glad to get back home!"

"Well, just bear that in mind when you go to stay in Crowtree. They share *some* of the benefits we have in the New Territory, but in many ways they're still a primitive community, because we haven't yet been able to get proper plumbing or electrical power to them. I don't want to hear you complaining because you can't live the way you're used to. Look on it as part of the adventure."

"All right Mum – I promise."

"Good. Now, go and fetch Emily's message from the loft. Let's hear what's happening in Crowtree."

As Krania took the outside stairway leading to the purpose-built loft, she recalled that her father had given up a valuable holiday week to build it for her several years beforehand. He wasn't a bad parent really. Perhaps her Mum was right. He was just too busy with his important job to lead the exciting life he'd known in his youth. If only she could have known him then, perhaps she might understand him better now. And her mother's idea that she should visit her cousin in Fenwold buoyed up her spirits no end. She checked her birds' food and water and collected the new message, unrolling and glancing at it as she made her way back to the kitchen.

"Here it is, Mum. It's brief as usual. Pigeon post messages have to be. Emily sends her love, has read some really good books, and wants to know about my latest boyfriend. Her Mum and Dad are well and the village expects a bumper harvest.

"In short, everything's perfect."

* * *

"And to wrap up, we're introducing field trips for the senior students, to give them a clear impression of the size and extent of the New Territory, as they were laid out by the Ancient Ones."

It was just before lunch, following a busy morning of meetings and further hearings of settlers' disputes, that the Governor had been pleased to welcome an old friend for the regular conference that he considered to be the highlight of his working week. His guest was Rajeev Shah, years earlier his trusty lieutenant and deputy marshal, an essential member of the little team who had trudged the length of Fenwold to conquer the Wall. After much cajoling from Bradley, his companion had been persuaded to take charge of the Knowledge Centre here in the settlement. Rajeev was no teacher, but had demonstrated outstanding skills of organisation and initiative during their now famous trek. He'd proved to be the ideal person to recruit instructors, then direct and organise the tuition of young settlers, either born in the New Territory or children of newcomers who arrived in their droves over the ensuing years. Now once a week Shah visited Bradley to keep him updated. Each would smoke a pipe – a lately acquired habit that they both found pleasant, even if it did stink out the office for the rest of the day. The meeting had become an essential ritual, and a real pleasure for both of them. Shah would deliver the usual catalogue of statistics – numbers of students, absences, test results and suchlike – while Bradley would listen, inwardly digest, puff away on his pipe and nod slowly.

"Ah yes," Bradley said, "Krania mentioned it over supper last night. She says her class is due to go on a trip in a few weeks time. She's been with us along the perimeter track in the car for some hunting, and we even took our horses and camped for a few days near the landing strip when she was younger, so there won't be much that she hasn't seen before. But we've never taken her the whole way round. She seemed quite excited at the prospect."

"And how is your lovely daughter, Dominic? Still fighting the boys off?"

The Governor's cheek twitched. "Hmm. Probably not hard enough, old friend. We've always allowed her the freedom to go where she wants and make friends. But some of the lads she brings home aren't necessarily the type I'd choose."

"Isn't that always the case with fathers, Dominic? No boy is good enough to take their beloved daughter away."

"Yes, but, damn it, man – she's only seventeen!"

Rajeev smiled, and even as he did so Bradley knew that it was one of those smiles that always preceded a piece of 'Shah wisdom' that couldn't be refuted.

"Just as a matter of interest, Dominic, how old was Sylvia when you two first – ahem – got together?"

Bradley pursed his lips. He was aware that Rajeev knew full well the answer to his own question, since he'd grown up in the village of Crowtree alongside Sylvia and her brothers. But he knew he must provide an answer, or appear to be the old fool that for the moment he felt he was.

"Seventeen when we first met – eighteen when we became – closer. But you've made your point, as usual."

Rajeev sighed. "I'm afraid you have to resign yourself to the fact that you're likely to lose your daughter sooner than you'd wish – and probably to some clueless, work shy…"

"Don't, Rajeev! I said that you'd made your point, didn't I?" Bradley held up his hands in defeat, and grimaced at his friend's self-righteous grin.

"Now, about these field trips – whereabouts will the tour take the students?"

"Oh, where you'd expect - along the track, first to view the acres of overgrown sheds and warehouses. It'll give them a sense of just how much more there is out there waiting to be opened up – both in terms of tools and knowledge. Then further on for a tour of the powerhouse, and finally out towards the landing strip. Though there's not a lot to see there – just a huge concrete area patrolled by mechanised dragons to keep it clear of vegetation. I suppose we've still no clue as to the purpose of the strip?"

Dominic shook his head. "You can ask Cara till you're blue in the face. All she ever says is that we're not yet ready for aerial and space flight. So we'll just have to be patient and enjoy the gifts she's seen fit to bestow upon us. Mind you, you have to admit that they're truly amazing, Rajeev. Virtually limitless electrical power for cars, bulldozers, cranes and all sorts of communication gadgets."

Shah chipped in. "And knowledge from the historical databanks. For me, that's the Ancient Ones' greatest gift to us."

"And printed books," Bradley said, "Don't forget them – hundreds and thousands of them. I can spend hours wandering around the library – I'd sooner do that than sit and search via a screen. Somehow it feels far more natural to hold a book in your hand and thumb through it. Though I have to concede, learning to read wasn't the easiest thing I've ever done."

"I know what you mean. And yet the children seem to pick it up without any difficulty."

"True. We've been blessed with all the technology and knowledge the Ancient Ones left for us to find here. And Cara's right to uncover it all for us at a measured pace. After all, there's the result of thousands of years of learning and discovery out there in the forest. It's not a lot to expect of us to be patient, and leave a little for future generations. Anything more to report?"

Rajeev shook his head, meaning that he had nothing left to say. He had never been one to spoil silence by unnecessarily filling it with facile conversation. Bradley of course was well used to his old friend's natural taciturnity, and by now had learned to endure these punctuations of quietude with patience and tolerance. He felt no need to jump in with any old platitude merely to interject some noise.

Then he remembered his earlier meeting with Forty-Two, so he told Shah about that, and they agreed they must all get together a few days hence. Then there was silence again.

Eventually Shah spoke. "We reached something of a milestone this week, Dominic. We took in our two thousandth student."

"Two thousandth? I didn't know you'd been counting."

Shah looked serious. "You can't control what you don't measure, old friend."

Bradley smiled inwardly at his own ability to be lectured by those who reported to him. Perhaps that was why they'd put up with him for so long. Oddly, he no longer worried about such things as status and seniority. He preferred to be allowed to be himself – open and honest. And he found, mostly, that people reciprocated. He enjoyed good relationships with most of those who worked for him.

"Quite right, Rajeev," he said. Then he added, almost reflectively, "I suppose we ought to keep similar tabs on the numbers of settlers."

"Well, last time I ventured out to the construction area," Shah said, "I noticed that the plot numbers were approaching twenty-five hundred." Bradley had good cause to confirm this fact and merely nodded, so Rajeev continued, "I'd judge the average household in the New Territory to number about four people, so we must have a population approaching ten thousand on this side of the Wall."

"That many?" Dominic replied. "And Fenwold's population must be diminishing as ours expands, so it's already likely that there are more of us over here than..." He puffed on his pipe again.

He didn't bother finishing his sentence. There was one subject, however, that Bradley felt he should broach soon with his friend for, apart from Sylvia and Cara, there was no one sufficiently qualified to discuss it with.

"Rajeev, do you ever wonder how this place will run after we're gone?"

Shah looked puzzled. "What do you want to worry about that for? We've got years ahead of us yet. With all the medical advances we've found here, barring accidents, we can expect to live far longer than we could ever have hoped back in Fenwold."

"I know, but we can't just wait until we're on our last legs, then suddenly announce it's time to introduce a New Order. Really Rajeev, I'm surprised at you, of all people. You're an organiser. Surely you don't think these things should be left to chance."

Shah smiled wryly. "If I didn't know you, you old campaigner, I'd take that as an insult. But I know you're just baiting me." Then he looked ponderous. "I've got to admit you're right though. We should at least start planning for succession. The trouble is, you run things so well here, and you're so highly respected that the people are more than happy for things to continue the way they are. Even the Fenwold Council – what's left of them – don't bother to interfere any more. Their last envoy was Tribune Pieter Jennings – and he only came because he's an old friend of yours. It was more of a pleasure trip than official business. If I recall, he went away having made no recommendation other than to carry on as normal."

Bradley laughed, partly to hide his embarrassment. "If I recall, he did suggest we persevere with driving a tunnel through the Wall as an alternative to the culvert. Although we made some headway we never did find the resource to re-start work after it collapsed. But I'm not going to argue with you, or we'll be here all day. The fact is that what we have here – like it or not – is a benevolent dictatorship. We've both studied the history files from the ancient times, so we know where that leads to in the end. Our population will grow to a point where it can no longer be ruled by decree. Then there'll be discontent, rebellion, anarchy and chaos. No. What we have to start thinking about is the introduction of democracy."

Now it was Shah 's turn to laugh. "Where have I heard all that before? It couldn't be Ancient Rome, could it? What was that fellow's name? Ah yes, I remember. Caesar, wasn't it? Julius Caesar?"

As usual, Dominic rose to Shah's bait. "That's not fair, Rajeev. I've no secret dreams to be made an Emperor – I sincerely mean exactly what I said."

"I know, Dominic. I was just pulling your leg. You ought to call a meeting of all the district elders, and see what they think. But one thing I would advise, quite seriously."

"What's that?"

"Don't take on all the work yourself. Get them to do it. In fact, if you can – and I know you can – make them think it was their idea in the first place."

Bradley nodded slowly. "You haven't lost the old cunning, have you, you sly dog?"

Shah only forced an innocent expression and said, "I'm sure I've no idea what you mean, Governor."

CHAPTER SIXTEEN
VENGEANCE IS BITTER

Had the ancient oak been blessed with the power of speech, no doubt it could have told some tales – perhaps even of events pre-dating the foundation of Fenwold, and the enclosure behind the great Wall of a thousand survivors of the plague that had wiped out the rest of Mankind. Being so close to Ashwell, it would certainly have witnessed the rise of the outlaw Red and his raider gang twenty years earlier. The unheeded pleas of the villagers, tortured and starved on his orders, would once have echoed through this now peaceful glade.

The red-haired youth slunk sullenly through the forest and lingered at the tree as arranged. He wouldn't normally put himself in harm's way, but the proposed meeting had sounded intriguing. Someone who knew of his parentage wanted to talk to him. So why not approach him openly at the tavern in Ashwell? He guessed the mysterious author of these tidings preferred to remain out of public view. An outlaw perhaps, as his father had been. His curiosity was aroused. How could he stay away? But still, his hand clasped the dagger at his belt, ready to defend himself in case of trickery.

"So you came."

The voice was a deep baritone – that of an older man.

"Step out where I can see you," the youth said.

A hooded figure emerged from the shrubbery.

"Show me your face."

"Not yet, lad. Perhaps when we know each other better."

"What makes you think I want to know you at all?"

"Because together we can avenge your father's death."

His interest quickened. "What do you know of my father?"

"I know you've never seen him. He was killed before you were born, by Marshal Dominic Bradley, now Governor of the New Territory. Don't tell me you've never dreamed of having your revenge."

The youth sneered, "You seem to know a lot about me too."

"I've made it my business. Rather than your given name, I know you prefer to be called Red, like your father. Your dead mother was an Ashwell village girl, who claimed he'd raped her during the occupation. She struggled to raise you with no man to help her. But your father's angry blood proved strong enough, guiding you from the grave to stand your ground and defy authority."

He wasn't sure how to take this. Was it a compliment, or an impudent appraisal of his character? Had any of his delinquent crowd of hangers-on uttered such words, they'd likely have earned a broken jaw. Yet this man spoke with authority. More than that, he seemed to admire his father, whereas most spoke only ill of him. And the man was right that he'd long looked forward to hastening the death of Dominic Bradley, hero of Fenwold.

"Who are you? What do you want?"

"You wouldn't know me. For now, call me Wolf. As I've said, I want to see Bradley's downfall."

"Why?"

The cold response came through gritted teeth.

"I have my reasons."

* * *

Crowtree's Marshal Jack Storey gazed out from his porch. He didn't look much like a lawman. Though he'd changed (at his wife's insistence) from his farming gear into clean woven trousers, shirt and jacket, he still looked every inch a man of the land. The day's toil finished, he relaxed now with his guest, both men enjoying a chat and a drink after a satisfying supper.

"You know, Andreas, even after twenty years it's hard to look at that stretch of ground without recalling the great battle that took place here. I can still hear the yells of the oncoming brigands, and the howls as they ran into our concealed spears and spikes – then Dominic's command for my sister Sylvia to sound the signal for the counter-attack. As you see, we never dismantled that old alarm bell. Can't you hear it too?"

The trader surveyed the peaceful ground and cocked an ear to humour his host, but then smiled as he lifted his face up to the welcome glow of the early evening sun.

"You forget, my friend, that I wasn't here. My home was on the coast, many leagues away to the east. But the news of Marshal Bradley's great victory soon reached every corner of Fenwold. They say that everyone can remember exactly where they were and what they were doing when the reports came. I was gathering berries in the forest with my future wife and some friends. The news gave courage to many other downtrodden villages to turn the tables on the brigand gangs."

Jack swallowed another mouthful of ale, and heaved a satisfied sigh.

Andreas continued, "And you've a second reason to celebrate, Jack – another successful harvest. It's the third year in a row that Crowtree's produced a surplus."

Jack nodded. "Aye, it's a good crop, all safely under cover. Every villager and slave alike has worked from dawn to dusk to get it all in. The Gods have been kind to us. We'll certainly have some excess to trade."

"Excellent. I'll have a look tomorrow morning at what you can spare if that's all right with you. There's a good market for your produce throughout Fenwold and the New Territory – even though they've reported a decent harvest too. But no one can match Crowhill cheese – it goes down especially well with the settlers beyond the Wall. If you've any more like the wedge that Lucy brought out tonight, you can consider it already sold. I'll pay you a good price too – even better if you'll take goods instead of coin."

"I'm unlike my dear departed father in that respect," Jack said. "He would never use the Council's coinage. But you know me by now – I'll take goods if we can use them, but since Fenwold has enjoyed peace for many years, I'm quite happy to accept your money as well."

He wondered why Andreas frowned at this last comment. But just then his wife came out to join them with their young daughter Emily in tow and with a contented sigh sat herself down on a spare seat. The girl kneeled on the porch deck beside her, clutching an empty mug and a book to which she immediately turned her attention.

"Well, that's my day's work all done," said his wife, and shot him a blank sideways glance.

"Sorry Lucy. You know I'd normally help you with the dishes. But when we've a guest and we've business to discuss…"

"It's all right, my dear," she laughed. "I'm only teasing."

Andreas asked, "I thought you two had a house man to help with your menial tasks."

Storey's face was set. "You mean Johanssen? The poor chap had a nasty accident in the woods earlier today. He was helping with some logging when he slipped and got his hand in the way of someone's axe, losing two fingers. He's still recuperating in his quarters, though he insists he's capable of light duties."

Andreas looked genuinely concerned. "By the Gods, what a thing to happen! Whatever will you do with him?"

Jack rubbed his chin. "I've been thinking about that. He's been the family's slave since he was sentenced after the battle of Crowtree. And he's turned out to be a willing and trustworthy servant. I suppose he was just a confused young man who was taken in by Red's promises of wealth and good living. Underneath he wasn't really bad. Anyway, he's part of the family now. I thought I might ask the village elders' permission to give him his freedom. I'd be happy to keep him as a paid help, if that's what he wanted. I haven't spoken to him about that yet though."

Lucy said, "It's funny, but none of the other families with raider slaves know anything about an accident in the forest. It's a bit weird. Still, some of Red's old gang members can be tight-lipped."

Then she smiled, nodding at the jug that stood on the table in front of her husband. "Is there any ale left? Or have you two guzzled it all? We've brought our own mugs." Both she and the child held out their vessels expectantly. Jack lifted the jug and poured them each a draught of the weak ale, from which they took generous mouthfuls.

Lucy wiped her lips with the back of her hand. "Ah, but that's good, if I say it myself. Well then, Andreas, have you brought us some nice things to trade for our produce?"

Jack frowned. "Don't forget we have the other villagers to consider, Lucy. The crop surplus belongs to all of us."

"I know that. But surely the headman's wife is entitled to the first pick, isn't she? I wouldn't mind a new dress and a nice brooch."

"Me too, Daddy!" Emily cried.

The trader smiled. "I'm sure we can find something for such a beautiful lady as yourself, Lucy. Though I'm afraid they might not do you justice."

Jack was by now well used to such mock flirtation by his friends. It was one of the penalties of taking such a young wife. Now twenty-eight, his junior by eleven years, she was also very attractive.

"We'll take a look at clothes and trinkets in the morning," he said grudgingly.

The two females exchanged knowing smiles.

He continued, "What else have you to tempt us with, Andreas – anything from the New Territory? I'm always amazed to hear about the wonders they're opening up there."

"You won't be disappointed," the trader said. "Though it's a shame that I can't offer you any of the powered gadgets they have. Not for a while anyway."

Lucy said, "They wouldn't be of much use seeing that we don't have any power – what's it called – *el* something?"

Emily looked up from her book. "Electricity!" she announced with enthusiasm. "The teacher told us. It comes from the Moon." Her certainty waned on this last word and she added with diminished authority, "Or it might be the Sun."

"I've heard something about it," Jack said. "I find it hard to understand. I think we're probably better off without it."

"Oh, I don't know, Jack," Lucy said. "It would be nice to have some labour-saving devices around the house. And I don't think I'd miss that dirty old wood burner."

Andreas said, "Yes, electricity will change everyone's lives before too long. The settlers have been promised portable powerhouses that could be used outside the New Territory. Just think about that – you'd be able to use chargeable communication devices to speak to your sister without waiting weeks or months for me to bring her letters to you."

The headman greeted this news with a stony face. "I hear what you say, Andreas. But I'm not sure we want to change our everyday lives. What's wrong with the way we live, after all? Yes, we all work hard and it's a struggle sometimes, but we've the satisfaction of knowing that our produce comes from our own sweat. And I reckon it tastes the better for that."

Lucy scowled. "Oh, Jack, don't be such a stick-in-the-mud. You can't hold back progress forever. Surely it's what Marshal Bradley's quest was all about, wasn't it? It's part of the destiny the Ancient Ones promised us."

Jack sniffed and said, "I won't deny there's a lot of good coming out of the New Territory. But we who've chosen to stay in Fenwold have gained too, even without the benefit of electrical power. With fewer mouths to feed, there's more of everything to go around. And I'm sure that was part of the Ancients' plan too. Still, I suppose if progress has to come, it will. But I won't be in a hurry to get rid of my horses."

The trader put a hand on Jack's arm and said, "Jack, I've brought you a whole lot of new books."

The headman's eyes lit up. "Ah, books! I'd say reading's the best thing the Ancient Ones have given us. It lifts you out of yourself." Then he winked at the trader. "But reading books is a bit like this ale here. Once you've had a taste, you fancy a bit more, don't you?"

Lucy said, "All right. I can take a hint. Pass me the jug and I'll be back in a minute. But Andreas, don't talk any more about what you've brought from the New Territory until I get back." And she went into the house to re-fill the ale jug.

While she was gone the trader's expression darkened. "Jack, you were saying how things are much quieter now than in our fathers' day. But just recently on my travels I've heard reports of gangs of escaped slaves causing trouble. Have you had any problems down here?"

Jack shook his head. "Most who were punished with slavery accepted their fate. We've never had a runaway from Crowtree – they have a pretty good life here. Some of the slave masters of Ashwell tend to be harder, but that's understandable after the treatment they suffered at the hands of Red and his hooligans. There've been a couple of fights among rowdies who got hold of some bad liquor. But people in these parts are mostly law-abiding. That's why my brother Liam moved up to Roundhill to be marshal there. It seemed a waste keeping him here as my deputy."

Looking relieved, the trader changed the subject. "You must be proud that Bradley chose your sister for his wife."

As he said this Lucy arrived back with a foaming jug of ale, and shook her head as she set the vessel down on the table. "You have that the wrong way round, Andreas. When he and Rajeev Shah set out on their quest to solve the Fenwold Riddle, marriage was the last thing on Marshal Bradley's mind. It was Sylvia who hounded him to let her join them, and it was she who set her sights on getting him too."

Andreas smiled. "Have you seen Sylvia and her husband since they settled in the New Territory?"

"Only once," said Jack. "Of course they were married here in Crowtree, but that was before they set off with the first batch of settlers. We were honoured that they were able to return to attend our own wedding. That's getting on for ten years ago. It's always good to get their letters of course. That reminds me – there's a bundle from Crowtree for you to take back with you tomorrow."

Young Emily tugged at his sleeve. "And don't forget there's a crate of pigeons, Daddy!"

"Oh yes," he laughed. "I know how you and your cousin Krania like to keep up-to-date with what each has been doing."

"It's quicker than letters, anyway," she pouted.

Still smiling, her father teased, "Only when the pigeons don't lose their way, get snaffled by a hawk or end up in some hunter's pie!" Then relenting he said, "But I'm sure Andreas won't forget to take them with him. He remembered to bring yours back from the New Territory, didn't he?"

"Yes. Thank you, Uncle Andreas."

The trader smiled and said, "That's all right, young lady. It's good company for me." And he made comical pigeon noises, which brought a broad smile to her face.

Jack scratched his head. "What was I saying? Oh, yes – the Bradley wedding. What a ceremony that was! Dominic's parents travelled over from the capital, and droves of folk came from all over Fenwold to join in the celebrations. My father was so proud – Mum too. By the Gods, I do miss them all!"

He succumbed to a mild choking fit on these words, and while he recovered a moment of silence was observed out of respect for his dead parents.

Then Andreas suggested, "Well, why not travel up to visit your sister and her husband? I'm sure Emily would love to really meet her cousin. It's only a four or five day journey, then a short ferry ride across the river and through the culvert in the Wall."

"I don't know, Andreas. As marshal and village headman I have a lot to look after here."

"Couldn't you delegate? What about Liam?"

"My brother? That wouldn't be fair. He'd want to come too."

"Well, someone else then. Surely you're not indispensable?"

Jack laughed nervously. "I don't know. I have lately been thinking that I'm a bit old to carry on as marshal here for much longer. One day perhaps."

The pigeons cooed from the loft above the store beside the house. This was a magical, peaceful time of day, when the village rested and reflected before retiring, and words between friends weren't really needed.

Lucy broke the silence. "I remember the wedding. And I remember Marshal Bradley very well. He was very kind to me."

"Oh?" Andreas said. "When was that?"

"I'd be about Emily's age at the time. It was the morning after one of the raids on our store by the outlaw Red. Don't you recall, Jack, when everyone went to deal with the fire at the outer barn? I didn't go because I had to shut up the chickens. I saw Red and another raider drive their wagon into the centre of the village while the fire took everyone's attention. I saw everything they did. They ran down two poor old women, Megan and Annie Beckett, before loading up their cart with our produce. Megan was killed and Annie seriously injured. Next morning Marshal Bradley and your father asked me what I'd seen. They were both really kind, but I think I fell under the Marshal's spell from that moment."

Jack said, "I recall the incident. It was the start of Red's brief reign of terror. His gang overran Ashwell barely two leagues away, and kept the villagers in appalling conditions. Several perished and some of their young girls were raped. They say that more than one Ashwell child was cursed with raider's blood flowing through its veins. Awful days, they were. We must thank the Gods that they're long past."

But as Lucy shared out the remainder of the ale and they watched the sun dip over the Wall to the west, the sound of clattering hooves interrupted their evening reverie.

Without warning, the slave Johanssen rushed out onto the porch and took a position directly in front of Jack just as two archers pulled up their steeds at the front of the house. In the blink of an eye their arrows were let fly and they galloped off. The slave crumpled onto the decking at Jack's feet.

Both Lucy and Emily screamed in terror as Storey yelled, "By the Gods! Johanssen!" Kneeling beside him, and horrified at the blood oozing from his chest wounds, he checked frantically for signs of life.

Andreas yelled, "Lucy – get some cloths to staunch the bleeding!"

But Lucy appeared dumbstruck, the back of her hand to her mouth.

"Lucy, didn't you hear me?" the trader said. "What's wrong?"

She lowered her hand.

"I – I think I've just seen a ghost!" she gasped.

CHAPTER SEVENTEEN
WAKING DESTINY

"Lucy was right, Jack. Red's come back to haunt us – in the guise of his bastard son!"

Liam delivered the news urgently as he dismounted directly outside the Storey's house. It was early evening on the day after the audacious attack.

The two brothers shook hands and then stepped across the porch and into the kitchen, where Lucy and Emily were preparing supper. Lucy looked up and smiled at Liam, her hands in a mixing bowl, while her daughter ran over to greet her uncle with a hug.

"Sorry to ask you to do all this running around, Liam," Jack said, pouring out some beer. "We're all at sixes and sevens here. I can still hardly believe what happened. What did you manage to find out?"

Accepting a mug of ale Liam took a long draught and then sat down by the stove. "As soon as your deputy gave me your message this morning I rode across to Ashwell to make enquiries as you asked. There's no doubt about it, Jack. From Lucy's description and from the villagers' accounts of who's gone missing lately, it's clear that one of Johanssen's slayers was the son of the dead outlaw Red. I know the fellow – a young tearaway, and the spitting image of his father. A girl called Mary went with him – they say she's the daughter of Red's second-in-command, that vicious brute called Clamp. Remember him?"

Jack said, "Yes, I remember Clamp. He went to his execution cursing the lot of us. And I know Mary. She's a crazy piece too – always in the thick of things when there's any trouble. Small stuff so far though – egging on boys to fight and getting drunk. The Ashwell villagers took to calling her 'Scary Mary'. I'm not really surprised she's taken up with Red's son. They'd be perfectly suited."

Liam resumed, "And two Ashwell slaves absconded recently as well. One of them could have been with Red last night. Did you manage to get a look at him?"

Jack shook his head. "No. The second archer was hooded."

"Were you able to track them very far?"

"No. We followed them into the forest. But you know what it's like trying to pick up tracks in the dark. They could have taken any one of a hundred deer trails. And I couldn't be sure there weren't others lying in ambush waiting to pick us off. I couldn't risk losing any of my men in a futile operation. I had to bring them out. I sent a deputy in at first light, but they'd covered their tracks well. I can only think they've a hideout somewhere deep in the forest."

His brother nodded. "I'm surprised these new raiders haven't had a go at our barns. We've taken in just about all our harvest at Roundhill – how about you?"

"Likewise. We're highly vulnerable. I've posted guards on our storehouses. I assume you've done the same."

Liam nodded. "Too right. But with the migration, our manpower's stretched to the limit and everyone's on double watches. I've stressed to my deputies and militiamen just how vital it is to stay alert, but it only takes one small distraction…"

"I know. It's a worry. I've been wondering whether to ask Dominic if he can spare any deputies. I could pin a message to one of Krania's pigeons. Andreas brought down a new crate load yesterday."

Liam said, "I'd put a hold on that, Jack. This might be just a flash in the pan. As I said, only a couple of Ashwell slaves have absconded – and we can't be certain they've both joined Red. There's Scary Mary of course, but otherwise, from my enquiries, nobody else is missing. We'd look foolish if we were overreacting. Why not keep the option in reserve in case trouble escalates?"

Jack said, "Hmm. Yes. I suppose you're right."

* * *

In a forest clearing far from the main trails, midway between Crowtree and Roundhill, the girl Mary and two older males listened in awe as young Red boasted about his assault on the Storey household.

"Wolf seemed pleased with last night's action – even though the pleasure of killing Jack Storey will have to wait for another time. It doesn't have to be Jack though – his brother Liam would do, if it brought Bradley down here to be a hero again. But who'd have thought that old fool Johanssen would sacrifice himself like that?"

One of the older men said, "Maybe we shouldn't have let him go when he overheard us yesterday."

Red picked up a stick and poked the campfire. "I couldn't risk killing him. If he hadn't gone home Storey would have had his hounds out and we'd never have had the chance to strike as we did. But we must have frightened him enough to keep him quiet. He must have figured taking Storey's arrow was his cleanest way out. Stupid sod! But what's done is done. Our immediate concern is supplies while we hold out here until we're ready to make our next move. Report please, Sperry."

The other man sat up straight when he heard his name spoken.

"That's taken care of, Red. Our brothers in Ashwell will send food and drink tomorrow at noon to a meeting place about four furlongs from here, as you asked."

Red smiled. "Good. I don't want anyone else to know about our hideout. Until we strike it'll be your duty to make sure we don't run out of stuff. You'd better take a horse with you though. I don't want any of you old men putting your backs out carrying more than you can manage." He sniggered at his mockery, as did the girl, who leaned closer to him to place both hands on his nearest shoulder while she shared his joke.

Sperry said, "They've just taken their harvests in, Red. Why don't we help ourselves to some of it?"

"No, no!" Red shouted, a sudden annoyance in his voice. "I told you what Wolf said. A raid on their barns is just what they'll be expecting now. They're not stupid. They'll have guards on them – especially after our visit last night. But that's all right. We'll just play a waiting game. We'll build up our numbers. After a while they'll relax their vigilance. Then with the men Wolf has promised us, we'll take them by surprise and have more supplies than we could wish for. What's the weapons situation, Banks?"

"Our friends in Ashwell have been stealing knives, crossbows and bolts for weeks now. They're building a hidden stockpile just outside the village, on the south-west side of the road to Crowtree. They'll be ready to do whatever you ask of them."

"Good. Then we'll have enough arms to strike when we're ready. You're certain you can handle crossbows, aren't you?"

"Sure, Red. Not longbows though – not since the elders took our bow fingers. But it's not hard to pull a crossbow trigger with your third finger – with practice."

Red pursed his lips. "Well, Wolf says his men are all skilled archers. But that doesn't mean you can just sit on your arses and leave them to it. So make sure you do practice – all of you!"

Banks nodded. "I'll put the word around."

The girl spoke, though her speech was slurred due mainly to the effect of wild mushrooms she'd been chewing. "What about Crowtree? They've got slaves there too."

Red turned to her. "I know, Mary. But the Crowtree slaves are tame in comparison. Just look at Johanssen. He was like a rabbit caught in the moonlight. They think their masters have done them a favour. But the Ashwell slaves are different. Because of the occupation, the villagers have been bastards to them. They have something to gain from rebelling. But don't worry. I have plans to make the Crowtree slaves see things in a different light."

She placed a wet kiss on his cheek and a hand on his thigh. "You're so clever, Red. Get rid of these two."

He got up and beckoned the runaway slaves to follow him.

"See to the horses, you two." Then, lowering his voice, he winked and said, "Then make yourselves scarce for an hour."

CHAPTER EIGHTEEN
SPREADING VENOM

The morning air carried the scent of early autumn, the sweet nuttiness of fallen leaves not yet decaying, as people drifted out from the village to gather at a near-by forest clearing and pay their final respects to the slave Johanssen. Two days after the attempt on Jack Storey's life, he and his family, together with several other Crowtree families and slaves, met where Johanssen's body had been raised to rest on top of its prepared funeral pyre.

Aside from a few muted greetings and pleasantries, the folk stood quiet and pensive. A full-throated blackbird entertained them as they assembled in the glade, a joyful finale to the dawn chorus, at once welcoming yet contrasting with the solemnity of the occasion. Before the lighting of the dried rushes at the base of the pyre, Jack stood in front of it to address the congregation.

"Friends, I know it's unusual for a slave's cremation to receive a formal eulogy, but I consider this a special case, and I hope you'll all bear with me while I say a few words in memory, not of the slave, but of the man Carl Johanssen.

"For Carl was a man whom I was proud to call a friend. He lived in my house for twenty years, and although he was a very private person in many ways, I think I came to know him better than anyone.

"From the little he told me, I know that Carl was born and raised in a northern village, and travelled south with a caravan of traders when he was thirteen years old, after his widowed mother was killed by a stampede of wild horses – a traumatic enough experience for a young boy. But then a band of brigands attacked the traders and he was taken prisoner – a slave to the callous outlaws until he was taken under the wing of the charismatic raider whom we all know as Red. From that point he knew no other life than one outside of the law.

"I make no excuses on Carl's behalf. No doubt there were countless chances for him to escape and find a place in normal society. But for whatever reasons he remained under Red's protection until he was captured here at Crowtree after the fateful battle that we all remember so vividly. Since that day he's worked diligently and without complaint as a slave in my household – until his untimely and selfless death at the hands of Red's son. It's ironic that the son of the man who first set Carl on his unfortunate career should prove the instrument of his death.

"I know nothing of his specific deeds before he came to live with us. That he took part in raids and no doubt other lawless acts while under Red's command, we must assume was inevitable. Certainly he never denied these accusations, nor did he make cowardly excuses for his behaviour, but accepted responsibility for his own actions. I only know that, during the last twenty years, he has been both a dutiful servant and friend to my wife, my daughter and me. I ask you to join me in honouring his memory before we return his body to the elements."

He then nodded towards two attendants who lit the rushes to ignite the fire that would render Johanssen's corpse to ashes.

After a quarter of an hour Jack and most of the villagers attending drifted away to resume their normal duties, for it was customary that those who came to a funereal burning didn't linger once the flames had taken hold. Usually only a couple of volunteers would remain to see the cremation completed. In Johanssen's case the pair who assumed this duty were two of his fellow slaves, Copeland and Treggano. In the light breeze the flames quickly ripped through the dry wood and foliage, soon hot enough to sizzle and burn through the dried flesh and bones that had been the slave Johanssen. After an hour all that was left of the poor fellow were a pile of hot ashes and an aroma reminiscent of roasting pork.

As the two slaves raked the embers to make the area safe, a rustling in the bushes made Treggano turn around. He gasped when he recognised the two men who emerged, armed with loaded crossbows.

"Red! What...?"

But the young fugitive interrupted him, keeping his voice low, though with no loss of authority.

"Quiet! We don't want to attract attention. And don't worry about these." His eyes swivelled towards the weapons. "They're just a precaution. I only want to talk to you. If you've done here, and you're certain nobody's in hearing distance, come into the cover of the undergrowth."

As the weapons were still pointed at them, the two slaves didn't argue. They nervously followed the outlaw into the woodland, his accomplice behind them. They looked relieved however when the bows were lowered.

Treggano addressed Red again. "Don't you realise the danger of your coming here? Everyone knows you killed Johanssen – every lawman around here is looking for you!"

Red lied, "That's why I had to come – to clear my good name! That lying bastard Jack Storey accuses me of murdering his slave, when in fact it was he who caused that poor man's death. It's true that I intended to kill Storey – and I don't apologise for that – but the coward pulled his innocent servant in front of him at the fateful moment to save his own skin! Isn't that right, Banks?"

With shifty eyes his accomplice only said, "Sure, Boss."

Red continued. "Listen. We can't stay here for long, but we came to ask the Crowtree slaves to rally to our cause, which is to free all slaves and break the hold of the lawmen in Fenwold. I have it on good authority that other groups are rebelling across Fenwold. We're organising in Ashwell, where we have a lot of support, and we'll be doing the same at Roundhill. I also have the promise of help from farther afield when we're ready. Meanwhile I need to be sure of your support here."

The second slave Copeland now spoke. "Look, Red. We understand why you feel bitter about your father's death at Bradley's hand, and that the Ashwell slaves have had it hard. But here in Crowtree we've been treated pretty well. It won't be easy to persuade the others to rally to your cause."

Red said, "I like the way you talk – very diplomatic. So, talk to the others for me. Tell them about Storey's treachery, and how these Crowtree folk see their slaves as dispensable chattels. By the Gods, man, haven't you any pride? Surely by now you've been punished enough for the misdemeanours of your youth! Isn't it time you all had your freedom? Well, these Crowtree buggers aren't going to give it to you – they've grown too used to having you as unpaid labour. You've got to rise up and take your liberty! All you need are weapons and courage. Be here tomorrow at this time and Banks here will bring some knives and bows to start you off. He'll be your contact until we're ready to make our move. In the meantime, start spreading the word. Well, what do you say?"

With Red's infectious fervour reflected in their eyes the two slaves nodded and shook hands with the outlaw. Before he turned back to the cover of the forest he said, "Go then – and prepare to win back your liberty!"

* * *

That evening at their woodland hideout Red and his three accomplices sat around their campfire. While Banks and Sperry sharpened knives, their leader and his girl lounged lazily, drinking beer and talking.

Red said, "You know, I reckon we'll win over the Crowtree slaves without much bother. I'd have preferred simultaneous uprisings in Ashwell and Crowtree, but Wolf thinks we should amass our forces and take Ashwell first."

He glanced at the two ex-slaves. "But we could do with some young blood on our side instead of just a bunch of old men."

"Leave that to me," Mary said. "I can think of at least three young hard cases and a couple of girls in Ashwell who are sick of the daily grind. I reckon I could sneak back and persuade them to join us if there was something in it for them."

"That would be useful. But be careful – I don't want you getting caught."

"What if I did? I've done nothing wrong. I'll just tell my folks I went off to dry out for a few days. They'll probably be pleased to hear it. By the way, they won't come to any harm when we strike, will they?"

"They've never kept a slave, have they?"

She laughed. "Only me."

He laughed. "Daughters don't count. But they'll be all right as long as they don't interfere."

"I'll see that they don't," she said. "When I've persuaded my friends to join us, shall I bring them here? We could fetch some more weapons with us."

He thought for a moment. "Bring weapons by all means. But no, have the group stay in the village. They'll be more use to us working on the inside. You'll have to serve as go-between so we can act in unison when the time comes."

"All right. I'll head back to the village tomorrow morning."

"When the lawmen know you've returned they're sure to ask you about me."

"I'll deny I've even seen you — that my going walkabout when you left the village was just a coincidence. They can't prove otherwise."

"Good girl. And as for what's in all this for your friends, you can tell them it's their only chance of joining the winning side. Plus of course, they'll have a share in the spoils. And they'll be well fed — which is more than I can say for the snivelling villagers!"

Sperry asked, "What happens after we've taken Ashwell? Do we move in on Crowtree?"

"Possibly. But Wolf says there are others plotting similar revolts across Fenwold. Working together, there's no knowing what we can achieve!"

He took a hearty swig of beer and rose to his feet, grabbing Mary's hand.

"Come on. Let's go for a walk."

* * *

"I don't understand what's going on, Lucy. It's been three weeks since Johanssen's murder and Red seems to have completely vanished. The militiamen guarding the barns are getting fed up. Autumn's here and they should be starting their ploughing before the frosts come. I can see their point, but… "

"But what, Jack?"

She handed him a dish to dry.

"I don't know. I just feel I'm missing something. Why has Red gone so quiet? I can't believe his attack was nothing more than an isolated act of bravado. I was expecting some follow-up action."

Lucy shrugged. "Maybe the answer's simple. Could it be that he realised what a terrible thing he'd done and became scared of the consequences? So he's made himself scarce. I'll bet he's far away from here, planning mayhem in some other marshal's district."

"If only that were true," said her husband. "But what of the two Ashwell slaves who absconded about the same time? What's become of them?"

"Maybe he killed them as witnesses, or just took them with him. Didn't you say that woman – what's her name...?"

"You mean Scary Mary?"

"Yes. Didn't you say she'd shown up again in Ashwell? And that you'd questioned her about Red's whereabouts?"

"That's right. But she had nothing to say, except that she didn't know where he was."

"And do you believe her?"

"I think she knows more than she's admitting, but I can't prove anything. She spends a lot of time mingling with the more gullible members of Ashwell's youth. I sent a spy in to eavesdrop on her but he was soon rumbled and had to withdraw. I wish I knew what she was up to."

"What does Liam think?"

"Like you, he believes the danger's passed, that the killing of Johanssen was an isolated act and that I should reduce the guard on the warehouses so that those farmers can get back to doing what they're best at."

"And will you? Call off the guards?"

"I'm going to sleep on it tonight and decide in the morning."

"Well, that'll make a change – if you manage to get more than an hour's sleep tonight. You've been restless as a pregnant sow ever since this business started. Honestly, Jack, it's making an old man of you. Can't you think about handing your badge over to someone younger? Either of your deputies would be more than capable."

Jack pursed his lips and sighed. "I know. I'll give it some serious thought. But right now I can't relinquish my duty while there's a mad outlaw still on the loose. Well, that's the last plate dried. If Emily's still doing her homework, lets go and sit by the stove and have some beer."

As he spoke these words there came an urgent hammering on the door. He opened it to see one of his deputies on the porch, holding his side and gasping heavily.

"Jack, I've been checking round the neighbours. Five slaves failed to turn up for supper from their work in the fields. I rode out to check and they've all gone. Sorry – I'm out of breath – my horse went lame on me – I've had to run the last six furlongs!"

"All right, Danny. Come in and sit while you get your breath back. Do we know how long they've been gone?"

Lucy offered the deputy a chair near the stove and he slumped into it. "Not exactly. One of the women took some beer out to them mid-afternoon and they were all accounted for."

Jack said, "So they could have been gone for anything between two and five hours. Did they have horses?"

"That's the other thing," said the deputy, now speaking normally. "They walked out to work in the fields, but five horses are missing from the farmstead near to where they were working."

"Did anyone see them take the horses?"

"No, Jack. Not as far as I know."

Jack thought for a moment. "All right, Danny. You did well to report all this. Go over to the barn and choose half the militiamen to take up defensive positions in the village. And get everyone else inside." Saying this, he grabbed his weapons that hung by the door.

"Where are you going, Jack?" Lucy yelled.

"To saddle my horse. There's just enough light to pick up their tracks. I need to know where they've gone and what they're up to."

* * *

When Jack reached the edge of the village he stopped and dismounted. Here the track met the main trail, leading northwest towards Ashwell or east in the direction of the Capital. The ground was still damp from an earlier shower, making his task a little easier. He crouched and quickly picked out their tracks. He counted five horses, headed for Ashwell. He tried to recall how long ago it had rained. The tracks weren't that fresh. He thought the slaves must have ridden this way between two and three hours ago. He swiftly re-mounted and kicked his horse to canter, mindful to prevent her straying from the trail in the fading light.

He had always hated night riding. There was barely half an insipid moon tonight and on top of that it was cloudy. At this pace he should reach Ashwell before it was completely dark. The journey back would be a different story, but he hoped he'd be able to take it more steadily. Right now, he needed to reach Ashwell as soon as possible. The feeling in his gut was probably just indigestion. But instinct told him something bad was about to happen. Maybe he should have brought more men with him, but that would have left Crowtree exposed. There wasn't much he could do on his own tonight. But he wouldn't take any risks. He would just observe what was happening. He had to know.

He glanced either side of him as he rode. The lowering forest seemed to be watching him. He hated the creeping shadows and whatever they might conceal. Not wild animals – he had no fear of them. But an ambush, or a sniper – if a crossbow bolt were flying towards him just now, there'd be nothing he could do about it. He'd be a dead man. Curse the darkness!

He knew the forest around Ashwell intimately. He'd spent many days of his boyhood hunting there with his friends from the village. He remembered them now, especially those who had passed on. Some had perished at the hands of Red's brigands during that cruel period of occupation. He decided he would take the deer trail that he'd picked out on that fateful night twenty years ago, when he, Dominic, Rajeev and the others had rescued those poor beleaguered villagers. Dismounting quietly he tethered his horse to a sturdy branch, then stealthily made his way towards the village stockade, which he knew lay at the end of this track. But it was dark – so dark that more than once he wondered if he'd veered onto another trail. He thought he heard shouting, but all this foliage muffled any incoming sounds.

Then all at once he saw a light. It was only a glimmer, but he moved towards it and kept on moving. Before he reached the stockade he realised what it was.

Fire! From his concealed position across the stockade he saw that several buildings were ablaze. The sound of burning timber crackled and smacked now from every direction, while the scent of smouldering hay wafted sweetly to his nostrils. Indiscernible yells and screams assailed the air. The villagers' corralled horses danced and snorted, spooked by the confusion, and pushed against the holding fence, snapping one or two spars in their frenzy. Then he heard clattering hooves as a single horseman galloped into the stockade from out of the heart of the village. In the flickering light from the blazing buildings he didn't recognise the rider, but he bore the cloak and hood of Red's accomplice from the night Johanssen was killed. The hooded man yelled and laughed as his horse dragged what looked like a sack on the end of a rope. It seemed smeared with red paint, some of which came off onto the dusty ground.

But when Jack looked more carefully his stomach turned. It wasn't a sack. It was a person.

* * *

"How many are they, Jack?" Liam asked.

"I'd say about twenty. Red, Mary, several slaves from Crowtree and Ashwell, plus a few youths and girls. They're all armed to the teeth and have Ashwell locked down. They've certainly killed at least one of the villagers – probably a slave owner. I saw a horseman drag him around like a sack. That's what I thought he was at first, Liam."

His brother placed a hand on his arm. "Let's hope they killed him quickly first. Surely they'd have had the decency to do that."

Jack looked at him apologetically. "I don't know, Liam. I arrived too late to see. I didn't lift a finger to help. And I'm supposed to be their marshal. What kind of a lawman allows this sort of thing to happen on his patch?" He leaned forward, letting his head loll into his hands, and mumbled, "It's the first time in twenty years as a marshal that I've felt so useless."

Liam gripped his arm more tightly. "Don't blame yourself. It was I that suggested Red was out of the picture. And you did right last night, Jack. If you'd tried to help they'd have taken you and made an example of you. Your villagers certainly don't need a dead marshal. I'm glad you came straight over here to tell me."

"You know how I hate riding at night, Liam. But I didn't mind, because nobody could see the tears falling while I rode here."

Liam stood up. Being single he kept erratic hours, so he'd still been awake when his brother arrived, though it was well after midnight. Now he took a kettle of boiling water from off the stovetop and made some tea. Handing a cup to his brother he said, "It's hard to know what to do now. We've barely enough able-bodied men between us to defend Crowtree and Roundhill. If we take men away to try an assault on Red's gang at Ashwell, we leave the other villages vulnerable. We really need help from outside – a lot of help. But just about every village in Fenwold must be in the same position. After twenty years of migration there aren't enough fit men left to defend their homes when trouble such as this strikes."

Jack sat up and sipped the reviving tea. Then he said calmly, "There's only one course of action open to us. We need to contact Dominic."

Liam sighed and said, "You're right. And we would have done so sooner if I hadn't persuaded you to wait. I'll make you a bed up. You should try and get some rest. But first thing tomorrow you should ride home and ask Emily to pick out the swiftest of Krania's pigeons."

CHAPTER NINETEEN
FIELD TRIP

"Hi there, Krania. Er, sorry. I've just..."

Krania smiled politely as her gawky fellow-student, Alexander, fumbled clumsily for the pen that he'd dropped on the floor of the bus. She was glad she'd chosen the emergency exit seat where there was more legroom – one advantage of being first pick-up. Thankfully he was able to retrieve his pen from beneath the empty seat beside her without resorting to grovelling. Then, clutching his schoolbag to his chest, he asked with a stammer, "Is ... is anyone sitting here?"

She forced a smile and peered up and down the bus. "Well, I was saving it for Geraldine..."

"Ah," he offered, "I just heard Miss Huntley speaking to her on the..."

She helped him out. "On the vid link?"

"Um, yeah. She has a cold – got to stay home," he said.

Fixing her artificial grin, she made room for him to settle next to her. She was disappointed. She'd been looking forward to some girl-talk and gossip with her close friend. Still, at least Alexander's quiet company would be preferable to that of some of her more precocious male classmates. Currently having no steady boyfriend, she was in no mood to suffer the pathetic overtures of immature youths wanting to fill the vacancy.

She peered out through the bus window at the clean, sharp lines of the little estate of settlers' prefabricated dwellings, where the bus had stopped to pick up the main group of students making today's field trip. The senior class was approaching the end of its graduation year, and she'd got to know everyone on the bus fairly well. Some she had grown up with, being children of the first settlers, which included her own parents. But not all had been born on this side of the Wall, as she had. Others were relative newcomers, whose families had more recently made the long trek from all corners of Fenwold, to make new and better lives here in the New Territory.

She exchanged greetings with her other schoolmates as they shuffled down the centre aisle, noting one or two scowls of disappointment from boys who were miffed that the class 'dork' had grabbed the seat next to her. She rather admired Alexander for his uncharacteristic initiative, and decided to be a good companion to him today, as fate had decreed that they should sit together.

"How are your Mum and Dad, Alex?" she asked him politely.

"They're both fine, Krania – thank you for asking." From the look of concentration on his face it took quite a bit of effort for him to frame the expected courtesy, "How about yours?"

She smiled and said, "They're fine too, thanks. Are you looking forward to the field trip?"

He nodded vigorously. "Oh, yes."

She'd hoped he might expand on the reasons for his enthusiasm, but it wasn't to be. Perhaps she should make an effort to rescue the flagging conversation, but she couldn't really be bothered. Besides they'd a long day ahead of them, and a spell of silence wouldn't hurt.

In any case she was rescued by the voice of their field trip leader, Amelia Huntley, which screeched over the public address system.

"Testing! Testing!"

There followed an ear-splitting shriek of feedback while Bill, the driver, studiously fiddled with the audio controls. After a while he nodded to the teacher, who continued nervously, "Good ... good morning, students!"

"Good morning, Amelia!"

This spontaneous greeting from the thirty young people brought a smile to her face.

"Well now, you appear to be able to hear me — and I can certainly hear you. However, for the benefit of everyone would you all please ensure the microphone on the console in front of you is switched on whenever you wish to address the whole bus or answer one of my questions?"

There were frowns all round as she kept smiling and asserted, "Oh yes, there will be questions — this may be a field trip, but it still counts as a class lesson. So pay attention — there'll be a lot to see and learn, and you'll be delighted to know that, as well as assessment by me here on board today, you can all look forward to a written test in class tomorrow!"

Krania thought the teacher relished her announcement with a hint of sadistic pleasure, as the student body emitted a collective groan. Then her features took on a vacant look as she spoke into the ether to an absent party.

"That goes for you too, Geraldine! Can you hear me?"

The driver fiddled with the audio controls again, and there followed a loud sneeze and the muffled words, "Yes, Amelia. I'm here."

Given the available technology, it took a pretty nasty illness to prevent a sick student from actually missing their lessons, even if from a distance. Today's comms link-up had required some swift organisation by the multi-skilled driver, who beamed a self-congratulatory smile. But this turned to a grimace when the sniffing student said, "I'm not getting any video though. Controls don't indicate any problem this end."

More fiddling at the dashboard by Bill, who then looked sheepishly at Amelia, with the admission, "Sorry - vision transmitter was off."

"Ah!" Geraldine croaked. "I've got it now. Yes, I can select front, right, left and, yes, inside view – though that's a bit dark... just a second... there, that's got it. All right, Amelia, I'm all hooked up. I'll try not to sneeze too much!"

The teacher resumed her preamble. "Right. I think you all know the purpose of today's excursion. First, the history – though I'm probably not the best qualified on board to cover this bit."

Krania always hated moments like this. She focussed on the back of the seat in front of her while knowing all heads were turned in her direction. And she tried not to grimace when Amelia added, "Don't worry, Krania. I'll do my best – but feel free to correct me if I make a slip."

She thought, "Yeah, as if..."

Amelia coughed. "Our interest today is in the wealth of technology that was promised – and delivered – by the Ancient Ones through the mouthpiece of the hologram, Cara. Though not a real person, Cara has remained with us and guided us to make sensible and gradual use of the many tools, machines, materials and stores of knowledge that have already propelled us a thousand years forwards in technological terms. There's no wonder that we all feel a great regard for Cara – or, more accurately, for what she represents."

Krania gave an involuntary nod and smiled at this reference to the other woman in her parents' relationship. She settled into her seat and relaxed as the vehicle made its way past acres of empty plots awaiting further expansion, and out onto the perimeter track.

"We're going to take an outer tour this morning, to give you a sense of the size of our treasure store and to visit the powerhouse. Then we'll stop at a safe clearing close to the landing strip for a picnic lunch – if you've any left..."

Several lunchbox lids closed quickly in percussive chorus.

"After lunch, we'll visit some of the warehouses. For obvious reasons some of the places we'll be going are normally subject to restricted entry. We have clearance as an authorised school field trip, but I must ask you to stay on the coach at all times unless we leave it to enter a specific site or building. On those occasions it's essential we all stay together and that nobody wanders off. Is that clear?"

"Yes, Amelia," came the droned response. Then the youngsters settled down to enjoy the scenery as the coach continued along the track, its electric motor softly whirring, carrying them towards the distant, forbidding forest.

* * *

Governor Bradley's regular weekly morning meetings with Rajeev Shah had lately become little more than opportunities to reminisce about the 'old days' and smoke without fear of criticism from their disapproving wives. Today Bradley had enjoyed their conversation so much that he ordered lunch to be brought into his office.

Downing his second mug of ale, Dominic wiped his lips with the back of his hand, and reached again for his pipe and tobacco pouch. Then, remembering his manners, he offered it to his old friend first.

Shah shook his head. "Thanks Dominic. My wife says it's a dirty habit and I should give it up. I'm trying to keep it to a reasonable level."

"Oh," said his host sheepishly, closing the pouch and replacing the pipe on its saucer on his desk. "Actually, Sylvia says the same thing to me. Quite right too, I suppose. We've no idea what muck we're taking into our lungs when we smoke this stuff. Why is it that the things that give you the most pleasure are always bad for you, Rajeev?"

"Ah," Shah replied. "I can offer you some consolation there, Dominic. Our wives have also been nagging us for years about our liking for a mug or two of ale every day, haven't they?"

"Yes," said Dominic. "Even though we used to drink it in great quantities as children. It staved off the hunger pangs when times were lean. Why, there's not enough strength in it to do any harm. So I've always held, in any case."

"Well, Dominic, you can keep on drinking your ale. Our scientists at the academy have conducted tests, and confirmed it's absolutely harmless – in reasonable quantities – say, a quart a day. In fact, in many ways, it's a valuable tonic."

"That's what I've always believed!" The Governor slapped a hand on his desk. "I tell you, Rajeev, we're becoming a soft society. A man should be able to do what he feels to be right, as long as he doesn't inconvenience anyone."

"Quite so, Dominic."

The pair quietly contemplated the wisdom of their discussion. Then Bradley shuffled uncomfortably in his chair, and got up to open a window.

"Mind you," he said, "it does tend to give you gas, especially as you get older, I find."

Rajeev also wriggled nervously, and just said, "Hmm."

Bradley changed the subject. "Look, I always pop in and have a chat with Cara about this time. Why don't you come with me? We'll ask her what she thinks about the democracy idea I put to you – or should I say, the one that the elders are going to come up with?" And he gave his old friend a wink.

As he opened the door, he smiled and added, "Cara's the one woman who never takes me to task for drinking, smoking, or any other minor human failing that might afflict me!"

The structure housing the computer equipment that produced Cara's hologram – known to everyone simply as 'Cara's house' – was very close to the Governor's Office, as well as to his family's dwelling. So within a couple of minutes the two men approached the deputy who stood guard at the outer door.

The guard nodded and as they entered Shah said, "I don't know why we keep a sentry on the door, Dominic. You decreed long ago that no settler should be denied access to Cara."

"I know, Rajeev, but I worry about frivolous contact. One or two mischievous youngsters have tried testing her patience by asking her nonsensical questions. Not that any have succeeded in confounding her wisdom. The software that drives her reasoning is robust, but it would be catastrophic if this contact with the Ancient Ones were lost due to some silly prank that somehow twisted her logic and damaged her circuitry. Better to be safe than sorry. The deputy is there as a deterrent."

They went inside. Though almost a daily visitor here, Dominic was always struck by the layout of the audience chamber. Like the building that housed it, it was in every detail identical to its counterpart back in Beverton, the town in the north of Fenwold, where Cara had first appeared to them both and Sylvia, young Toby and the outlaw Red, twenty years before. Here were the large batteries and illuminated consoles arranged around the edge of the circular room, and the five black circles on the floor, pressure upon any one of which had never yet failed to rouse Cara from her slumber. He and Rajeev stepped forward, and the familiar attractive figure flickered magically into life in the space in front of them.

"Good afternoon, Dominic. And also to you, Rajeev."

"Hello, Cara," said Dominic. "Rajeev and I wanted to discuss a political issue with you today."

"Governor, Director – forgive me, but there is something much more important that I have to say to you. Something you should know."

"Oh?" said Bradley. "If you say it's so important, Cara, then please speak."

"Very well. You are aware that, eight hundred and twenty years ago when your ancestors were enclosed within the walled region that you know as Fenwold, it was in an attempt to ensure humanity's survival following the period of plague, and to allow their subsequent re-colonisation of Earth."

Bradley thought Cara's announcement might have been referring to some abstract planet. But he nodded. "As you say, we are familiar with the Ancient Ones' plan for our future, Cara."

"Correction, Dominic. Your earlier understanding was that your survival was planned and inevitable. It was not."

Shah spoke next. "You mean you contemplated the possibility of failure?"

The hologram nodded. "Yes. The probability of success was computed at less than thirty-two per cent. The risk of extinction from the recurrence of plague, civil war or famine was greater."

"Oh," Bradley said. "Extinction? That's – er – interesting."

But Shah was ahead of him. "Not just interesting, Dominic. What do you think the Ancient Ones would do if the chances of their achieving something one way were less than even?"

He turned to his friend. "Why, they'd lay a second plan, of course ... By the Gods!"

Then he addressed Cara. "Go on. Tell us."

"I was programmed to keep this from you, because failure of the parallel strategy need not have concerned you. However, a huge craft – we called it a star liner – housing another group of survivors was sent off into space at the same time as Fenwold's enclosure. That group's primary aim was to seek another planet, similar to Earth. If found, their descendants were to attempt settlement."

Though he didn't want to contemplate her inevitable response, he knew he must ask the next question. "And if they were unable to find such a planet?"

"They had the option to return to Earth, no sooner than eight hundred years later. We never expected both groups to survive, Dominic. I am so very sorry."

His mind was racing. "Are you telling me that they're coming back? And why do you say you're sorry?"

"My latest information is that their mother ship the Salvation is at this moment holding a position in orbit on the far side of the Moon. They intend to invade and colonise."

"Invade? You mean, they know about us?" But he answered his own question. "Yes, of course they do." It took him a few seconds to form his next query. "Can't we persuade them to take some alternative course?"

"They want what you have, Dominic. Your people have made huge advances during the past twenty years, and learned to use the technologies that I have been programmed to show you. But these people have had the benefits of those technologies – and others not yet revealed to you – since the time they left Earth. They are scientifically far superior in every respect."

Dominic feared what was coming, so he hurriedly fished for more information while there was still time. "Answer three questions for me, please, Cara. How many do they number? What kind of weapons do they have? And what will be their most likely offer?"

The hologram was silent for a moment. Then she spoke solemnly. "Dominic, I will answer these questions, but after that

I can speak to you here no more. I am faced with a huge dilemma, because I am charged to assist the development of humanity. I was never programmed to make a choice, and therefore I must not. I cannot take sides. It is best that I shut down rather than show any favouritism. They number about twelve thousand. They have advanced weaponry – handguns and bombs that can stun or kill. I calculate that they will require your people to vacate the New Territory and re-locate back behind the Wall. If you do this they should have no reason to harm you. For your people's safety, I suggest that you accept such an offer. I must now close down this portal."

"But, Cara ..." Bradley's voice trailed off, because he knew it was useless to continue. She couldn't hear him now, in any case. Already the lights on the consoles around the room had dimmed, while Cara's image flickered into oblivion, leaving only a cold and lifeless room that emitted an artificial plastic and metallic odour, the smell of finality, which for Bradley would forever represent the stench of loss, disappointment and betrayal.

CHAPTER TWENTY

TOUCHDOWN

Half an hour into the field trip the bus had left the sprawl of settlers' dwellings behind them, but Amelia hadn't allowed her charges' attention to wander. She'd been keeping them alert by quizzing them on the subject relating to their first scheduled stop – the powerhouse.

"That's right, Katie – good. And do you know how electrical power used to be delivered in ancient times?"

The student responded, "I've read that it was by wires and cables – though that's hard to believe. Just think of all the thousands of leagues of plastic and metal – all the insulation and grounding – how could they possibly manage it all without accidents and leakage?"

"Well, they did manage it, for quite a while," Amelia said as she moved down the aisle to the rear of the bus. "Thankfully transmission accidents were far fewer than you might think. Though the cost of maintenance must, as you say, have been considerable, especially as the physical networks aged. But that was before the great energy crisis forced a radical re-think of power production and distribution."

At this point Krania noticed that the bus was slowing. As Amelia turned to make her way back to the front, Krania craned her neck to get a closer look at the long, low powerhouse complex on the right hand side. She was already familiar with its outline, clearly visible from the housing estates at the edge of the city. It comprised a flat, dark rectangle nestled between two taller buildings, the first supporting a large metal mesh dish pointing skywards, and the second a tall tower resembling a radio beacon.

Two armed guards – one male and one female – approached the bus as Bill brought it to a halt.

"I want you all to step outside and line up in an orderly fashion," Amelia said. After documentary formalities, the party moved towards the main building. The uniformed guards, attractive and in their mid-twenties, were already receiving close attention from some of the students, but had the good sense to hang back.

As the group progressed, Amelia singled out one of the boys. "Brian, your father's on the maintenance team here, isn't he? What can you tell us about it?"

The young student wasn't fazed by the sudden question. "Well, for a start, it's not really a powerhouse – the energy isn't produced here, it's only stored – in all these batteries."

With a wide sweep of his arm he indicated a huge metal framework housing row upon row, tier upon tier of matt-black boxes, each about a stride in length and almost as tall, but only half as wide.

As if rehearsed he continued, "If you look you'll see there's a two-inch ventilation gap between every battery in each row, and a half stride wide maintenance channel between the rows. Those thick cables in the gap carry the current to the transmitter house." He ended his tour guide's brief by adding, "Oh, and that building we passed on the way in – with the big metal scanner on top – that's where the power is collected."

"All right – thanks, Brian – an excellent description," Amelia said. "Now, to save you having to count them, I can tell you that there are more than a hundred thousand batteries here. Believe it or not, each one has the capacity to supply the daily energy needs of an average household of four people even in the depths of winter. So this configuration should easily cope with the needs of the expanding city for the foreseeable future."

Her statement was met by an appreciative collective murmur.

The group then made its way to the far end of the building, and past the transmitter tower where Bill had brought the bus round via a service road.

After extracting some of the teenagers away from flirting with the guards, Amelia ushered them on board, made a quick head-count and signalled to Bill to drive off. But before they re-joined the perimeter track, she had them look back at the transmitter tower.

"You probably know that the building at the foot of the tower houses the conversion equipment, creating energy bundles for transmission to the city for everyday use.

"We can all grasp the concept when stated in such simple terms, but although we have people studying the science, we still don't fully understand the technology involved in wireless power transmission. As with many of the treasures provided by the Ancient Ones, we've learned how to use and maintain the equipment, but we're not yet able to do the reverse engineering and create it for ourselves from scratch. No doubt these secrets will be revealed to us when Cara feels we're ready to use them sensibly."

The students seemed content to chew on this thought, for all that was heard for the next few minutes was the *whir* of the electric motor of the coach, and the hum of its tyres on the concrete perimeter track.

Twenty years had seen a considerable area of ground cleared for agriculture and construction. Even at this distance from the present city suburbs Krania noted teams of bulldozers doing just that. But it wasn't long before the perimeter road skirted the edge of the forest. Here, eight centuries' absence of human activity had allowed the vegetation and wildlife to thrive without check, and it was with an almost primordial sense of unease that she peered into the dense, inky blackness. Fear of the wild forest was somehow coded into everyone's genetic make-up. For here, so close to civilisation, was potential danger from wild animals such as wolves and even bears.

"Ooh, look! What's that?" one of the girls announced loudly, resulting in a crowding on her side of the bus.

Looking where she was pointing, Amelia said, "It's only a rabbit."

Then, seconds later, one of the boys pointed out a young deer on the other side, so that the centre of gravity shifted once more. Krania's stomach gurgled, and she silently praised Bill's skilful driving, as he managed to maintain a steady speed, while steering deftly to compensate for the trim of his erratic cargo.

"All right, keep to your seats now!" Amelia said. "We'll see plenty of wildlife from the perimeter track, but that's for another lesson as well. In a few minutes we'll be reaching a place where we can have our lunch. It's a cleared area, patrolled by the machines that we still call dragons."

A ripple of excited anticipation ran through the class, and Amelia was quick to add, "But I'm not going to guarantee that you'll see one!"

She continued, "You'll notice a change in the composition of the roadway here. That's because we're now on part of the original cleared area. Cara refers to this as the landing strip, and we assume it's where we'll construct and operate flying machines some day, when she reveals the secrets of aerial transport. Unlike the main perimeter track, the surface of the roadway here has the appearance of smoothed-out earth, not concrete or hard core."

Timothy, a student seated not far from her, offered a correction. "It's not earth, Amelia. It's ash."

"That's right," she said. "The surface is covered with ash — the compacted remains of burnt vegetation, shoots and saplings that would otherwise have soon overgrown and obscured the track. These days we bring in compactors to make it firm – or we'd never get a bus like this over it. But otherwise this must be exactly like the very roadway that led Marshal Bradley's party north from the Great Bridge to Beverton. He found it passable all the way to the outskirts of that town – and, if you've read your history, you know how it was kept clear by the dragons. Timothy?"

The students to the left of the aisle were lucky, for from the coach on that side they looked down on the powered metal rail that served as the dragons' track way.

Timothy responded, "They emit controlled bursts of flame to burn back any encroaching vegetation."

"That's right. Bill, would you stop the coach for a minute so the students can safely move across to this side and have a look too? But remember everyone, although we've stopped, nobody is to leave the coach – we still have dense forest to our left and there's always potential danger from wild animals."

Timothy suggested with a cheeky grin, "But wouldn't one of the dragons come along to scare them off, Amelia?"

Many of his friends laughed, but she seemed determined not to make light of a hazard that was patently real. "You might like to reflect that no fewer than thirty people have been killed or injured in attacks by wolves since settlement began. And before any budding statistician among you observes that that's less than two per year, let me say that none of those happened to be safely shut up inside a coach at the time."

The class noise subsided as she sealed her message with one terse, unequivocal command.

"Nobody leaves the bus!" she said.

The students quietly digested the importance of her words. Krania recalled her earlier visit here with her parents, when she'd experienced that first real sense of untamed wilderness. Although the stretch of vegetation on the right was fairly narrow, before it gave way to the emptiness of the landing strip, she had the impression of being totally surrounded by the forest. Even from the safety of this motorised cocoon, ancient memories were awakened, sharpening her senses and magnifying that life-preserving presence of fear; the instinctive gift of stealth and keen awareness that had meant life or death to the forty generations gone before.

The forest spoke to them. The songs and alarms of birds, the sighing of vegetation touched by the breeze, the rippling of a stream on its way to the river estuary, the scurrying of small animals – all these distilled into a natural symphony that few of her classmates had experienced first-hand. It seemed to hold everyone spellbound.

But suddenly the magic was violently shattered and the air split asunder by an almighty *roar* from somewhere high above them, shaking the ground, the trees, the coach and every one of its occupants to the very core. It was like a terrifying clap of thunder, only many times louder, that once begun, seemed destined never to end. This was accompanied by a series of bright flashes on all sides, only gradually obscured by a huge cloud of dust that enveloped forest and coach, making everyone cough and cover their faces with scarves and hankies. Then at last both noise and light show subsided, leaving the class and the forest outside alarmed but apparently unharmed, though now effectively silenced, and still shrouded by the swirling dust cloud.

Some of the students whimpered, and most found a colleague – of whatever sex – to hug and hold on to. Krania looked at Alexander and saw that he was as terrified as she was. She gripped his hand and tried to smile at him, but his expression remained gaunt and pallid. She raised herself up to glimpse their trip leader, deathly white, grasping her seat tightly with both hands, and staring out of the window in an apparent state of shock.

Nobody spoke for a while until the crackling communications link emitted a whine, followed by a sneeze and the voice of Geraldine, speaking from the safety of her sick bed.

"Hello! Hello! Amelia, can you hear me? In the name of the Gods of the Wall, what was that! Are you all right? Has there been a crash?"

Seeing that Amelia sat stiffly, clearly still traumatised, Krania answered for her. "Geraldine! It's Krania. Yes, we seem to be all right. We haven't had any kind of accident. But something's happened – some sort of explosion outside. We can't see, because of this dust cloud."

Then she heard Bill say, "I'm trying to contact the city administration office. Damn!"

Krania saw that Amelia was recovering and exchanging some anxious words with the driver. Although she couldn't hear their conversation, it was obvious from the ethereal crackle from the speakers that the communications were disabled.

Alexander found his voice. "I don't know what that was, Krania, but from what I've seen on the science videos, I'd say it was some kind of aircraft landing."

She was perplexed. "But we haven't built any aircraft yet. Cara says we're not ready."

He shrugged. "Perhaps it's a prototype the boffins haven't told us about."

She nodded, but guessed he was merely clutching at some straw of consolation. He must know that, had that been the case, no field trip would have been sanctioned today.

Then Amelia stood shakily and addressed them from the front of the bus.

"Listen, everyone! I've just discussed with the driver what we should do next. There isn't room to turn around just here, because the track's too narrow. In any case visibility's too poor to go anywhere until this dust settles. We're not far from the clearing we were heading for. We're going to wait until visibility improves, then carry on to just inside the landing strip. Bill thinks he should be able to turn around there."

Krania stood up and said, "But Amelia, if something has set down on the strip, aren't its occupants likely to see us? They could be hostile raiders. What if they should come after us?"

Bill turned around and shouted down the bus, "Then all clip on your safety belts, because I'll be ripping this coach back down that track just as fast as she can go!"

$$* * *$$

"By the stars, Captain! I thought we were going to crash! Still, we seem to be in one piece. You never said it would be so noisy, though. Have we landed in the right place?"

The nervous shuttle passenger had just removed his helmet, and now wiped a handkerchief across his sweating face, betraying the effect that terrestrial gravity was having on his generous body weight.

Captain Des Riley exchanged glances with his co-pilot. Then he looked out of the window, barely concealing a disdainful grin. "Well, Councillor Cropper, I think I said that if we miscalculated, we'd hit the trees and be engulfed by a raging inferno."

The Green Watch Councillor hadn't much of a sense of humour. "That's all very well, Captain. I can obviously see we've not collided with anything. What I can't see is where exactly we've landed. Not through all this dust."

Riley sighed. "I also said that, if we made either the landing site or some other open area, we'd probably kick up a great deal of ground debris. As you've already observed, Sir, that's exactly what we appear to have done."

"Hmm," the Councillor sniffed. "I don't understand why you can't be more specific about where it is we've come down."

"We haven't just come down, as you put it," the Captain snapped. Then he added tetchily, "We've achieved a controlled landing. What you heard was the outside air pressure and the reverse thrust of our fusion drive. Without that, we'd all of us be roasted at the bottom of a very deep crater. But Co-pilot Deene and I have spent our entire careers to date preparing for this moment. We've each had thousands of hours practising on simulators, spent years studying aeronautics, been honed and toned in the classroom and gym to keep our minds and bodies in tip-top condition, all to get you safely to where you want to be. But you have to understand that this is a space shuttle, which needs to approach at a shallow angle to avoid burning up, and – while I *think* this is the right place – I can't be absolutely certain until the dust settles. So you'll have to be patient for just a little longer."

This seemed to calm the Councillor somewhat, though he still mopped a bead of sweat from his brow. "Oh, I see. How long do you think that will be?"

"About fifteen minutes, I'd guess."

Colin Wakefield of Red Watch sat next to him, quietly amused by the interchange between Cropper and the pilot. The shuttle's crew and contingent of four guards, comprising two females and two males, were drawn from the other three watches. Wakefield had argued hard and long in Council to win a place on this ambassadorial mission, and he was determined to make his presence felt. But, for the time being, he was happy to allow his gauche fellow-Councillor to stumble through his amusing dialogue with Riley.

Cropper drummed his fingers on the console beside him, and emitted a low, tuneless whistle as he peered out into the still swirling dust cloud.

"I wish you wouldn't do that, Councillor," said Riley. "I need to listen out for any signs of movement outside." Cropper didn't argue with him on that point, though from the pilot's tone Wakefield suspected he was just getting on his nerves. In any case, he stopped his drumming.

"Will they know we're here yet?" he said.

It was the co-pilot, Graham Deene, who answered. "Only by direct observation. It's unlikely they'd have radar facilities yet. We're too far from their main settlement to have been seen from there, since we made our approach from the west. They might have heard and seen something like a thunder flash – but any freak of the weather could produce that. No, only if they had people in the immediate vicinity would they suspect anything. And as our fusion drive will have interfered with radio transmissions for a league in all directions, any chance passer-by wouldn't be able to phone home to report us for a while."

"I see. When the air clears and we can see well enough, I want our landing party to start moving. Pity you couldn't provide mechanical transport, eh?"

Deene shook his head. "There was never a chance, Councillor. The weight of eight of us on the shuttle – Captain Riley and me, you and Councillor Wakefield plus the guards – leaves no room for fancy land vehicles. I'm afraid some of us have quite a walk ahead of us. I trust you've both prepared for this with a few extra hours in the gym?"

Though this mischievous question was posed with a straight face, Riley and Wakefield exchanged a muted smile. The pilots were, of course, at the peak of fitness, and Wakefield's habit of daily exercise had prepared him well for the effects of gravity. There was no doubting the physical condition of the military contingent. Cropper, on the other hand, bore the typical physique of an administrator who had spent all his life in the low-gravity environment of an interstellar space cruiser, without the benefit of much physical exertion. In short, he was overweight, physically weak and flabby. The trek to the settlement was going to be something of an ordeal for him.

"How far do you reckon we'll have to walk?" he asked nervously.

"Can't say for sure," answered Riley. "Two or three leagues, I wouldn't wonder."

"Two or three..." Cropper's brain could almost be heard trying to work out how many times around the admin section corridors that represented.

"How long until this dust settles, did you say? Fifteen minutes?"

The Captain shrugged. "Ten, maybe."

* * *

Sylvia Bradley shot out of the front door of the Governor's dwelling as if propelled by some explosive force. At thirty-seven, she was still extremely fit – slim, strong and agile in body and mind.

It wasn't far to her husband's office, and she soon reached the door. Clerk Cooper rose up from his seat as she flashed past him, allowing no time for any greeting as she rushed into the Governor's chambers. Finding his room empty, she immediately emerged and, showing little sign of breathlessness, said, "Where is he, Stephen?"

Not entirely flummoxed by her whirlwind entrance, the clerk replied, "The Governor and Director Shah went to consult with the hologram, Mistress Bradley."

And without a further word she was gone.

Close by, Bradley and Shah were just leaving Cara's house and looking deflated following her devastating revelation. But the sight of the wild woman racing towards them temporarily broke their mood. Thankfully she came to an abrupt halt in front of them. Bradley took hold of her left arm as gently as he could, while she addressed him urgently.

"Dominic, I just had a call from Geraldine – you know, Krania's friend."

With a furrowed brow he snapped, "I'm sorry, Sylvia, I've no time to discuss teenage gossip just now..."

She scowled at him. "Gossip? Gossip? Do you think I'd race round here to interrupt your little chat with your girl friend in there, just to pass the time of day with idle gossip? Honestly, Dominic, you can be really pig-headed sometimes!"

He looked at her worried face, and said, "All right, I'm sorry Sylvia. Tell me what's wrong."

She didn't stop to draw breath. "Geraldine couldn't make the field trip – she's sick – but she's been attending by vid-link. She says there's been some kind of explosion, and the phones have gone dead."

Dominic and Rajeev exchanged glances. They'd learned long ago that, whenever bad news came in bundles, there was usually a connection. Then he asked his wife, "Did she say where, and when?"

"They'd stopped to look at the forest, close to the landing strip. She called me as soon as she'd lost contact, and that was only a few minutes ago. Less than five minutes, I'd say."

Bradley turned to Shah. "Must have been while we were with Cara. Go back to my house and fetch my car, will you? It's been on charge all night. I'll go and arrange an escort."

He rushed to the admin building and instructed his clerk, who immediately called the Militia Commander for a platoon, fire appliances and ambulance trucks. Then he went into his office where he unlocked his gun cupboard, and took out a rifle, a couple of side arms, ammunition and – almost as an afterthought – his crossbow and quiver of arrows. Clutching this arsenal, he returned to where Rajeev had brought the car, and saw that Sylvia already occupied the rear passenger seat.

"Oh, no, my girl. I'm not putting you in harm's way as well."

But with fixed expression Sylvia said: "You're forgetting that's my daughter out there, Dominic. Now shut up and get in, if you're coming!"

CHAPTER TWENTY-ONE
FIRST CONTACT

"Captain Deene, there's still interference from the debris, but I'm fairly certain my portable sensor's picking up a large metal object – possibly a stationary vehicle – about a furlong due south, behind those trees over there."

As the female guard pointed towards the narrow strip of woodland concealing the field trip bus, the shuttle Captain checked his on-board display panel.

"Can't see anything here. No, wait a minute, you're right – there is something. Yes, I've got it. Metal, with multiple heat sources inside."

Cropper nervously mopped his face again with his near-saturated kerchief and blurted, "Humans, Captain?"

Deene fiddled with the controls and said mischievously, "Either that or circus animals."

Cropper said, "Really? I've seen video of circuses. Oh, I see. You're making a joke. So they're humans. How did they know we were coming? Are they armed?"

Deene shrugged. "I can't see how they'd know about our landing. We know their portal shut down an hour ago, and in any case it was programmed not to interfere."

Wakefield suggested, "It would have to have told them about the Salvation. Perhaps they figured that we'd send a shuttle, and that here would be the obvious place to touch down."

Cropper rounded on him. "What utter rubbish! Don't forget these people are little more than savages! They wouldn't have sufficient intelligence!"

Wakefield sighed. There was much he wanted to say, but he wasn't prepared to waste either time or energy arguing. Besides he knew full well that his Green Watch counterpart's mind was already made up.

Deene said, "I can't tell if they have weapons. It's best to assume they do." He turned to speak to the guards behind him. "Visibility's better now. Would two of you go and investigate?"

Colin Wakefield wondered what must have been going through the young soldiers' minds just then. Like everyone on board the Salvation, they'd each have opted freely for their chosen careers, studied and drilled watch upon watch in dutiful preparation for a situation such as this. But their entire lives to date had been spent in space, cocooned inside the star liner's massive protective hull, with no opportunity to experience a different environment, let alone deal with a real, potentially dangerous situation. Yes, they'd have spent countless hours in simulation, but could computer-generated scenarios even come close to the cold reality of their first real-life encounter?

He knew their leader Janine fairly well, even though she belonged to Yellow Watch, their families having met frequently in recreation. He turned and looked into her eyes now, hoping she understood that his kindly smile wished her well in her first contact with the Earth people. He thought he detected the slightest response on her lips before she set her jaw, checked her weapon and said, "Copy that, Captain."

She touched the colleague next to her and said, "Come on, Ben. Better use our shields to cross that open ground." Then she addressed the other two guards. "Stay on board. And don't risk coming after us – remember, the shuttle and its passengers are your number one priority. And Captain, if we're not back in five minutes, I suggest you return to the Salvation and consider alternative strategies."

* * *

As the dust gradually cleared Krania noticed signs that her fellow students were getting restless. Now that the thunder and flashes had abated, everyone must be wondering what was going to happen next.

Her companion Alex – having been typically silent so far – peered across her for a better view through the window.

"What's happening? Can you see anything?"

Krania put her face close up to the pane. "It's not easy. There's a film of dust covering the glass." A thought crossed her mind, and she leaned across her friend to look down the centre aisle towards the driver. But Bill had obviously had the same thought, for the wiper blades were already in motion to clear the film of debris from the front screens.

Then the bus intercom crackled and she heard him say, "No, Amelia, I can't see anything but forest. I reckon the source of the ruckus is on the other side of the strip of trees to our right. I'll need to get out and find a way through on foot."

"You'll do no such thing!" the trip leader insisted. For some reason, most likely a release of the general tension on the bus, this exclamation brought forth a collective nervous giggle from the students.

"Ah," Amelia observed, "It looks like we have our comms back. I think we should have a go at contacting the city again. Could you try please, Bill?"

The driver fiddled about with the controls and gave his call sign. He tried this a few times before shaking his head and saying, "Sorry. Looks like our on-board transmitter's out."

There was more crackling after which Geraldine's voice cut through the interference. "Hello, can you hear me, Amelia?"

A look of relief crossed the teacher's face. "Oh, Geraldine! Thank goodness! Yes, we're hearing you." She looked at the screen in front of her, which emitted only a foggy image. "There's no video though."

Geraldine spoke again. "Hello. Amelia, anybody on the bus, are you receiving me?"

Once more Amelia responded. "Yes, we're here, Geraldine. We're all right."

"Hello, hello. This is Geraldine calling the field trip bus. Is anybody hearing this?" Then, as if addressing a third party, she was heard to say, "It's no good, Marshal. I don't seem to have contact. Pardon? Oh, I see. Well, yes, if you think it's worth a try. Hello, Amelia. I'm not receiving you, but in case you can hear me, I can tell you that help is on the way. Meanwhile stay where you are and remain inside the bus."

She repeated this last message several times.

Then suddenly a couple of girls sitting at the front of the bus screamed out. Even from where she sat Krania saw the cause of their hysteria. Two helmeted figures who could only be military and wielding what seemed to be riot shields – she'd seen something similar on ancient newsreels – had come around the front of the bus to stand by the main passenger door. She couldn't imagine where they'd come from, because they looked nothing like any soldiers she'd seen in the city.

Bill must have seen them first, for she now noticed that he was holding a handgun. She guessed he must be a member of his local militia and therefore authorised to bring one along to defend those in his care. Her mind raced at the sight of the gun, and she quickly realised the potential danger for all of them in this situation. It was impossible to know what kind of weaponry these strange soldiers carried. If Bill made a hostile move now they might react with devastating consequences.

In response to an enormous rush of adrenaline and an overwhelming feeling that Destiny was at last calling her to action, she made a snap decision.

In a flash she reached for the lever on the emergency door beside her, released the retaining catch, turned the handle and pushed the door panel, which swung open propelled by its own weight. She then jumped onto the ground and raised her hands as the nearest soldier turned towards her, shield to the fore and a weapon in his right hand.

"Don't shoot!" she yelled. "I'm Krania Bradley. My father is Governor of the New Territory. Take me as a hostage but please don't harm my friends. Bill, put the gun down!"

She couldn't see the driver now but hoped he'd have the sense to do as she said. She also prayed that the soldiers would take her at her word.

Amazingly the other soldier, clearly female, answered her plea by saying, "Very well. Stay there for a moment. My colleague is armed as you can see, so please don't attempt any heroics."

"I promise you I won't," Krania said meekly.

Janine then turned and rapped on the passenger door with her weapon, and Bill opened it.

"Give me your gun please," she said.

As he passed down the handgun, the on-board speaker crackled loudly once more and this time it was Dominic's voice that was heard to say, "This is Governor Bradley. Don't worry, we'll have you all home safe and well very soon. I'm already on my way with the emergency services!"

When nobody responded Janine said, "Well, aren't you going to reply? Who's in charge here?"

Amelia stood and gave a nervous cough. "I am. Something disabled our transmitter. These students are in my care. Please don't harm any of them."

"Of course we won't," the soldier assured her. "Is this some kind of school lesson then? Is that why you're here?"

The teacher nodded and said, "But who are you? Where have you come from? And what will happen to Krania? You won't hurt her, will you?"

"She's a brave girl. She's offered herself as hostage, so that's just what she'll be until our leaders can settle this matter. She'll be safe – don't worry. As to who we are – well, I can't say too much just now. I'm not really authorised." Then she asked, "Is your vehicle immobilised?"

Bill answered, "No, I don't think so. Are we free to go then?"

"We'd rather like to speak to your Governor if he's on his way. It's best you wait here until he arrives. Tell him to approach our shuttle alone and unarmed. He'll be in no danger if he makes no hostile move."

She turned to leave and indicated to her colleague to do likewise. Then she paused and said, "It will help a lot if you remember to tell him we have his daughter."

* * *

"Well done, Janine! It was a smart move to take such a valuable hostage. What did you say to the vehicle's occupants?"

The female guard hesitated in her response to the man who, Krania assumed, must be in charge of the vessel. Many would so easily have made personal capital out of his misplaced praise. Her honest reply made Krania smile with admiration.

"I can't take full credit, Captain," she said. "This girl offered herself as hostage. She said she was the Governor's daughter, and I took her at her word. It was – still is – a bit of a gamble on my part, actually."

Deene flashed a serious look in Krania's direction. "I see. Well, young lady, can we rely on your claim that your father really is the Governor of the New Territory?"

Still floating on an adrenaline high, Krania looked around her, eagerly surveying the form and contents of the craft that had been the cause of all the recent commotion.

Wide eyed she said, "What is this? An aeroplane?"

In kindly tones Colin Wakefield said, "Sort of. We call it a shuttle, and it's our means of travelling between our mother ship, the Salvation, and the Earth. If you'll just answer the Captain's question, I'll be happy to tell you more."

Cropper interrupted him. "I think you've told her enough, Councillor! Just answer the question, girl!"

Sensing the mixed feelings towards her, Krania could only say, "It's true. I'm Krania Bradley. My father, Dominic Bradley, is the Governor of the New Territory, and from what I just heard over the bus speakers, he's on his way right now to see what's happened."

The Captain turned to Janine. "Is that right? Is their Governor coming here now?"

The guard nodded. "I heard him address them over the vehicle's comms system. I told them to send him to parley with us when he arrived."

Cropper looked relieved. "Well, that's one piece of good news anyway. At least we'll be spared that awful trek to the city!"

Even as he spoke one of the other guards said, "I think he's coming now."

All eyes turned towards the copse just under a furlong away across the landing strip. Even from that distance Krania recognised the three figures of her parents and Uncle Rajeev emerging from the woodland. They appeared to be having a heated argument resulting in Rajeev holding her mother's shoulders to prevent her from following her father. He, brandishing a crossbow, then marched determinedly towards the shuttle, which he entered via the steps at the open doorway.

He stood resolutely in the entrance, his stature that of a leader of men, who commanded authority. "Who are you and by what right do you invade the New Territory? And what do you mean by abducting my daughter?"

The Captain addressed him. "I assume you are Governor Bradley? To answer your question, we represent the survivors aboard the star liner Salvation. We exercise our right to land here through our contract with the Ancient Ones. Your daughter has bravely offered herself as a hostage. And I have to say that, in doing so, she has averted a potentially dangerous confrontation."

At this Sylvia arrived at the foot of the steps, with Shah standing a few strides behind her, looking apologetic. She spoke breathlessly.

"Krania! Whatever are you doing? Come out of there at once!"

Her daughter answered, "I don't think they'll let me out just yet, Mum. But don't worry. They seem quite nice."

Clearly her father wasn't concerned with further preliminaries.

"All right," he said tersely. "What do you want from me?"

Cropper preceded his response with a warning. "If you don't stop waving that bow and arrow around, neither you nor your daughter will live long enough to find out!"

Krania watched her father silently take stock of the assorted weaponry being pointed at him. She knew various courses of action must be flashing through his mind just then, the first of which probably involved pumping a bolt into the gut of the horrid man who had just addressed him. But then he looked at her with a reassuring smile, and slowly reached down and lowered the bow to rest it on the floor of the shuttle.

Cropper continued, "That's better. Here's what's going to happen. You and your people will leave the New Territory and return to Fenwold. If you need help in doing this, we will give it. In any case, you have two weeks to meet our demand, which is non-negotiable. Meanwhile we will hold your daughter as – insurance. Please don't insult us by suggesting any kind of compromise. I'm not authorised to make any concessions in any case."

"How can I contact you?" Dominic asked coldly.

Wakefield handed him a small object. "Take this phone. I'll contact you in forty-eight hours from now. That'll give you time to explain the situation to your people, and work out a plan for your peaceful migration. When it buzzes, press the green button. Allow for a few seconds' delay – the signal has to bounce off satellites and pass behind the Moon."

Dominic turned the device over in his palm.

"And your name?"

"Councillor Colin Wakefield. Please return to your friends now, Governor. Captain, when they're at a safe distance, take us back to the Salvation."

Dominic cast one last loving glance in Krania's direction saying, "Don't worry, my sweet. You'll be back home with us in no time."

Then her mother burst past him to hug her daughter. "That's a promise, darling. We'll all be back together again very soon."

Then, his arms around his wife and daughter, Dominic singled out Cropper, and looked straight into his eyes, speaking slowly and deliberately.

"But think on this before you go to sleep each night, my friend. If you cause any harm to come to my daughter, I swear I will hunt you down and slit you open like a squealing pig."

CHAPTER TWENTY-TWO
CAPTIVE

Why didn't she feel afraid?

Only an hour ago she'd been riding in a comfortable bus enjoying a tour with her friends, looking forward to a picnic lunch and with hardly a care in the world. Now here she was aboard a space shuttle, surrounded by strange people, forced hurriedly to don a protective suit and helmet and on her way to captivity in what was likely to be an alien environment – and looking out onto the most exhilarating spectacle she'd ever seen in her hitherto boring life!

Who had time to be scared amid all this excitement?

Wakefield's voice broke into her thoughts through the headphone in her helmet.

"It's quite a sight when you see it for the first time, isn't it, Krania?"

His use of her given name was a comfort to her, as if she had a friend on board. And yet she knew she must be wary. She'd read many a story where a captive was disoriented by a Mr Nice / Mr Nasty scenario. But then, she must try not to be always so cynical. This man did seem genuinely concerned for her well-being. She didn't want to appear rude. She'd just have to remember to be careful not to disclose too much information.

"I've seen it on video, but looking at the whole of one side of the Earth spread out below us makes me feel so tiny – and privileged!"

"I agree. This is our first trip to Earth as well, remember."

"How long will it take us to reach your spaceship?"

"About an hour and a half."

She couldn't hide her disbelief. "But the Moon is a quarter of a million miles from Earth, isn't it?"

Wakefield chuckled. "You've obviously been paying attention to your studies. Of course you're right. But, fully charged, our batteries can power our fusion drives to produce tremendous acceleration once we're free of Earth's gravity. I need to warn you about that, because Captain Deene will be engaging thrust very shortly."

"Is it dangerous, then?"

"No, not dangerous – just a little uncomfortable. You might feel nauseous for a few minutes."

Cropper chimed in with, "But try and control yourself, girl, because the inside of a space suit and helmet isn't the most convenient place to be sick!"

Wakefield shook his head. "If I recall, Councillor, you complained of feeling unwell on the trip out, didn't you? Perhaps you should heed your own warning!"

This had the effect of silencing Cropper momentarily, while amusing Krania who, resolving not to disgrace herself, was now glad her picnic lunch had been postponed.

"How fast can we go then, Councillor Wakefield?" She'd paid heed to the earlier introductions, because she'd learned it was empowering to be able to address people correctly.

"It might sound incredible, but our shuttles can attain velocities of up to one million miles per hour. We'll be reaching half that speed on our flight to the Moon."

"Wow! The fastest I've been on Earth is about forty miles an hour in my Dad's electric car. I thought that was pretty scary, but…"

"I promise you there'll be no danger," Wakefield reassured her. "You won't even feel any motion once we've stopped accelerating. Just relax and enjoy the ride."

Relax? A thousand questions milled around inside her head. She hungered to learn more about these people's science and everyday lives.

"What about space debris, such as meteors and asteroids? Couldn't they damage the craft's hull?"

"The large stuff is easy. It's detectible by radar from far enough away for the shuttle's computer to adjust course accordingly. Smaller particles are deflected by the vessel's high impact ceramic shields."

"Er, Councillor!"

Krania wondered if Cropper ever opened his mouth without sounding annoyed. Perhaps he still smarted from her father's parting threat. She hoped so anyway.

"You'd do well to remember that this girl is our prisoner. Please limit your conversation to practical matters. Or, better still, don't talk to her at all."

The sense of hostility between these two men was undeniable. She ought to exploit it if she could. She shifted her position to face Wakefield's adversary.

"I don't know your name, Sir, nor the rules of social etiquette on board your spacecraft, but on Earth it's considered rude to shout all the time."

Cropper was clearly taken aback by her rebuke. But unable to see that she was goading him, he rose to her bait. "Well, when it comes to rudeness, aren't Earth children brought up to show some respect for their elders?"

Quick as a flash she replied, "Where I come from, respect has to be earned."

The Green Watch Councillor addressed Wakefield. "You'd better keep this little savage out of my sight when we reach the ship. I think I'd be tempted to teach her some real manners with a good thrashing."

Wakefield said, "Well, you haven't exactly made her welcome, have you? My wife and sons will be pleased to have her as our guest until she can be returned to her family."

Sounding distinctly uncomfortable as the fusion drive thrusters kicked in, Cropper merely said, "I think you mean, *if* she's returned to them, don't you, Councillor?"

* * *

"Oh, Dominic! What are we going to do?"

Sylvia sat huddled on a chair in their living room, all cried out, her head lolling into her open palms.

Again her husband wrapped a comforting arm about her trembling shoulders. For once in their devoted marriage of twenty years, he was unable to find the words to bring her any comfort. He felt completely and utterly helpless.

He stood up and suggested, "Could you drink a cup of tea, dear?"

"Tea?" she sniffed. "My whole world's been turned upside down, and you offer me tea again! I'm beyond tea, Dominic. If I had any of my grandfather's potato whisky, I might have a go at that – nothing else could put me put of my misery!"

He shook his head. "You know we finished off the last of that at Jack and Lucy's wedding. I could ask around and see if any of the settlers have brewed something similar. I've heard rumours…"

"Don't bother," she sighed. "I need to keep a clear head anyway. Pour me a mug of that weak beer."

He went into the kitchen and brought out two foaming glasses of ale. He handed one to his wife and sat beside her.

She sipped at the soothing liquid and then said, "You've got to do something, Dominic."

"I am doing something. I've asked Rajeev to call an urgent meeting of all the district elders. We've been considering introducing democracy and now is as good a time as any to start. A situation as serious as this merits concerted action. I have to put the best interests of the New Territory first."

She rounded on him. "You have to put your daughter's life first, Dominic Bradley! Sod the New Territory!"

How could he explain the inner turmoil he was also suffering, torn as he was between his loyalty to his office and love for his family? He so wanted to tell Sylvia how he was being ripped apart inside, but he needed to be strong for her just now.

She leaned her head on his shoulder. "If I could just speak to her – to know she was all right!"

He squeezed her to him. "I'm sure she will be, my love. Councillor Wakefield seems a decent sort – hardly the kind of man who'd allow a young girl to come to harm."

"That's as may be," she said, "but I didn't like the look of that other fellow – Cropper, I think he was called. He looks like a nasty piece of work. I shudder to think what might happen if she were left alone with him. Oh, Dominic, is there no way we could make sure she's safe?"

Dominic took the phone that Wakefield had given him out of his tunic pocket.

"This is our only means of communication with them, but he said he'd call in forty-eight hours. I should have asked how I could call him. What a fool!"

She kissed his brow. "Don't beat yourself up, my love. He probably wouldn't have told you anyway. Here, let me have a look at it." She took the phone and held it in her palm. "It looks like a simple comms device, with a display screen and a keypad. There's no reason to think it can only receive calls – there has to be a way to reach them with it. I can't wait two whole days for news of Krania!"

They both stared at it. "You'll need to switch it on," he said. "Try pressing the red or green buttons."

"All right. Ah, it's the red one. Oh, bugger!"

"What's up?"

"It's asking for the pin code. Well, I hope it's like just about every other comms device we have in the New Territory." She keyed in four digits, and for the first time in hours, she smiled.

"One-two-three-four?" he grinned.

She nodded, then pressed a few keys at random and held the phone to her ear.

"What are you doing?"

"You never know. Beginner's luck."

"Is it ringing?"

She sighed. "No."

"How many numbers did you press?"

"Four, I think."

"Press another one."

She shrugged. "Why?"

"Maybe they have five digit numbers. It's worth a try anyway."

She pressed another key and shook her head.

"Give it a few seconds."

Her eyes widened. "I think it's working – it sounds something like a ringing tone anyway. Wait."

Dominic's basic reading skills were sufficient for him to see why she then pressed a key labelled 'SPKR', and then lay the instrument down on the near-by coffee table. Now any response would be audible to both of them. Then they heard what sounded like a loud *yawn* and an irate male voice saying, "Hello, what time…? By the saints, this had better be urgent! Who the hell's calling a Blue Watch number at this hour? Don't you know it's our sleep period? If it's you Orange delinquents messing about again, I'll be reporting you first thing…!"

Dominic spoke across the ranting. "I'm really sorry to disturb your sleep, Sir. I must have the wrong number. I didn't want Blue Watch."

"Well, which bloody watch *did* you want, idiot?"

He and Sylvia exchanged grimaces and, for a moment, Dominic wondered if bad tempers were the norm on board the star liner. Then he thought about the angry man's question. From what he'd said, it seemed the Salvation's crew must be organised into watches, apparently designated by colours. When he'd stood in that shuttle doorway, he recalled that each of the occupants sported a small coloured insignia on the breast of their space suit. He concentrated hard to bring to mind which colour was Wakefield's. He couldn't be certain, but thought he might hazard a reasonable guess.

"It's Red Watch I'm after, Sir."

"Well, every child knows all Red Watch numbers start with a five! It's supposed to be a foolproof system, which doesn't say much for your intelligence, does it?"

"Er, no," Dominic said sheepishly. "Sorry to have troubled you, Sir. I hope you get back to sleep…"

The line went dead.

Then he immediately keyed in a five digit number beginning with a five. After a few seconds the message 'NNR' appeared on the small display screen.

After his earlier success in making a contact – albeit unpleasant – his shoulders drooped and he scratched his ear.

Sylvia said, "Number not recognised. I'll bet that's what it means. Try another one."

He did, but only elicited the same response.

Then she said, "Wait. Let's reason this out. How many people are there on board of the Salvation?"

Dominic didn't quite follow her line of thought but had learned long ago that his wife could somehow cut a logical path through many a mental maze. He cast his mind back to what Cara had said at that final devastating meeting earlier that day.

"Twelve thousand," he said.

She pursed her lips. "Right. I don't know how many of these *watches* they've split themselves into. Let's guess it's four. That would be just three thousand per watch, give or take. Five digit phone numbers would allow as many as a hundred thousand combinations, but if every Red Watch number must start with a five, that reduces your choice to ten thousand."

Dominic now followed her reasoning. "That's over three times more than they need. So trying five digit combinations at random should, on average, result in a valid number after three or four attempts."

"Unless the numbers are bunched together."

"Explain please."

"Well, we know that Red Watch numbers start with a five. Yes?"

He nodded.

"Given that, it's logical to start with five-zero-zero-zero-zero and continue from there. Allocating successive numbers to three thousand individuals would only require you to use numbers starting five-zero, five-one and five-two. So I think you should try combinations starting with numbers in those ranges.

"All right my clever little squirrel – let's test out your theory."

He keyed number five-zero-one-two-three. There followed the expected signal delay before the ringing tone sounded.

"Thank you for calling Red Watch catering. For today's menus please press one or log on to rwc.menus.sal – updated daily. To leave a message about special dietary requirements, please press two. For careers information please press three. In case of complaints, we suggest you try an alternative service and wish you the best of luck in finding one."

Sylvia smirked. "Well, at least someone in their kitchen has a sense of humour. Come on, let's get on with this initiative test."

Dominic turned towards her and smiled, grabbing her gently by the shoulders. "That's just what this is, Sylvia! Don't you see? Wakefield expected us to try this!"

"Why?"

"I don't know – perhaps to test our intelligence and determination. So far he's been considerate towards us – unlike Cropper. Maybe he's going out on a limb for us, and wants to be sure his gut feelings aren't misplaced."

She raised her eyebrows. "In that case, we'd better not disappoint him. But it occurs to me that if we keep contacting random Red Watch personnel or asking for Wakefield's number, someone's going to get suspicious, which might land him in trouble."

She picked up the phone and clicked a few keys.

"What are you doing?"

"If he wants us to contact him as you suspect, he won't have made it so difficult. Who's to say he hasn't left his own details in its contacts directory?"

While she pressed a few more keys he said, "It couldn't be that easy…"

She replaced the phone on the coffee table, with only a smug smile to refute his misplaced supposition. After the usual delay a male voice spoke to them.

"Oh, hello, Governor Bradley. Colin Wakefield here. I somehow knew it wouldn't take you long to get through to me."

* * *

"Mr Wakefield, please let me speak to my daughter!"

The brief signal delay that followed Sylvia's demand seemed interminable. To their delight and amazement, the next voice they heard was Krania's.

"Hello, Mum, Dad. I'm fine and the Wakefields are treating me well. Things are so fascinating here – it's like being on holiday! So, there's no need to worry about me. Are you two all right?"

"Of course we are, except that we've been worried to death about you. I'm glad to hear you're safe, darling. Are they feeding you properly?"

"Mum, there isn't time to go into details. I think Councillor Wakefield wants to speak to Dad."

Dominic said, "I'm here, Councillor. I thought you were going to make us wait forty-eight hours for news."

Wakefield coughed. "Much of what I said to you on the shuttle was for other ears. I think you'll understand that. And

I'm sorry I had to use that ancient mobile phone. I did what testing I could before we landed on Earth, but I wasn't a hundred per cent certain it would work from there."

"It seems to do the job," Dominic said. "But why so keen not to give me something you could be sure *would* work? Ah, wait. I assume its signal isn't traceable?"

"Correct. Cara monitors all our communications made on modern equipment. I didn't want that."

Sylvia interrupted. "So Cara runs your lives too, eh?"

They heard the grin in his response. "She's indispensable – as I'm sure she has been to you. But in this matter I'd sooner keep some things to myself. You see, I don't concur with our present course of action regarding you and your people. We're a democracy of sorts here and currently the balance – which is by no means solid – favours the Green Watch proposal to encourage you to leave the New Territory."

In the slight pause that followed Dominic injected, "Or to use force to eject us if necessary?"

"Unfortunately, yes. But I wanted confirmation of my assumption that you were rational, trustworthy people, and that – given the opportunity – you would be willing to work together with us to develop new cities across the Earth."

Dominic's sigh as he took in Wakefield's words was so forceful, he was sure it must be clearly audible across the void. "Sorry, Councillor. That's a lot to take in. I appreciate your being so candid with me, and of course my family and I will treat your remarks with the utmost confidence. But we are working towards a democratic society here too, and I'm sure you'll understand if I tell you I must at least gauge the feeling among my district elders before making any important commitments. I'll do this when I meet them this evening."

"I understand. The support of your people would of course be crucial. Let me know the outcome of your meeting."

"I will. But there's one other thing. I want you to organise a face-to-face between me and your overall leader – if there is such a person."

"That would be Commander Boone. He's a decent and intelligent man. When the forty-eight hours are up, I'll request a meeting on your behalf."

Sylvia now jumped in. "And while that's going on I'd like to come and see Krania!"

A female voice was heard to say, "Of course you would, Mrs Bradley! You wouldn't be a mother otherwise. This is Rigella Wakefield. I have two sons of my own – the younger one six and the older nearly twenty – and I'm sure my husband will do his best to allow you to visit your lovely daughter."

Wakefield coughed and said, "I'll see if that's possible."

Dominic said, "Thanks for that. By the way, do you keep the same hours as we do?"

"We operate on a weekly five watch system – four days on, three off. Currently Red Watch matches your own daily routines. But during this emergency period I suggest we each be prepared for contact by the other at any time, day or night."

* * *

From behind his office desk Dominic surveyed the array of dumbfounded faces. The silence was hard to take. He'd expected more of a reaction to the bad news – had even been prepared for their criticism. He was the person in authority here, after all. The responsibility for what had happened was down to him.

Then one of the elders spoke, a long-term man by the name of McMahon who had settled in the New Territory with his family soon after the first crossings.

"Governor Bradley, you say they've taken your daughter as a hostage?"

He nodded. "Yes, though by all accounts they're not mistreating her."

"And they want us out of the New Territory within two weeks?"

He didn't bother to answer – he'd made the Salvation's demands clear enough already.

Another elder, a more recent settler, merely said, "So, Sir, what have you decided to do?"

He took a sip of water. "I've requested a meeting with their Commander. I won't know if that's possible for another two days. I think they'll allow it."

The same man asked, "What will you say to him?"

"I'll state our case for being here – that we were invited by the Ancient Ones, through the Fenwold Riddle and with the support of their own representative, Cara. Obviously I'll also ask him to release my daughter, though if I were in his shoes, I wouldn't give up such a precious bargaining tool."

Now Rajeev, so far standing silently at his side, said, "Do you think there's any way we could organise a snatch, Dominic?"

He turned to his old friend, a smile in his eyes in spite of his inner sadness, and said, "When I visit their ship I'll look for every opportunity, but the odds are overwhelmingly in their favour. Their weapons and technology are far superior to ours. Crossbows and hunting rifles aren't going to be much use against their firepower." He sighed heavily. "But, of course, I won't rule anything out."

Another of the founding elders asked, "What do you want of us, Governor?"

He chose his words carefully. "For me to represent your wishes I need answers from you to two important questions. First, if I could negotiate a settlement whereby we share the Ancient Ones' legacy with these newcomers, would you accept it?

"The second question only applies if a compromise can't be reached. If that were the case, in the face of their superior weaponry, would you agree to withdraw peaceably back into Fenwold?"

The room was hushed again, except for the shuffling of feet as the New Territory elders turned these questions over in their minds.

"I realise you'll want some time to consider what I've said. Rajeev and I will withdraw to my home for thirty minutes. Meanwhile my clerk will bring you all something to drink. Please choose a spokesman and, when we return, let me know your decision."

* * *

"Hello, Councillor Wakefield?"

"Governor Bradley, how are things going?"

"Not too well, I'm afraid. I've just come from a meeting with the elders. I hadn't expected them to be quite so resolute so quickly. They've invested their lives in helping develop what the Ancient Ones left for them here. They can't face going back to the poverty and drudgery of life back in Fenwold. Nor are they willing to believe that sharing these resources would result in anything but effective submission. I'm inclined to agree with them on that score. While I don't doubt your own sincerity, I see no reason to trust your other colleagues."

"So they wouldn't be willing to accept a compromise?"

"No."

"Then, what do they propose to do?"

"Almost to a man, they're ready and willing to stand their ground!"

CHAPTER TWENTY-THREE
IMPASSE

Dominic, isn't this wonderful?"

Two days after the call to Wakefield, Sylvia stared out from the shuttle at the Earth's face below them.

"It's an amazing sight," he replied. "There's no wonder people are so willing to fight for its bounties."

"Do you really think it'll come to that? Fighting for the New Territory, I mean? After all, from up here the world seems such a huge place. You'd think there'd be room for all of us."

"I know, but unfortunately the Ancient Ones only left one store of their treasures. They didn't count on two separate human groups wanting exclusive use of it."

"Dominic, you don't think we're being foolhardy taking this trip, do you? How do we know they won't take us as hostages too?"

"I believe in the main that they're honourable people. Colin Wakefield has given me his word that we'll be returned unharmed. Besides, they already have what they know to be more precious to us than our own lives. But if we don't come back, our people are well able to fall in behind Rajeev's leadership."

"I can't wait to see Krania. It's incredible how well she's taking all this. It's almost as if she's enjoying the experience."

"I'm glad she's taking that attitude. It'll help her through the ordeal. She's a very special girl, and we're lucky to have her for a daughter."

Sylvia sighed. "It was courageous of her to offer herself as hostage and prevent a violent confrontation at the landing strip.

Things could have turned out so differently if she hadn't. Have you decided what you're going to say to their Commander?"

"More or less, though I'm more interested in what he'll have to say to me."

"Promise you won't try anything silly, Dominic."

"I told you, I'm merely going to talk and listen. You'll be taken to the Wakefields' quarters to see Krania. Remember to give her my love in case I don't get the opportunity to see her."

The voice of the shuttle captain cut into their conversation.

"I'm about to engage thrust. Please relax and prepare yourselves for slight nausea."

* * *

"Welcome on board the Salvation to you both, Governor and Mistress Bradley."

Gideon Boone's face was lined and care-worn, but kindliness shone from his old eyes as he shook hands with his guests.

Dominic said, "I'm pleased to meet you, Sir. Though I'd have preferred different circumstances."

They'd been escorted to what seemed to be a public area where the Commander waited for them, along with Colin Wakefield and an attractive woman who looked to be of similar age to Sylvia. Other people passed by in both directions but there were no guards present as far as he could see.

Wakefield offered his hand and said, "This is my wife, Rigella. She'll take Mistress Bradley by rail shuttle to see your daughter. They'll return here in two hours. I hope you'll both be comfortable in those space suits. I'm afraid it didn't occur to me to provide a change of clothing." Then with a smile he added, "We don't get many visitors on the Salvation!"

Sylvia laughed nervously. "These suits are quite comfortable, Councillor – even stylish!" She looked around at people passing by. "I notice many of you have similar clothing – hardly anyone seems to be taking much notice of us. Are you forever popping out for space shuttle trips?"

Wakefield laughed. "You're very observant. We're still close to the shuttle port here. A lot of those you can see wearing suits are technicians involved in repairing the lunar sunlight collectors. Eight centuries of meteor bombardment have left the array of panels working at far below their potential. There's several months of repair work to do to bring them up to full strength."

Dominic said, "Before the shuttle swung around to the rear of the Moon I made out a large black area – I thought it might be an artificial sea, but now I realise it must have been the panels. And the two huge towers at either end must be the energy transmitters, right?"

The Commander coughed and Dominic noticed his male hosts exchange glances, clearly uncomfortable with this line of talk.

Wakefield looked embarrassed as he said, "I'm sorry, Governor. I'm not authorised to discuss such technicalities. I'm sure you understand." Then he smiled and said, "There's an office along here where you and Commander Boone can talk in private. I'll be waiting outside in the corridor. You were auto-scanned for weapons on entering the shuttle, and I'm pleased you chose to come unarmed. The Commander carries no weapons, though of course he has the means to summon immediate help if he needs it. I hope you don't mind my mentioning this."

Dominic smiled. "Of course not, Councillor. You can never be too careful."

Sylvia kissed Dominic on the cheek before leaving for the rail shuttle with Rigella. Wakefield opened the door to the office and motioned for him to enter followed by Boone. Then he closed the door after them.

Dominic was surprised how basic the room was, with only an air vent and no window, barely illuminated by low ambient lighting, and containing just two worn moulded plastic chairs, which nevertheless proved to be comfortable enough. There was also a low table with a jug of water and two beakers. Again he was surprised at the absence of guards, but their reasoning was plain. Krania was their security.

"Forgive the austerity, Governor," Boone said. "We've been sixty years making the return trip to the Solar System, and since we need stars to charge our batteries, we've had to carefully prioritise our use of resources during that time. Of course it's better now that we're so close to the Sun, but for many of us older ones frugality has become a habit."

He shuffled in his seat for comfort, as if preparing for a fireside chat. "Now, Dominic Bradley, Governor of the New Territory, tell me something about yourself. I take it you weren't always a Governor?"

He realised the Commander had already skilfully manoeuvred the conversation into interview mode, and was content to humour the old man – for the time being, at least.

"No, Sir. I was born the son of a wealthy merchant trader in Fenwold's Capital. We relied on agriculture, and our farming communities came under increasing harassment by raider gangs. I trained as a Council marshal along with several others and helped subdue the outlaws. That was twenty years ago."

Boone sat forward, his imagination clearly stimulated. "I see. I wish there were more time to hear about your exploits. But where did these raiders come from?"

"Mostly they were just boisterous and disgruntled young men. Farming life was hard and some were unwilling to accept sweating for a subsistence living. It just needed a few nasty characters with promises of an easy living to tempt them away from their communities. Some of them created small armies that threatened the structure of our society."

"But you and your colleagues defeated them. How was that?"

"We trained the decent village youngsters in weaponry and combat, and helped them fortify their villages against attack. When the inevitable onslaught came, we were ready to face the enemy."

"What happened to the raiders then?"

"Those found guilty of murder were executed."

The old man's face blanched as he reached for a beaker of water.

"I see you find the concept of execution unnerving, Commander. I can assure you we only used it when there was no alternative. We're not barbarians, whatever some of your people would have you believe."

Clearly Boone wasn't going to be drawn on this remark. "What about the others?"

What a clever old bastard this Commander was. By creating an affable atmosphere in which an uncle might be reminiscing with his nephew, he had drawn Dominic on the one subject that could so easily justify the views of hardliners like Cropper that the Earth dwellers were little more than savages. But he was determined not to lie.

"They were put to work alongside the other villagers."

"You mean, condemned to slavery."

"That's a very emotive word, Commander. It conjures impressions of ill-treatment or even cruelty."

"But some of your slaves are chained up in the fields, aren't they?"

"Only if there's a likelihood they'd abscond and make trouble. But, wait a moment. How do you know all this?"

Boone was silent for a while. Then he said, "Your daughter is a very intelligent child – and also open and honest. She's struck quite a rapport with the Wakefields. She seems naturally inquisitive about our ways, and has been more than willing to reciprocate on the subject of life in Fenwold and the New Territory. Please don't blame her for her openness – it's a great gift."

Dominic wondered if Boone was merely repeating what the Wakefield's had told him, or if their living quarters were bugged. He suspected the latter – or perhaps he wanted to believe it. But, whatever the truth, he wondered – could he really count on Colin Wakefield as an ally?

Boone must have read the unspoken question in his face, even if the answer was non-committal. "Your daughter's hosts have enjoyed her company. Wakefield is by nature a non-adversarial fellow. But in the end his loyalty is towards the Salvation. Please understand that. Now, tell me how you became Governor of the New Territory."

He felt he'd already divulged too much information. He decided to keep his answers short and move towards his own agenda.

"It was a kind of reward for defeating a particularly nasty outlaw."

"We know. Red. But weren't you also instrumental in waking Cara and breaking through the Wall to the New Territory?"

Dominic shrugged. "I happened to be in the right place at the right time."

"Hmm, I see. There's just one more question I have for you, Governor."

"What's that, Sir?"

"Do your people have no relationship with God?"

Dominic gave his host a puzzled look. "God? Some of us had fanciful notions that Gods created the Wall, though now of course we know that humans built it for our safety."

"But what of the Earth, the Sun and the Universe?"

Dominic tried hard to recall some of the teaching modules he'd begun, but let fall by the wayside in the face of pressures from his official duties.

"I seem to recall reading that many of the Ancient Ones' scientists believed the Universe was created by something they called the Big Bang. That's as near to a concept of God that my mind can accept."

"But, without a God to guide your life, what makes you a moral man?"

"I think morality comes from within, Sir. It's about living harmoniously with your fellow human beings to achieve a better life for all. The ancient newsreels tell us that some believers in your God had opposing agenda and were capable of horrific atrocities. But our time is moving on, Sir, and there are important matters that I wish to raise with you."

The Commander didn't reply, but shuffled in his seat.

"First, I want you to understand just how hard my people have worked under Cara's guidance to create the growing city that we now have in the New Territory. Men, women and children have toiled to make a new life – and all propelled by the Ancient Ones' promise enshrined in the Fenwold Riddle. We see this as our birthright. And though it may appear trite to point out, we did get there first. We should be allowed to finish what we started. To try and take it from us by force – just because you can – would amount to unjustified aggression – a case of might over right. Where would that leave your superior morality? Would a moral God really condone such an act?"

Boone said coldly, "Because you haven't the capacity to understand, I will pray that God forgives your words of blasphemy. Was there something else?"

"Yes. I want you to release my daughter. When she offered herself as hostage, it was to prevent carnage on that school trip bus. She knew the driver had a weapon and would have used it if necessary. It was an act of goodwill to remove that threat and almost certain retaliation by your guards. To hold an innocent girl merely as a bargaining tool amounts to terror tactics in my book."

The Commander sighed. "I will note your argument and convey it to our Joint Watch Committee." He stood up, clearly wanting to bring the meeting to a close.

"There's just one final thing, Commander," Dominic said.

Boone now looked very tired, and though he hadn't exactly warmed to the old chap, Dominic thought he now had a better understanding of his position. He stood and tried to sound as respectful as he could.

"I'd like to speak to Cara, Sir."

He'd been expecting his request to be dismissed out of hand, but instead the Commander merely shrugged and said, "I don't see why that can't be arranged. There's a portal only a few corridors from here."

He opened the door. "Wakefield, take Governor Bradley to meet Cara, will you? I'm feeling a little tired, so I'll take a rail shuttle back to my quarters." Then he turned to Dominic. "It's been a pleasure meeting you, Governor. Please pass my apologies to your wife for not staying to say goodbye. I hope we can resolve our differences." A rail shuttle stopped close by long enough for him to climb in, and Dominic watched it accelerate and carry him away down through the warren of corridors. He wondered if he'd given the old man food for thought. He hoped so, anyway.

"Want to talk to Cara, do you, Dominic?" He thought he detected a mischievous smile cross Wakefiled's face. He also wondered if their relationship really yet merited first name terms.

"I'd like to, yes."

"All right. Please follow me."

It didn't take them long to arrive at an unassuming door with a sign on it simply saying: CARA. There was no guard. Clearly everyone had free access to the hologram. Wakefield ushered him in.

The layout was familiar to that of the portal in the New Territory, except that no batteries were in evidence. He guessed that power must be derived from the ship's central energy source. He stepped onto one of the black circles on the floor, and then waited for the familiar hum and formation of Cara's figure from the three beams of light. He smiled, for the hologram's form was so familiar that he had the impression of meeting an old friend. He prepared himself for the usual exchange of greetings, but found her words at once disappointing.

"New supplicant. Middle aged adult. Please identify yourself."

He laughed nervously. "Cara, it's me – Governor Dominic Bradley of the New Territory. Surely you recognise me?"

"Negative. The New Territory portal is closed. Identity data has not been downloaded to me. I am taking readings now so that I know you again. What do you want of me?"

"I want you to help sort out this mess. As you know about the New Territory, you also know they're already occupied by my people. The Salvation contingent want to force us out and take the lands for themselves. Can't you mediate in this somehow?"

"Computed predictions suggest the best outcome for your people is to evacuate peaceably. That is my advice. My loyalties must be with the survivors aboard the Salvation. Please withdraw. This audience is terminated."

* * *

"What do you mean, she didn't recognise you?"

McMahon, the senior elder, spoke with such force that Dominic almost recoiled at his outburst. He couldn't blame him. The settlers were clearly worried about what was going to happen.

"Just that," he replied, as calmly as he could manage. "We have to remember that the various versions of Cara aren't identical – except in appearance. There's a certain amount of information that each portal shares, but the hologram on board the Salvation doesn't know any of us here. Apart from me, now, of course."

Another elder asked, "How did their Commander react when you asked him to reconsider? And about releasing Krania?"

"He was non-committal on the first point. But I think I rattled him when I said that holding my daughter hostage was a barbaric act. They appear to set great store by their belief that we're morally inferior to them. It sort of justifies their actions that we execute murderers, keep slaves and don't believe in their God."

Rajeev said, "That's a bit of an over-simplification. Historically…"

"I know," Dominic interrupted. "But I didn't waste time arguing with him. I got the impression his views were fixed in that area."

McMahon said, "All right, Governor. What else emerged from your meeting?"

Dominic sighed. "Negatives first. I don't believe we'll shift their opinion that they have more right than we do in colonising the New Territory. If it comes to a shooting war, there'll probably be many casualties on our side. We have nothing that can bring down their fighter shuttles. And finally, they have nothing to gain in releasing Krania."

His voice lowered in tone as he said this, and there followed a moment of awkward silence.

Then Rajeev said quietly, "Any positives at all, Dominic?"

"Perhaps. They seem used to a low security environment. They allowed me to see Commander Boone alone. And the shuttle they sent for us carried no guards – just a pilot and co-pilot who looked to be little more than children. On the Salvation itself – at least near the shuttle dock area – it seems that if you're wearing a space suit, nobody questions your right to be there."

Another elder suggested, "They've probably never known a real combat situation. Perhaps they'll find it hard to use their weapons on live targets, if they're not used to the concept of killing."

Dominic shrugged. "You might be right. But I wouldn't like to test that theory. What military they do have come over as professionals, who are trained to follow orders."

The same man asked, "Do you think we could attack them from within?"

"The thought had crossed my mind to attempt a kidnapping raid of our own, perhaps their Commander, rescuing Krania into the bargain. But we'd need access to a shuttle – and to someone who'd pilot it for us. We have neither."

McMahon sighed. "What do we do then, Governor?"

"For the time being, we wait for Boone's response to my requests. He has to report back to the ship's governing committee. Colin Wakefield is a member. I'll be talking to him later."

As the room cleared Sylvia barged in through the emerging elders, waving a scrap of paper in her hand.

"Dominic, I think you'd better see this. In fact everyone should hear what it says."

He took the paper, and noticed that it was wrinkled, as if having been repeatedly folded. Guessing its origin, he carefully scanned the brief message it contained. His body froze. His voice faltered for a second but then he yelled out, "Wait, friends! This is important!"

The elders turned to reassemble, and he fought to regain his composure.

"Some of you know that my daughter keeps a pigeon loft. It's a childish hobby but she likes to stay in touch with her young cousin, daughter of my wife's brother Jack, who's Marshal of Crowtree and Ashwell. I don't know how long this message has been up there."

He glanced at Sylvia, who shrugged and said worriedly, "Anything up to a couple of days."

"I'll read it," he said, and then his voice rang sombrely around the otherwise hushed meeting room.

"DOM PLEASE HELP – SLAVE REVOLT LED BY SON OF RED – SOME ASHWELL CASUALTIES – NEED REINFORCEMENTS – JACK."

CHAPTER TWENTY-FOUR
DRASTIC ACTION

"It's good of your family not to keep me shut away, Martin – and of you to give up your day to show me around. What's this place we're in?"

"It's our college refectory. We seniors take our meals here. It's pretty quiet now, but in five minutes you'll think you're in a madhouse, when the students come in for their brunch break. When they do, I'd like to introduce you to a couple of my friends. And, as for not confining you to the family quarters, we have Commander Boone to thank for that."

"Really? How so?"

"After your father's meeting with him last week he told my Dad to let you have more freedom. What he actually said was, 'Governor Bradley's daughter shouldn't be kept cooped up like a caged animal. After all, we're not barbarians.' Dad suggested I choose a day when I could afford to skip my studies and show you around. So today we're free to go wherever we want – so long as it's not outside the ship – and I'll get you back to our quarters in time for supper."

Krania smiled. "Your Mum and young Declan have been nice to me these past seven days, but I must admit it'll be good to have some company closer to my own age. Do none of the senior students live in with their families?"

"No, we make better progress staying in dorms near the lecture halls during term time. It's supposed to have something to do with bonding – most of us prefer it anyway. It's just as well because it means you can use our room at home. Declan won't have minded sleeping on a cot in our parents' room for a few days. Are you finding my bed comfortable?"

Krania suppressed a giggle as he blushed at his gauche remark.

"It's fine," she said, straight-faced as she could manage. Further embarrassment was avoided by a sudden influx of what seemed like hundreds of boisterous students seeking mid-morning refreshment. In less than a minute there was a cacophony of shifting furniture, raised voices and clinking crockery. Out of the melee a teenage girl and boy approached their table. Like Martin, she judged them to be a couple of years older than her.

"Hi, Martin," they said, staring wide-eyed at Krania.

"Hello, you two." He stood up. "Krania, I'd like you to meet my friends Jessica and Leonard." They each shook her hand in turn.

Jessica seemed especially excited. "Krania, I hope you don't mind my saying this, but I really love your hair!"

Knowing that the Wakefield males were completely bald, and suspecting Rigella wore a skilfully crafted wig, she now understood that real hair must be a rarity on the Salvation.

Instinctively her fingers went up to her short, straight black mop and almost apologetically she said, "Oh, it's nothing special. It feels like a bit of a rag sometimes."

Jessica said, "Oh, no, Krania, it's wonderful! Do you think…? Would it be all right if…?"

She felt awkward, but realised it could do no harm. "Go on then. Touch it if you want to." Jessica put out her hand, and then hesitated, as if uncertain whether she'd overstepped some undefined social boundary. Only lightly brushing Krania's fringe, she quickly withdrew her hand and smiled shyly.

The boys shuffled uneasily, and Krania hoped they weren't going to ask the same favour. Though enjoying the attention, she was beginning to feel a bit of a freak. For a moment she thought she might turn things around by commenting on their false hairpieces, but had second thoughts.

Instead she asked them, "Are you all studying the same things?"

Leonard said, "These two are doing history and politics. My fields are science and computing. Shall I get some drinks and stuff?"

Martin replied, "Good idea. Why don't you bring some tea and cake while I tell Krania the purpose of our meeting?"

"Meeting?" she said. "I thought we were just socialising."

Jessica explained, "We are socialising, but it's also a good cover for our real agenda. There's so much noise in here that nobody can eavesdrop. It's the ideal place for a private chat."

"I'm intrigued," Krania admitted. "You're not planning a teenage revolution, are you?"

"Nothing like that," Martin said. "But we're worried about what might happen to you if your people don't roll over. We need a contingency plan."

Krania laughed nervously. "But everyone seems so kind and civilised. Even your Commander was concerned about my welfare. Why should anything happen to me?"

Martin frowned. "For a start, Commander Boone is really only a figurehead. Senior people from all of the five watches decide policy. Your main experience so far has been of Red Watch. Traditionally we've always been liberal in our outlook. You met Cropper on the shuttle, didn't you? Well, he's typical of Green Watch thinking – very hard line. And just now, he has the ears of the other three watches. He's frightening them into believing your people will turn on us if we give them any leeway. He'd be happier if the Earth settlers just stopped existing."

Krania stared at him, realising the implication of his words. "But what can you do? I wouldn't ask you to put yourselves in danger on my behalf. I volunteered to be a hostage, remember."

Returning with the drinks and snacks, Leonard said, "We only want to ensure no harm comes to you if Cropper gets his way."

"How will you do that?"

Passing her a beaker of synthesised tea Martin said, "If necessary, we plan to steal a shuttle and take you home."

* * *

"No! No! No!"

Colin Wakefield drove his fist down hard onto the conference room table top, causing the water jug and beakers to perform a frenzied dance, and drawing gasps from the other watch representatives, clearly amazed at his uncharacteristic display of anger.

"What you're suggesting goes far beyond what's necessary! These are our fellow human beings, not dangerous aliens!"

Irwin Cropper smirked. "But the deadline we set has arrived, Councillor. It's clear they lack the intelligence to understand that their inaction must have consequences. And there's not much difference, so far as I can see, between these people and aliens. Their beliefs, habits and standards differ widely from our own. We're superior to them in every respect."

Wakefield lowered his voice. "That, if I may say so, is a very simplistic and subjective judgement. We know hardly anything about them. Governor Bradley's daughter has been in my family's care for two weeks now and appears most charming and self-assured, in spite of her hostage status."

The Green Watch representative sniffed and said, "I've met Governor Bradley's daughter. She smells. So does her father. I'll wager they all do. They're nothing but savages, and we need to distance ourselves from them. If it takes an aerial attack to persuade them to move back behind their Wall, then so be it."

Wakefield gritted his teeth. "They smell of the Earth – of the soil. Their modern resources are limited. If they haven't yet adopted the habit of showering daily, that hardly makes them inferior. I find the Councillor's observations mean and petty."

The other watch representatives had contributed little above an earlier exchange of pleasantries. Unfortunately his colleague Herbert Harrison was absent through sickness. But now one of the Blue Watch delegates coughed nervously and said, "Though I'm not sure about our tactics, I must say that I concur with Green Watch that we mustn't allow ourselves to become contaminated by these people. In saying this I'm not judging them, you understand. I only think it would be sensible to remove them from the New Territory. They're bound to carry many germs and bacteria unknown to us since our ancestors left Earth."

Wakefield sighed. "And if we colonise Earth, don't you think we'll come into contact with such things in any case? We'll have to learn to adjust in so many ways. If we adopt a policy of cooperation the present inhabitants could help us to make the transition – teach us about the new environment and how to cope with it, just as we could teach them how to improve their lives."

Cropper said with sarcasm, "I'm sick of hearing all this wishy-washy drivel about how we can help each other. We don't need their help. We just need the resources our ancestors left for us. They're ours by right and I'm amazed we're even discussing the possibility of sharing them with these primitives."

Wakefield's hackles rose again. "I must object to the Councillor's insistence in referring to the Earth dwellers in such derogatory terms. As I've said before, we know hardly anything about them."

"We know that they fight among themselves continually and keep slaves," Cropper retorted. "On top of that, we know that some of them have reverted to the disgusting habit of smoking. And they freely imbibe alcohol – adults and children alike! I've already mentioned their general lack of personal hygiene. Also they kill and eat meat, just as you'd expect savages to do. They're poorly educated and undemocratic – Bradley lords it over them like some self-proclaimed deity. And worst of all, even God has forsaken them. Their only concession to a higher power appears to be a vague notion of their 'Gods of the Wall' – a supposition based on little more than a children's fairy story!"

Again Commander Boone's bass voice interrupted, "It's to be hoped that we can bring our religion to them, once we have them subdued."

Wakefield couldn't allow the Commander's choice of words to go unchallenged. "Once we have them subdued, Sir? Isn't that a rather arrogant attitude to take?"

The other representatives shuffled uncomfortably in their seats, but Cropper spoke for them all. "I am sure that Professor Wakefield would wish to retract his disrespectful outburst, Commander."

"Sir, I meant no disrespect. But I feel strongly that we haven't the right to impose our presumed superiority on the Earth dwellers, and that we should seek a more cooperative approach."

Cropper said, "And I, Sir, consider Professor Wakefield's interpretation to be not only wrong, but also dangerous. Our survival is paramount, and nothing should be allowed to get in the way of that. But I am not a brutal man, however much he may think so. I believe that any force we have to use should be minimal. And although it may sound harsh, I believe the least painful way to convince them of our resolve is obvious, if you will only reconsider one small point regarding Governor Bradley's daughter."

Boone frowned and regarded him darkly. "And that is?"

Cropper paused to glance around the table at the ship's leaders. Then he said determinedly, "It's far preferable to make one small initial sacrifice, if in so doing we can prevent the carnage of an extended conflict. We must be true to our word, or else we'll appear weak.

"Much as it goes against my nature, I propose we make an example of Krania Bradley."

* * *

The Salvation's main shuttle dock throbbed with early morning activity. Space-suited personnel milled around in their dozens, either gossiping on arrival or waiting to board departing craft. The big airlock acted as a virtual bottleneck. Its doors seemed to be forever *swishing* open to disgorge passengers from emptying shuttles or closing after consuming groups of fresh boarders. Krania saw little sign of any order in the coming and going, other than a rather bored looking couple of attendants who Martin explained were checking the job details of each technician en route to the damaged lunar energy collectors.

She'd been sceptical about his plan from the outset, and now the thought of the risk they were taking made her distinctly jittery. She was especially worried about her appearance – or more accurately, about the loss of her hair. She'd had to agree that keeping it would have blown their plan completely. So Jessica had offered to do the deed that morning, adding an attractive flimsy red hairpiece, so that she wouldn't stand out in the crowd. But now the cool air of the shuttle dock made her feel naked, and she couldn't help thinking people were looking at her. So far though, no one had regarded her strangely, other than with mildly admiring glances. Still she felt highly self-conscious.

Their main concern was being allocated a dedicated shuttle. Martin had explained this to her earlier.

"Most technicians fly down to the lunar surface in groups of five or six. Many by now have passed their basic pilot's test, and clever old Leonard has managed to hack into the registration database to have me listed. Don't worry – it's really only a formality. Whatever the career pilots would have us believe, it's the on-board computer that drives the shuttle. A child could fly one. But we need a shuttle just for the two of us. So I asked Leonard to create a job number on the maintenance database for a repair somewhere as far away from the main cluster as possible. It's less complicated for the attendants to allocate shuttles for one-drop trips, so that's what I'm hoping they'll do. Leonard's also registered us both as maintenance personnel – me, under my real name, and you, under a made-up one. They may not even ask your name, but if they do, it's Rachel Reese. The only risk is that someone does a check between the main ship's database and the technicians listing. But even if they do, by the time they discover the discrepancy, we'll be long gone. Once he knows we've succeeded, Leonard will delete all the dummy data."

The way he said it made it sound credible, if a little complicated. They joined the end of the queue until it was their turn to request a shuttle.

"Hi there," Martin said brightly. The dour male attendant yawned and said, "Stand still while I scan your job details." While Krania looked on intrigued, he then held a small device to Martin's temple while observing a near-by screen.

"Clip data validated – job location extreme south-west," was all he said, while Martin turned nonchalantly to indicate his companion saying, "She's with me."

The attendant stifled another yawn and smiled. "Name please."

Krania took a deep breath and lied, "Reese – Rachel Reese."

"Don't think I've seen you on the maintenance squad before. You look a bit young for fixing heat receptors. Are you a trainee?"

She hoped she wasn't blushing. She hadn't expected an interrogation.

"Yeah," she replied as nonchalantly as possible. "First time, umm, moon-side."

She guessed the grimace Martin was trying to suppress meant her attempt at shuttle crew slang was probably not a good idea.

But the attendant smiled. "Moon-side? I like that. Well, Rachel, why don't we get together for drinks next time you're ship-side, eh?"

She forced a smile. "We'll see."

"All right. You'll need a dedicated shuttle, I suppose. You can have the one just coming in." He spoke flatly to Martin. "Take the token and enter the airlock after all arrivals have disembarked."

A device at desk height spat out a plastic disc, which Martin grabbed. The airlock doors opened and several technicians emerged, a couple of whom cast admiring glances in Krania's direction. The couple stepped into the airlock.

"Put your helmet on, Kra – Rachel," Martin said, doing the same.

They entered the shuttle and took the two front seats. Martin clicked the disc into a slot on the console. The shuttle doors closed automatically, and there was a different kind of *swish* as the cabin pressurised.

"What was all that about clip data and waving that gadget around your ear?" Krania asked.

"We have tiny implants fitted at our temples to take all kinds of clips – for leisure, study, or any activity where we need to access specific apps or a lot of data. Technicians have them loaded with their job details. Leonard cloned one for me."

"I never noticed. Can I see? What kind of stuff can you clip in?"

"The implants are hardly visible – just two tiny holes. You can clip in any kind of data – music, books, newsreels, simulator programs. Anything. I've brought along a box of clips that might come in useful."

She was still getting her head around all this when she heard the airlock doors behind them close and saw the outer doors open.

"Can we take our helmets off now?" she asked.

"We could," he said, "but it's safer to leave them on. It's a principle we call 'belt and braces' – though I'm not sure why."

She wondered whether to explain the origins of the old metaphor to him, but her mind was in too much of a whirl. Then he pressed a button on the console, and she felt a gentle lift as the craft shot out into the void.

Smiling she turned to face him and said, "We did it, Martin!"

"We got out anyway," he said. "But if we don't change course we'll be heading for the south-west corner of the sunlight collectors on the other side of the Moon. After a minute or so you can't change the autopilot coordinates without going manual. That's where being a professional pilot does come in handy – these craft are buggers to handle manually."

"How are you going to change course then?"

"The on-board computers share a database of previous destinations. I just need to search the lists for the one we want." His nimble fingers navigated their way through the on-screen menus. "Ah, this'll be it – East Britain Landing Strip." He touched the screen to make the selection. "That's done," he said.

Krania frowned. "Is it really that easy?"

"As long as neither of the attendants notices we've changed course."

"What if they did?"

"They'd probably call us on the comms and ask us what the hell we're playing at."

A light flashed on the console.

"What's that?" Krania asked.

"That's somebody calling us on the comms," he said flatly. Then he flipped a switch and said, "Hello?"

A tinny voice said, "What the hell are you playing at?"

Krania's heart went cold, until Martin said, "Hi there, Leonard. Still playing computer games, eh?"

"Nothing beats the real thing, Martin," his friend replied. "Anyway, I just thought I'd call to wish you both the best of luck. It's only just occurred to me that we might not see each other for some time. You're not going to be able to come back, you know."

Krania gasped. She hadn't fully thought through the potential consequences for Martin – or for his family. She rested a hand gently on his arm.

"Martin, you've taken such a big risk for me."

"It's the right thing to do, Krania. And my father has given his blessing. We couldn't let them harm you the way Cropper was planning. And believe me – he was. But we've been careful. In the first place, Leonard has all the computer stuff sorted."

She studied his face seriously. "And in the second place?"

"We've concocted an alibi to protect my family."

She saw his hand hover above the *thrust* button. "It would have to be a good one. Tell me," she said.

Even through his helmet visor she knew he was taking a deep breath. "This is the story. I fell head over heels for you the first time we met, and knew I needed to be with you for the rest of my life. I couldn't stand to see you come to harm, so I planned this without any thought for the consequences. My family don't have clue. I left a goodbye letter for them to show the authorities."

For once, Krania was speechless.

Martin said to the console, "Cheers then, Leonard, and thanks. Watch your back, and say 'cheerio' to Jessica for me." Then he smiled at Krania, hit the *thrust* button and said, "Relax now. We're on our way."

CHAPTER TWENTY-FIVE
CAPITULATION

After the dust had cleared at the landing strip and she'd removed her helmet, Krania was amazed to see her parents hurrying across the open ground towards the shuttle. Martin released the door catch and followed her down the steps to meet them.

Krania fell into her mother's arms, both of them sobbing and unable to speak. Dominic shook Martin's hand vigorously and hugged him saying, "Thank you, thank you. You're forever in our debt, young man!" Then they changed partners, Dominic embracing his daughter while Sylvia smothered her embarrassed young rescuer with grateful kisses.

Finally the group walked back to the forest and Dominic's car, which he'd left parked on the perimeter track.

"You obviously got my father's call, Sir," Martin said.

"Yes," Dominic replied. "It must have been a hard decision for you all. It was also a very courageous act on your part. But you realise you've effectively burned your bridges?"

"I understand what you're saying, Governor, but we're still hoping the other watches will come to their senses. My father will continue to press for a more cooperative outcome."

"I'm afraid it's more complicated than that, Martin. My own people are just as unwilling to compromise. You'll meet the elders later on. They're good folk but their blood is up at the moment. It would help if you would talk to them and let them know we have friends on board the Salvation."

"I'll be happy to put our case to your elders, Sir."

They all climbed into the car and headed for the city, Sylvia and Krania in the rear seats. By now Sylvia's joyful tears had subsided and her vision cleared.

"By the Gods, Krania, what happened to your hair?"

Krania's eyes went up and she laughed. "It was a precaution. Nobody up there has real hair, Mum. Look, Martin's as bald as an egg."

"Yes, but he's a boy. It doesn't look so peculiar on him!"

"Oh, thanks, Mum. I didn't think I looked peculiar."

Sylvia hugged her to her. "I'm sorry, dear. I didn't mean it. At least you'll be able to grow it back. You can wear a headscarf in the meantime."

"Oh, I don't know," she giggled. "I might get used to the hairless look. What do you think, Dad?"

Dominic caught his daughter's reflection in the rear view mirror. "We've got you back, my sweet. That's all that matters to me – even if you have left all your hair behind on the Salvation. By the way, Martin, what happens to something like that? Would you incinerate it?"

"Unlikely, Sir. We don't waste anything. If I know Jessica, she'll probably stuff a cushion with it."

Dominic laughed. "Are you telling me that, after whizzing around the universe for eight hundred years, your women still have a thing about collecting cushions?"

Martin smiled. "It sounds as if our people have a lot more in common than we'd imagine."

Dominic nodded. "Well said, young man. Well said."

* * *

"Friends, I want to introduce Martin Wakefield from the star liner Salvation. He may only be nineteen years old, but he's risked his life to bring Krania back to us."

The elders applauded and some even cheered the embarrassed looking young man, while those standing closest crowded in to shake his hand.

Dominic's expression darkened as he continued, "With their two weeks deadline for us to clear out having expired, it grieves me to tell you they were contemplating Krania's execution by lethal injection."

The elders gave a collective gasp of disbelief.

"I've promised myself there's one of their number who'll sorely regret making such a proposal. But Martin's father has been arguing for cooperation with us. Before you give me your final decision as to what you want to do, I ask you to give the lad a fair hearing."

Martin began awkwardly. "Sirs, I'm a political student, so I've had some practice at public speaking, but never in a real situation like this. I'll do my best.

" My father – among others – believes there can't be much difference between us. We've all been set on a course by our ancestors – the Ancient Ones – to inherit the same legacy. And of course, we can't both have all of it. But we could each have some of it. All it takes is cooperation and understanding. If you were willing to talk about sharing these bounties, a lot of pain and suffering could be avoided."

McMahon said, "That could be interpreted as a veiled threat, young man." Some of the others murmured their agreement.

"It wasn't meant to be," Martin insisted. "I have no authority, to make either threats or treaties. I'm just looking for a way to avoid conflict. I can't even promise that my people will listen to you now, but it may not be too late. If you'd only let

Governor Bradley call my father and tell him you're willing to negotiate, there might still be a chance that the rest of the Joint Watch Committee will see sense."

"Young man, I think you're genuine," McMahon said. "But I fear your view is naïve. We've spoken of nothing else for the past two weeks, and it always comes down to the same thing. In spite of what you say – and probably believe – we can't accept that your people would ever share the Ancient Ones' bounties with us. But we know how to fight to defend what's ours – and that's what we're ready to do, to the best of our abilities."

He looked around at the other elders. "For the last time, do I speak for us all?"

Though one or two shook their heads, a clear majority either nodded, said, "Aye!" or raised their hands in agreement. Their spokesman turned to Dominic. "Governor, if you will, please call the lad's father on board the Salvation and give him our decision."

But the phone was already buzzing on Dominic's desk. He pressed the *receive* button and engaged speaker mode, so that all could hear.

"Yes, Councillor," he said.

Wakefield's voice was subdued. "Governor, I've been ordered to tell you that, as the deadline is well past, we're unable to give you any more time. Armed shuttles are already on their way to you. I advise you to get your people under cover without delay. In particular tell your district elders to vacate their dwellings, as several of their homes will be targeted. The safest place is out in the open and away from buildings."

"I'm sorry, Dominic."

"How can you possibly target the elders' dwellings?"

"Our technicians have been able to remotely access your migrant files and housing allocations. The elders' have been selected as exemplary targets."

Dominic gritted his teeth. "How long do we have?"

"I'd estimate no more than forty-five minutes. While you're getting people to safety, may I speak with my son?"

Fully understanding a parent's concern for his child, Dominic picked up the phone, cancelled speaker mode and handed it to Martin. Those elders who had brought personal comms with them were already contacting their families. Others waited impatiently to borrow phones in use.

"Use the office comms if you wish," Dominic said. "Or go to my house and use ours."

Then he turned to Shah. "Rajeev, can you put out a general message that everyone should get well clear of their dwellings?"

"I'll get onto the military to organise it. Is there anything they can do to set up a defence?"

"With pop guns against space shuttles? I don't think so. Besides, I wouldn't want them to do anything that might attract fire on our people."

McMahon overheard this. "Governor, are you saying we've just got to stand by and watch while they destroy our homes? Can't we at least use that boy as a bargaining tool?"

But when he turned to look where Martin had been standing, Dominic was glad to see that he'd had the good sense to slip silently away.

* * *

The attack came precisely as promised. The thunderous roar of the shuttles' engines was almost deafening, even though they moved and hovered several furlongs above the city. With almost sinister grace and precision the two craft performed a fascinating dance in the sky, moving swiftly to take up fixed positions directly above each target in turn. So rapid was the despatch of their missiles that no trail was visible from firing to delivery, only a spurt of dust above each imploding building, which seemed to fall in upon itself as if devoured by a vacuum. Within the space of no more than five minutes, seven of the elders' houses were thus obliterated, while ten thousand terrified citizens cowered in the streets and open spaces. Each burst of fire was met by a concerted cry as perfectly aimed artillery demolished pre-fabricated roofs and walls as if made of matchwood. The accuracy and total destructive power of the weapons used was breathtaking, and beyond the understanding of the vast majority of horrified onlookers. The entire operation was perfectly executed, frighteningly cold and clinical.

Then as quickly as the shuttles had arrived, they were gone, and all was silent once more.

The silence prevailed. Hardly anybody spoke, but most clung to their loved ones, or if close to a target site, some wandered among the rubble as if they needed to see with their own eyes that the destruction was complete. But thankfully no casualties were reported.

Eventually several of the elders drifted back to the Governor's office, where Dominic and Rajeev sat in quiet contemplation. Dominic looked up.

"Are your families safe?"

He took their collective mumble to mean that they were.

McMahon slouched towards Dominic's desk, and spoke in lowered tones. "Governor, it's taken this attack for me to realise that we have no way of directly opposing these people. It's been an expensive lesson, I'm afraid."

Dominic stood up. "I know. Well, at least we can be thankful that no lives have been lost. We have to decide what to do next."

"More to the point," the elder said, "what will *they* do?"

"I think I'm best qualified to answer that question." The voice came from the back of the room.

"Martin!" Dominic exclaimed. "Where were you hiding?"

"In a boat down by the river. With the talk of using me to bargain with, I thought it best to make myself scarce."

McMahon turned to face him. "Don't worry lad. I didn't intend that you come to any harm. Well, what will your people do next?"

"Today has been a mere indication of their capabilities. If you continue to defy them, you can expect more of the same – only more devastating next time."

"What? You mean they'll target people?"

Martin lowered his head. "There are some, like Cropper, who consider that to be a legitimate course of action. You've seen how destructive those armed shuttles can be against buildings. Imagine that sort of firepower directed at human beings."

The elder said, "You can pilot one of those things, can't you? How about the one you brought Krania home in? Couldn't we use it to fight back?"

Martin shook his head. "I can only fly on autopilot. Anyone could. But I've never flown manually, which you'd have to do in combat mode. Besides which, the craft we came in carries no weapons."

Dominic rubbed his chin. "Nevertheless I think we should send a team out to the landing strip to drag it somewhere out of sight. You never know, it might prove useful to us some day. Can you organise that, Rajeev?"

"I'll get onto it," he said, and rose to leave the office.

"Just a minute. Wait to hear what I have to say first."

He placed both hands on his desk and faced the elders.

"Though I'm sorry to say this, I had contemplated the situation we're now in, and I've thought about what we should do if we had to leave.

"First, I want you all to know that I'm not admitting defeat. I don't know how we're going to regain our share of the Ancient Ones' bounties, but I swear I'll dedicate the rest of my life to trying. For now though, we'll have to be patient, study our enemy, find their weaknesses and use them to our advantage.

"When this meeting is over I'll contact Martin's father and tell him you're prepared to leave the New Territory and go back through the culvert. I'll ask for a month to complete the withdrawal."

McMahon straightened and said, "Why that much time, Governor?"

"Because we're not going away from here empty-handed. For one thing, there's a good harvest in the stores and I don't see why it should feed those who haven't worked for it. We'll raise new barns on the other side of the Wall and store enough to feed any who are prepared to establish a settlement there. The rest can be shared among the families who elect to travel back to their home villages. We should also take anything that might prove useful – not the gadgets or vehicles of course, because we'll no longer have access to electrical power. But of manual tools and weapons, we should take all that can be carried."

Another elder said, "There's dried foods and emergency rations in some of those warehouses, Governor. I tried some once – not all that tasty but it filled my belly for the day!"

This produced a weak spasm of laughter from around the room. But Dominic's expression remained serious.

"We must deprive them of anything that's useful – even dwellings if there's time to dismantle any of them."

McMahon said, "The culvert is bound to prove a bottleneck, Governor. How will we get all this stuff through in time?"

"We'll organise ourselves into watches, as they do on board the Salvation. We'll work day and night. I'll talk to the ferrymen about adapting their biggest barges to carry the maximum cargo through on each trip, with an empty one ready to send back for immediate loading. And there should be a rule – nobody goes through the culvert empty-handed."

Rajeev said, "You know, Dominic, sooner or later they'll realise what's happening. What if they try to stop us taking everything?"

Dominic scratched his head. "Yes, I know that's a possibility. I'll try to persuade them to keep out of the way during the evacuation. It's possible they'll agree, if I give them my word we'll be gone by a fixed date. From what Martin tells me, they're still focussed on repairing the lunar energy cells, so that'll take their attention for a while. But if they do decide to interfere, we'll have to make do with whatever we can shift in the meantime. That's why we have to make a start this evening."

A voice from the middle of the room shouted, "How will we decide who stays on the other side, and who goes back to their home villages?"

"Nobody will be pressed to stay. The purpose of the settlement here will be to make life as difficult as possible for the newcomers. I'm not suggesting we provoke or challenge them openly, but I'm sure we'll find ways to frustrate their objectives – become a thorn in their sides. And, as long as we keep a foothold here, we'll live in the prospect of eventually turning the tables and regaining our birthright.

"Well, what do you say? Are you with me?"

McMahon looked around and obviously saw what Dominic saw – an array of smiling faces that for once bore a trace of hope – hope that had been denied them these past catastrophic weeks.

"Aye, Governor," he said. "We're with you to a man!"

"Good. I'm appointing Rajeev Shah as Deputy Governor to oversee all of this while I'm gone."

The man's jaw dropped. "Gone, Governor? Why? Where are you going?"

"It's two weeks since my brother-in-law sent news of the slave rebellion. Obviously my hands have been tied by events here. But now I have to go to Crowtree and help him if I can, and I'll need volunteers to come with me. Rajeev is more than capable of organising the evacuation here. Meanwhile the good folk of Crowtree and Ashwell are suffering. I can't ignore their pleas. I'll be leaving the day after tomorrow. Now, if you'll excuse me, I need to send Jack a note by pigeon post."

But what he didn't tell them – because the thought was still just a ghost of an idea in his mind – was that he sensed a connection between the resolution of their challenges here and the source of the present troubles in old Fenwold. And that had to do with Jack's mention of the recent rise of an offspring of his old archenemy – the vicious and murderous outlaw who had been known simply as Red.

CHAPTER TWENTY-SIX
EXODUS

"Looking at this river, Sean, I wonder how many conflicts it's seen over the millennia."

"Several, I should think, Marshal."

It amused Dominic that the former fisherman and long-term ferry port master still used his old title. In their meetings – too infrequent these days – neither Sean nor his son Toby had grown used to addressing him as 'Governor', and he'd long ago given up bothering to correct them.

Toby said, "According to their history books, the people even fought with other nations over the right to take fish from the sea! Can you imagine it, when there's plenty there for everyone?"

Dominic took a swig of beer. "I gather it wasn't always so, Toby. But wars are usually about an unwillingness to share resources – though they're often dressed up in other clothes. I suppose it'll always be so."

Sean nodded. "That's clearly the case with the present confrontation. Mind you, I can fully understand why you've had to back down, in the face of their weaponry. Do you know, we could see and hear yesterday's attack clearly from this side of the river, and we're almost two leagues off? We feared for you all, and we were ready to come across and help you. But as nobody lit a beacon we assumed our services weren't needed."

Dominic smiled. "The old systems always work best. But I'm sorry to have to bring you such bad news, Sean. You and your kinfolk have kept the ferry service going for nigh on twenty years. After most of the families migrate back to Fenwold you'll not be seeing much traffic, I'm afraid."

Sean placed a friendly arm on his shoulder. "Don't you worry about us, Marshal. If all else fails we can always go back to fishing. By the way, how long are they allowing you to evacuate?"

"Just two weeks. I'd asked for a month, but at the rate our people are working, I'm hoping it'll be enough."

"Well, I'm certain in time you'll find a way to prevail. Then we'll have more passengers than we'll know what to do with. Meanwhile I'll do as you ask and send a couple of big cargo barges across straight away."

"Thanks for that, Sean. Our settlers have been working hard through the night piling stuff up at our end of the culvert ready to transport through. Our plan is to strip the settlement and warehouses of everything that's useful. There's no point in making the newcomers' lives any easier for them – nor ours any harder."

"That makes a lot of sense."

He paused for a moment, as if searching for the right words.

"How did your people react when you told them you'd be travelling south tomorrow?"

Dominic's brow furrowed. "Not too well. I half expected it though. After all, few of them know where Crowtree is, let alone feel any duty towards its inhabitants. I believe they understand my feelings, though I overheard some criticising me for deserting them. I can't tell you how that made me feel."

Sean stared into his beer. "You're faced with an impossible choice, Marshal. No man can say whether you're right or wrong. In such a position, you have to follow your heart."

Smiling again, Dominic said, "I knew I'd come to the right place to hear some words of wisdom. Well, there's no doubt where my heart lies just now. The people of Crowtree – my old comrades – are asking for help. There's little more I can do here for a while. I have to go to them."

"Right then," said Sean. "To practical matters. How big a force will be going with you?"

"I've chosen six serving law officers, plus an equal number of militiamen who can handle a hunting rifle. And we'll be taking some extra weapons for our friends in Crowtree. There'll still be a decent force staying to defend the new settlement, under Rajeev's leadership."

The ferryman screwed up his eyes as he took in the numbers. "I suppose you'll be bringing horses and wagons across. You do realise it'll take a while to fetch you all over?"

"I didn't expect we'd do it in a single trip. I thought you could take most of the horses and riders first, then the munitions wagon and four guards with their mounts."

Sean looked at the sky. "It's a pity you couldn't have started out this morning – the weather's fair and there's a good breeze."

"I know. I'd like to have made a start today, but there are too many preparations to take care of – such as organising the munitions wagon. We'll need as much fire power and as many spare shells as we can carry."

"I'm surprised the Fenwold lawmen have never taken to the modern firearms, Marshal."

"It's true they've preferred to rely on their crossbows. Then again, until now things have been fairly peaceful across most of Fenwold. There hasn't been a need for the modern weaponry."

Then Toby, who had been listening intently, said, "I can fire a rifle, Marshal. I'd like to come with you."

His father looked stunned. But after a few moments he said deliberately, "When you were five years old you were man enough to withstand all the foul treatment that that bastard Red handed to you as his hostage. You're more than man enough now to help Marshal Bradley bring the outlaw's spawn to justice. If the Marshal will have you, then go with my blessing!"

"I'll be glad to have you along, Toby," Dominic said. "I'll need men I can trust to guard our munitions wagon – you can be one of them. Be ready to join us here tomorrow morning."

Toby stood to attention and proudly declared, "Yes, Marshal!"

Then Dominic added, "I recall I made you an honorary deputy marshal after your ordeal twenty years ago, but I think we can now make your appointment official!"

* * *

"Sylvia, can you find me some better stirrups than these? This left one looks like it's about to snap."

"I'm busy packing just now, Dominic. Have a look in the tack shed, won't you?"

"Packing? There's no need. I have all I need in my horse's saddlebags."

"There's every need. Krania and I can't travel without at least a change of clothing. Then there's…"

He shook his head. "You're not coming."

"Oh, yes we are."

"Sylvia, don't be silly."

"But why shouldn't we come? Can't you understand that I want to see my brothers again?"

"Of course I understand that, but you must see that it's just not possible under the present circumstances. Besides, what if all the other families wanted to follow their men into battle?"

"But that's different, Dominic. They wouldn't be going home!"

"But this is your home! Why can't you and Krania wait here till I return? Then later, when things are settled, we'll all go and visit your family together."

"I'll tell you why – because we'll be worried sick wondering what's happened to you. Besides, I can fight as well as any…"

"I know – as well as any man."

"Yes. And you know that's true."

"That may have been true twenty years ago, but…"

"Oh! So, you're writing me off as an old woman, are you? I bet it would be a different story if it were Cara who wanted to go with you!"

He checked his temper and grasped her wrist, pulled her towards him and circled his free arm about her. "Darling, you know that's ridiculous. I'm only concerned about your safety, you know."

Tearfully she said, "I know. But my brothers need me. And seeing you go to join them in that cauldron of danger, without knowing your fate – it's going to drive me crazy. Can't you see that?"

"We all have to make sacrifices," he said.

She rubbed her eyes, dried them on the sleeve of her tunic and sniffed. "Very well, Dominic. You're right, of course. I'm just being a silly woman. You'd better finish getting ready. Your ferry leaves in an hour. Your platoon will be waiting."

His cheek twitched as it did on those rare occasions when he was annoyed with her, but he saw no purpose in further discussion. He thanked goodness she'd come around to his way of thinking. He went into the shed where their riding gear and harness were kept, and rummaged around to find the best of a neglected bunch of well-used leathers. He wished he'd given more time to riding, but over these latter years he'd somehow drifted out of the habit, often deferring to the speed and comfort of his electric car.

Still rattled by his words with Sylvia, he heard heavy footsteps approaching from behind, and turned to see a uniformed figure standing in the shed doorway.

"Good morning, Governor!"

He screwed his eyes against the glare of early morning sunlight behind the imposing silhouette. Then a smile of recognition crossed his lips, and he held out his hand in welcome.

"Why, if it isn't my riddle messenger, Forty-Two!" he said. Then he frowned apologetically. "I'm afraid that, what with all that's been going on, we never did find time to have our planned get-together. I'd ask if you and your family got settled in to your new home, but I fear all that's irrelevant now."

"It's unfortunate, Sir, but at least we haven't been here long enough to get our roots too firmly fixed in the ground. I feel sorry for the families who've invested their lives in this place though – it'll be hard for them to give up what they had here."

"Aye, that's true, lad. I see you're kitted up for action. Have you come to volunteer your services?"

The young deputy shuffled his feet. "I'd have come before now, but my wife wasn't happy about going back to Roundhill." He looked glum. "But I explained to her that it was a matter of duty."

"That's very loyal of you," Dominic said, and then thought for a second. "She needn't go back though. You could be as much help defending the new settlement just beyond the Wall. And before you start that job, there's something else that I want you to do. I was going to select someone from my own troops, but there aren't that many of them. Besides, you'd be the ideal man."

"Oh? What do you want of me, Sir?"

"I want you to take a message to the Capital. The Council ought to know what's going on. We'll find a good horse for you. You're to deliver my letter into the hand of Councillor Pieter Jennings. He's a Tribune of the High Council, and an old friend of mine."

"Should I bring his reply to you in Crowtree, Governor?"

Dominic picked up the stirrups he'd selected. "No - come straight back here where your family needs you. Take one of my niece's pigeons for Jennings' reply – it'll reach me sooner. Look, come into the house. I'm better at wielding a sword than a pen. It'll be quicker if I dictate something for my daughter to write down. Tell your superior I've commandeered your services. Then say your farewells to your family and ride as soon as you can. If you're quick you can have a lift across the river on one of our ferries. Follow me."

* * *

When the ferry was loaded with horses and supplies, as well as his courier Forty-Two, Dominic boarded and turned to address a small crowd of well-wishers on the shore. He was disappointed that he didn't see his wife and daughter among them. His old friend Rajeev and Krania's rescuer Martin were there though, and their smiles cheered him to a degree.

"Friends, I'll keep this short, because we're keen to get going. As you know Fenwold once more faces the threat of terror from outlaw gangs. But armed with superior weapons it shouldn't take us long to suppress the slave uprising. I promise you we'll be returning very soon with news of victory!"

A modest cheer rose from the crowd, and he signalled the shore hands to slip the retaining ropes. Then the gathering dispersed as the ferry put out to cross the river.

Once out of earshot of the dispersing crowd, he called his men together and addressed them.

"I think you all know Marshal Owen McMahon."

He beckoned to a ruddy-faced, stocky but tough-looking man of about thirty, who stepped forward to stand beside him.

"Marshal McMahon carries the authority of his father, the senior district elder of the New Territory, and will act as my second-in-command on this mission. You will take orders directly from him. You are all carefully selected marshals, deputies and crack militia, in whom I have every confidence. For speed we're dispensing with a provisions wagon – you've all had instructions to carry your own rations. You'll be able to supplement these with game from the forest. I estimate – barring any unexpected delays – that we'll make Crowtree in four days. Marshal McMahon will be checking your weapons soon, but in addition we're taking a wagonload of munitions along with us. As these constitute artillery that's far and away superior to the bows and arrows of the insurgents, they'll be crucial to the success of our mission. I've already assigned four guards to the security of that wagon. Three of them will accompany it on the next boat, and the fourth will join us at the ferry port.

"Please carry on, Marshal."

As McMahon assumed authority and set about giving out detailed orders to the troops, Dominic sniffed the air and wondered if the weather would, in fact, be kind to them on their journey. Though late in the year, the day was fresh but fair, and a benevolent wind filled the sails to carry them to the southern shore. As he watched the skill of the helmsman at the big tiller he half regretted that he'd never taken up Sean's offer to teach him sailing. But there was no time for such fanciful thoughts now. After twenty years of settling trivial disputes and routine administration he was back doing what he'd been trained to do

– to lead warriors into battle, to fight, to defeat an enemy and, if necessary, to risk his life for what was right.

* * *

No sooner had the last trooper set foot on the southern shore than the wind freshened considerably and black clouds mustered along the northern hills. Toby presented himself for duty, accompanied by his father, who offered his hand to Dominic.

"I wish your cause good fortune, Marshal, and a safe and favourable outcome for you and all your men."

"Thank you, Sean. The hunting rifles will assure our victory."

The fisherman smiled. "As you see, Toby carries his own – and he knows how to use it. I hope and believe he'll prove an able and worthy warrior."

"Of that I'm in no doubt, if his skill matches the courage I know he possesses."

He called McMahon to his side. "We've a tedious wait of an hour and a half for the empty ferry to return and collect the munitions wagon and guards. Tell the men they can wait in the tavern, but they're to have no more than a quart of beer apiece. If they want anything more to drink, it'll have to be tea."

"Yes, Sir," McMahon said, and went to do his bidding.

The time then dragged until at last the Marshal gave the order to line up and move off, while the first heavy drops of rain stung the cheeks of horses and men, dampening clothing and threatening to tarnish the sheen on polished leather.

* * *

"You'd think they'd turn round and go home, Sean."

"After travelling all this way, Luke? Would you?"

The two cousins took a draught of ale at the little tavern barely ten strides from the quayside, watching the latest batch of hopeful Fenwold emigrants waiting in the rain to undertake the last stage of their long journey to become citizens of the New Territory. The dreadful news of the recent capitulation hadn't yet travelled south of the river – so still they came. Today there were about a dozen of them.

"You've explained the situation over there, haven't you? Well then, what's the point of making the crossing? There's nothing for them there now."

The boatman shrugged. "Many of them have never sailed before – even on a ferry. Perhaps they'd been looking forward to the experience."

Luke laughed. "In this foul weather? I know where I'd rather be!"

"Don't get too cosy. If they want to go, I have to take them. With Toby gone off with Marshal Bradley, and the fellow who helped me with the last two crossings away to tend to his ploughing, I'm in need of a rudder man."

His cousin halted in raising his mug to his lips. "So that's why you offered to buy me a drink! You sly old dog!" He drained his mug in one draught. "Well, I'm sorry to tell you the full price of my services includes three more drinks – one more on the other side and two when we return!"

"All right," Sean grinned, and finished his beer. "Looks like they're getting restless. We'd best get going. Break out some of those waterproof sheets from Cara's stores, will you?"

As he got up Luke said, "I wonder how much longer we'll hear that phrase repeated. Cara's stores have fed the growth of that city over there – and the crumbs from their table have been welcome here in old Fenwold too. Waterproofs, weapons, books and learning – all sorts of things we'll have to get used to doing without again. It's a sad time for us all."

Sean said, "We'll see. When Marshal Bradley returns, he'll maybe have some ideas. He's not let us down yet."

"But his best days are behind him. Sooner or later an old warhorse is happier being put out to grass."

His cousin shook his head. "Not the Marshal, Luke. I'd put my last ounce of faith in him. Anyway, unfasten that rope and let's push off."

The two men did what they'd been raised to do. They mastered the wind and waves to take their craft where they wanted it to go – Sean working the sails and Luke on the tiller. Their cargo of refugees from hardship huddled under the waterproofs they'd provided, clinging desperately to their meagre possessions and peering out at the opposite shore, their hearts full of expectation in spite of the ferryman's disappointing tidings.

At last the boat made shore and the bedraggled passengers got up to disembark. Usually, once cargo – human or otherwise – was set down on the bank, it only remained to release the retaining rope and make the return journey. Occasionally they'd collect goods for use by residents at the ferry port, or there'd be traders crossing with produce or examples of Cara's bounties to barter or sell on their sojourns throughout Fenwold. None were expected today, so Sean beckoned through the rain to his cousin to cast off.

"Wait! Hold on there!"

Three hooded figures approached the quayside on horseback, dismounting – in one case, less than gracefully – on arrival. One of the three – a woman, Sean thought – fumbled with a purse to extract some coins.

"How much is it now, Sean? I've not used your ferry for a few years."

He started. He recognised the voice but wouldn't have expected to hear it in these circumstances, nor today of all days.

"Why, Sylvia, is that you? Whatever are you doing, wanting to cross the river in such foul weather?"

She sighed. "I'm going to visit my family in Crowtree with my daughter and her friend. And as my husband is clearly unwilling to let us travel under his troops' protection, we're forced to follow at a distance. Now, how much to take us across – with the horses, of course?"

"I wouldn't take your money, Sylvia. We have to go back no matter what. Put your purse away. But – are you certain you want to make this trip? It looks like winter's coming in with a vengeance, and Dominic told me it's at least four days journey in the best of weather."

"I've travelled in worse conditions than this, Sean – as you know full well. Now, are you going to let us on board, or do you expect us to swim?"

He didn't answer, but merely stood aside and watched the three sorry looking travellers board, tether their horses in the purpose-made stalls and take their seats close by.

The two seafaring cousins exchanged glances with raised eyebrows, and knowing Sylvia to be a headstrong woman, Sean realised there was no point in further discussion. He looked at the sky and checked the direction of the wind, then shouted the expected command to Luke, though for once it lacked its usual enthusiasm.

"Cast off!"

And as the fresh breeze filled the mainsail, they skilfully and silently steered their craft through the foam-topped waves of the untameable river.

CHAPTER TWENTY-SEVEN
QUAGMIRE

"This is marvellous, Krania!"

Martin flung back his head and let the rain cascade onto his face. It hadn't let up since the heavens opened twenty-four hours earlier, but this was the first section of their journey where they couldn't resort to woodland trails for some degree of shelter. They'd spent the night at Nearbank, where Sean and Toby had lived before establishing the ferry port, several leagues to the east of the New Territory, beyond the great bridge, on the southern shore close to the mouth of the estuary.

Sylvia had explained the geography to Krania before they'd fallen into the cots provided by Sean's kindly relatives.

"When your father, Rajeev and I stumbled on this place twenty years ago, there wasn't a road in or out. The villagers had voluntarily quarantined the entire area years before because of a suspected plague outbreak. We had to machete our way through from the west – and we weren't even sure there was a village here at all. Since then they've cut a new road to the south, which I'm unfamiliar with, so it'll be best not to deviate from it."

This meant that, without even the partial cover of the forest, they'd taken the full force of the rain since leaving Nearbank.

Krania's jaw dropped at Martin's observation.

"Marvellous? Are you joking?"

"Not at all," he said. "Can I remind you that it doesn't often rain in space? This is a new experience for me."

Sylvia said, "But surely you have showers on board the Salvation."

"Yes, we do, Mistress Bradley. But use of water is strictly rationed. Each shower burst is timed. You get fifteen seconds to wet yourself, then you apply soap substitute, then you get thirty seconds to rinse off."

Krania said, "That can't be enough – how can you get a proper shower in so short a time?"

Sylvia laughed. "It may not have occurred to you yet, but very soon the luxury of running water and showers is going to be a thing of the past for all of us. So make the most of these natural downpours. Anyway, if you don't like the rain, pull your waterproof over you properly. And try not to slouch in the saddle."

Krania gave her a sideways glance and made a pointed display of adjusting her posture.

"How are you coping with your first time on horseback, Martin?" Sylvia asked him.

"I'm enjoying the experience, though the saddle's a bit hard."

Krania muttered, "It's not the saddle that's hard – it's your bum that's too skinny."

"Krania, that's not very nice," said her mother.

"No, it's all right, Mistress Bradley," Martin said. "Most of us on the Salvation are on the thin side – it's an observation I've made during the few days I've spent among your people on Earth. Don't misunderstand me – no one goes hungry on the Salvation. But our foods are carefully prepared to provide the maximum nutrition with minimum weight gain. You see, living as we do in low gravity, it keeps us trim for when we eventually migrate to a high gravity planet."

"That Cropper bloke must have slipped through the net then," Krania observed. "He looked to me to have a serious weight problem."

"He claims to have a clinical metabolic imbalance," Martin said. "But he's probably a secret overeater."

"That reminds me of something I was wondering about at supper the other evening," Sylvia said. "What do you people eat? You don't keep livestock, or grow crops in the fields like we do."

"We do grow some crops, using hydroponics – feeding them nutrients, light and moisture artificially. But you're right about animals. We have some pets and a sort of zoo – to maintain certain genetic examples. But none of us have tasted meat for centuries. Most of our food is synthetic – or recycled."

"Recycled?" Krania said. "I don't think I like the sound of that, if it means what I think it means."

"Most of what you ate while you were with us was recycled food, Krania. You didn't complain about the taste, as I recall."

She looked strangely thoughtful following Martin's observation, so Sylvia asked him, "What about you? How do you like the food you've been eating here?"

"I found it strange at first – eating cooked animal parts in particular. But if I'm to make my life here, I realise I have to get used to eating what you do. And I can't deny I'm coming across flavours I've never experienced before. It's as if I'm discovering my sense of taste for the first time."

As Sylvia thought about the changes Martin must be going through, and how adaptable he seemed to be in the face of all these new experiences, she was suddenly snapped out of her train of thought by a shocking realisation.

"Oh, by the Gods of the Wall, something's just struck me!"

"What's up, Mum?" Krania asked.

"It didn't occur to me to ask our hosts if and when your father's troops passed through the village."

"So?"

"Look at the ground here. It's been raining for twenty-four hours and it's muddy. But do you see any ruts made by a heavy artillery wagon? Or the hoof marks of several heavily laden horses?"

"Oh," Krania said. "No, I don't. The track ahead looks as though it hasn't been used in months."

"Could your husband's troops have taken another route?" Martin asked.

"They must have," Sylvia said. "I should have checked with Sean before we left the ferry port. But he and his cousin went straight into the tavern. Dominic's brigade must have headed directly south, along the western trail that runs closer to the Wall."

"Is there a proper trail there?" Krania asked.

"There's always been one, but as far as I know it's seldom used. I suppose he must have wanted to take the shortest route. I'd sort of hoped to catch up with them in a day or two. That's obviously not going to happen."

Krania said, "But at least we'll be keeping to the safe trails, even if our route isn't a straight line. Do you think the western trail will be passable in this awful weather?"

Sylvia merely pulled her waterproof sheet closer to her and said, "I don't know, Krania. Let's hope so."

* * *

"I'm beginning to think this was a bad choice, Marshal."

McMahon shrugged. "It should be the most direct route under normal conditions, Governor. It's just our bad luck that this rain looks to have set in for the duration. It hasn't let up these past three days. We can only hope it eases off soon."

274

Dominic checked his horse as it stumbled in the mud. "I'd expected this road to be better maintained. We send enough in taxes to the Capital each year to pay for this sort of thing. Well, we're too far on to justify turning round and crossing over to the central trail. It was about this time yesterday that we passed the western junction, so that would mean losing at least another two whole days. We'll just have to make what progress we can. Look for a break in the woodland where we can stop and rest the horses for a while. I'm going to backtrack down the column and offer the men some words of cheer – if I can think of any!"

As he did so, tarrying alongside each pair of bedraggled riders in turn to say something to raise their spirits, he noted how stretched out the platoon had become since leaving their overnight campsite earlier that morning. By the time he reached the back markers, he judged that he'd ridden at least a furlong and a half from the head of the column. It was understandable in a way, because travelling was miserable for men and horses in this weather. It was so easy to adopt a sluggish gait. But he decided not to make an issue of it, because they'd be re-grouping soon anyway. That would give him a chance to warn them to stick closer together.

Then something occurred to him that made his blood run cold.

Unable to conceal his agitation he said to the back-markers, "Where's the munitions wagon?"

The two riflemen exchanged sheepish glances, and the one who looked the elder straightened and said, "I last saw them half an hour ago, Governor. They were about two furlongs behind, but it was a long straight stretch and there didn't seem to be a problem."

The younger militiaman smiled and said, "There's nothing but dense forest to their left and those big hills to their right, Governor. There's nowhere else for them to go. They're bound to make up their lost ground before too long."

Dominic bit his lip. He wasn't about to criticise the lad merely for his lack of experience. So he said, "I want you two to ride back and check that they're all right, then report straight back to me."

"Yes, Governor," they responded in unison, and turned their horses' heads ready to carry out his instruction.

But before they could complete the manoeuvre, there came a deep rumble from back along the trail, which grew in volume until it resembled a mighty peal of thunder. Dominic peered down the muddy track for as far as he could see, until some movement on the hillside far off to his left grabbed his attention. Now focussing through the rain, he couldn't believe what his eyes were telling him.

The whole hillside was collapsing.

* * *

"Did you hear that?"

Krania sat up in the saddle and collected her reins in reflex to the sound.

"Sounds like distant thunder," her mother said.

"I'm not so sure, Mum. It sounded sort of spooky. Do you think we've done right in taking this cross trail?"

"Why not? It's a well-kept surface."

"So was the road we were on, and if we'd stayed on it we'd have come to Crowtree eventually."

"But we know your father's taken the western trail."

"I don't know why you're so eager to catch up with him. You know he's going to be livid when he sees we've disobeyed him."

"Disobeyed?" her mother snapped. "I didn't marry your father to spend my life as his servant! And if you ever have plans to trade your freedom just to get a man in your bed, you'll sorely disappoint me, girl!"

Krania looked embarrassed, her eyes skewing towards Martin, who appeared to be studying the forest on the opposite side of the trail. In lowered tones she said, "All right, Mum! I'm sorry. I used the wrong word. I meant, well, there's going to be a row between you two, and I'd sooner put it off as long as possible. I don't like it when the pair of you argue."

"Oh," Sylvia said more calmly. "I see. I'm sorry if I flew off the handle, dear. I don't want to quarrel with your father. You know I love him very much. It's just that sometimes he's over-protective. I promise I'll try and smooth things over when we meet. Does that make you feel better?"

"A bit. But what if he's right and we are riding into danger?"

"Raiders don't like the rain any more than we do. Besides, we're armed and we have Martin to protect us." She tried not to remind herself that, given his background, though intelligent and courageous, Martin had probably no experience of combat situations.

At the mention of his name their young companion smiled, touched his backpack and said, "That's right, ladies."

Krania asked, "What exactly have you got in there, Martin?"

Still smiling, he merely said, "Useful things."

Seeing that he wasn't about to elaborate, Sylvia said, "So you see, we've nothing to fear. Cheer up. It won't be long now till we reach the junction with the western trail."

Afternoon saw them riding south along the looser, muddier track that led directly towards Crowtree, though they knew in these conditions that their destination must lay at least a day and a half ahead of them. Sylvia was thankful that the rain was now less intense, as they made their way through countryside that would have looked pleasant on a fine day, with the woodlands to their left and grassy slopes on their right hand.

Suddenly Sylvia pulled up and signalled for the others to do likewise. Then she drove her horse under the cover of the woodland, ensuring Martin and Krania followed her.

"What's up, Mum?" Krania asked urgently.

"I saw horsemen ahead."

"Are you sure? I didn't see anyone."

"That's because you're slouching and not paying attention."

Krania sighed. "All right, Mum. What are we going to do?"

"They were coming this way. Dismount, keep the horses still and let them ride past."

Krania said, "We should pull further in. Their horses might smell ours."

"It's good to know you're thinking smart for once. Take mine and I'll hide here."

"What for?"

"Because I want to see who or what they are."

So Krania led her own and her mother's horses deeper into the forest, followed by Martin with his mount, while Sylvia concealed herself behind a blackthorn bush and peered through its branches at the approaching riders.

It was only when they'd ridden a further ten strides that she heard the rattle and clatter of wagon wheels. She looked more closely as it passed. It looked familiar. She was certain she'd seen the wagon being loaded the day before the troops had embarked. She recognised the shape of the boxes – four long wooden ones for the hunting rifles, and several cubic metal containers for the spare ammunition.

She emerged and stepped out onto the track.

"Whoa!" A third rider pulled his horse up abruptly to avoid running her down. Startled, she turned around.

"Miss Sylvia!"

There was only one person in the whole of Fenwold who would address her thus. She stared at the startled horseman.

"Toby! What are you doing here? And where are you taking my husband's munitions wagon?"

"I joined the Marshal's platoon at the ferry port. He assigned me to the detail guarding the wagon. But all this rain's started a landslide along the trail. It's completely blocked, and there's no way we can drive it through the forest. So he wants us to take it all the way back to the cross trail and bring it around to Crowtree using the central route."

By now, Krania and Martin had left the cover of the forest to see what was happening.

Martin stepped forward. "Excuse me, but by my reckoning that's going to take you an extra two days. What about the rest of the force?"

Toby said, "They were well ahead of us when the hillside came down. They're pushing on, because Marshal Bradley doesn't want to waste any more time in getting help to Crowtree."

Krania said, "But this wagon could make all the difference! What are they going to do when their ammunition runs out?"

Martin spoke again. "Let me understand this. Governor Bradley and his platoon are further along this trail and on their way to Crowtree?"

"Correct," Toby said. "We were forced to stop and shift the wagon when it got stuck in a rut. It took a while because we had to unload the munitions to shift it, and then re-load them again. Then the landslide cut us off from the main party."

"So between the platoon and the munitions detail, half of that mountain…" Martin pointed to the hills to the west. "…is now blocking the trail."

Toby nodded.

"So, how did Governor Bradley give you the order to backtrack?"

"There are deer trails in the forest. Marshal – I mean Governor Bradley is an excellent woodsman. Though it meant a six furlong detour, he found a way through the woods to get to us."

"So why not take the wagon through using the deer trails?"

By now all six of the mounted munitions detail had gathered around the wagon, and to a man they laughed raucously at Martin's suggestion.

He, however, was clearly unimpressed by their reaction.

"Well, why not?"

Krania helped him out. "Even I know that deer trails are too narrow for a horse-drawn wagon, Martin."

Sylvia added, "And widening them is a long and arduous job. Believe me, I know this from experience." She took a machete from one of her saddlebags. "By the way, how many of these do we have among us?"

Toby produced the only other machete from his own gear, while the rest of the platoon shuffled in their saddles. One of them protested morosely, "Nobody told me machetes were meant to be part of our kit."

With raised eyebrows Sylvia said, "Well, I estimate that two machetes will see us through the job in four to five days. I expect my husband made a similar calculation. I have to say that I agree with his decision to send you round the long way. You'd better carry on."

But Martin persisted. Swinging off his backpack he said, "No. Wait, please. I have something here that might help."

While the others stood by amazed, he took out a metallic object resembling a broad-barrelled handgun.

"What's that?" Krania asked.

"Something very versatile. I took Governor Bradley at his word when he encouraged us to take anything that might be useful from Cara's stores. I believe these were originally designed for agricultural use, from what I've seen on the newsreels. It's an electronic multi-tool driver. You clip various devices to it, depending on what you want to do. As what we need is a cutting tool…"

He extracted another instrument from his knapsack, and clipped it to the driver. Then he held it up for everyone to see.

Krania said, "Didn't you say it was electronic?"

"Yes."

"But you're forgetting that we don't have the benefit of electricity way out here."

He smiled. "I know," he said. Then he rummaged in his bag and produced what appeared to be a small black box. "Hence, the third and most important element."

Sylvia grinned. "A battery. Clever boy. How fast is this going to work?"

He inserted the battery into a cavity in the handle of the driver. "Well, let's try it." He spoke to Toby. "Take me to where these deer trails begin."

"It's a good way back," Toby said, leading them down the trail until they reached the first incursion of the landslide. Sylvia saw that it was massive and would certainly require an extensive detour. She thought it ironic that the rain had now virtually ceased, and that patches of blue showed through gaps in the cloud.

"We'd have to begin cutting here," Toby said, making way for Martin to step forward.

"All right," he said. "I haven't done this before, so you'd better stand back. He pointed the cutter at the undergrowth on the left hand side of the trail and squeezed the handle. An enormous flame leapt from the tool, which immediately engulfed the target shrubbery, igniting the surrounding foliage. Quickly he depressed a button, and a spurt of white gas erupted from the nozzle, quickly dowsing the fire.

"Sorry," he said. "I had the setting too high. I'll reduce the temperature."

He made an adjustment to a dial on the driver and aimed the cutter at the next section of undergrowth. Within a matter of seconds he had reduced it to a pile of gently smoking ash that covered an area about two strides square.

He turned and asked, "Is this wide enough to pull your wagon through?"

"Yes," Toby said. No one else spoke.

"I'll continue then, shall I?"

Sylvia said, "Yes, please, Martin. Do you think you can keep this up at the same rate?"

"Yes, though my wrist might tire. I'll let you know when I need someone to take over."

"This is incredible," she said. "I calculate – without hitches – that you can cut a trail through in a matter of hours."

"What about batteries?" Krania asked. "They obviously won't last forever."

"Ah, yes," he said. "To be honest, I have no idea how long a battery will last. This is clearly a high energy job, so I imagine I'll get through quite a few."

"How many do you have?" Sylvia asked.

He hesitated. She suspected he was being careful.

"Ten."

"All right, you lovely boy. Go for it."

CHAPTER TWENTY-EIGHT
RECALL TO ACTION

Jack Storey peered out from his kitchen window into the evening gloom.

"There's more than a half moon, Lucy. See how it lights up the clearing whenever the clouds clear."

"Is that good or bad?" his wife asked anxiously.

"Good, I suppose. It means that if they come, we should see them. Based on that alone, I'd say they'd choose to stay away tonight. On the other hand, I reckon their maniac leader doesn't think like a normal man. He could decide to attack just because he thinks we're not expecting him to. And after five solid days of rain his rabble will be itching for some action."

"Oh, Jack, I'm sick of all this waiting. All the slaves have joined him now. Sooner or later he's bound to attack our stores. Do you think our defences are good enough?"

He couldn't bring himself to give her a straight answer.

"Every able man stands a nightly vigil guarding the village entrance or the main store. But they're ploughing in the fields by day, so by nightfall they're pretty well exhausted. Our defenders are few enough, but worse than that I fear they'll not be fully alert when the raiders attack – as they surely will. We can only hope we have the strength to hold them off."

His daughter Emily went over to him by the window. "Daddy, Uncle Dominic is coming to help us though, isn't he?"

He smiled down at her. "Yes, my sweet. And I'm sure he'll be here soon – along with the rifles he promised us. But be a good girl and stay away from the window."

Obediently she went back to her mother by the fire.

Lucy said, "At least the houses are protected by the old fortifications."

He nodded. "Yes. And I've done what I can over the past couple of weeks to get the spikes and pits back up to standard. But I wish we'd had the labour to do the same around the storage barn. There are quite a few gaps. I'm hoping they won't know where."

"Some of the runaway slaves know where the weak points are," she said, biting her lip.

He made no comment, but moved towards the door and removed the retaining bar. "I'm going over to the store now. You have your crossbows and plenty of bolts. Emily, remember always to keep one bow primed ready for your mother to shoot if an attack should come."

His daughter showed him a serious face that almost brought tears to his eyes. "I will Daddy. It's hard work but I've been practising."

"Good girl," he said, and then smiled at his wife. "I don't expect them to attack the house, but you know what to do if that should happen. Bolt the door after I've gone."

"I will," she assured him. "You go now – and be careful."

With the door closed behind him he waited, crossbow in hand, for the moon to disappear behind a cloud before moving across the open space towards the main barn. As he approached the building he gave a low whistle. The echoed response came from Danny, his deputy, who stood back in the shadow at the side of the building. He went over and stood beside him.

"Any sign of movement?" he asked.

"Not yet, Marshal. For a frontal attack they'd have to come down the track from the village entrance, so we'd be sure to see them.

"Who's watching the rear?"

"Dan Benson and Archie Forrester."

"Dan? Our old blacksmith's a bit long in the tooth for this sort of thing."

"You'd think so, but you know how stubborn he can be. He insisted. Says he's doing it for Ryan."

"He's a good man. It must have been hard when he lost his son in the battle all those years ago – the only fatality on our side."

Both men took a second to remember their brave companion.

Then Jack said, "Cover me while I go and see what's happening at the village entrance."

He walked down the track towards the place where it twisted through a thicket before joining the main trail leading to the outlaws' stronghold at Ashwell, barely two leagues away. Again as he approached the junction he gave the familiar whistle, and waited for the expected response before proceeding.

"Anything?" he asked one of the two men guarding the entrance.

"No, Marshal. We've a pretty good view of the trail from here and we've seen no movement."

"You know what to do if you see anything?"

"One of us runs back and sounds the alarm bell to rouse the rest of the village. The other stays here to judge the size of their force before falling back."

Jack put a hand on his shoulder and said, "Good man. Carry on then." Then he turned away to head back to the barn.

As he did so the other guard yelled, "Wait! I see something, about four furlongs off – mounted men, I'd say. But they don't seem in any hurry."

Jack peered down the trail and caught a glimpse of the approaching riders in the moonlight, though they were still too far off to identify.

"I reckon they're riding in file, two by two," said the guard with surprise in his voice.

"How many men?"

"Can't say yet – at least six. Could be more."

"All right," Jack said. "Go sound the alarm. I want everyone battle alert."

The senior guard ran back to strike the bell that had last rung out to warn of a raider attack twenty years earlier. Soon men and a few feisty women ran out of their houses, some pulling on clothing and all clutching bows and other weapons.

The lawmen and part-time warriors took their places in the shadows, with bows primed and ready to face the enemy once it reached the village centre. Jack sensed the tension in the air as each man and woman waited in silence, as he did, no doubt riding waves of emotion ranging from exhilaration to gut-wrenching fear.

The column of riders turned into the village.

"Don't shoot till I give the order!" Jack hissed.

"Take aim! Choose your targets!"

"No. Wait!"

He stepped out into a pool of moonlight.

"Dominic – is that you?"

Bradley dismounted and approached with arms outstretched, hugging his brother-in-law to him with gusto.

"Jack, it's good to see you! Thanks to the Gods we're not too late to help. I'm only sorry we left it so long. But we've had a few troubles of our own. I'm sorry there aren't more of us."

Jack stepped away sporting an enormous grin, while the Crowtree militia emerged from the shadows and greeted the arriving platoon members, as if they, too, were long separated relatives.

So pleased and grateful were they for the help they'd all hoped and prayed for.

* * *

"Wait. I recognise the road here. We're approaching Ashwell. The main trail goes right through the village."

Martin sounded puzzled. "Why should that be remarkable, Mistress Bradley?"

"Oh, for the sake of the Gods of the Wall, would you please stop addressing me so formally? Call me Sylvia."

"Oh, sorry, Sylvia."

She grabbed his horse's halter. "No, I'm sorry. I'm worried for my husband, my brothers – and for us. I shouldn't have brought you two here at such a time. I sense danger."

Martin smiled. "But why should we be in danger? We have the protection of six brave riflemen, we have a wagonload of guns and ammunition, and I…" He reached over his shoulder and tapped his backpack. "I have my little bag of tricks. There's no reason to be afraid – Sylvia."

"You're right, of course," she said. "But I can't forget the awful things that happened in this village twenty years ago. The outlaws used it for their headquarters. I don't think we should go in."

"But Mum," Krania said, "that was then. That doesn't mean…"

Martin interrupted her. "No. Your mother's right. Remember that pigeon message from your Uncle Jack? It said something about Ashwell casualties. This place might not be safe. Our destination is Crowtree. We should find a way round."

He looked at Sylvia. "You grew up around here. Can we get the wagon to Crowtree avoiding Ashwell?"

Sylvia sighed. "Yes, by taking deer trails, but you'll have to use your cutter again."

"Oh," was all he said.

"What's the problem?"

"Low on batteries," he muttered. "How far do I need to cut?"

"About a furlong," she said.

He stopped to think.

"All right, but not tonight. The flashes might be seen from the village. I suggest we find a place to camp in the woods. I'll start cutting at first light."

* * *

The fire had gone out in Jack's kitchen. Lucy and Emily had gone to bed. Jack and Dominic warmed themselves with mugs of hot tea.

"You don't have the rifles, Dominic?"

"I'm afraid not – nor or our spare ammunition. Is Liam here?"

"No. The stores at Roundhill may be less tempting, but they need guarding too."

"Have you stood your people down?"

"Yes, and I appreciate that – they can all do with a good night's sleep."

"I hope they'll get it. Meanwhile my men can take four-hour watches. They know to strike the bell if anything happens."

"I suppose you all carry spare rifle shells?"

"Some, yes. But I'd feel much better going into battle knowing I had enough ammunition to finish the job. Without the other rifles and ammunition, we lose our advantage."

"When do you expect your munitions wagon?"

"Two days from now at the earliest. I'm sorry, Jack."

"Don't apologise, Dom. I'm grateful you even managed to get down here, especially with all the turmoil you've spoken about. By the way, how are my sister and Krania?"

"They're well. Unfortunately though, I left the New Territory in the middle of an argument with Sylvia. She wanted to come with us, and I forbade her."

Jack looked askance. "Forbade? Would I be right in guessing *argument* to be something of an understatement?"

Dominic merely rolled his eyes and sought solace in his hot tea. "Don't say anything, Jack. We'll work it out. Is there somewhere I can get my head down for a few hours? I'm bushed."

Jack made him up a spare cot in the corner of the kitchen, and within minutes he was sleeping soundly.

* * *

They came at dawn.

There was nothing subtle about the attack. The rabble of runaway slaves and disaffected youngsters galloped noisily down the main track from Ashwell, giving the lookouts plenty of time to warn the villagers of their approach by sounding the alarm bell loud and long.

As the second peal subsided Dominic stood on the kitchen floor. Quickly he pulled on his breeches, boots, tunic and sheepskin coat, and swung his ammunition belt over his shoulder. He grabbed his rifle and made for the door, with Jack literally two steps behind him, clutching a crossbow and quiver of bolts.

At each inhabited cottage the story was the same. Every able-bodied adult male – and a few brave young women – reacted to the alarm, emerging from their dwellings bearing whatever arms suited them best.

In the few minutes left before the expected onslaught, Jack Storey reminded them to take cover and avoid offering their bodies as easy targets. They took him at his word, seeking the protection of walls, doors, overturned wagons and barrels. Meanwhile Dominic spread his riflemen among the villagers, echoing Jack's advice to take advantage of whatever shelter was available. But he added the order, "Conserve your ammunition. Don't fire until I tell you."

From their positions of comparative safety the Crowtree defenders took heart in the supposition that their attackers must be inexperienced and poorly led. Their battle tactics appeared to consist of an unreserved frontal attack without a thought for personal safety. And if the underlying strategy relied on their opponents' pity, it was ill conceived.

Jack hardened his warriors' resolve with the exhortation, "Shoot at will!"

Dominic counted no less than six attackers who fell to well-aimed bolts from Crowtree bows. It amazed him that the oncoming hoard seemed to have no coherent attack plan. The weapons they bore were cudgels, short swords and other hand weapons that could only be effective at close quarters. None had the chance to use them, though their wild assault brought their contorted features close up to the defenders. Any who saw them must know, from their glazed eyes and wild expressions, that they were under the influence either of hallucinatory herbs or strong spirit – perhaps even both.

There could be only one explanation. This vanguard was expendable. Their task was to test the opposition, to establish its strength. Dominic's decision to delay deploying his riflemen was vindicated.

But what next?

The answer came in the form of a single command from the rear.

"Pull back!"

As if mesmerised the attackers withdrew to take shelter beyond a point half way down the track towards the village entrance. Astonishingly here three ranks of pallets had been swiftly erected, protecting an unknown number of prone archers, who immediately let fly a volley of arrows. From his cover behind an upturned wagon Dominic saw that the attackers' horses had been tied in the hedgerow lining the track, ready for a rapid exit if needed.

From shouts on either side of him he knew that at least two of Jack's people had taken hits. He also noticed that the oncoming arrows varied in length and approached at different angles. This could only mean one thing. Some of the archers out there were firing longbows – and with precision. Because of the higher trajectory he suspected it was their arrows that were doing the most damage. He ran his eyes carefully along the line of the assailants' protective pallets. Not only were the tops of the longbows visible, but occasionally so were the crowns of the archers' heads. This must be because, to deploy their bows, the archers must adopt at least a semi-kneeling position, whereas the crossbowmen were able to lie prone, shooting through slits in the pallets.

Keeping low, he wasted no time in moving deftly to each of his riflemen to tell them where to place their fire. Though he'd never had a chance to test their skill, it was obvious from the result that they were no novices with their weapons. Within thirty seconds virtually all the longbows were out of action – due either to shattered bows or dead or wounded archers. He thanked the Gods for the precision of Cara's rifles.

He sensed consternation among the enemy ranks. But after only a brief hiatus, the crossbow volleys recommenced. However, now clearly wary of their opponents' 'secret' weapon, the bowmen couldn't risk taking such careful aim, for fear of being hit by rifle shells through the arrow slits. As a result their shooting became erratic – although still prolific. The Crowtree army continued to match the onslaught, until the exchange settled down to a slogging match, in which further casualties were thankfully few and purely the result of luck – good or bad, as the case may be.

Dominic looked for Jack and McMahon and beckoned them over behind the wagon to discuss tactics.

Dominic said, "Are you surprised to see longbows in use here, Jack?"

"Yes. Slaves can't use them – that was the point in removing their bow fingers. They must have help from some unknown quarter – which would also explain their numbers."

McMahon said, "I thought they were just a mad rabble at first, but that rush was clearly a calculated sacrificial move to assess our resources. Fortunately we hadn't engaged our rifles, so that part of their plan didn't work. But it also bought them time to set up those pallets, which I have to say look to be quite effective."

Jack said, "I agree. It also suggests some tactical thinking at the root of their battle plan."

Dominic asked him, "Does that square with what you know about this son of Red?"

Jack shrugged. "He's no dimwit. But I'd say there was a trained military mind behind this."

"What happens now?" McMahon asked.

Jack said, "Our two sides seem fairly evenly matched. It's going to depend who runs out of ammunition first."

Dominic nodded. "As I said, our spare rifle shells are limited. How are your troops off for arrows?"

"Fairly well. We've been preparing for this for several days now. We can also collect their spent bolts – as they can ours."

"Any chance of getting behind them?"

"I think not. They'll have lookouts posted on the main trail. We'd never get close enough to do any damage."

McMahon said, "So we just continue to slog it out?"

"Yes, but I'll pass the word to conserve arrows."

About mid-morning, McMahon reported that his riflemen's store of spare shells was almost exhausted. "They've been concentrating on the arrow slits, hoping to hit flesh through the narrow apertures. We think a couple of shots found their mark, but overall we've made little impression on their rate of delivery."

An hour later the Crowtree artillery was reduced to arrows only.

Then a breathless villager approached Jack Storey with a strange report.

"Marshal, there's a wagon and seven riders approaching from the north fields."

He relayed this to Dominic, who said, "Lend me three archers and I'll investigate. It could be a trick." Recalling the village layout from his time here twenty years before, he took a back lane to the track that separated the north and south fields, many of which had been ploughed ready for the frosts.

He watched the rig approach and as it drew closer felt certain he recognised it as the diverted munitions wagon. Although baffled as to how it could have arrived so soon, he was elated that it was here and apparently fully laden.

But who were the three horsemen accompanying Toby and the three other guards?

Closer still, all became clear – or partly so. He spurred his horse on, trying not to let his initial good spirits give way to anger.

As he approached with gritted teeth, Sylvia shouted, "Don't say anything, Dominic. We're here, and there's nothing you can do about it. And if we hadn't met your wagon going north, and if Martin hadn't cleared a way through the forest, you'd still be waiting for your spare ammunition. And, from the look of things here, I'm guessing you're probably in need of it."

He didn't pretend to understand everything that she was saying, but he couldn't bring himself to chastise her. He merely rode up to her side, leaned over and kissed her, did the same to Krania, shook hands with Martin, then smiled and said, "Why am I not surprised? Follow me."

He led them down the track behind the Crowtree dwellings, bringing them around behind the barn, from where the four guards distributed spare shells to their fellow riflemen, which greatly increased the returned assault on the opposing bowmen.

Very soon cries of "Retreat!" and "Pull back!" were heard and the enemy force quickly mounted and turned tail, back to their stronghold in Ashwell, leaving their arrow-festooned and splintered pallets behind them.

CHAPTER TWENTY-NINE
A SPY IN THE CAMP

"How would you assess today's action, Marshal?"

Owen McMahon accepted the mug of beer that Jack Storey handed to him. Both family reunion and battle post mortem, lunch had been a lively gathering comprising the Storey and Bradley families and guests, who also included Martin Wakefield and Toby.

"Thanks, Jack. And thanks to you, Mistress Storey for your excellent hospitality. Though from now on I think, to be fair to you, Toby and I should find billets with other families while we're here in Crowtree. I'd say we acquitted ourselves well, under the circumstances. Our casualties were few and thankfully minor. They didn't get near the store – whose defence was our main objective."

Dominic said, "I agree. I'm very pleased with the skill of our riflemen. And your people seemed well drilled, Jack. Everyone knew what was expected of them."

Jack smiled. "That's because we've been providing basic training whenever possible. A few things I learned from my old teacher."

Dominic brushed aside the compliment. "I'd say the enemy seemed well prepared too, if you discount that rabble they threw at us first off. They must have been out of their heads on something."

Jack said, "That would be the red-haired lad's influence. My deputies warned him a couple of months ago for passing hallucinatory mushrooms around."

McMahon said, "To get people high to use them sacrificially in battle – that's sick, but it also suggests a military brain. Did anyone see who was shouting the orders on their side?"

There was a general shaking of heads.

But then Martin said, "Just give me a moment and I'll check."

Every face regarded him blankly as he reached into his tunic pocket and withdrew an object no bigger than a thumbnail.

"What's that?" Jack asked him.

Excitedly, young Emily yelled, "I know! It's a clip! I've learned about them in class, but I've never seen one. Are you going to clip it in? What does it do, Martin?"

"It's just a basic sound and vision recorder," he said, pressing the device into the two tiny holes just behind his right temple. "Forgive me if I shut my eyes, and I'll have to ask you to be quiet."

That was hardly necessary, because his audience was dumbfounded.

"Just a second while I find the place. Ah, here it is. I'm just at the point where someone ordered the retreat. It came from the left side, I think. I'm going to zoom in. Ah, I think I have him – but it's not of much use, I'm afraid. He's wearing a cloak and a hood."

He opened his eyes. Everyone stared at him as if he were crazy.

He sounded suddenly embarrassed. "Oh, I'm sorry. We use these things all the time on the Salvation. I should have realised it would shock you to see it in use for the first time. Look, it's not so weird. It just uses your eyes as a camera and your brain as the controls."

Jack said, "What's a camera?"

There followed a babble during which at least three others at the table tried to tell him.

But he held both hands up. "Never mind. I don't really want to know. Is there any more beer, Lucy? Or, better still, some of that liquor that Andreas brought with him last year?"

His wife touched his cheek, and then got up. "I'll go and see, dear."

Dominic said, "That's some gadget you have there, Martin. I don't claim to understand how it works, but is there any way you can show us what you saw?"

He shook his head. "Sorry. Not with this alone. I brought some other stuff with me, but not a conventional camera."

"In that case," Dominic said, "we'll have to rely on you to be our secret eyes and ears."

* * *

As Martin crossed the yard to brush and talk to the horse they'd loaned him, Emily watched wide-eyed and whispered to her cousin.

"Isn't he wonderful, Krania? He's so clever and cute with his coloured hairpiece. And he loves horses, I can tell." She sighed heavily. "But I doubt if he even notices me."

Krania made a face. "Yuk! How sickening. Some people are impressed very easily. You do realise he's more than twice your age, don't you?"

"Yes, but Mum says I'm mature for my years. Anyway, she's a lot younger than Daddy. Do you think he'd wait for me?"

"Of course not. He probably has loads of girl friends on board the Salvation. I met one of them, called Jessica."

"Ah, but Aunt Sylvia said he couldn't go back there – not after rescuing you."

"Why does everybody have to keep reminding me about that? I can't go through my whole life feeling forever grateful to him."

"I bet he wouldn't expect you to – he's too nice."

Krania's eyebrows went up. "Honestly, Emily! I really don't know what you see in him. He's not even especially handsome. He's just an ordinary boy. He's also skinny – and a bit nerdy."

"Not to me, he's not."

"Well, you're welcome to him. I know. I'll go over and ask him if he wants to marry you." She grabbed her cousin's hand and dragged her towards where he stood grooming his horse, while Emily leaned backwards, her face like a beetroot.

"Oh, Martin," Krania said, smiling cruelly at her cousin. "There's something important Emily wanted to ask you."

Still brushing, he said, "Oh, really? What's that, Emily?"

"Nothing," she protested. "I don't know what she means!"

"Oh, well," said her cousin, "if you haven't got the nerve, I'll ask him for you."

"No!" Emily protested.

"It's all right," said Krania glibly. "I don't mind. Martin, Emily wants to know if…"

He stopped brushing. "Yes?"

"She wants to know – if we hadn't better find a wig for you if you're going to go prowling around Ashwell."

She turned and grimaced at Emily, whose expression shifted from relief to indignation.

He smiled at the younger girl. "I hadn't thought of that, Emily. You're right. They might be suspicious if I turned up looking like this. Thank you very much – that's really very clever of you. Do you know where I can get one?"

Now embarrassed again, Emily muttered, "There's a lady in the village who makes them. Shall I ask Mum if you can go and see her?"

"If you like," he said. "But only if you promise to come with me."

* * *

"Are you sure you want to go through with this, Martin?"

"No one else can do it, Governor. It takes minor neurosurgery to fit one of these." He tapped the implant at his temple, and affixed the clip. "Anyway, it's not really so dangerous. They don't know me. I'll pretend I'm a new recruit. I just have to find an opportunity to leave before I overstay my welcome."

He, Dominic and Jack Storey stood with their horses tethered on the forest trail leading to the Ashwell stockade – exactly where Jack had stood a month before and witnessed the savage scene of retribution on an unfortunate village slave owner.

Jack said to him, "Remember, don't attempt any heroics. Just go wherever they'll let you and have a good look round. Try not to stay any more than a couple of hours. We'll be waiting for you here. And keep your hair over your ears, whatever you do."

Dominic said, "Let's see how you look. Hmm, the clothes are right and the wig really suits you, but your face is too clean." He stooped to rub his hands in the damp earth, and smeared some of it on Martin's cheek. "That's better – now you look just like any scruffy village lad. You'll be fine. Ready?"

He nodded, and slipped through the half overgrown trail entrance and into the clearing. Three youths stood talking close to the corral gate. As he walked across the open ground towards the village, one of them yelled out to him.

"Hey, you! Come here a minute!"

He tried to look and sound nonchalant. "Who, me?"

"No, the bloke behind you!" the lad shouted, and all three laughed when he checked to see if there was anyone there. Then he remembered reading about irony in colloquial speech among uneducated terrestrial teenagers, and tried to react accordingly. He laughed too, to show he accepted being the butt of their pathetic brand of humour. Maintaining that smile, he walked towards them.

"Can I help you?" he asked.

"Dunno. Can you?"

More hilarity. Already he was finding this tedious. Still, he held onto his friendly expression, and merely looked the speaker in the eye.

"Know anything about horses?" the boy asked.

He tried to keep it simple and stick to the truth. "Not much. They have four legs, a head at the front, and a tail at the back. I think there are some over there." He pointed – helpfully, he thought – at the small herd in the corral.

He didn't understand why their expressions at once turned serious, as the same boy said, "Are you tryin' to be funny?"

This didn't seem to be going very well. All he could say was, "Well, yes, I suppose I am really. I thought we all were."

Now they looked confused. But they must be in genuine need of help, because another lad asked him, "Which one's the Arab stallion? Red wants us to take it to him."

But it rattled Martin when he added, "Tell us and we won't break your legs."

How had he arrived at this point? If they were serious, he must act quickly. His studies had extended to ancient working and draught animals, and he was fairly sure he remembered what an Arab horse was supposed to look like. He went over to the corral and counted at least four animals that matched the fine, trim image in his mind. Three were among the main group, while the fourth was held in a separate pen, along with a few others of various types. They said that Red had asked for 'the Arab stallion', so there could be only one. Unfortunately he had never come across the word 'stallion' before. He studied each of the four horses. He compared the physical attributes of the three in the main group with the one in the pen. He quickly deduced what a stallion was.

Pointing he said, with questionable confidence, "That's it."

Then he took a deep breath and added, "Shall I take it to him?"

He was aware that some complex thought processes were going on inside at least one of the brains in front of him.

At last the first youth said, "All right. Get it and follow me."

From what he'd recently learned from Krania he knew that leading a horse required at least a halter and also preferably a lead rope to attach to it. He noticed that very few of the corralled horses had halters – including the one he'd just pointed out.

"Have you got anything to lead him with?" he asked.

"I've got a bit of rope here," one of them said, handing it to him.

Cautiously he opened the gate to the stallion pen. The occupants jigged about as he approached the Arab. He spoke lightly to the animal and slipped the rope over its neck, bringing it round so that he was able to clutch the two ends underneath its chin. Then he pulled gently, still muttering coaxing words, until it followed him through the open gate.

"Secure that gate, will you?" he said to the three youths, and amazingly one of them responded.

"Where's Red?" he asked. The trio shifted and led him away from the clearing and through the village until they arrived at one of the more salubrious dwellings. Here the red-haired youth, a girl and a hooded man sat drinking beer in the front yard of the house, while warriors practiced combat and target shooting in the open space before them.

Red got up and approached him.

"Ah, here he is. This is the horse I promised you, Wolf. What do you think?"

The hooded man stood up and stepped towards Martin. He stroked the stallion's muzzle and scratched its head.

"Nice beast," he said. "He'll do for me. My men will need better horses too. See to it, will you?"

"Sure, Wolf," Red said. "I'll see what we can get hold of."

For a second the angle at which Wolf held his head revealed his face to Martin. He fought a natural reaction to look away and said, "Shall I take him back now?"

The hooded man, his features once more concealed, said, "Yes. Thank you, lad."

Martin turned to pull the horse away when Red's voice sent a chill through his body.

"Hey, you! Wait a second!"

He stopped and turned around.

"I don't think I've seen you before. What's your name?"

"Martin, Sir," he mumbled.

In the brief silence that followed he envisaged having his cover blown, and the inevitable consequences of that. Perhaps it had been foolhardy volunteering for this assignment.

"Where do you come from?"

He wondered how Red would react if he responded, "The Salvation, a star liner moored on the far side of the Moon." But what could he say? He realised that, for once, he had no choice but to deviate from the truth. He must use the only other Fenwold village name he could call to mind.

"Crowhill, Sir."

"Really? Well, you're obviously too young to be a slave. Just fed up with village life under the marshals?"

"Something like that," he lied.

Then the girl approached him and put her hands to his hair. He hoped she wasn't going to ruffle his wig.

"You're a nice looking kid," she said. "You stick around – we'll look after you. Ain't that right, Red?"

Though he said, "Oh, yeah," Martin didn't think he meant it.

Tentatively he said, "I'll take him back then, shall I?"

"Yes, yes," Red said impatiently.

On the way back to the corral he made sure to swing his vision in all directions, to record as much information as possible about the layout of the village, numbers of raiders, weapons, horses – and villagers. He thought it strange that he'd so far seen no sign of any. When he arrived at the clearing no one else was there. He assumed the three youths had stayed in the village centre to look for someone else to humiliate. He hoped they were in some way responsible for the horses' well being, because before leaving he wedged open the gates to the corral.

Not only that, but having taken a strong liking to the looks of the Arab, he led it through the foliage and onto the forest trail where Jack and Dominic waited. Laughing, they rode to the main track and cantered back with the stallion in tow before Red's raiders had a chance to miss their escaping horses.

* * *

Emily ran out to meet her father on the group's return, and handed him a piece of paper as he dismounted.

"What's this, child?" said Jack, turning it over in his hands.

"I just went up to the loft to feed my birds and found one of my pigeons with this clipped to its leg – it must have flown in this morning. I think it's for Uncle Dominic."

"Who's it from, Jack?" Dominic asked.

"Wait a minute. The writing's all wrinkled."

"Read it out, would you?"

"DOM – REGRET NEED TROOPS DEFEND CAPITAL – OUTLAW GANG ATTACKED ONCE COULD RETURN ANY TIME – SORRY – PIETER."

He scratched his head. "I don't get this, Dom."

"Before leaving the New Territory I dispatched a courier to the Capital to ask for help down here. That's their reply. Seems they have troubles of their own."

"Oh," Jack said. "Well, at least we know our limitations now."

"Yes. Let's go inside and see what Martin can tell us about the enemy's."

It was now late afternoon, and Lucy brewed some tea while Jack stoked the kitchen fire with logs.

Dominic was first up with a question for Martin.

"Can you estimate their numbers?"

"There are two distinct groups – the adolescents and the warriors. I'd say the first group numbers about twenty, and the second around thirty. I didn't see any older men – those you referred to as slaves – or any of the villagers."

Jack said, "The slaves are probably guarding the villagers. You wouldn't waste crack troops on that. And those kids are worse than useless. Did you see any clue as to where they might be holding the villagers?"

Martin closed his eyes. "Let me just replay my walk back to the corral. What should I be looking for?"

Dominic said, "Bars on doors, boarded up windows, perhaps armed men standing in front of houses."

"Wait. Yes, I think I have it – a house with planks of wood across the windows. There are no armed men though."

Jack said, "If I sketch a plan of the village afterwards, could you pinpoint the house?"

"Probably, yes. I think so."

In a similar way he was able to give them other valuable information about the raiders' resources. Finally Dominic asked him the question that had been nagging him ever since the previous day's battle.

"And the hooded man – what of him?"

"Wolf. That's what Red called him. And he wears that hood all the time – for a very good reason."

"Why's that?" Jack asked.

"Because half his face is burned away."

"Really? Can you draw him?"

"Well, I've got the picture centred in my mind. I just need to keep on trying until I get it right."

"I'll ask Emily for some paper and charcoal," Jack said.

Thirty minutes and fifteen crumpled attempts later Martin handed a sketch to Dominic. "That's as near as I can get it," he said. "I'm sorry the burnt side isn't very good."

"Don't worry about that. Jack, do you have any pieces of mirror?"

"Lucy keeps a square in the bedroom for beautifying herself. I'll fetch it."

He brought in the glass and handed it to Dominic, who placed it at right angles to reflect the unburned side of Martin's sketch of Wolf, thus producing a complete, unblemished image.

"What's up, Dom?" Jack asked, for his brother-in-law's own face was suddenly as pale as the morning mist.

"I'd hoped never to see that man again."

* * *

"It's odd now, looking back, but with the excitement of the wedding and overseeing the migration to the New Territory, the squalid affair of Rankin's and Miller's trial and Carson's court martial sort of got parcelled up and stored in an obscure corner of my memory. I now clearly recall my day on the witness stand, and the crooked Councillors' sentences – long enough for them to expect to die in prison. As for Carson, he admitted conspiring to subvert the political process and received a twenty years sentence. About ten years ago I heard of a break-out attempt by setting fire to the prison, but it went wrong and he was badly burned – though it was never proven that he was directly involved. I suppose I should have expected him to hold a grudge and come seeking revenge some day."

Jack frowned. "I'll bet he and his gang had something to do with the attack on the Capital that Pieter Jennings mentioned in that note. But Dominic, you're not suggesting Carson's gone to the trouble of raising a small army to lure you down here just to settle a personal grudge?"

Dominic pointed at Martin's sketch. "Like most men of a criminal disposition, he's an opportunist. When he got out of jail, he'd look for anything that didn't involve sweating for a living, so becoming a raider boss was always on the cards. It's common knowledge that I killed young Red's father, and I can almost understand the boy's twisted loyalty. But when Carson heard he'd gone off the rails he must have seen a chance to bring me within his reach. And, let's face it, his plan worked, didn't it?"

Jack said, "I'm sorry, Dominic. I didn't think…"

"No, Jack. Don't apologise. I'm glad you asked me to come. This is my fight as much as anybody's."

He smiled and placed a hand on Martin's shoulder. "But if he thinks he's dealing with old-fashioned warhorses, he's very much mistaken. With Cara's rifles and this young man's gadgets and courage, we've a clear advantage over Carson's archers and Red's layabouts."

Martin asked, "Could I make an observation based on my professors' teaching?"

Dominic said, "I was once a raw youngster, relying on what wise people had taught me. I'd value your contribution to our discussions."

Martin coughed. "It's true we have superior weapons. But to use our advantage in a brutal way would mean a bigger, bloodier battle costing more lives and suffering. I don't believe that's acceptable, even if it means victory for our side. What I saw in Ashwell today were large numbers of gullible people controlled by two evil and charismatic men. If I thought those people were united by some tangible cause – religion or political doctrine, for example – then I'd agree that only a decisive strike would deter them. But they're not. Their loyalty to Red and Wolf – or Carson, as you call him – is based on dependency and fear, verging on mass hysteria – hero worship, if you like. Remove the objects of that loyalty, and the ragged army should break up and dissolve back into civil society."

Jack said, "So what you're saying is that we should forget major battle preparations, and concentrate on taking Red and Carson out of the equation?"

Martin nodded. "Yes, and we have to move fast, because they're sure to want to strike again soon."

Dominic picked up the sketch of his old enemy. "I follow your logic, Martin. But there's one important element your textbook formula has ignored."

The lad looked at him quizzically.

"The good people of Ashwell. Removing Red and Carson would leave them at the mercy of that ragged army. And even if your theory is right, and their followers did disperse eventually, they would first naturally look to exact revenge on the nearest available target. No, son. Before we move against their captors, we have to snatch those innocent people out of there."

CHAPTER THIRTY
RESCUE MISSION

"Once again, Mistress Storey, I must say you set a fine table."

"Thank you, Marshal McMahon. It's a shame we only see you for your councils of war, nevertheless you're most welcome. But all the women in the household have a hand in preparing these meals. I couldn't do it on my own."

"In that case," the Marshal said, raising his beer mug, my compliments to all of you ladies!"

Martin lifted his mug too. "I'll second that. Now that I'm getting used to Earth food, I see what we've been missing on board the Salvation."

Jack said seriously, "This is all very well, but we still don't have a plan for releasing the Ashwell villagers. We can't just walk in and let them out like we did twenty years ago. We used fire arrows then to cause a distraction, but these days most Ashwell roofs are like ours - tiled rather than thatched or timbered."

Dominic added, "Besides, the prison cottage then stood away from the main village. From Martin's observations, the house they're in is visible from where Red and Carson are billeted."

Martin said, "That's true. It's over on the north side, but in the big circle of main dwellings. It does back on to the forest though."

Dominic put down his beer mug. "That has to be our approach then – from the woods. Jack, do you know the trails on that side?"

Through a mouthful of potato his brother-in-law mumbled, "Yes, I think so."

"Good. So what we need is a way to get to the guards and immobilise them without causing too much of a stir. That rules out a direct assault, of course."

Sylvia said, "I wonder?"

"Wonder what?" Dominic asked.

"Remember all those years back, after we'd taken Red and you were captured by the few survivors of his gang? I traded Red for you and left the remaining raiders a few bottles of Grandfather's liquor. It doped them enough for Jack and Rajeev to go in a few hours later and round them all up."

"Of course I recall that episode – thank you for reminding me in front of all our friends."

"Oh, don't be so touchy, Dominic. It's common knowledge anyway. It wasn't your fault they took you – you'd gone in to help young Adam Genney."

"That may be so, but it still chills me to think of the risk you took on my behalf. In any case, if my memory doesn't fail me, Jack and I drank the last of that poison the night before…"

"Before our wedding," Lucy said ironically. "It's a wonder he was fit for…"

"Lucy!" Jack said sharply.

Dominic coughed, while Sylvia said hurriedly, "Lucy, didn't you tell me there was someone else in the village who brews similar stuff? We'd need half a dozen bottles of something really potent."

Jack said, "When Red's gang were sentenced to have their bow fingers removed the tribunal of elders stipulated it should be done as humanely as possible. We managed to get hold of some fortified wine based on valerian root oil. It put them out for a couple of hours – they didn't feel a thing."

Dominic asked, "Can we get some?"

Lucy smiled. "I'll go and see her after dinner."

Sylvia said, "If the guards can be immobilised, how will you bring the Ashwell villagers out of there?"

Dominic thought for a moment. "We'll take a couple of wagons and ferry them a safe distance – there are clearings we can use as staging posts. Those that can walk will make their way here using the forest trails. I suggest we take some food for them – they may be in need of it."

McMahon said, "But who's going to deliver the liquor? They'd have to pass themselves off as one of Red's hangers-on – preferably a young woman."

Without a pause Krania said, "I'll do it!"

But Sylvia was already shaking her head. "Oh, no, my girl. I'm not having you walking into that pit of danger."

Her daughter didn't conceal her frustration. "But that's exactly what you did for Dad! Why is everybody allowed to take risks except me? Marshal McMahon said it has to be one of Red's female misfits. I'd hardly need to act to pass myself off as one of them!"

Sylvia turned to her husband. "Dominic, tell your daughter she can't do this!"

He picked up her hand and looked into her eyes. "I've learned that both my women are courageous and know their own minds. Krania has your fire and spirit, my love. And she's right for the part – and it needn't be that dangerous. We'll have a small army in the woods as backup. At the first sign of trouble, we'll be in there and snatch her out to safety. Trust me."

She put her other hand out to Krania and with tearful eyes said, "Very well, Dominic. But if anything goes wrong, I don't think I'll ever be able to forgive you."

* * *

As she followed her escort of six riflemen through the forest, Krania felt the same excitement as when she'd been taken hostage and given her first ride in a space shuttle. But as they came nearer to their destination, her exhilaration became tinged with anxiety. She consciously fixed her expression, determined not to show any sign of fear.

"We've taken a risk, leaving it this long, Governor. They must be ready for their next strike by now."

"I agree with you, Owen, but what else can we do? According to that old crone who makes the liquor, it doesn't brew in just a few hours. Besides, the Crowtree defences are in good shape, and our forces are primed and ready."

Jack turned to whisper to them. "Keep your voices down. We're skirting the main part of the village now. They're only a few strides away from us."

They followed Jack through the warren of forest trails that led to the wooded north side of Ashwell. He looked up from the sketch he'd made from Martin's description of the village layout.

"We're here," he hissed. "Wait and I'll find a way through."

He disappeared momentarily into the undergrowth but soon re-emerged.

"Right, Krania. Are you ready? Hold your basket while we load you up. I hope they're not too heavy for you."

She smiled at him. "Don't worry, Uncle Jack. I can manage." But her expression was strained now that she had the six heavy bottles in her basket.

"There's a back door. I suggest you knock. You know what to say?"

She nodded eagerly. "I should do. I've had five days to practice."

They exchanged nervous smiles.

"Good girl," he said. "And don't worry. We'll be watching and listening. Remember to whistle if you think you're in trouble."

She put two fingers to her lips. "I've been practicing that too," she said.

"Good. All right. Off you go."

Her heart beating almost to burst, she pushed through the foliage where Jack held back the branches of an elder bush, and soon stood at the back door of the house. There was no point in peering through the windows, because they'd been well boarded up. Struggling to hold the heavy basket steady with one hand, she knocked with the other on the door, hoping her wig would stay in place.

A gruff male voice demanded almost immediately, "What do you want?"

She said, "I'm from the camp. Red sent me – with a gift."

Heavy bolts and locks rattled on the other side until the door opened a crack and Sperry's face looked out.

"What is it? Did you say Red sent you? I thought he'd forgotten us."

"No, no," she said as convincingly as she could manage. "He's worried about you. He's sent some drinks for you all." With difficulty she raised the basket to give him a closer look at its contents. As she did so, she tried to get a look inside to confirm that the villagers were there, but the place was inky black and there was little to see.

"Huh!" he said. "It's about time. Here, let's have 'em then."

314

She passed the basket through the crack and he grabbed it, slamming the door in her face. But he shouted to her, "Better tell him 'thanks' – but our stores are getting low here. Tell him… No, ask him to send us some more food. The villagers are in a bad way."

Relieved to have confirmation that this was the right house, she turned away, saying, "All right. I'll tell him."

She returned to her friends.

"Did you hear all that?" Krania's voice shivered with excitement.

"Yes," said her father. "Well done. I'm proud of you."

His smile and appreciative words filled her heart, and it was all she could do to hold back a tear.

"I want you to do something else," he said. "Go back with Toby to the wagons and fetch a couple of baskets of the food we brought. I'm hoping one or more of the villagers will seize the opportunity to break out, once the wine's taken its effect. But just in case, what that slave said offers us a contingency plan."

* * *

They waited two hours and there was still no sign of activity from the prison house.

"Krania," Dominic said, "I'd hoped this wouldn't be necessary. I want you to take these baskets of provisions and knock on that door again. This time though we'll be just in the undergrowth behind you, and as soon as the door's ajar, Marshal McMahon and I will push past you and into the house. When that happens get back into the woods as fast as you can. Can you do that?"

She forced a smile to mask her apprehension. "Of course, Dad." She picked up the baskets and stepped out towards the door. Placing one of them on the ground, she knocked.

There was a long pause. Then an anxious voice said, "Who is it?"

"It's me again," she said. "I've brought some of the food you asked for."

Eventually, as before, she heard the bolts being unfastened. After a further pause the door opened, but only the slightest crack. Then she gasped as she heard someone say, "Who is it? Is it a trick?"

The person on the other side of the door answered, "No. Red's sent food for us."

The gruff response came. "Grab it then."

The door opened wider.

There was a rustle behind her and Owen McMahon rushed past her followed by her father. Both carried primed crossbows.

"Get back to the others, Krania!" her father yelled, but she was rooted to the spot.

She heard the short *swish* of a crossbow bolt, followed by a *thud* and a sharp sigh. As the person who had opened the door slumped to the ground, she heard exactly the same sounds and – forgetting her father's instruction – stepped over the body at the door to follow him and McMahon into the main room of the house.

She only had a glimpse of the misery and suffering in that room before Toby's strong arms scooped her up and whisked her away. She glimpsed her Uncle Jack and the rest of the force charge past her, crossbows drawn, as Toby returned her to the safety of the undergrowth.

Jack sipped his evening tea. "So what happens now? Do we wait for them to attack?"

Dominic poured himself a mug. "They might just decide to sit tight. After all, removing the villagers probably relieved them of a problem – the slaves too; they'd be of little use in battle. Now we have to use men to guard them. Carson may be happy to bide his time, as long as he knows I'm here. Oh, hello, Martin."

"Hello. May I help myself to some tea? By the way, that was a smooth operation today. Is it all right to say 'well done'?"

They smiled at him.

Jack said to Dominic, "So, what are you saying? Do we attack them?"

He shook his head. "I'd rather avoid it. As Martin reasoned so well a few days ago, there'd be a lot of bloodshed – as there would if they tried another assault on Crowtree. No, it'll be better to target Red and Carson in their nest. With them out of the picture, their rabble should fold and go home."

"How do we do that? I know we have rifles, but to get a clear shot we'd need to be inside the village. You or I would be recognised, so we'd have to sneak a couple of your riflemen in."

"I wouldn't ask any of them to go in there armed – if discovered, they couldn't expect any mercy. Besides, there's one small complication."

"Complication? What sort of complication?"

"Without going into details, it's important that I leave here with Red – alive."

"Ah," Jack sighed. "That's some complication."

"Excuse me," Martin said. "And forgive me if it's not my business. But would I be right in understanding that you need to immobilise Red and Carson without killing them?"

The two men regarded him quizzically. "That's right," Dominic said. "Why do you ask?"

* * *

The tree they selected was a tall horse chestnut, whose upper limbs protruded above the surrounding canopy. Though Martin, as the owner of the weapon, offered to take the shots, Dominic thought it best that one of his marksmen do the job.

"I'll do it," Toby said. "As well as an excellent shot, I'm also an expert climber of trees."

So, with the other riflemen guarding the area around the base of the tree, Martin handed Toby the components, which he secured under his tunic, before grabbing the first limb and finding a foothold to start the climb.

"Good luck, Toby," Martin said. "You're sure you can assemble it?"

Toby smiled. "I think so – you had me practice for two hours."

"I've set the power level to 'stun', but remember to check it before you fire – and also to lock onto your target. And make it count – that's my last battery."

"I will, Martin."

The climb seemed interminable. In fact, it took about ten minutes. They'd timed the operation for just after mid-day, when Red and Carson generally had lunch while Carson's troops drilled in the centre of the village.

Once at a point where he could see them, Toby wedged himself in a twist of a firm limb and reached inside his tunic for the components – monopod, stock, power pack with battery installed and telescopic sights. He clipped the parts together as he'd rehearsed countless times. Then he checked that the power level was set to *stun* mode. He tried to ignore the alternative embossed letters, which coldly spelled *kill*.

Checking his posture – Martin had told him to stay relaxed and try not to tense up, as there would be no recoil – Toby raised the assembled gun and pointed it in the general direction of the two men, and extended the monopod to give support on a lower branch. Now he looked through the telescopic sights and, when Red's torso sat behind the cross hairs, he clicked the 'lock' button. Now, amazingly, no matter how the gun waved from side to side, Red's figure remained in the sights. But Toby knew he must fire within a few seconds.

He fired.

He heard a gentle *hiss* as the weapon drew power from the battery, followed by a satisfying *zip* as the energy was discharged. Screwing up his eyes he looked across the treetops to see Red fall from his seat.

Now he had no time to waste, because people were starting to react to what had happened. Carson was already on his feet, so Toby quickly but more clumsily repeated the preparation sequence, this time targeting Carson, then locked the sights and fired.

Carson went down.

He disassembled the weapon and replaced the parts under his tunic before descending. At the foot of the tree he handed the components back to Martin.

"Well done, Toby. Our lookouts say their camp is in turmoil. They don't know what's happened. Some of Carson's men are already mounting up to leave."

"That's good, Martin. Our people should be able to walk in and bring their leaders out for trial."

Martin gasped. "Wait. Are these settings as they were when you fired that second shot?"

"I think so," Toby replied. "Why?"

Martin showed him the power selector switch. There could be no doubt.

The indicator pointed directly towards *kill*.

* * *

Late the following evening after everyone else had retired Dominic and Martin shared a nightcap of hot tea.

"It's been a busy day, young man. We've not had a chance to talk. Tell me about that gun. What went wrong?"

"There was obviously a fault with the selector switch. Once locked, the switch shouldn't move. Toby isn't to blame."

"A fairly serious defect," Dominic observed. "Was it just a fluke?"

Martin shrugged. "Probably not. My father insisted I bring that gun with me. I think he got it from some dubious contact in the military. Perhaps it was a reject. I'm sorry it meant we didn't take Carson alive."

Dominic shook his head. "I admit I'd sooner have seen him tried for his crimes. But I doubt that anyone will shed a tear that he's dead. As you predicted, most of his archers have dispersed. Some may re-form as smaller gangs, but without a leader the Council's forces will soon deal with them. I'll send couriers to the Capital to let them know. I'm sure they'll be relieved."

"As for Red's disciples," Martin said, "they seem at a loss what to do. Some have wandered off, but a few appear to be carrying on using the village as if nothing's happened."

"I know. We'll have to move them out for their own safety. When their hostages recover and return home, they're unlikely to feel hospitable towards them."

"And the slaves?"

"We should really call them convicted raiders. But oddly, on questioning the villagers, their guards appear to have treated them as well as the cramped accommodation allowed. Certainly nobody's suggesting they be severely punished. It'll be up to the village elders, but I'm recommending they be freed. They've served twenty years in bondage. I think they've paid for their misguided youth."

"And what punishment can Red expect?"

Dominic sighed. "There's no doubt he's a killer. Lucy and Jack can bear witness to that. The usual sentence for murder here is death by drowning. But I'm going to ask the elders to release him into my custody."

Martin's jaw dropped. "Really? Wouldn't that mean taking a big risk?"

"Yes, it would, Martin. But I believe the son of the original Red could be a vital factor in the resolution of our problems in the New Territory."

"Really? How?"

Dominic poured them both some more tea.

"Let me explain."

CHAPTER THIRTY- ONE
FIGHT OR DIE

"You're lucky to have a fine day for the crossing, Dominic. The weather's been foul this past week."

A strong breeze filled the big white sail as the ferryboat cut a clean trough through the choppy waters.

"Aye, Sean, and I'm thankful for it. As you know, I'm not the heartiest of sailors – especially when the boat rocks about a bit."

The ferry master smiled. "You should come out fishing with us on the Great Sea some day – that 'ud help you find your sea legs!"

Sylvia, seated next to her husband, took his arm and drew closer to him. "I doubt if he'll have time for fishing trips, Sean. Now the raiders have been subdued in the south-west, we've the small issue of the Salvation invaders to sort out."

"You did well to take their leader alive," Sean said, nodding towards the sullen red-haired figure slouched amidships, hands bound, with a rifleman either side of him. "I couldn't believe my eyes when he stepped on board. He's Red's double, without a doubt. But I'm surprised he got off with his life. By all accounts, he's as much of a devil as his father was."

Dominic said, "You'll remember, twenty years ago, how I was forced to strike a bargain with his father, to gain access to Cara using the tiles that opened up the culvert through the Wall?"

"I do. At the time I didn't understand why you'd done it, for if a man deserved to die for his crimes, it was he. But later I realised you'd higher things on your mind."

"Aye, well, let's say history sometimes repeats itself. That young villain could be as valuable to me alive today as his father was back then. But if you're looking for heroes of this expedition, it should be your own son, our daughter and her friend."

He'd already stood Toby down from duty, last seen enjoying a beer at the ferry port tavern. But he nodded proudly towards Martin and Krania, seated opposite, and said, "If Sylvia hadn't brought these two along, things mightn't have turned out quite so favourably."

Sylvia smiled as he kissed her on the lips, their earlier differences forgotten.

Sean's cousin shouted from the tiller, "Did you find your family well, Sylvia?"

"As well as could be expected, thank you Luke," she replied. "And after the conflict we had some weeks to enjoy their company free of any worries."

While Krania and Martin chatted, Dominic and Sylvia looked out over the mighty river towards the northern shore, appreciating the altered perspective as it drew nearer. From their vantage point out on the water there were signs of development on the eastern side of the Wall. What had previously been an empty bank now supported buildings – the warehouses that Dominic had commissioned plus several pre-fabricated dwellings cheekily stolen from the incoming space settlers.

Sylvia pointed and smiled. "Look, Dominic! Aren't those tents?"

"By the Gods, I think you're right. There must be a hundred of them. I recall Cara giving the code for the outdoor equipment container only a few months ago. They'll provide instant shelter while more permanent dwellings are being built."

Sylvia said, "I wonder how they're coping without the modern conveniences left behind in the New Territory. It'll be hardest for the children, I expect – they've known no other life."

"They'll get used to it," he said. "And if we can all face the winter with a common resolve, perhaps we can look forward eventually to having things the way they used to be."

"We'll be disembarking soon, everyone!" Sean shouted. "Please stay where you are until we've moored up!"

"You've wasted no time creating a sturdy looking jetty on this side, Sean," Dominic observed.

Taking in the mainsail the ferry master said, "It's just a floating timber mole, but it serves its purpose. Hey, you! Secure that rope, will you? Thanks. Now, walking passengers should disembark first, please, then those leading horses. Our crew will manhandle any heavy luggage. Don't strain your backs."

As Dominic led his horse onto the jetty, as always it took him several wobbly steps to get used to the absence of motion before he could proceed with confidence. But the sight of Rajeev waiting to greet him made him forget the rigours of the journey.

"Dominic, my dear friend, welcome! Sylvia, Krania, Martin! It's good to see you all back safely. How was your journey? No, don't answer – I'm sure it was dreadful. You're all to come to our house for a hot meal. My wife is preparing it now. And I'm sure you'd all like to clean up. Here, let me take your horse, Krania. We've put up some lean-tos to serve as stables for the time being. I've asked a couple of lads to feed and water your animals, so you don't have to worry about that. Here they are. That's right. Now, just follow me. We're over here next to the Wall."

He led them into a standard prefabricated house, which as he'd indicated abutted the gigantic concrete structure.

As they entered he said, "By the way, yours is next door. It's exactly the same as this one."

"But Rajeev, I didn't expect you to sort out a house for us," Dominic said. "That's very kind of you."

"Not at all," he insisted. "I'm sure you've had enough on your plate these last five weeks. The last thing you want is to worry about where you're going to live. Besides, the people here are concerned to have you back in harness. They're looking to you for leadership."

Dominic suppressed a smile at his friend's confused metaphor, but on reflection thought it valid. During his twenty years as Governor, he'd come to realise that it was his people who held the reins, driving him on to fulfil their needs and realise their expectations. If, as Rajeev had suggested, they still had confidence in him, he only hoped he deserved it.

Sylvia was first to use the Shahs' bathroom facilities, and after ten minutes emerged looking less travel-worn.

"This is amazing, Rajeev. I'd no idea you'd have hot water!"

"Being so close to the New Territory, the built-in power receptors still work here. I thought the Wall might block the energy flow, but it doesn't seem to affect it. Of course, the further east you get, the less reliable the voltage. It's a shame we could only bring thirty living units through. We allocated five to the remaining elders, reserved twenty for general use, and held a lottery for the other three."

"That sounds fair," Dominic said. "But I feel a bit uneasy grabbing one for my own family."

His daughter sighed heavily. "Oh, no. I knew it was too good to be true. Please, Dad, don't throw it back in their face."

"Krania's right, Dominic," Rajeev said. "The elders insisted you and I have these two powered units. They want us to concentrate on leading them out of this situation. Worrying about our families' comfort isn't going to help us meet that objective. So you have to set aside your natural modesty and accept the inevitable."

"All right. But I want the people to know that we're grateful for that gesture."

Rajeev shook his head. "They already know that, Dominic."

Over the meal Dominic quizzed Rajeev about the progress of the evacuation during their absence.

"You must have worked like beavers in the two weeks they gave you. These thirty prefabs are a real boon. And having hot water makes a big difference."

"Yes, but there's a drawback. We're not connected up to the mains water supply. We have to use electric pumps to raise river water up to our holding tanks for washing and showering."

"I see," Dominic said. "Is the system sustainable?"

"As long as people remember to boil water for drinking, yes."

"Well, water's plentiful here and we have electricity to boil it, so that sounds workable. What's been happening on the other side?"

"For the first few days, not a lot. That was frustrating for us, because we felt we could have used that time to bring more stuff over. But clearly they didn't want us to take anything else."

Martin asked, "What was to stop you just going through and helping yourselves?"

"When our two weeks were up, they placed armed guards at their end of the culvert. We sent a foraging party through, but they were forced back with no illusions as to what would happen if we tried it again."

Dominic asked, "And since then?"

"They've been ferrying settlers in – or so we assume. We hear the roar of shuttles landing more or less continuously during daylight hours. But as we can't get through or over the Wall, we don't really know what's going on over there."

Martin said, "Don't take this as a criticism, Deputy Shah, but didn't you consider installing a few concealed cameras and mini transmitters before you left?"

Rajeev sighed. "It sounds as if we could have done with you here, Martin."

Dominic said, "Never mind – this young man proved his worth to our mission in Ashwell. Unfortunately, we only have one of him."

Martin looked suitably embarrassed.

Then Rajeev turned to Dominic. "Have you had a chance to think about what happens next?"

His old friend smiled. "Very diplomatically put, Rajeev. You mean, do I have a clue what I intend doing? Well, I've had a couple of ideas. First, in general terms, we need to think of ways to hamper the Salvation settlers' plans."

"Difficult," Rajeev said, "as we have no way to reach them."

"True. But, do you remember that we started digging a tunnel under the Wall several years ago? We stopped because of a collapse and lack of resources, as I recall."

Shah sat up. "Yes. But it'll require an immense amount of manual labour."

Dominic said, "It's winter. I assume those stores you've built are full of provisions. If everyone has shelter and basic necessities, I'm guessing we have more than enough labour to resume digging."

Rajeev said, "We brought plenty of tools through – I'll get something organised tomorrow."

"Good. Because, with a way through – especially if we can keep the exit out of view – there's all sorts of mischief we could get up to. For example, we could climb up to the reservoir and disrupt their water supply. We could even resort to some basic vandalism, like smashing their power receptors. There must be a lot more chaos we could create."

Holding a potato-laden fork in mid-air Martin said, "I also have an idea. It involves a lot of 'ifs' though."

Dominic said, "Go on, young man."

"Well, if we could get through the Wall using your tunnel, and if we could locate the shuttle I stole, and if we could draw some missiles from Cara's stores, and if I knew how to fly the shuttle manually – I could knock out the powerhouse energy transmitter. That would deprive them of electricity for a very long time."

The potato having completed its transit he devoured it slowly, while everyone focussed on the champing of his jaws, spellbound.

Sylvia ventured, "Er… Martin, how much of that is… feasible?"

There was a pause while he swallowed his potato. Then he said, "Well, Governor Bradley has already put the case for a tunnel. Deputy Shah organised the concealment of the shuttle. Among the clips I grabbed on leaving the Salvation is a shuttle flight-training module. That's three out of four, which just leaves persuading Cara to release the weapons store codes."

"Oh," Sylvia said vacantly. "Is that all?"

Dominic dabbed his lips on his napkin, folded it neatly and pressed it to the table beside his plate.

Then to an astonished audience he said, "Do you know, I believe we could work on that?"

* * *

Almost exactly one week later the expedition was ready.

Its essential contingent would comprise Dominic, Sylvia, Rajeev, Toby and the young convict, along with three riflemen to guard him round the clock.

At the Bradley family's evening meal the night before their departure Dominic said to their guest, "Martin, I'd like you to come with us."

"I'd certainly like to, Governor. How can I be of use?"

"Last time we were in Beverton Red's father smashed up a couple of the rooftop batteries, so we're taking some spares along with us. I was hoping you'd have a clip that explained how to fix them up."

Martin smiled. "Fitting new batteries is a simple operation, Governor. Do they have connection leads?"

Dominic nodded.

"Then I'll be pleased to come and do it for you."

"Also, at the end of the trail we'll need to cut a way through to Cara's house – wide enough for the small wagon carrying the batteries. It'll be much easier for us if you can bring along your power cutter."

"You're people brought plenty of the smaller hand tool batteries through the culvert. I'll grab a half dozen to take with me."

Sighing heavily Krania said, "It looks as if everyone's invited but me! Am I supposed to stay here on my own, then?"

Dominic looked across at his wife, who merely raised her eyebrows.

He saw no valid reason to leave their daughter behind. The mission shouldn't present any serious dangers, and so to keep the peace he replied, "Of course not. You'll be company for Martin. But get an early night – we leave an hour after dawn."

Everyone helped clear away the supper plates, made their final preparations for the morning's journey, and retired.

Later before she and Dominic went to sleep Sylvia said, "Explain it to me again – why Beverton?"

"It's the only portal left where there's still a possibility she'll talk to me. Also it's the only one currently accessible to us."

"What about young Red? Do you really think he'll fool Cara?"

"I can't be certain. But she once said that her recognition routines aren't infallible. Red's son is a close double for his old man. I'm hoping that whatever her monitors look for will be similar enough in the son's case to pass for his father."

"You have the key safe, I suppose?"

"Of course. It's in my tunic pocket."

"Last time you saw Cara she dumped you. What makes you think she'll change her mind? I hope you're not relying on her being a woman."

"No, I'm going to try and reason with her – appeal to her logic."

"It sounds like a long shot, Dominic."

"It's all we have, my love."

* * *

"Ladies and gentlemen, we've been flying in settlers for almost four weeks now. Naturally I've read all the log reports on the operation, and I congratulate you all on your contributions. I have been hearing rumours though, that some of our settlers are experiencing difficulties. Would any of you care to elaborate?"

The Salvation's Joint Watch Committee's monthly session had glossed over shipboard issues to concentrate on the overriding topic of the settlement of the New Territory. Commander Boone studied the faces of the representatives gathered around the table. There were ten of them – two from each Watch – and protocol demanded he take heed of whatever advice they had to give him. However, as the ship's Commander in Chief he had the respect of everyone on board, whether passengers or crew.

Herbert Harrison, still weakened from his recent illness, respectfully raised a hand and watched for Boone's almost imperceptible nod of acknowledgment. He spoke slowly with frequent pauses for breath.

"As you know Red Watch didn't support the enforced evacuation of the terrestrial settlers. However we accepted the majority decision – and indeed some of our families were eager to join the first wave. But reports suggest actual conditions have fallen far short of their expectations."

Irwin Cropper sneered and didn't bother requesting permission to speak. "I'd expect such negative comments from Red Watch. From what I'm hearing from our people things aren't that bad."

A Blue Watch member said, "They're not that good, either, Councillor. We didn't prepare our people well enough for all the work there is to do in the fields. They're finding it hard to handle the ploughing and harrowing equipment. Very few seem to have any natural skill in making a direct trench."

"Ploughing a straight furrow," Harrison muttered.

"Yes, quite. Well, it's something you can't learn on a simulator – not unless the ground's completely level. There isn't an acre that's ready yet for the winter frosts. That could affect spring sowing and ultimately next year's harvest. It's worrying."

Cropper interjected, "We can always provide recycled food from the Salvation until they acquire these skills. And there's game in the forest for them to shoot."

Now Yellow Watch pitched in. "But nobody seems to have the stomach for killing wild animals – let alone eating their meat. Besides there's a dearth of hunting rifles – the Earth settlers seem to have taken most of them."

An Orange Watch representative added, "It's not only rifles – they've stripped their houses of cutlery and hand tools. Every can opener has been taken – personally I think that was a vindictive move. And when we asked Cara, she said they'd had all of her stock, and, no, the Ancient Ones didn't think we'd need electric openers. We're having to saw the tops off food cans – those that haven't been taken, that is."

Blue Watch added, "And our people are nervous of the Earth folk choosing to re-settle just on the other side of the Wall. It makes them feel uneasy."

For once Boone allowed his irritation to show in the form of a dark scowl. But he didn't raise or change the tone of his voice. "Did nobody think to negotiate with them as to what they should take or leave for our people, and how far away they should go?"

A circle of blank expressions gave him his answer.

Then Cropper said nervously, "But our settlers aren't going to starve. They have shelter and heating. These problems are just minor irritations."

Before closing the session the Commander sighed and said, "I very much hope they are, Councillor."

* * *

The journey from the coast to the outskirts of Beverton was uneventful. The ash-covered road was clear – evidence that the housemaid dragons were still doing their job of continuously burning off new growth. This didn't surprise Dominic, because to his knowledge nothing had happened over the past twenty years to interfere with them, their supporting rail or solar power modules.

Recalling that the mechanised guards were programmed to blast any large creature that approached them, whenever he heard one snorting on the trail ahead, Dominic had the travellers lead their horses into the undergrowth until it had passed.

As had been the case twenty years earlier, on reaching the outskirts of the town the cleared road gave way to unchecked growth, but both Dominic and Rajeev were fairly certain where Cara's house was located.

"We've not far to go now," Dominic said. "But it's too late for Martin to begin cutting. We'll camp here and start after breakfast."

Later the next morning saw them standing in front of the building housing the portal where Cara had first appeared. Toby helped Martin manhandle the spare batteries onto the roof by the rear staircase. As he'd predicted, it was a simple matter to connect them up.

Dominic then examined the variously patterned tiles around the doorway, looking for the four that matched the motifs depicted on the key. For the key to work, the palms that pressed those tiles twenty years ago must do so again today. Only three of them would satisfy that requirement. His theory that Red's genetic makeup was close enough to his father's to provide the fourth match would now be tested.

He beckoned to the guards who held the young raider.

"Untie his hands and bring him over here."

When Red stood before him he said, "You know what I want you to do?"

"I think so," he mumbled.

"You understand that I asked the Ashwell elders to release you into my custody just so that you could perform this task? And that, as long as you do as I ask, I won't take you back to stand trial – which would, we both know, result in your execution by drowning?"

Red nodded.

"Good. This is the tile." He indicated the one bearing a six-pointed star.

He handed the key to Toby, who approached the door and offered it into the slot beside it. Then he stood poised with his thumb ready to depress the button just underneath. Dominic had never known for sure that a unique thumbprint was critical to the process – but it would be careless to assume otherwise.

"Now, let's place our palms against our tiles and – when I say 'press' – then press and hold until I say 'release' – likewise with the button, Toby. All right?"

All nodded.

"Toby, why not count us in the way you did twenty years ago, in your ancient tongue? Do you remember?"

Toby smiled. "Yes, Marshal. Here goes. Yan – chan – thether – mether – pip!"

Almost simultaneously Dominic said, "Press."

After a few seconds he said, "Release."

He couldn't breathe. The twenty years separating this moment of suspense from that other one were suddenly condensed into a few seconds. But that fact alone didn't ensure the opening of the door before him. It took faith as well.

He heard the *click* and breathed again. Next came the *hiss* as the two halves of the door drew apart.

He stepped inside and signalled the other four to follow. All but Red knew upon which of the black circles they'd stood all those years ago, and did the same today, leaving him only one choice. As before, the backlighting died as Cara's transparent form materialised.

Dominic had expected to be quizzed as to what he was doing here – what were his expectations? But instead the hologram launched into a monologue that could only have been prepared for this moment.

"Your ancestors – those whom you call the Ancient Ones, and who you know constructed the Wall around Fenwold – had one objective: to assure the survival of Mankind.

"To achieve this goal they set wheels in motion that would deliver the Earth to the surviving group. They calculated that the probability of one or other of the groups outliving the estimated quarantine period was more than fifty per cent. I can find no record of their having computed the likelihood that both groups would survive.

"Because time to complete preparations was limited, no programming resource was allocated to my ability to direct a shared settlement should the need arise. I was, however, provided with a complex algorithm which – taking account of several factors – enables me to calculate the probability that any surviving human group might achieve a successful settlement. Given the present circumstances, I am able to employ that algorithm for either group – Earth dwellers or star liner refugees. Simple logic dictates that I concentrate my advisory resources on the group with the greater probability of success.

"When I made that assessment nine weeks ago, results favoured the group on board the Salvation. Therefore I was forced to break off communications with you. The best that I could do was to counsel your withdrawal from the New

Territory, and that you abandon the treasures that I had opened up for you over the past twenty years.

"But – as I have repeated to you frequently – I am not a person, but a computer. As a result I re-run the algorithm constantly. I have no choice in this – it happens whenever new information becomes available. This being the case, the result is subject to change. Every step forward, every mistake made by one group or the other affects the relative likelihood of either group's survival. But when I review my programs for guidance should I need to reverse my earlier decision, I find none. I become caught up in logic loops and repetitive sub-routines. This could adversely affect my processing capacity, so safety overrides cut in and prevent my going round in circles forever. All that is left to me is to revert to the Ancient Ones' ultimate objective and make an appropriate judgement. And it is this.

"I now calculate that either group is fully capable of restoring civilization to Earth. Therefore I cannot favour one side or the other. But neither will I withhold any information that might assist either group to successfully colonise the New Territory. All you have to do is ask me. So, what do you want to know?"

Though her reasoning sounded complicated, Bradley thought he understood what Cara had told them. But he needed clarification before he barked out the series of questions that were already forming a bustling queue in his mind.

"Tell me Cara, is this information available at the portals on the Salvation and in the New Territory? And if so, are the Salvation's settlers aware of it?"

"It is available at the New Territory portal, but the new settlers have not yet consulted me there. The portal on the Salvation does not fully share my functions and has no knowledge of my recalculations."

"Thank you. In that case, I have several questions. First, how many mini power plants are there and where are they stored?"

"There are one thousand and they can be found in container number five-zero-one-six."

Bradley decided it was time to dispense with niceties, so he didn't bother to thank Cara this time. "What's the code for entry?"

"Alpha-two-November-five."

Before he asked his next question, he had a mild panic attack when a thought occurred to him. He turned around and noticed that Rajeev was noting down Cara's responses. Relieved, he turned back to face her image.

Even in spite of her earlier promise not to withhold information, he doubted that she would give a truthful answer to his next query. But, nothing ventured…

"Where are the shuttle missiles and electronic weapons stored and what are their entry codes?"

Without hesitation she replied. "The shuttle missiles are in container number five-four-two-seven. Code four-hotel-Mike-seven. The electronic weapons are stored in container number five-four-two-nine. Code seven-Lima-Oscar-two."

Though he knew such niceties to be illogical, he couldn't help himself.

"Thank you, Cara," he said.

"You are welcome, Dominic. Do you have any further questions?"

"No."

For once he didn't wait for Cara's image to flicker and fade. Instead he turned to the others and gestured that they should leave.

337

Once outside he barked the general instruction, "Come on. We must break through into to the New Territory before they speak to Cara and deny us what we need to win this war!"

CHAPTER THIRTY-TWO
GUERRILLA TACTICS

All the way home questions whirled around in Dominic's mind. Why hadn't the newcomers consulted Cara? Had the shipboard hologram provided them with their settlement plans – or were they just too arrogant to think they needed further guidance? If they did decide to consult her, and she told them she'd be assisting both sides, would they clear out the weapons stores just as a precaution? And how could his people gain access to those stores meanwhile? He knew that Rajeev's tunnel workers had only succeeded in breaking a short distance into the fabric of the Wall. In the absence of a tunnel, there remained only one way through.

He spurred his horse to bring him up beside Rajeev, who rode a few strides ahead of him.

"Rajeev, were you able to establish the strength and routines of the guards at the far end of the culvert?"

"We made some observations. There are six guards on duty during the day, changing every four hours. But this is reduced to just two between eight at night and four in the morning, changing at midnight."

"Only two? Why is that, do you think?"

"I've wondered about that, Dominic. I can only assume it's because, in the hours of darkness when there's little activity or noise of shuttles landing, any craft floating through would be heard as soon as it moved in from our end. The slightest motion in the water echoes like anything. As soon as they heard anything they could easily call up reinforcements and be ready to deal with whoever was coming through. The only concession seems to be that they use male and female guards on the daylight watches, but only males at night. A nod to old-fashioned chivalry, I suppose."

Dominic smiled and shook his head, bemused by his friend's reasoning. "We'll speak more about this later, Rajeev. Thanks."

He reined back his horse and waited for Martin and Krania, deep in conversation. "Can you spare a few minutes, Martin? There's something I need to discuss with you. Do you mind if I tear him away, Krania?"

"No," she smiled. "I'll go and bother Mum." And she trotted forwards to ride with Sylvia.

Martin seemed in good spirits. "How can I help you, Governor?"

"I want to understand the mentality of your people."

The young lad shook his head. "That might be difficult, Sir. Because we're separated into five watches, there are probably as many political outlooks, if that's what you mean."

"Not exactly. Rather than the differences between the watches, I need to appreciate the common qualities that result from being cooped up in a spaceship with twelve thousand other people. In terms of relationships, ignoring political differences, what sort of mentality does that produce?"

Martin sighed heavily.

"Trust, I'd say. The knowledge that, however much an adversary might dislike you, they would never break the basic rules of honour."

"You mean your word is your bond. And you wouldn't ever cheat."

"The Salvation is a wonderful craft, Governor. It's been our home and protected us for more than eight hundred years. But we all know it's fragile. If someone neglected their duty, they could jeopardise the ship and everyone on it. So we do things by the book, without question. And we trust everyone else to do the same. Cheating isn't a concept that would occur to us naturally."

Dominic smiled. "Thank you, Martin. That's what I hoped you'd say."

Then he said, "I've never really thanked you for what you've done, Martin. But I often wonder how you found the courage to leave your friends and family on the Salvation to rescue my daughter and help us in our struggle."

Martin looked embarrassed. "I appreciate your thanks, Governor. I could say I was motivated by a yearning for justice and a peaceful settlement of the differences between our people – and although that's partly true, it isn't the entire story."

Dominic frowned. "I don't understand, son."

The youth took a deep breath. "I'm sure you know I left a note to protect my parents, saying I was besotted with your daughter, and that my feelings for her drove me to steal that shuttle and bring her back to you."

"Yes, I know that. It was a very clever plan."

"It wasn't just a plan, Sir. It was the truth."

Dominic caught his breath, and then smiled. "Have you told her?"

Martin stared into the distance. "Not exactly."

"Really? What on earth have you two been talking about for the past three hours?"

"Oh, general things."

"Well, we'll be home by mid-afternoon. I suggest you spend the next couple of hours being a bit more specific."

* * *

Approaching what currently passed for home, the travellers were greeted by the distant roar of shuttles, still presumably bringing in new settlers and their luggage at the landing strip further up river. Though this was to be expected, they were treated to two immediate surprises. The first was that Red – who so far had acted morose and withdrawn – was capable of a wide, boyish grin and a joyous cry.

His outburst was in response to the other surprise.

"Mary! It's my Mary!"

Owen McMahon was on hand to help them dismount and explain her presence. "After Red's capture she wandered off along with most of his other followers. She arrived on foot at the ferry port this morning, with only the clothes she stood up in and no money for the ferry fare. I think Sean took pity on her and turned a blind eye."

"Let me down to her!" Red pleaded.

Weary from the journey, Dominic's only thoughts tended towards a hot meal, even though it was nowhere near suppertime. In any event he didn't relish an argument with Red over a simple reunion. So far the outlaw had been cooperative – even compliant. There could be no harm in it.

Turning to the guards he said, "Let him down and untie his hands. But watch him. Red, I'll give you five minutes."

The couple kissed and stood locked in a prolonged embrace, saying little.

As Sylvia dismounted she said, "Isn't it strange that even wicked people are capable of such affection?"

Quietly Dominic replied, "The longer I live it seems the less I understand about good and evil, love and hate. When I was younger they were like black and white. Now all I see are shades of grey."

"That girl doesn't look as if she's had a proper meal in days, Dominic. Let's offer her supper and a bed tonight."

He was too tired to argue. "All right. If you're happy to set another place."

"I'll ask her in a while," she said. Then she looked around. "Where's Krania gone? If you see her, ask her to come and help me in the kitchen, would you?" Then she handed her horse's reins to a waiting stable lad and walked towards their dwelling.

Dominic had seen Martin and Krania take their horses to the lean-to stables a few minutes earlier. The image had lodged itself in his mind. They walked side by side, Krania's piebald gelding on her left, and Martin's fine Arab to his right. And it gladdened his heart to recall one simple detail.

They were holding hands.

"I'm not sure where she's gone," he called to Sylvia. "I'll come and help you."

* * *

"I'm sorry we've only rabbit," Sylvia said.

Their guest thrust her fork into the pot and speared a leg, which she transferred to her hands and voraciously stripped of its sinewy flesh.

Tactfully Sylvia said, "As it's stew, I'll ladle it out, shall I?"

Laying the bare bone on the side of her plate, Mary said, "Oh. Sorry, missus. First proper meal in five days."

While her hostess dished out the stew, the girl shuffled in her seat and asked Dominic, "What are you going to do with him?"

"Well, you know he's guilty of some terrible things, don't you?"

343

She didn't answer, but only pursed her lips.

"Because I wanted him to help me with something important, I asked the Ashwell elders to place him in my charge."

Fumbling with her fork, she put it down and picked up her spoon to scoop up the juicy bits of meat and vegetables. "And has he done what you wanted him to?" she slurped.

"Yes," he replied tetchily, "but that doesn't mean he's paid for his crimes. He'll have to remain in custody. We've converted one of the units into a cellblock for him and his guards. It's better than he could have expected if he'd gone on trial."

She seemed more or less satisfied with his answer, and continued shovelling down her stew.

He was glad about that, because there were more important things on his mind just now.

"Well, Martin – have you had any time to study your shuttle piloting clip in between – um – other things?"

"Oh yes, Governor. I'm as confident as I'll ever be."

He'd never found Martin's confidence lacking – except in the courtship of his daughter - although he felt from looks that had passed between them during the meal that the lad might have recently addressed that particular issue. He hoped so anyway, because he genuinely liked him, and occasionally glimpsed his younger self in his actions. Regardless of all that, piloting a shuttle could be no trivial task, and over-confidence might be a very dangerous thing. But what could he do but take the boy at his word?

"That's good," he said. "On another issue, that weapon you used in Ashwell – does the battery pack have any power left in it?"

"The second shot would have used a lot of its power, Governor. But there'll be some charge left."

"Enough for two stun shots?"

Martin looked thoughtful. "I believe so, yes."

"Splendid. In that case, are you up for a mission tonight? I'll ask Marshal McMahon to go with you."

"Yes, Governor. What do you want us to do?"

"Two things. First, your people's shuttles are still making enough noise to mask the sound of movement in the water. So when you're done here I want you to get your gun and take a small boat to the far end of the culvert, but not so far that the guards can see you. Then I want you to wait for the second night watch to come on – around midnight. Move out, then stun, bind and gag them. That'll allow us to send more people through to do what's necessary before the first day watch turns up at four o'clock."

"That's a long wait, Governor. Why not act during the first night watch?"

"Because settlers will still be moving about. There's less risk we'll be noticed in the wee small hours."

"I see. Yes, that makes sense. There's just one thing that worries me."

"What's that?"

"Well, it'll take a few seconds to row our boat out of the culvert so that I can take a clear shot. That's enough time for the guards to get one in first."

"Hmm. Good point," Dominic said, and tapped the table as he thought about the problem.

Before he could think of a solution Mary said, "You need a distraction, so the guards will have their backs to him. That'll help him get his second shot in as well. I suppose there's some kind of jetty on the other side?"

Wide-eyed, Dominic could only answer her truthfully. "Er, yes. The guards will probably be on it."

"So if something took their attention from the shore, they'd be looking away from the culvert?"

"Yes," Dominic drawled. "And that something would be…?"

"Me. Or better still, me and her. There'll be more chance of it working if there's two of us." She nodded in Krania's direction. "She's your daughter, isn't she? I heard what she did at Ashwell. That must have taken some nerve."

Then she addressed Krania directly. "Well, are you up for it? Can you swim?"

Krania sat up and blinked a couple of times. Then she said, "Yes. Why not? I've often swum in that part of the river. It's quite safe. What will we have to do?"

"Nothing much really. Just slip out of the boat, swim underwater to the bank and then walk towards them on the jetty. They're bound to turn round. Then your boyfriend can…" She made a pointed gun shape with her hand and uttered a soft *puff*.

Sylvia said, "Wait a minute, Mary. You're not suggesting any – er – physical contact with those guards, are you?"

"No, missus. I just want them to look at us. She won't come to any harm. And I don't intend to neither."

Sylvia bit her bottom lip. "None of them have any hair. Yours is growing back, Krania, and Mary's could do with a chop."

Mary looked concerned and argued, "It'll be dark and there's no moon tonight. They won't be looking at detail. Just our being there will distract them. It'll all be over in a few seconds. I don't think it'll make any difference."

Martin said, "You'll need to come out in the boat with Owen McMahon and me – in which case, I think we'd better get going. Oh, but what was that other thing you wanted us to do, Governor?"

"Only this. Find the container where Cara told us the missiles were kept – Rajeev has the number and the code – take a couple, make your way to the shuttle, take it up and destroy the powerhouse energy transmitter as you suggested – and get yourselves back here before the next change of guard!"

"Oh," Martin said. "Is that all?"

CHAPTER THIRTY-THREE
NIGHT OF ACTION

The waiting was almost unbearable. And it was cold. Of course, she'd known it would be – it was mid-winter, after all. Her mother had made them all take along plenty of warm clothing and blankets, as well as some bits of food to nibble. She'd also managed to rustle up a couple of thermos flasks taken from Cara's stores, which she'd hurriedly filled with warmed up rabbit stock, and they had plenty of bottled drinking water. Because of the long wait though, none of them seemed eager to consume much liquid.

But the hardest part was not being able to talk, at least not after the shuttles had ceased their row. Ever since Martin had declared his feelings on their way back from Beverton, she'd wanted nothing more than to tell him again how she felt for him. Her earlier mask of indifference had been nothing more than a wall of defence, meant to soften the blow of his apparent coolness towards her. Though his declaration today had come out of the blue, somehow it had released all of those secret wishes that she'd kept locked away, destined for oblivion once she was certain all hope was lost. She had even convinced herself that he and Jessica had been emotionally involved, and that she would wake one morning to the news that he'd returned to his old life on board the Salvation.

As they couldn't talk, for a while they found solace in exchanging loving, longing glances. But this soon proved frustrating, so instead in her mind she went through over and over again what she and Mary were supposed to do. This didn't pass much time, because it wasn't so difficult – slip out of the boat, swim under water to the bank, walk onto the jetty and attract the guards' attention so that Martin could stun them from behind. What could be simpler? The water would be very cold, she knew, but she'd swum in this river before in all seasons. It wasn't something that bothered her.

At last they heard the short conversation that signified the change of guard. As the sound of the retiring soldiers' boots on the jetty's timbers gave way to silence, Mary looked at her and whispered, "Ready?"

She nodded.

"Strip off then."

She suddenly panicked, and turned to see Martin and Owen staring at them. Mary's sign language left them in no doubt that their attention was unwelcome, and they had the decency to turn around and face the other way. McMahon gazed at the night sky while Martin closely studied his gun.

Krania realised she hadn't prepared herself for this bit. She'd glossed over the detail in her mind. She grimaced and whispered, "Everything?"

Mary nodded and in fact was already half undressed. Of course it was logical. Their task was to distract the guards. What could be more distracting than two naked women? What else could she do? She took off her clothes, drew a deep breath and followed Mary silently under the water.

She'd been wrong about it being cold. It wasn't. It was absolutely freezing. To take her mind off the acute discomfort she concentrated on keeping her body below the surface. Very soon she was touching the riverbed – she must be in the shallows. As gracefully as possible she raised herself out of the water and joined Mary at the landside end of the jetty. The guards lounged at the far end, no more than twenty strides away, dutifully watching the culvert and the river. It was obvious they hadn't yet seen or heard them.

Mary took her hand, smiled and whispered, "Come on – you'll probably never do anything like this again."

Despite the serious nature of their mission, suddenly she wanted to laugh out loud – at this ridiculous exploit, the sheer thrill of their bravado – and because their audacious plan might actually work.

They walked towards their quarry.

The repeated *thud* of their bare feet on the boardwalk was loud enough to turn the heads of the guards, whose faces registered at first surprise, then disbelief, followed by two burgeoning grins. Those appreciative smiles were not to develop fully, however, because first one, and then the other bemused victim crumpled onto the decking like sacks of potatoes.

Krania saw Martin put down the gun, and then turn around and grab an oar, joining McMahon in rowing the boat towards the shore, their backs towards the two women. For a moment she bathed in the satisfaction that their part of the mission had succeeded. But then almost immediately she realised the predicament they were in. Mary's knowing glance was sympathetic, and she said softly, "Don't worry."

As the boat touched the bank she said harshly, "Don't either of you two dare to turn round! I've got hold of the prow!" And she grabbed and held on to the front end of the craft.

"Now, without turning your heads, hand out our clothes and blankets from the back."

To their credit the men did as instructed and looked away, while the women dried off as best they could with the blankets and hurriedly pulled on their garments. Once dressed, Krania hugged her clothes to her, relishing their warmth.

"All right," Mary said. "We're dressed. Now we swap places, I think."

As planned, the two males climbed out of the boat and held it steady while the girls stepped aboard and grabbed the oars.

Before pushing them off Martin bent down and kissed Krania on the lips, and then whispered in her ear, "I nearly missed them – you looked so gorgeous."

She gasped and scowled, but relaxed when she realised he must be teasing her. He and McMahon manhandled the boat around and she flashed him a smile over her shoulder. Then she bent her back with Mary to row back through the culvert, and give the signal that the next phase of the raid could begin.

For much of that night she prayed to the Gods of the Wall for his safety. And when she wasn't praying, she was trying to decide whether he'd really been teasing her or not.

* * *

Martin and McMahon exchanged beaming smiles as Krania and Mary disappeared into the culvert, though not a word was said as to what each thought he might have glimpsed momentarily.

McMahon reached inside his tunic and produced a length of rope, took a knife from his belt and set about binding the guards' hands and feet. Martin handed him a couple of rags, and soon the soldiers were suitably gagged. They dragged their unconscious bodies a few strides along the quay to a small shed where wharf ropes had been kept before the evacuation. They leaned the two men against its door, so that they'd remain out of sight for the time being, but would be easily located when missed.

Martin said, "You have the numbers, Marshal?"

Nodding, McMahon produced the piece of paper that Rajeev had given him. He handed it to Martin saying, "No need for formality, young man. Call me Owen."

Martin took out a torch and studied the paper. "Lead on then, Owen."

As he did so McMahon said, "My family settled here when I was ten. The growing city and the woods were my playground. It grieved my parents to be turned out so readily. It grieves me too. So I'm more than eager to be a part of tonight's mission.

"If we head for the Wall and stick to it for fifty strides we'll be in a copse that'll provide good cover. From there we'll follow a forest trail for a couple of furlongs until we come to the eastern limit of Cara's stores. All the containers are consecutively numbered but cover a vast area. It might take us half an hour to find the ones we're looking for."

"We'd best get a move on then," said Martin. "The others won't be far behind. Do you know what they're after?"

"Wheelbarrows to start with. That container's open already – third row in, I think. The barrows will help them move what they're really after – miniature powerhouses and guns like yours. What did you do with it, by the way?"

"I left it in the boat – battery was spent."

"Have you no spares? I thought we'd grabbed as many batteries as we could when we had to clear out."

"Not these. They're specific to this model. They should be in the same container as the weapons."

"How did you come by yours?"

"My Dad got it from a contact in the military. He insisted I bring it – though I thought nothing of it until I realised it could actually save lives if we used it to target Red and Carson."

Owen said, "If I were your father, I'd have insisted you bring a weapon too. As for now, don't worry – I have my rifle." He touched the weapon that hung from his shoulder.

"Let's hope you won't need to use it," Martin said. He looked around. "Governor Bradley was right. At this hour of the night, everyone's indoors and most likely asleep."

"Good," McMahon said. "Let's go."

Twenty-five minutes' easy walking brought them to the vicinity of the shuttle missile container. Flicking his torch Martin read Rajeev's note again and said, "Over there. I'll key in the code." He did so, turned the door handle and pushed the door open. The container illuminated automatically. It was packed with metal boxes.

"How many in a box?" Owen asked.

"Not sure. Let's have a look."

They lifted one of the boxes down and lowered it to the floor. Martin pulled a quick-release catch and heard a feint *hiss*.

Owen remarked, "It always amazes me how boxes like these can stay airtight for over eight hundred years. How many then?"

"There are six in here. Governor Bradley suggested we take two, but they're not that big." He lifted one from the box. "And not too heavy. I reckon I could carry two in my knapsack. Could you take another two, just for insurance?"

"Sure, Martin."

They loaded two missiles each into their bags and closed the container.

"Where to now, Owen?"

"I was on the team that hid your shuttle. We towed it away from the landing strip and into the forest, just beyond the western limit of the containers. I reckon it's about an hour's trek from here. Are you up for it?"

Martin smiled. "It's longer than my average exercise walk on board the Salvation. But I think I'll manage it."

353

They walked in silence for ten minutes or so. Then Martin said, "It's weird walking between these containers in the middle of the night, don't you think, Owen?"

"Spooky, I'd call it. I'm no coward, but I'm glad to have your company. I suppose it's knowing they were put here centuries ago, and that the people who packed them are all dead and gone. It gives me the shivers."

Martin said, "Likewise."

It was approaching two o'clock when they reached the shuttle. It stood at the centre of a clearing about five chains across.

Owen said, "Can you lift off from here without setting fire to the trees?"

"Probably. I might scorch the grass and shrubs a bit, but on autopilot it'll be a perfectly vertical lift, so there should be minimal spread of ignition blast."

"Shall we go for it then?"

"Yup. But first we have to prime and fit the missiles."

This wasn't too difficult a task, but as Martin insisted on checking and re-checking that they'd done it properly, the operation took them about forty minutes.

Martin then examined the area around the ship.

"What are you looking for?" McMahon asked him.

"I'm checking there are no loose rocks that might be thrown up and damage the undercarriage on take-off."

Then he pressed a button on the side of the shuttle. The door *swished* open and steps automatically unfolded inviting them to step aboard.

Directing Owen to the co-pilot's seat on the right, Martin took his place in the pilot's chair. He took the plastic disc from his tunic pocket, and placed it in its slot on the dashboard, which immediately lit up.

"I need to do a few safety and system checks," he said. When I left the Salvation, the shuttle dock attendants did it all remotely. Down here I'll have to do it myself. It won't take too long."

Taking a variety of clips from his pocket, he selected one and attached it to his temple implant. Then he spent a few minutes going through the checking routine as directed by the clip software. When he'd finished he detached the clip and put it away.

"Everything all right?" Owen asked.

He hesitated. "It shouldn't be a problem, but there's been some power seepage while the shuttle's been standing." Then he grinned. "But I'm sure there's enough for what we have to do."

"Well then, shall we go?" Owen asked, rubbing his hands.

"I've been thinking," Martin said. "As soon as we take off, the racket we make will be sure to rouse the relief guard. To give our people time to collect as much stuff as possible, we should wait until the change of guard at four. Our people should be back through the culvert by then."

Owen nodded. "That makes sense." He looked at his watch. "So, we have an hour to kill. Tell me all about life on board a star liner."

* * *

"It's time, Martin."

"Oh, right. You're supposed to strap yourself in with that belt thing, but as it's unlikely we'll survive a crash, I wouldn't bother. Engaging autopilot."

He pressed a key on the dashboard.

"Ignition."

An almighty *roar* accompanied the shuttle's fight against gravity. Rigid in his seat, Owen gripped the armrests, his face contorted, while Martin thought it strange that such a hardened lawman should find a simple lift-off so terrifying. But then he realised that this must be McMahon's first experience of flying.

He smiled and yelled, "It's all right to be scared, Owen. I felt the same way the first time I got on a horse!"

The craft gained height until it was clear of the forest canopy.

"Here goes, then," said Martin who, although a declared agnostic, silently prayed for divine protection. "Engaging manual control."

The shuttle lurched downwards, its lights illuminating a big horse chestnut that seemed to be reaching out to embrace them. Martin struggled with the controls to regain the lost altitude while Owen, white faced, tried frantically to fasten his safety belt.

The craft lurched upwards again in a slow spiral until at last it levelled out.

"I think I've got the hang of it now," Martin said.

McMahon gulped and said, "I'm glad. That was – an interesting experience, Martin. I thought you'd flown this from the Moon?"

"I didn't – the autopilot did. This is my first manual flight. I had the simulator clip to teach me, but without real controls it's just theoretical. Now I know where things are, I'll be fine."

McMahon heaved a sigh of relief. "Where are we?" he said. "I can hardly see a thing."

"That's an advantage in a way," Martin said. "It'll be easier to pick out the power house lights. They should be to the west – that's two hundred and seventy degrees on that circular indicator."

Owen studied the compass. "In that case, we're going the wrong way."

"All right. I'll turn her round." Now more confident, he made a wide, gentle turn to point the craft towards the west. "Can you see any lights?"

Owen peered through the cockpit window. "Nothing yet. Wait a minute. Yes. I think I can." He glanced again at the compass. "Head about ten degrees to your left."

"Port," Martin said.

Owen smiled. "Same as a boat," he said.

They grinned at each other, and Martin felt a real liking for this man, sensing an empathy that transcended the difference in their ages. "I see it now," he said, tapping keys on the console and reading data from the screen just above it. "We should be there in three minutes."

"How do you fire the missiles?" Owen asked.

"You see those switches numbered one to four?"

"Yes."

"Each controls a different missile. Sorry – you probably guessed that. You flip the switch to arm the missile you want to fire, select your target on the screen by aligning the cross hairs, press the button above the switch to lock onto the target, and press it again to fire."

"Sounds as if you can't miss. Whereabouts do you plan to concentrate your fire?"

"Best would be to blast the building at the base of the transmission tower, but there's a dilemma."

"What's that?"

"I can select human detection mode, so that if there's anyone in there – maintenance personnel, for example – the missile won't fire."

"Oh," said McMahon. "And what if that happens?"

"I'll have to target the tower itself, but as it's a broad mesh latticework structure, I can't guarantee a good strike. The missile might even pass through."

"But you'd have three more shots at it."

"Yes. Well, we're nearly there. What do I do?"

Owen looked shocked. "Pardon?"

"Well, I'm just the pilot. For important decisions, I defer to your seniority."

The Marshal's brow wrinkled. "You don't mind putting people on a spot, do you, Martin?"

"I didn't want to have you worrying about it for too long. You'll have to make a snap decision."

"Thanks very much. All right. Well, we haven't set out to kill anyone tonight. I think you should have the detector on."

The powerhouse was now directly ahead. Martin hit the keyboard. "Detection mode engaged. Selecting number one missile. Selecting target – locking on. Firing!"

Nothing happened. They zoomed over their target.

"Someone must be in there," Owen said.

"All right. I'll wheel round to port ninety degrees and have a go at the tower."

As he approached from the south he said, "I'll have to disengage the detector, or else the computer might still pick up the human and disable the shot. I'm assuming whoever's down there is in the building and not climbing up the metalwork."

Owen peered out into the inky darkness. "Sounds like a reasonable assumption to me," he said.

"Here goes then. Re-arming number one – targeting – locking on – firing!"

The missile sped away towards the target, but as Martin had feared it passed through the latticework and struck the open ground about fifty strides beyond, its implosion throwing up a minimal amount of debris.

As he pulled away to the north Owen asked, "Was that a dud?"

"Not at all. These are implosive missiles. They suck material inwards – that's why they're so good for demolishing buildings. But they have to hit something first."

This last remark was tinged with disappointment.

Owen said. "All right. Well, we're not beaten yet. Can you go back and fly over for us to have a look?"

"Sure," Martin replied. "I'll hover for a bit and engage the shuttle spotlight."

Moments later they hung in the air above the powerhouse complex.

"Look there!" Owen said. " He pointed at two figures running from the building below the tower. "They're leaving. Let's have another go at the base."

"Right you are, Skipper!" Martin enthused, pulling away to prepare for another approach.

McMahon said, "How's our battery holding out?"

Martin consulted the dashboard screen, and his exuberance quickly diminished. "Oh, curses! Not too well I'm afraid. We'd better launch this one and go."

"Let's do it then, Martin!"

He wheeled the craft around again and locked on to the target. "Firing!" he said at last. "Switching to rear view."

Though receding, the image on the screen showed the base building imploding and the metal tower slowly toppling until it smashed onto the concrete below.

The two men locked hands in the air and cheered gleefully. But Martin's concentration lapsed momentarily and the craft wobbled, causing him to check his enthusiasm and fight to regain control.

Then McMahon peered at the screen.

"What's that?"

"What's what?"

"I don't know. Behind us."

Martin looked. "Oh, blast!"

"What's the matter?"

"We have company."

"Why is it getting bigger? Are you zooming in?"

"No. It's getting closer."

"Well, if you can make this thing go any faster, I'd appreciate it. It's another shuttle, isn't it? One of theirs, I suppose?"

"This is the only one that isn't. They must have heard us."

"From behind the Moon?"

Martin grimaced. "No. For some reason the crew of the last shuttle that landed must have decided to stay overnight. I wonder…? I haven't looked at a calendar lately – you know about months and years, don't you?"

"Yes," Owen said. "Cara told us. We keep the same calendar as you. Why?"

"Well, I know it's December, but what's the date?"

McMahon thought for a moment. "It's after midnight, so it's the twenty-sixth."

"Ah, that explains why the settlement's so quiet."

"What do you mean?"

"For the devout ones amongst us – to be fair, most of us – yesterday was the assumed birthday of our major prophet. Traditionally families stay in their quarters on Christmas night – that's what we call it – for a sort of bonding experience. It's quite pleasantly sentimental actually, even if you're not religious. I bet the crew have family down here."

McMahon said, "I hope they're not too upset about us breaking up their party."

As he said this Martin heeled the craft over to starboard while a missile *swished* past, just missing the port wing. "I think they probably are," he said.

"Are we heading for home?" Owen asked, reaching for the dashboard for support.

"Hang on," Martin said, swinging the shuttle violently to port as another missile *whizzed* by on the starboard side. "That's the general idea."

"I wonder what it's like being imploded?" McMahon mused.

"Try not to think about it," Martin said. "Oh, bugger!"

The expletive only just preceded an urgent claxon-like sound that now filled the cabin.

"That's something bad, isn't it?" McMahon said dryly.

"You could say that. As the battery's nearly spent, in thirty seconds the autopilot will take over and make a controlled landing."

"Why is that bad?"

"Because we're on the wrong side of the Wall, Owen. We'll be captured."

"Ah. Do we have any choices?"

"We're about a half a league from the Wall. I can override the autopilot and try to hop over."

"Do it, Martin. Do it!"

"All right. Hold tight."

He tapped a few keys and worked the controls. The Wall loomed ahead, its rim about fifty strides lower than the craft.

"If I can just hold this altitude, we'll be fine."

Suddenly everything sounded different.

"What's happened?" McMahon asked. "It's as if I can only hear the air outside."

"You *can* only hear the air outside, Owen. The engine's stopped. The battery's dead. We're losing altitude."

As the Wall loomed larger through the cockpit window, Martin noticed the shuttle behind them turn aside. "Well, at least they're not bothering with us any more," he said.

"They probably think we're going to crash anyway," McMahon observed.

"They know we're going to crash, Owen. The only point for debate is whether we crash into the Wall or into the river."

"Just get us over the Wall – we'll worry about the river later. How are we doing?"

"We're lucky the wind's in our face. We're gliding on the wings. But we're still losing altitude. The Wall's two furlongs away – fifteen chains… We're going to hit it!"

"If the power's gone, why is the console still working?"

"Different battery – too weak though – we couldn't fly on it."

"How do we hook up to it?"

"But, Owen… Oh, what is there to lose? Just flip that switch up there."

McMahon reached for the switch Martin had indicated and flipped it. The cockpit and external light went out. At the same time they felt a little *kick* as the engine coughed back into life. Though its revival lasted only a few seconds, Martin was able to use them to gain some vital altitude. But would it be enough?

"I can't see anything, Owen. It's too dark. No, here it comes! Hold on!"

With a *swish* the shuttle overshot the Wall with inches to spare. In the sheer blackness they didn't see the approaching shallows off the river's northern shore. Their only sensation of contact was the initial *splash* and increasing churning of the disturbed waters that magnified to become a deafening wall of sound, until the resistance finally flipped the shuttle over into the freezing river.

CHAPTER THIRTY-FOUR
RESOLUTION

"Commander, I move that Red Watch be formally censured for the actions of Councillor Wakefield's son!"

News of the wanton disabling of the powerhouse transmitter came as a blow to everyone on the Salvation, but especially to Boone. Could its timing signify that their God was displeased with how they were conducting the settlement of the New Territory? He wouldn't yet share such doubts with the Committee, but neither would he condone the Green Watch representative's increasingly wild outbursts.

"Councillor Cropper, I fail to see how an entire watch can be held responsible for the behaviour of one wayward youngster. And quite apart from that, what would there be to gain from such an action, other than to drive wedges between us?"

Red faced, Cropper replied, "With all due respect, Commander, it might help concentrate their minds on raising their children to be more loyal to the Salvation!"

Colin Wakefield tried to keep his cool. "Sir, I resent the implication that Red Watch is a cauldron of disloyalty. While I regret Martin's involvement in damage to property, I am certain his motivation is for a peaceful and cooperative solution to the settlement issue."

Cropper leaned forward. "What utter rubbish! Peaceful and cooperative? The savages are laughing at us! Not only have they disabled the main power supply, they've even stolen the portable generators from under our noses! And those they couldn't carry, they made useless by stripping out their receptors! What are our settlers going to do without electrical power? Now tell me that!"

An Orange Watch representative said, "It does seem to demonstrate how underhand they can be. Should we send some troops in and take back what they stole?"

Boone said, "They took many powerful weapons too. If we attack, there's every chance they'll use them against us. I couldn't condone risking loss of life."

Wakefield said, "Let me go down and talk to them. I realise the damage is done, but as Martin's father they'll probably listen to me. Perhaps I could persuade them to return the receptors."

His offer sounded genuine. But Boone suspected his real motive must be to ascertain the fate of his son, last seen piloting a disabled shuttle straight into that Wall of Death.

* * *

Well over a month having elapsed since the last evacuees came through, any traffic through the culvert was a significant event. Only one shuttle had been heard landing today, and Dominic's settlers assumed the newcomers were still licking their wounds after last night's audacious expedition. The general euphoria east of the Wall was tempered though by a brooding expectation of some form of reprisal.

The first that Dominic and Sylvia knew something was happening was when Rajeev ran into their house shouting, "Dominic, come quick! They're sending guards through the culvert!"

He grabbed the stun gun he'd been examining and hurried outside with his friend to see three figures drawing up to the shore in a small boat. From where he stood he saw that two of them were armed and from their demeanours that none was used to travelling on water. When he looked closer he was sure he recognised the unarmed figure, so he briskly stepped forward.

"Colin? Is that you?"

Wakefield extended a hand, which after helping him ashore Dominic shook vigorously saying, "It's good to see you! How are your wife and young son?"

Recovering from the rocky crossing – albeit short – Wakefield huffed and said, "It's nice to see you again too, Dominic. My wife and son are well. I hope the same is true of your family?"

Dominic nodded and turned to find both Sylvia and Krania at his shoulder, each smiling their greetings for the visiting Salvation Councillor.

Wakefield lowered his voice. "But I'm here mainly for news of Martin. Just a minute while I get rid of these two."

He spoke to the guards. "I'll be all right. Come back for me in two hours."

They pushed off and disappeared into the culvert.

Dominic led the group towards his house as Wakefield said, "Your little escapade last night caused quite a stir. But I'm sure you guessed that."

"I'd have been disappointed if it hadn't. Your people can't expect us just to sit here and do nothing."

Wakefield laughed. "It amazes me that many of them do. We're not used to dealing with adversaries as clever and determined as you are. But please, do you have news of Martin? His mother's been sick with worry. We heard that the shuttle had crashed, and he's the only person who could have piloted it."

"Don't worry," Dominic said, leading him into the house. "He sustained a few bruises, but otherwise he's fine. I'm afraid the shuttle's a write-off though. Martin's resting in one of the tents – I'll take you to see him shortly. He's proving to be a very brave and capable young man. He's been invaluable to me."

While Sylvia and Krania prepared some food and drinks for their guest, Dominic went on to describe Martin's exploits in Crowtree and Ashwell. Wakefield's pride in his son was evident.

As Krania handed him a mug of tea and some jam and buttered scones she said, "You should be very proud of Martin, Mr Wakefield. He's been – wonderful!" And she blushed before returning to the kitchen.

Wakefield looked quizzically at Dominic, who smiled and said softly, "They've become very close friends, Colin. I've not seen her so happy in a long time."

Their visitor frowned, as if he'd learned something completely new about his son. But then he smiled too and said, "That's – really good to hear, my friend. Forgive me. I'm a little overwhelmed. Food of this quality on board the Salvation is reserved only for very special occasions."

He took a knife and spread some jam on the scone. He picked it up and regarded it for a few moments, as if wanting to relish and remember the look of it before he took a bite. When he did, a look of ecstasy washed across his face, his mouth motionless for a while as he savoured the subtle mixture of delicious flavours and textures.

Sylvia came in with some fruit and said, "I'm sorry it's only simple fare, Councillor. If ever we get our lands back we'll serve you up some proper food."

"Sylvia, if you'd had to exist on recycled food, you wouldn't say that. This is marvellous, and I thank you for it."

He set aside his plate and took a mouthful of tea.

Then he said, "Before we see Martin, I do have something to ask you. You'll understand I had to have another reason for coming here, and it's this. I'm asking you to return the receptors your people removed from the generators that they couldn't – um – take away last night. Before you answer let me say that such a gesture is likely to quell the warlike ranting of our more excitable committee members. And don't take that as a veiled threat, Dominic. It's an honest observation."

"I'm sure it is, Colin. But I'll have to consult the elders about such an important issue. Sylvia, would you mind asking Rajeev to get them to come here in half an hour?"

She nodded and left.

"If you've had enough to eat and drink, Colin, I'll take you to see your son now."

As they walked along the shore to where the tents were erected, Wakefield commented on the neat way in which the temporary settlement was set out.

"That's down to Rajeev. I was absent while the evacuation took place, as I explained to you earlier. When I came back it was all sorted. He's a gifted organiser. Well, here's the hospital tent. Martin's just in here."

He pulled back a canvas flap and said, "Visitor for you, Martin."

Martin sat up in his cot with some difficulty, and father and son embraced.

After preliminary greetings Martin said, "I'm sorry I didn't phone you again, Dad. I feared they'd pick up our messages, and I didn't want to get you into any trouble."

"You did right, son. Cropper's been looking for the slightest excuse to incriminate me. But luckily no one's pointed a finger – at me or your friends. As far as anyone's concerned, you took that shuttle for your own reasons. And, from what I'm hearing, that might not be far from the truth."

He smiled while his son looked bashful. Then his expression turned serious. "But honestly, Dad, I believe what

I'm doing here is right. We can only move forward if we cooperate."

"I agree. And I want you to know that your mother and I are very proud of you. It's confusing for little Declan, because there's not much we can say to him without incriminating ourselves. But he still misses and loves you."

"Tell the little stinker I miss him too – and give him a big hug from me."

"I will. Well, we have some business with the elders, so I'll leave you to rest some more."

"Before you go, Governor…"

Dominic smiled and said, "I'll tell Krania you're awake."

"Oh, thanks, but there was something else. Can I see Owen?"

Dominic's face blanched, and he crouched by Martin's cot, taking his hand. "Martin, there's no easy way to tell you this, but I'm afraid Marshal McMahon didn't make it. What you two achieved last night will stand as testament to his courage. He'd have been proud to call you his comrade."

Martin lay silently and stared at the canvas above him, while the two men took their leave. On the short walk back to Dominic's house he explained to Wakefield what had happened.

"Everyone was awake when the shuttle overshot the Wall. Though it was dark we heard it skimming along this side of the river till there was an almighty *splash* further downstream. We launched all the boats and found that Martin had managed to swim clear through the broken front window. Unfortunately Owen McMahon was still in the cabin. It's possible he made Martin swim out first, but took in too much water to follow him. Martin obviously doesn't recall that he tried to swim back but our people wouldn't let him. It would have been too late by then anyway. Owen was a good man and is a sad loss to our community. His father's the senior elder, so you'll meet him shortly. Obviously I've already spoken to him today and his attitude is 'business as usual'."

They went into Dominic's house where the elders had already convened. Dominic introduced Wakefield to them all and he offered special words of sympathy to Owen McMahon's father. He then explained his proposition.

"I understand and support your claim to a share in Cara's treasures. On the other hand I hope to convince my colleagues that we must cooperate on equal terms if we are to settle on Earth. If we begin with conflict, we'll never achieve a peaceful co-existence. My ultimate wish would be for complete integration of our communities – but first things first.

"In taking the receptor tubes from the remaining portable generators, you leave our settlers little hope of coping through the winter. I'm sure most will opt to return to the Salvation until the main powerhouse can be repaired. When that's done they'll return, but they'll be far less trusting and probably more hard line. I know these sound like threats, but that's not what I intend them to be. It's just my logical reasoning.

"If you make the gesture of returning the receptors, my people will understand that you're willing to compromise. What you achieved last night shocked us all – but also made some of us respect you, for your bravado and cunning. Most of us are now unwilling to think of you as inferior. Oh, there are a very few whose minds will never be turned, but that's always the case in a democracy. I believe that if we can generate a mood of compromise and mutual respect, we can all look forward to a wonderful future for ourselves and our children."

Most expressions appeared favourable, and there were no questions. The elders retired to a corner of the room while Colin Wakefield and Dominic waited outside. After only a couple of minutes Owen McMahon's father came out to speak to them.

"This has been a hard day for me, as you both know. But I feel my son will have died in vain if nothing good came out of this. We accept your proposition, Councillor Wakefield, and we are willing to talk with your Council about the next steps forward. However if your people refuse to compromise, we have a sustainable community here and are quite able to continue making your settlers' lives a misery.

"We'll bring the receptors to the jetty and load them into a boat. They'll be ready for you to take through when your guards return."

* * *

"I don't much like this snow, Dominic."

"Which snow did you ever like, my dear?"

"Good point. None, I suppose. I just wish we were back on full power again. I feel cold all the time."

"Yes, well, these portable powerhouses are all right, but they don't charge up the batteries enough to have the heating blasting out day and night. Here, pull another blanket around you."

"Thanks, Dominic – you're always so thoughtful."

"We'll have a stroll to the camp area later if you like. I love a mug of ale around that big fire of theirs, and you can get really warmed up. We can call at Krania's and Martin's tent."

"But, Dominic, they've only been married for three days!"

"So?"

"So they'll probably have other things on their minds. When they want to socialise, they'll let us know. Let's not spoil things for them."

He shrugged. "All right, my dear. Come over here and sit beside me."

She cuddled up to him and said, "Tell me again about today's meeting."

"It couldn't have gone better. We've signed a cooperation agreement. We'll be electing a sub-committee to take charge of Cara's warehouses, and decide what gets used when and where. The existing city will be expanded, and all housing re-allocated so that Fenwold and Salvation settlers occupy alternate dwellings. It's what Colin and I always wanted."

"And they really want you to carry on as Governor?"

"Only because of Boone's age. He was quite happy not to put himself forward. I think he's had enough of the politics. I was disappointed in a way that Colin Wakefield turned down the position of Deputy Governor. But when he explained why, I understood."

"Wouldn't Rajeev have been upset to lose that job?"

"He knew my appointing him was only a temporary measure. He'll be happy to go back to running the Knowledge Centre. They have some brilliant teachers on board the Salvation, you know."

"How do you think you'll get on with Cropper?"

"As Deputy Governor? I can't say I relish the thought. But once he's down here and I can talk to him more, perhaps I'll pull him round. He's resigned to the fact that his ideas went out the window – at least, I think so."

"And this all starts when the powerhouse tower's fixed?"

"That's right."

"But you can't shift them on their decision about Martin?"

"I'm afraid not. Though he was on the right side – and crucial to our winning all the arguments – too many of his people still see him as a traitor. A horrible word, I know, but a label he'll have to learn to live with, wherever he chooses to go."

"And that has to be outside the New Territory."

"Yes – and his family have elected to go with him."

Sylvia said sadly, "And Krania, of course."

He squeezed her to him. "And Krania."

"Where do you think they'll go?"

"There's plenty of room in Crowtree – they're both already known and respected there."

Sylvia smiled. "It's good to know they'll be among friends. But can you really see Martin as a farmer?"

"Funnily enough, yes I can," he said. "I can also see him as a marshal some day. Well, shall we go for that walk?"

She snuggled up and kissed him on the lips.

"No," she said. "Let's have a night in."

ABOUT THE AUTHOR

Dave Evardson spent most of his working life as an accountant. Finding the work too exciting he also took up internal auditing. Prior to that he worked for a short spell as a chemical process operator. Concurrently for forty years until 2012 he and his wife Julie performed as a semi-professional folk duo, Dave playing guitar and composing many of their songs. Latterly he has concentrated on writing stories, in between travelling and enjoying retirement with Julie and their dog Droushia in the quiet seaside resort of Cleethorpes in the county of Lincolnshire.

Lightning Source UK Ltd.
Milton Keynes UK
UKOW06f1953121115

262623UK00008B/155/P